Praise for Jeremy Robinson's *Instinct*

"*Pulse* was a video game in print form, and [*Instinct*] is a tribute to James Cameron's film *Aliens*. Intense and full of riveting plot twists, it is Robinson's best book yet, and it should secure a place…on the A-list of thriller fans who like the over-the-top style of James Rollins and Matthew Reilly."
—*Booklist*

"If you like thrillers original, unpredictable, and chock-full of action, you are going to love Jeremy Robinson's Chess Team. *Instinct* riveted me to my chair." —Stephen Coonts

"Jeremy Robinson is a fresh new face in adventure writing and will make a mark in suspense for years to come."
—David L. Golemon, *New York Times* bestselling author of *Ancients* and *Leviathan*

"*Instinct* is a jungle fever of raw adrenaline that goes straight for the jugular."
—Thomas Greanias, *New York Times* bestselling author of *The Atlantis Revelation* and *The Promised War*

"Robinson's slam-bang second Chess Team thriller [is a] wildly inventive yarn that reads as well on the page as it would play on a computer screen." —*Publishers Weekly*

"Jeremy Robinson has done it again. *Instinct* is a knock-down, thought-inducing, all-out-thrill-fest with enough testosterone to put hair on even the wimpiest of chests. The Chess Team is back and once again they'll travel to the ends of the earth in an effort to save it."
—thenovelblog.com

"The action and the pacing were spot on with spills, chills, and surprises throughout. Thriller fans get ready because Jeremy Robinson is the next A-List thriller writer!"
—*Megalith Book Review*

"Here's a neat twist: a young adventure thriller writer—whose heroes save the world—saves the world of adventure thrillers. In a genre glutted with popcorn gimmicks and tired rip-offs, Jeremy Robinson dares to craft old-fashioned guilty pleasures—far horizons, ancient maps, and classic monsters—hardwired for the 21st century. There's nothing timid about Robinson as he drops his readers off the cliff without a parachute and somehow manages to catch us an inch or two from doom."

—Jeff Long, *New York Times* bestselling author of *Deeper*

"I think *Pulse* is Jeremy Robinson's best yet. A really intriguing premise, frightening consequences, wrapped up in roaring adventure."

—Stel Pavlou, bestselling author of *Decipher*

"An elite task force must stop a genetic force of nature in the form of the legendary Hydra in this latest Jeremy Robinson thriller. Yet another page-turner!"

—Steve Alten, *New York Times* bestselling author of *MEG: Hell's Aquarium*

"A pulse-pounding adventure genetically engineered to mythic effect."

— Thomas Greanias, *New York Times* bestselling author of *The Promised War*

"*Pulse* is fun, edge-of-your-seat action laced with questions about humanity and immortality... mixed with witty humor and even something to stimulate my intellect and love for ancient mythology."

—ThinkHero.com

St. Martin's Paperbacks Titles
By Jeremy Robinson

Pulse

Instinct

INSTINCT

Jeremy Robinson

St. Martin's Paperbacks

This is a work of fiction. All of the characters, organizations and events portrayed in this novel are either products of the author's imagination or are used fictitiously.

INSTINCT

For information address St. Martin's Press, 175 Fifth Avenue, New York, NY 10010.

Library of Congress Catalog Card Number: 2009047572

ISBN: 978-0-312-53425-7

Printed in the United States of America

St. Martin's hardcover edition / April 2010
St. Martin's Paperbacks edition / February 2011

St. Martin's Paperbacks are published by St. Martin's Press, 175 Fifth Avenue, New York, NY 10010.

10   9   8   7   6   5   4   3   2   1

For Mom, even though I know
this one will freak you out

ACKNOWLEDGMENTS

Over the past few years I have come to learn that without a core group of supporters, the job of being an author (and all the self-promotion that goes along with that) would be impossible for me. The time, skills, and knowledge required to pull off big promotions and even bigger stories is immense. So it is with great appreciation that I thank the following folks, my core.

Though I'm sure my twists on science sometimes make him cringe, Todd Wielgos, senior research scientist with MS Chemistry, makes my genetics tinkering not just believable, but also cutting edge. You make me look smarter than I am.

Major Ed Humm, U.S.M.C. (Ret.), your advice on everything from military tactics to weapons and even nit-pick details like foreign uniforms, is invaluable. Brigadier General Anthony Tata, your insights into the world of Delta and knowledge of field gear has been exactly what I needed to keep things real.

Stanley Tremblay (aka Rook) and Walter Elly (aka sucka) you make PR, web analytics, and social marketing fun and challenging. You are also the best idea soundboards an author could have. Your unceasing excitement about the books and other media projects I dream up is contagious and often keeps me on track when I would normally be in a slump.

Roger Brodeur, you are one of my biggest supporters, my

favorite father-in-law, and the best grammar/typo checker I know.

Scott Miller and the gang at Trident Media Group, your advice is valued and judgment sound. With the exciting projects we have brewing; I look forward to a long and prosperous journey with you.

And now for the folks who truly make dreams come true. Peter Wolverton, you're an awesome editor whose insights are sometimes brutal, but always appreciated. Readers have noted how much better the Chess Team books are, and that is in part thanks to you. Elizabeth Byrne, an e-mail from you is always good news, and I greatly appreciate your quick replies and diligent answers to my many questions. Rafal Gibek, production editor, and Christina MacDonald, copy editor, you took my rough prose and made them shine. And Jerry Todd, as an artist myself, I am a harsh judge of cover art and I am thrilled with what you have done for *Instinct*. A hearty thank you to all of you.

And finally, to the people who are always last in my acknowledgments, but first in my life: my wife, Hilaree, whose years of sacrifice helped make this dream of being an author possible. My children, Aquila, Solomon, and Norah, while I spend my days dreaming up tortures and tension you fill my mornings and evenings with creativity, joy, and love. You are the ying to my writing yang. Love you guys.

There is no law of progress. Our future is in our own hands, to make or to mar. It will be an uphill fight to the end, and would we have it otherwise? Let no one suppose that evolution will ever exempt us from struggles. "You forget," said the Devil, with a chuckle, "that I have been evolving too."

—William Ralph Inge

Man…is a tame or civilized animal; nevertheless, he requires proper instruction and a fortunate nature, and then of all animals he becomes the most divine and most civilized; but if he be insufficiently or ill-educated he is the most savage of earthly creatures.

—Plato

Life is a sexually transmitted disease.

—R. D. Laing

PROLOGUE

The Annamite Mountains—Vietnam, 1995

Three months had gone by since Dr. Anthony Weston began his search for the elusive creatures, and now that he'd found them, they were going to kill him.

A cascade of sweat followed a path of crisscrossing wrinkles down his forehead and dripped into his wide eyes. The salty, dirty sweat stung and brought forth a welling of tears, blurring his vision. He couldn't see the creatures clearly, nor the ground on which he ran, but he could hear them all around, calling out to each other.

The sheer volume of their booming hoots and hollers filled him with a kind of primeval dread that quickened his pace and made his heart pound painfully in his chest. He feared a heart attack for a moment, but the crunch of dry leaves all around signaled that his life was fleeting, heart problem or not.

Weston rounded a bend on the overgrown path that wound its way through the jungle and eventually up into the mountains. He picked up speed as the trail straightened out. If not for the assistance of gravity and the steep grade, the beasts would most assuredly have already overtaken him, but as it was, Weston found himself running much more quickly than on level ground. Even still, the task of outrunning the savage tribe was taking a grim toll on his body. With each labored breath, his ruddy brown beard and mustache, which had grown long and ungainly during his months in the bush, were sucked in and pushed out of his mouth. His light blue eyes sparkled with wetness, and his hands, which held off approaching tree limbs and bushes, shook violently, smearing the blood drawn from his fresh wounds.

Brush exploded to his right as one of the creatures toppled through it. They were tumbling and tripping as they barreled clumsily in pursuit, focused more on their quarry than their surroundings. They were single-minded hunters. He knew this from watching them take down yellow pigs and the antelope-like saola—even that fine creature's keen horns couldn't fight off the savages when they were hungry.

And they were hungry now.

Weston first knew something was wrong when, that morning, the creatures began sniffing vigorously at the air. He'd been watching them from a distance, higher up on the mountain, for an entire week. He'd observed them hunting, grooming, sleeping, and playing. But it hadn't been enough. Seeing through binoculars and hearing only distant calls could not quench his thirst for discovery. So, the previous night, he'd worked his way carefully, silently, down the mountainside until he was a mere fifty yards above with a clear view of the glade and mountain cave that served as their home. After carefully concealing himself with brush and debris, he waited eagerly for daybreak.

As the morning sun burned off the previous night's fog, the group emerged from their cave, stretching and yawning. Typically, grooming would come next, but a new smell had caught their nose—Weston. As a cool breeze tickled the back of his neck, he realized the winds were rolling down the mountainside from above, and since he was so close, the odor of his unbathed body was fresh in the air.

He'd only just begun debating what he should do next when the group started jumping up and down, slapping the earth. A moment later, each and every one of them, forty-three in all, charged up the mountain. Their brown hair stood on end, bouncing madly as they ascended. For a moment, he sat still, stunned by the display, but as the creatures made eye contact with him and began their wild hoots, he too began to climb. Upon reaching the top, he wasted no time looking back to see how close they were. He knew them to be excellent climbers. They were no doubt already nipping at his heels.

And now, not two minutes after reaching the mountain's peak and beginning his frantic descent down the other side, they were on top of him.

Weston lost his footing for a moment and screamed. He was surprised by the volume and high pitch of his voice. It sounded as inhuman as the noises made by the unclassified creatures pursuing him. As he sensed the front-runners of the group closing in he searched for any hope of escape. In the movies this was the point where the hero would trip and slide down a perfectly formed mud-covered waterslide and escape. But the forest was an unending assemblage of tall tree trunks, the occasional low-level scrub, and a detritus-coated, downhill-sloped forest floor. There was nowhere to go but down.

And then where? The river was two days out on foot and from there it was a week, at least, to the nearest pocket of civilization. And what weapons did they own that could defeat such a group as this?

None.

Hopelessness settled in and his limbs grew weary. He thought of his wife and only regretted not having been able to tell her how angry he was that she'd left. In the end, she had grown to hate him and taunted his profession; said that being a cryptozoologist was a job far better suited to children or imbeciles prone to flights of fancy. He thought she'd understood him, but he'd been wrong. And he would have never known if not for—

Shaking his head, Weston banished his thoughts of his wife. She was not the image he wanted to see when he died.

With sure footing beneath him and the slope growing steeper, Weston felt himself moving faster. The pain in his lungs began to subside and the sweat on his forehead evaporated before it reached his eyes. He'd never before experienced a second wind but recognized it, and for a moment, felt some degree of hope.

That's when he saw the flickering shadow surrounding him, as though something above were blocking out the sun that filtered to the forest floor between breaks in the canopy. He glanced up into a pair of red-rimmed, deep yellow eyes. The beast shrieked at him and reached out. Its fingers found his field vest and gripped tightly. A moment later, Weston's feet left the earth and he found himself airborne, propelled through the air with stunning ease.

As the forest spun, he saw the entire group descending toward him, some charging, some taking to the trees, and some rolling clumsily through the brush. What may have been a ten-foot flight took Weston much farther as the ground continued to drop away. Twenty-five feet later he landed, but the same grade that made his fall farther also minimized the force of his impact. He rolled and slid another fifty feet and came to rest at the foot of a tall, slender Aquilaria tree.

Weston knew he was lucky to be alive, but even luckier to not have sustained any broken bones. He hadn't even lost consciousness. He struggled to his hands and knees, acutely aware that the wave of hair-covered flesh roaring down the mountain was almost upon him. He stood on wobbly legs and held the tree for support. It was shaking.

Weston looked up and found the same deep, red-rimmed eyes staring back at him. The creature, suspended upside down on the tree, reached out and backhanded Weston's head. He fell to the ground, stunned and despairing. They had him. Escape was impossible.

He began weeping as the creature climbed down the tree with an agility he'd witnessed all week. In many ways the creatures were more suited to a life in the trees than on the ground. Once on the ground, the beast stood erect, stretching its height to a mediocre five feet. If not for their physical strength, Weston might even have been able to fight his way out. But he remembered how easily he'd been thrown, as though he were but a child.

As the beast stood above him it hollered to the others, who quickly surrounded his prone body. They hooted and slapped the ground in a wild display, the likes of which he had not observed in the last week, even when they were hunting. A few stayed in the trees where they shook branches and shrieked. The one who had caught him, Red Rim, stood above him and looked into his eyes. Red leaned in close and smelled him, moving slowly from his feet to his head, sniffing diligently.

Perhaps they're trying to decide if I'm edible, Weston thought. He tried to think of a way he could make himself less appealing, but that was impossible. Inside his pants, his legs were already coated in shit, and his urine had leaked through the front. He smelled terrible; though, he noted now, not as terrible as the creatures standing guard around him. Their scent was fecal and raw, like moldy egg salad. As Red sniffed Weston's head and blew its breath onto his face, he could taste the decaying flesh of some previous meal that clung to its two-inch-long canines. While Red sniffed his hair, Weston became aware of a gentle caress upon his chest. He glanced down, past his matted beard, and saw two large hair-covered breasts dangling down onto his body. Red . . . was a female.

Then she was up and hooting again. The cacophony reached an apex and the group descended on Weston like a starved pack of hyenas, yelping and reaching for him. As his clothes were torn and yanked away from his body by tooth and claw, he began to scream and fight. It did little good and only seemed to work the group into more of a craze. Then one was on top of him, straddling his naked waist and pinning him to the ground. The creature's face leaned in close.

Red.

She howled and then bit into the meat of his shoulder.

DEVOLUTION

ONE

Annamite Mountains—Vietnam, 2009

The open sores covering Phan Giang's feet looked like the craters of the moon. They'd long since stopped oozing, but the dried flaking skin itched relentlessly. Yet he kept walking. Stumbling really. He'd been moving like a machine for the past three days, shuffling through the jungle like a zombie. His bloodshot eyes, half closed, stung and saw the world through a haze. His feverish, parched body was slick with moisture that clung to him yet failed to penetrate his skin. His tattered clothes, those of a peasant villager, hung from his bones in damp tatters, like meat hung to dry. Though he was near death, his heart soared when the jungle broke.

He emerged from the sauna that was the jungle of Vietnam and stepped into an open field. He saw an array of gleaming metal hangars, several parked green helicopters, and groups of men in uniform patrolling the outer fringe of the facility. A military base. *Who better to help,* the man thought.

As the only surviving man in his village, Anh Dung, he had left in search of help. For generations his people had dealt with *cái chết bất thình lình*—the sudden death. Occasionally one of the men in the village would fall over dead. Regardless of health or age, the man struck would die suddenly where he stood, sat, or lay. They'd always believed that angry spirits looking for vengeance on the living sometimes targeted men, taking their souls. But the solution had always been to dress and act as a woman. This knowledge had saved the village, as the spirits never claimed more than one man.

But this time . . . the spirits that visited Anh Dung were furious. Regardless of dress or duty, the spirits had slain every man in the village, first striking them with a mild fever and coughing, then death. Whether sleeping, tending the field, or washing clothes, men were struck dead. Some in midsentence. Others in their sleep. The spirits were relentless . . . to the point that the villagers realized it wasn't *spirits* killing the men.

It was a plague.

In a single week twenty-three men, some of them very young, had died.

Seeking to save his own life and possibly bring back help, Giang had fled into the jungle. When his father fell dead he simply turned and ran. He had no food. No clothes. And no idea where he was headed.

But after three days in the dark jungle, he'd emerged like Jesus from the tomb, back into the light of the world, where men, alive and well, stood guard.

He was spotted immediately, rounded up, and brought to the infirmary. The men, well trained as they were, saw Giang's condition and kept their distance. The decision saved their lives.

Hours later, Giang woke from a sound sleep. He'd been fed and hydrated. He was feeling much better despite the sore throat, bouts of sneezes, and severe headache. The room the base had him quarantined in was small, but the cot was comfortable and the food edible. A single bare bulb hanging from the ceiling lit the four white walls.

Giang jumped when a man suddenly appeared in front of the window that looked out into a barren hallway. The man's expression was placid, almost friendly, but his uniform, olive green with a single gold star on the shoulder, revealed his importance. This would be the man who could help him.

Giang stood. An intercom next to the window crackled to life. "I'm Major General Trung. You're feeling better?"

Giang looked at the intercom. He'd never seen anything like it. The man's voice had come through the wall via the device. He squinted at it, inspecting the speaker and single white button. He tried looking through the plastic slats. There had to be a hole in the wall behind it.

Giang jumped back as the speaker came to life again. "Push the white button to speak, and I will hear you."

Doing as he was told, Giang slowly related his story. The village. The sudden deaths. The fear of plague. Trung listened closely, nodding, but asking no questions. When Giang's tale came to an end Trung pursed his lips. "The doctors who tested you last night found only a flu, which is typically treatable."

A smile crept onto Giang's face. He would survive!

"But . . ." Trung's face turned deadly serious. "We exposed some men to your saliva last night. Two fell dead this morning. Three others are feeling fine, but we believe they will die soon enough, just as you will."

Giang sat on the cot, his mind a swirl of emotions. The military could help. They had special medicines. Surely they could cure him. He stood and pushed the white button. "You must do something!"

"Perhaps," Trung said. "Is there anything you overlooked in your story? Maybe something entered your village a few days before the first man died? Did anything strange happen? If we can locate the source . . ."

Trung paused, watching through the glass as Giang's eyes rolled back in his head. Then the man disappeared below the window, slumping to the floor. Trung peered down at the body. Dead.

Trung rolled his eyes in annoyance.

He exited the small two-room building on the outskirts of his base. As he closed the door behind him, he turned to the four men waiting for him. "Burn it down."

As the four men doused the building with gasoline, Trung advanced across the dirt-covered central quad of the base. Technically, this was a training facility for the Vietnam People's Army, but two years ago it had been acquired by Trung and his elite Death Volunteers. The unit had been formed during the Vietnam War and as a tribute to this, they still referred to themselves as part of the Vietnamese People's *Liberation* Army, as an homage to those who came before.

His men were the best Vietnam had to offer and had been since the Vietnam War. They trained in jungle warfare, preparing for what they felt was the inevitable invasion by the west . . . again. Trung's own father had been a soldier with the Vietcong and his stories of defeating the superior forces and technology of America had inspired Trung's childhood fantasies. And now he was in a position to defeat them himself, should they be foolish enough to return.

Whatever Giang had brought out of the jungle was new, of that he had no doubt. The symptoms and tests revealed a flu, but the end result was unheard of. What he did know was that, once exposed, his enemies would simply fall over dead before realizing anything was amiss. Entire armies or cities could be wiped out without a shot being fired. It was the perfect weapon. But it could not be used in combat. Not yet. Not until he had the cure.

Twenty men, his best, stood waiting for orders; he issued them without pause, telling the men about the strange virus that infected Giang, and what they needed to do about it.

They entered the jungle and hiked for three days before reaching the Annamite range. A day's hike into the mountains, a mere half mile from where Anh Dung was shown on the map, the man on point called a halt.

He'd heard something.

Trung trusted his men implicitly, and the man on point had ears like a dog's. The sound that came next could have been heard by the deaf. It was a shout. A scream really. But not human. And the source . . . it rose up all around. His men took up positions, forming a circle around him, covering the jungle in all directions.

The sound came in cascades, washing over the men as the trees above them swayed in a fresh breeze.

Then, tearing through the din came a voice. A man. He shouted a single word . . . in English. "Now!"

The jungle exploded. Tree limbs fell from above. Ground cover burst into the air. Stones and branches soared at them from a distance. For a moment Trung believed the attack, primitive and ineffectual as it was, came from the frightened women of Anh Dung. But the male voice—commanding, as though speaking to soldiers . . .

Trung realized too late that the chaos concealed an advancing force. A diversion. His men, trained to hold their fire until acquiring an actual target, had waited calmly for the enemy to appear. A mistake.

"Open fire!" he shouted.

The enemy descended.

From above.

Falling among branches and severed leaves from the canopy, they arrived. Through the debris filling the air, Trung saw figures—their exposed tan flesh and ruddy orange fur. Then a flash of white skin. A long beard. Perhaps glasses. The man appeared and disappeared as the chaos erupted.

Against roars and brute force his men fell one by one. Few shots were fired. Several attempted to fight hand-to-hand, but they lasted mere seconds. In less than half a minute, ten of his best fell to the savage yet incredibly organized attack. They were severely outmatched. As his remaining men fearlessly engaged the enemy, he slunk down and slipped behind a tree. Sure he hadn't been seen, he turned and ran.

Four days later he emerged from the jungle, his feet swollen, his body craving water. He looked little better than Giang when they'd first found him stumbling from the jungle. When his men saw him, they kept their distance, fearing he'd been infected. After demanding a water bottle be thrown to him, he drank its contents and related his story. Still fearing Trung might be ill, but fearing his wrath even more, the soldiers helped him to his quarters, where doctors tended to him.

A week later, cleared of the mystery illness and feeling strong, Trung met with some of the nation's best doctors, scientists, and government officials. The scientists were stumped. The disease confounded their attempts to understand it. Without discovering the source of the infection, they wouldn't be able to understand it . . . or find a cure. Even with the source they doubted whether they could solve the riddle.

They needed help.

Loath as he was to admit needing assistance, he could think of only one nation with both the scientific and military capabilities that would be required to track down the source and develop a cure—America. He left the meeting having said nothing of the plan brewing in his mind. But he put things in motion that night. The Americans would bring their best military and scientists . . . and *he* would be waiting.

TWO

Beverly, Massachusetts, 2010

Daniel Brentwood had never fancied himself a family man. To be a family man, in his mind, you first had to be a ladies' man. After all, procreation only happened with a willing partner. And throughout his life, willing partners were not lining up. He'd been a glasses-wearing, pocket-protecting geek in high school. An Apple IIc and a pirated copy of the kung-fu game Karateka had been his best friends. Throughout college he'd been a perpetually mocked virgin and the butt of more than a few shower room pranks, though he'd managed to trade the Apple in for a brand-new PC featuring Windows 3.1 and a pirated copy of Doom. And now, ten years later, he was CEO of Elysian Games, one of the top video game developers in the world, alongside Blizzard, Microsoft, and EA. At thirty years old he'd built an empire and made more money in a year than most people did in their entire lives.

His glasses had gone the way of the Tasmanian tiger, replaced by contacts, and his pocket protector had been displaced by a PDA, but he was still a geek to the core. There was a time when nothing could distract him from the games he created. Then he'd met the proverbial "her." Actually, he'd hired her. Angela O'Neill. A brilliant programmer. He admired her talent. Few women got excited about creating realistic gaming physics, but this one did. But that wasn't what pulled his eye away from the computer screen. It was her penchant for tight T-shirts that accentuated her chubby love handles. He wasn't sure why, but those love handles drove him crazy.

As it turned out, she had a thing for PDAs. They'd married a year later—a grand spectacle and perhaps the only event away from the world of computers that half the guests had ever attended. Then, two years ago today, they'd had a child. Ben. A little runt with light blue eyes, pale skin, and jet-black hair. Angie liked to joke that God had turned up the contrast when Ben was formed.

And now that Ben was two, they were tearing themselves away from the business. Away from the computer screen. Away from the chaos. Lynch Park was their destination, a park full of green grass and tall trees with two small beaches, a half-shell theater, a Dick & June's Ice Cream, and a sea breeze that couldn't be beat. All they'd brought was a few towels, some toys, and plenty of sunscreen.

Daniel had just returned from a week-long, round-the-world business trip that started with meetings in Tokyo and Hong Kong and finished in Washington, D.C., where his team photographed the Oval Office for a level that would be featured in a new first-person shooter, Army Ranger: Advanced Strike Force. Inspired by the current president's exploits as an Army Ranger, the game featured a look-alike president, though the character's name was different. The highlight of the trip had been when he met the president in the Oval Office. They'd been publicizing the meeting for months and it was everything he hoped for and more. Not only did President Duncan welcome him warmly, but he also said he was looking forward to playing the game! The president! Of course, the low point of his visit had been sneezing on the president. He'd picked up a bug while in Hong Kong that stayed with him for the week. Embarrassing as it was, the president shook it off with a joke.

But now, being home again with his family—nothing could beat that. Not the president. Not seeing *Godzilla* in a Tokyo theater. Not the release of any new game. With the cold all but gone, he was free to enjoy the summer weather and time alone with the people he loved most.

They'd just driven by the large Beverly cemetery where Daniel's grandparents had been buried, when Ben began to serenade them with a rousing rendition of "The Wheels on the Bus," a song to which he had created at least twenty distinct verses. And Daniel knew them all by heart. The sound of his son's voice, no matter how repetitive, was more magical than the welcome chime on his computer. Ben was his finest creation. Nothing could compare.

Daniel had surprised even himself when he turned out to be an excellent father. Loving. Energetic. Fun. He was the kind of dad all kids want. Infinitely trustworthy and endlessly playful. His one flaw was that he was also very busy. Which was why they were getting away, alone, as a family, for Ben's second birthday.

Daniel steered the black Jag, which he'd bought five years previous as a gift to himself when his first game had sold a million units, onto the steep hill leading down to the park's wide parking lot. He noted the lot was fairly empty for such a nice summer day. Motion above the lot caught his eye; the trees bending, as though reaching for some invisible desire. It was windy. Perfect day for a kite.

The Jag picked up speed as it rolled down the hill, but before Daniel could lift his foot off the gas and onto the brake, he froze. Eyes glossed over. Jaw slack. Gravity pulled his body forward. His head hit the steering wheel as his foot descended on the gas. The Jag launched forward, held straight by the weight of his head on the wheel.

The kids checking for park stickers jumped from their umbrella-covered lawn chairs just before the car plowed through, destroying the chairs and a cooler full of sodas. It continued across the parking lot.

In the backseat with Ben, Angie screamed and shook

Daniel's shoulder, pleading for him to wake up. She tried to climb over the front seat to get to the brake, but the car hit the curb and launched into the grass. The jolt smashed Angie's head against the ceiling. She fell back into her seat, head spinning. If the seawall had been straight, the car would have plowed into the Dick & June's, but angled as it was, the Jag was headed toward a six-foot drop into the ocean. Angie realized this, snapped her seat belt into place, and held Ben's hand.

The green chain-link fence at the top of the seawall didn't stand a chance when the car struck. It snapped free from the support poles and rolled over the side with the car. Angie's quick mind worked through the scenario as they fell upside down. Water would seep in while she unclipped Ben and—

The car struck with a grinding sound of metal on stone that made Angie sick to her stomach. Or maybe that was the seat belt yanking on her abdomen? They'd landed upside down on the mass of boulders that surrounded the park, revealed by a low tide. As her mind cleared she became aware of the most dreadful sensation. Silence.

She could see Daniel, who never wore his seat belt, crumpled on the ceiling in the front seat. And next to her, Ben dangled in his car seat.

With shaking hands she unbuckled herself and fell to the car's ceiling. She fumbled to Ben and unclipped him. He fell into her arms. As a whimper escaped her mouth, she checked for a pulse. Nothing. She put her hand in front of his mouth and held her breath. She sighed with relief when she felt her baby's breath on her finger.

The silence was shattered by shouts from above and an acrid smell that told her the same thing: "The car is on fire! Get out!"

She tried her door. It was jammed tight. Deformed by the impact. She tried the door on Ben's side. It too was wedged closed. In fact, the whole roof of the car had crumpled down.

They were trapped.

And as smoke poured in through the heating vents, she realized they'd be suffocated or burned alive.

A loud explosion shook the back of the car and she screamed. But it was followed by a shout. "Take my hand, lady!" She looked back and found two young men. They'd smashed in the window with a large stone. Before she had time to think about how to get Ben out and then go back for Daniel, she was grabbed by the arm and yanked out of the car. She began screaming about Daniel, about how he was still in the car. As she was pulled over the rocks, which skinned her ankles, Ben began to cry. He was okay.

Her senses returned with the cry of her child and she demanded to be put down. Why were they treating her so roughly? Heat and odor brought her eyes back to the car. It was an inferno. Daniel was gone.

Her two rescuers pulled her and Ben over the rocks and into the ocean. When the car exploded they fell under the protective water. They were safe. But Daniel was dead. And no one would ever know what killed him.

The official ruling: fell asleep at the wheel. The cost of all that success. The news covered it for a night, focusing most of their attention on little Ben, now fatherless. Just another death to pad the nighttime headlines while folks waited for their reality TV.

THREE

Gulf of Aden—Somalia

A stark white motorboat bearing no national symbols, name, or markings of any kind rose up over a wave, catching air for a beat. The motor buzzed as it left the baby blue water before being muffled once more as the boat descended and the blades bit into the sea. The fifteen-foot craft leaped from wave to wave, dancing over the ocean as fast as the old engine could push it and its five occupants.

The five passengers were dressed in loose clothing and head wraps; only their eyes could be seen. Four sets of eyes were locked onto a single target—the *Volgaeft,* a Russian cargo ship. The only one of the five not looking at the cargo ship sat at the back, guiding the flat-hulled boat through the maze of five-foot swells. The seas were rough for such a small craft to handle, but as they closed in on the cargo vessel, none on board thought about the threat of capsizing; their thoughts were on the violence that would soon begin.

The *Volgaeft* was at full speed in a bid to outrun the band of pirates, and had no doubt issued a call for help, but the pirates knew they could catch the sluggish, heavily laden vessel. And, with some newly acquired technology, they would easily board it before help arrived. And help would arrive. After a short period of successful pirating that brought in an estimated thirty million dollars, the international community had cracked down. Warships from India, the European Union, the United States, and China patrolled the waters off Somalia, sometimes escorting ships from their various homelands, but always rushing to the aid of any ship in distress. And the *Volgaeft* wouldn't have waited to put out a call.

The pirates' sources put the nearest warship, a Chinese destroyer, roughly thirty minutes away. But with the *Volgaeft* now making a beeline for the destroyer and the destroyer for the *Volgaeft,* that half hour would be cut in half. And it had taken five minutes to pull up alongside the freighter.

Ten minutes left.

Typically, once a cargo vessel was boarded and the crew rounded up, there was nothing a destroyer could do. The ransom would be paid. And after returning to port as hostages, the ship and crew would be free to go. But this was no ordinary pirate raid. They were after something specific, and they needed to be gone by the time the Chinese arrived.

As the freighter crew watched the small pirate ship far below, preparing to cut grappling hook lines, they saw something they'd never seen a pirate do before. All five of the pirates raised what looked like handguns, but were tipped with solid black cylinders. Pirates typically fired warning shots at the crew, forcing them away from the rail while they scaled the side, but these devices weren't weapons at all. All five fired as one. The black cylinders arced up over the rail, trailing thin black wires. They landed atop a large metal container and snapped up into standing positions as their magnetic bases engaged.

One of the Russians armed with a machete tried to cut through the thin black wires, which were already taut with weight, but his blade could do no more to the wire than a plastic knife could. Before the crew could discuss what to do next, the pirates were pulled up and over the rail, landing on their feet and drawing pistols. The stunned crew stared for a moment. Then ran.

Ignoring the fleeing crew, the pirates entered the maze of metal containers covering the deck of the massive ship. They were looking for one container in particular. Its contents were worth more than the bounty received from all previous pirate attacks in the last year combined.

They wove their way through aisles created by the looming towers of containers, scanning the variety of labels, serial numbers, and I.D. codes. They knew what they were looking for. ID-432 out of Vladivostok.

Three minutes later, they found it.

A pair of bolt cutters emerged from beneath one of the loose robes worn by the pirates. The lock fell to the deck a moment later and the large metal doors opened. Flashlights rose to meet the darkness within, illuminating a single metal carrying case.

"Over there," one of the large men said, his English perfect, though tinged with a New Hampshire accent.

"I'm on it," the shortest replied, her voice feminine. The cheap black ski mask she wore covered her face and the black face paint beneath concealed her skin color. The only aberration in her pirate disguise was her indigo eyes.

The man—Stanly Tremblay, call sign: Rook—stepped inside the container, flashlight up, followed by the woman— Zelda Baker, call sign: Queen.

Queen knelt down by the silver case and inspected the area around it. "No traps. Looks clear, King."

Jack Sigler, call sign: King, stepped around Rook and unwrapped his face mask. His hard jaw was covered in stubble. His eyes glimmered with what his mother called mischief, but what the U.S. military called intensity.

Outside the container, the last two "pirates" kept watch. Erik Somers, call sign: Bishop, brimming with muscles, and the smaller man, Shin Dae-jung, call sign: Knight, kept their silenced pistols aimed down either end of the hallway formed by walls of shipping containers.

King pulled the case free from the bungee cords that held it securely to the back wall of the container. A digital touch screen and ten numbered buttons, zero through nine, were inlaid on the side of the case. Low-tech travel and storage, meet high-tech security. The case could not be opened without the correct code, and though there were no traps guarding the case itself, no one wanted to test a last-recourse defense mechanism by opening the case without the right code. "Deep Blue, you there?"

"Right beside you." In fact, the Delta team's handler, Deep Blue, was half a world away, watching them via satellite. Named for the chess-playing supercomputer that trounced world champion Garry Kasparov in 1997, Deep Blue was the only member of the team whose identity was unknown. The man was an enigma, but he had access to U.S. military resources that were unparalleled, an impressive strategic thought process, and an understanding of military tactics that only someone who had previously seen combat could have. "I can see Bishop and Knight outside the container. Are you in?"

"Affirmative. I'm about to access the locking mechanism," King said as he used his KA-BAR knife to pry off the touch screen. He plucked the cable free from the back of the screen, removed a small touch screen of his own, and attached it. Once connected the screen lit up, a similar light blue to the ocean outside, and scrolled through a series of numbers. Unlike other mechanisms that tried a myriad of codes, looking for the right one, this device actually rewrote the software so that a new code could be added.

"Once you confirm the contents, you need to bug out," Deep Blue said. "The Chinese destroyer will be at your doorstep in five minutes and it looks like they're warming up a chopper."

King shook his head. It was never easy. "Armed or transport?"

"Gunship."

"Shit."

"Bishop, Knight, the crew is getting brave," Deep Blue added. "Looks like they're armed."

"Just let us know where to aim," Knight said.

Bishop, as usual, remained silent at his post. Watching and waiting. Unlike the others, he had nothing to fear from bullets, not physically anyway. Thanks to an unrefined serum created by Manifold Genetics, Bishop's body could regenerate from almost any physical injury short of decapitation. The downside was that every injury, from a paper cut to a bullet wound, pushed his mind farther to the brink. The test subjects before him all became what the team called "regens"—mindless killing machines. It was only Bishop's history of anger management and a regimen of mood-enhancing drugs that kept him stable. It had been almost a year since their run-in with Manifold and the regenerated mythical Hydra, but this mission was Bishop's return to active duty. He'd been deemed fit for duty only a week ago.

The numbers on the display stopped, and a blank screen with ten empty spaces appeared.

"Ready for the code," King said.

"Hey guys, Lew here." The new voice in their ear belonged to Lewis Aleman, their tech-wizard who was not only hardened on the digital battlefield, but also on the physical battlefield as a Delta operator. "The legendary CD Key for Office 97 is the code."

"Lew," King said, "this really isn't a time for—"

"All zeros," Rook said.

"And the winner is . . ."

King didn't hear the rest. He was already typing in the ten zeros. Upon finishing the code, the screen went black. "Uh, Lew . . ."

The locks clicked open. They were in.

"Knight, now would be a good time for a warning shot." Deep Blue's voice was cool, but the speed with which he spoke conveyed urgency. The crew of more than thirty men were closing in on what they believed were five Somali pirates.

Hoping the noise would intimidate, Knight removed his silencer from his .45-caliber Sig Sauer 220 handgun and fired off a round. It pinged off the deck where a crewman's shoe was poking out from behind a container. The man shouted and they heard the sound of feet shuffling away.

"That did it," Deep Blue said. "But they haven't given up. Chinese heli is in the air. ETA, two minutes. The destroyer will be right behind it."

King ignored the time line. It would only make him nervous and slow him down. He opened the case. Steam hissed from inside, rolling over the edge and out across the floor of the roiling hot case. When the steam cleared, twenty small vials were exposed. King removed a small kit from his cargo pants, which were hidden beneath his robe, and opened it. Moving with extreme care, he then untwisted the cap of one of the vials, inserted a Q-tip, and soaked up a small amount of the clear liquid within. He rolled the Q-tip across the white surface of a small device that absorbed and analyzed the liquid. Normally, to identify a mystery liquid would require more processing power and equipment, but they were looking for one specific liquid, or rather, what was contained within the liquid medium. A small light on the device flashed green.

"Confirmed," King said. "We've got ourselves enough Russian-made smallpox to wipe out the populations of ten major cities."

"Great," Rook said. "All headed for our buddies in Iran."

Cases of smallpox could be traced back two thousand years in human history, emerging in China. The virus moved across the Asian continent to Africa, claiming the lives of thousands, including Pharaoh Ramses V. After arriving in Europe in 720 B.C. it crossed the Atlantic to the New World along with Hernando Cortez and an army of conquistadors. Contrary to popular belief, it was not the brutal tactics of the conquistadors that wiped out the Aztec civilization, it was smallpox. Nearly four million Aztecs died from the virus. The last case of smallpox was recorded, ironically, in Somalia circa 1977. Since then the world has been smallpox free . . . and more susceptible than ever. There is no cure for the virus and though the mortality rate of the infected is ten to thirty percent, ten percent of the population of New York City is eight hundred *thousand* people. In the wrong hands, these small vials could be weaponized and kill millions.

"So much for Putin's assurance that their smallpox cache was secure," Queen said.

"I believe that as much as I believe Putin saved a film crew from a Siberian tiger," Rook said. "If the guy had been born and raised in the U.S. he'd probably be on Broadway by now. What I don't get is why this is still kicking around."

"Human nature," Queen replied. "We've been dousing the world in chemical and biowarfare for thousands of years before we even understood what the stuff was. And the U.S. is just as guilty as any other nation. Just because we don't use chemical and biowarfare now doesn't mean we never did. It's only because we have better tech and bigger bombs that we no longer need to fight dirty."

"Amen to that." King nodded as he placed the Q-tip and small device on the floor. He took out a long cylinder that had been strapped to his leg, opened it, and doused the Q-tip and device with Thermate-TH3, a ruddy brown powder made from an iron oxide variant of thermite, barium nitrate, sulfur, and PBAN as a binder. The powder would burn at 2500°C, incinerating all traces of the smallpox and melting a hole in the container and a portion of the decks beneath. He closed the case as another shot rang out from outside the container.

"Another warning shot," Knight said. "No worries. Scratch that. Big worries, incoming."

The *whup, whup, whup* of an approaching helicopter rose in volume. The Chinese had arrived. King stood and shook the remaining Thermate onto the open case. Though more than a few science boys in the United States would like to examine the old smallpox plague contained in the vials, Deep Blue's orders were clear: destroy it. The world would be a better place without another smallpox strain floating around, even in U.S. hands.

As King wrapped his scarf over his face once more, he headed for the exit with Queen and Rook. He popped a flare and tossed it into the container, then quickly closed and latched the metal doors. The Thermate would quickly suck the oxygen out of the small container space, but the flames would not be smothered. The powdered hell contained its own oxygen source and could burn just as easily at the bottom of the ocean or in the vacuum of space. Once lit, nothing could put it out.

Outside the container, Knight pointed to the sky. A black Zhi-11 gunship was approaching low over the sea, headed straight for them. As bursts of yellow flashed from the helicopter's twin 12.7mm machine guns, King shouted, "Go! Go! Go!"

The Chess Team darted down a side alley, hiding them from view as rounds chewed up the deck where they had stood only moments before. Hidden from the chopper, they ran without fear of being cut down from the sky, but they ran with weapons out in case the crew still lingered about. As they reached the port rail it was clear that the crew had hid with the chopper's arrival. They knew enough to not get caught in the cross fire.

The gunship roared above and out to sea, turning in a tight circle. It would be back in seconds.

The team hitched themselves onto their cables, still tethered to the cargo container, holstered their guns, and slid over the side of the ship, rappelling with large leaps down to the small, white, and defenseless motor boat. Once aboard the craft, they disengaged the magnets, which automatically reeled in. Without looking up, King gunned the engine, which looked old, but was actually top-of-the-line U.S. military. The small boat shot forward just as a line of 12.7mm rounds traced across the waves and ripped into the side of the *Volgaeft*.

King steered the small boat out and away from the cargo ship as the helicopter swung around for another pass. But the helicopter didn't return. It just circled at a distance.

Too easy, King thought.

"King," Deep Blue's voice returned. "Cut hard to starboard."

King glanced to port. Closing in was an ominous Chinese destroyer, its cannons swinging toward them. "They can't be serious."

"The Chinese have been in the Gulf of Aden for a year without any major conflicts," Deep Blue said. "They're eager to test their mettle. I think they—"

BOOM!

The ocean in front of the small boat burst skyward as a 100mm cannon round struck the water. The small boat launched off the resulting wave and cut through the mist, landing on the other side. King cut to starboard, but with the *Volgaeft* moving away they were exposed. If not for the boat's small size and speed they would be an easy target.

"You're looking good," Deep Blue said. "Keep your current course for thirty seconds."

"Easier said than done," King replied.

BOOM!

The second round struck just behind them, pitching the boat up and forward, bringing the engine out of the water. If not for the quick thinking of Rook and Bishop, the team's two giants, who threw themselves to the stern deck knocking the back end back down, the bow would have caught water and flipped them too soon.

"Wait for the next round," King shouted. "Then—"

BOOM!

The round struck just off the port side. The small boat became lost in a plume of seawater. When it cleared the boat appeared—capsized and immobilized.

Rather than apprehend the pirates involved, the Chinese destroyer tested its aim on a still target.

BOOM!

The small boat shattered and burst as the massive round, powerful enough to sink the multi-hulled *Volgaeft,* struck home.

Thirty feet below the explosion, five bodies descended, unmoving after the shock wave struck. Then a hand flashed up.

Hold position.

A dark shape loomed below. Waiting. Listening.

King gave the crewman monitoring the hydrophone inside the submarine a moment to recover from the impact and explosion above. Then he shouted, expelling the last of his air, "Open the damn door." The message was garbled by the bubbles escaping King's mouth, but it was received. The side dry dock of the still-classified HMS *Wolverton* opened. All five swam inside. The doors closed as the small cabin pressurized and filled with air.

The Chinese searched for the remains of the pirates they'd wiped out, but found only debris of the small boat. Regardless, the front page of China's most popular newspaper, the *Southern Metropolis Daily,* heralded the encounter as a bold Chinese naval victory. And despite the pirates' best efforts, the only losses were minimal damage to the *Volgaeft* and the total destruction of one container destined for Iran, reported full of toys donated by a charitable Russian organization.

FOUR

Catoctin Mountain—Maryland

A brisk pace.

That had been his campaign motto. It was catchy, to the point, and reflected the kind of lifestyle led by Tom Duncan, the president of the United States. Not only was he a proponent of whirlwind reform on everything from abortion to taxes, but in his foreign policy as well. Some called the ex–Army Ranger and Desert Storm veteran ruthless, and at times he was, but he preferred the term "efficient," like a surgeon cutting away the world's cancer. In the three years he'd been president, he'd put massive dents in three terror organizations including Hamas and Hezbollah, which brought the opportunity for establishing peace in the Middle East. But his tactics and in-your-face brute force policy brought criticism from several world leaders who feared the president's "efficiency" might turn in their direction. But when push came to shove, no one denied that the world was a safer place with Duncan in the Oval Office.

And his pace never slowed, not even while jogging, which his security team knew all too well.

Duncan checked his pulse and then the time on his wristwatch. He was thirty seconds faster than his best time and felt far from tired, though his army green T-shirt was soaked through with sweat. He could hear the heavy breathing of the two Secret Service men following behind him as they struggled to keep up with the most physically fit president the United States had ever known. He didn't drink, never smoked, and ate less sugar than a diabetic. And his good looks reflected his health. His short cropped brown hair, though balding slightly, when combined with his wry smile, drew swoons from the female press corps and graced the covers of very un-presidential magazines. It was theorized that his good looks had helped win the female vote and squelch the notion that a single man could never win the presidency. He was a modern American hero in his prime and a shoo-in for the next election.

But these things were far from his mind on this summer day. The scenery of the wooded trail that wrapped its way around Camp David had been a favorite walk of Roosevelt, Bush Jr., and occasionally Clinton, but not one of them charged through the scenery like a man on a mission. And all the while he was enjoying the view. The foliage was lush and the woods smelled of wet earth and decaying leaves. The atmosphere was slightly humid, but here in the mountains, eighteen hundred feet above sea level, the air was crisp compared to the near-tropical moisture of Washington, D.C.

This was the second day of his visit to Camp David and he would remain here for two more weeks, entertaining staff and heads of state, and at the end of the two weeks, putting the finishing touches on the peace accord to be presented to Palestine and Israel. But for the next three days he was here to relax. And he was determined to do just that, clear his mind, maybe even read a book. He'd heard *Ice Station* by Matthew Reilly was a good read and was looking forward to an action-packed story that would remind him of his time as a U.S. Army Ranger.

With that, his thoughts turned to some good news. Upon taking office, he had coordinated with the military to strike terrorism down hard. But he didn't want to attack with a blunt weapon. Countries wouldn't be invaded. Innocents wouldn't be killed. And they would never make front-page news. Instead, he wanted to oversee teams of surgeons who would carefully remove terrorist organizations like cancerous cells from the body . . . with brutal efficiency.

To this point, only the Chess Team excelled. And they had won another silent victory the previous day. The world believed a band of pirates had attacked yet another cargo ship and that the pirates responsible had died at the hands of a Chinese destroyer. For this reason, he looked forward to meeting Jack Sigler and his Chess Team, though Deep Blue would not be making the engagement, which would surprise no one. His success required that his identity remain veiled.

Deep Blue or not, Duncan felt it was high time the Delta team that had helped his presidency flourish be rewarded, though that too could never be disclosed. The funny thing was, King didn't want a medal. No one on the team did. Said they didn't believe in them. All they wanted was a barbeque . . . so a barbeque it was. And Duncan was determined to make it the best damn barbeque the Chess Team ever enjoyed. He wasn't bringing in top chefs or having a catering company come. He was doing one better. He'd had a new professional Lynx grill installed, ordered the freshest prime cuts to be delivered that afternoon, stocked up on the team's preferred brew—Sam Adams—and was flying in the best stick-to-your-ribs barbeque master he knew: his brother Greg.

When he thought about the good food and relaxing time he'd have with King and crew, who served the country so well, he smiled and lay back. He was looking forward to his time with them and hearing about their exploits from a firsthand perspective.

Rounding a bend in the path, he took note of the brilliant lime green leaves clinging to the maple trees that lined the trail. Between the leaves he could see the azure sky and beaming sun, which set the leaves aglow. The only smudge in this otherwise pristine day, which was the beginning of what would be a very good week, was something conjured up by his imagination the night before. He'd dreamed of being chased through the jungle—not chased, hunted. He watched from above as his child self ran from pursuing shadows that shrieked and wailed. Then he *was* the boy, panting, terrified, running as though submerged in mud. Before waking with a scream that brought armed Secret Service agents rushing into the room, he saw a flash of yellow teeth shoot toward his face.

He'd never experienced a night terror before, but knew that dream had to be close. He woke, covered in sweat and all scratched up, presumably from where he'd scraped himself with his nails while struggling to fight off his imagined assailants. He'd seen a doctor shortly after who attributed the nightmare to the president's ensuing downtime. The doctor knew Duncan was a workaholic and thought the idea of relaxing was actually stressing the president.

While Duncan didn't buy the "fear of downtime" theory, he couldn't think of a better reason for the nightmare, either. Of course, he had watched James Cameron's *Aliens* a few nights back in the White House theater. That seemed as likely a candidate as any physical or psychological ailment. But he was happy to forget the nightmare altogether. And the scenery was helping him do just that. It was a beautiful day, after all. A perfect day. He took it as a good omen.

Then a pain racked his chest. He stumbled and stopped, suddenly dizzy. He checked his pulse . . . and found *nothing*.

His heart had stopped.

As he fell to the ground, wondering how someone had been able to poison him, he heard the two Secret Service men calling out orders. But as bright spots danced before a black curtain in his vision, he knew there was nothing they could do. He never felt the pain of his head hitting the earth.

President Duncan was dead.

FIVE

Fort Bragg—Cumberland County, North Carolina

"Holy horseshit!" Rook said as he handed Knight a jack of spades. "That's five in a row! You better not be cheating."

Knight flashed a cocky smile and leaned back in his chair. The smile, in combination with his chiseled jaw and the perfectly smooth, never-been-shaved tan skin of his cheeks, not only won over many women, but it also really pissed off Rook. It wasn't that Rook was unlucky with women; he just wasn't a "pretty Korean boy" like Knight. "I would never cheat. Knights are honest and true."

This got a chuckle from King, Queen, and Bishop, who were sitting around the card table, holding their cards secretively. Each player, except Rook, had a small pile of cards laying facedown on the table in front of them.

"Honest and true, my ass," Rook said. "I just haven't figured out how you do it yet. And when I do . . ." Rook held out his fist. "I'm going to jam this right up—"

"Okay, okay, enough with the fantasizing, little man," Queen said. In the field, Queen could be a demon, but at home she often found herself being the peacemaker. It wasn't that the guys didn't get along, but they were like brothers . . . and sometimes brothers fight. "You're up."

Rook sighed and looked at his cards. His instincts told

him to look for pairs, wilds, and flushes, but they weren't playing poker. In their first year together, the team found poker to be a frustrating game, mostly because King couldn't be beat. He had a way of reading people's faces and intuiting how good their hand was. After the team collectively lost twenty-three hundred dollars to King in a single game, Rook, his face beet red with anger, had taken the chips, doused them in gasoline, and lit them on fire, melting them down into a red, white, and blue blob of singed plastic. After that, they agreed to play something less competitive . . . something that was more a game of chance than skill. But in the past month, to Rook's ever-increasing frustration, Knight never lost. Though no money was at stake, it was worse than King's poker run because it was supposed to be a game of chance. But somehow, Knight had figured out a system . . . at least when it came to Rook, who was always the first person out.

Rook focused on his three remaining cards. Ace of hearts. Ten of diamonds. Three of spades. He had to pick one.

"Knight. Ten of hearts," Rook said. "Fork it over."

Knight glanced at his cards, then slowly shuffled through them. "Nope . . . nope . . . nope . . . Sorry, big guy. No can do."

Rook raised his eyebrows as his face turned a light shade of pink. He stroked his two-inch-long blond goatee. "Don't piss on my leg and tell me it's raining, Knight."

"Cats and dogs."

"Damnit."

"Oh, and Rook? Go fish."

Rook took a card from the center pile while muttering obscenities. Then he smiled. Ten of hearts. "Ha!" He slapped the cards on the table, announcing his first pair. "Fish this, Knight."

Knight laughed. "That makes no sense."

"Hey, Rook," King said, trying to contain a smile.

Rook looked at King, who was dressed in his usual uniform, blue jeans and a black Elvis T-shirt. What Rook saw in King's orange-brown eyes was something few people ever got to see—humor. And it made him nervous.

"Ace of hearts," King said.

Rook handed him the card, his face cast with suspicion. "Are you two working together?"

"No," King said, leaning back so that his curly moplike hair fell out of his face and revealed his widening smile. "I just figured out Knight's secret."

Knight's and Rook's eyes both went wide.

"Behind you," King said, pointing to the back wall of the rec room, twenty feet back, where a month ago Knight had installed a small mirror next to the ceiling-mounted television. Rook saw the mirror and, though it was far away, had no doubt that Knight's eagle eyes could see his cards across the distance.

Men from other units who had been watching TV, playing pool, or reading books stopped and turned to watch as Rook stood up, towering over Knight like a Swiss giant, and shouted, "You little bitch."

Knight hopped out of his seat as Rook came around the table for him. He began whipping his cards at Rook, biffing him in the forehead with each shot. As Knight laughed hysterically, he stumbled over King's extended foot. This was all the time Rook needed to catch Knight by his silk button-up shirt.

Knight suddenly stood still and stopped laughing. "Don't mess with my shirt, Rook."

Rook began hocking up a wad of spit, snorting loudly with his nose for good measure.

"Rook . . ."

Even the normally silent Bishop was laughing. This confrontation had been brewing for a month and the three members of the Chess Team not involved were enjoying every minute of it. It was the beginning of what was to be a nice week of R & R, kicked off the following day by the barbeque at Camp David, no less. They were scheduled to leave that night and their bags were packed. Of course, they might be delayed pending any injuries. Rook was stronger and bigger, but Knight was fast and a skilled fighter . . . and apparently, had luck on his side.

"King!" The voice was commanding. Urgent. Which wasn't unusual for the one-star Brigadier General Keasling, but the person accompanying him into the lounge was very unusual.

Not only was Queen the only female Delta operator, she was the only woman in all of the Special Forces units at Fort Bragg. With a population topping twenty-nine thousand, there were plenty of other women on base, but they didn't enter the barracks very often, and they certainly weren't seen in the company of the short, grisly faced general now storming toward King. But this one stuck to the general's side like a prom date, and she looked, in every way, to be Queen's opposite. Power suit. High heels. Stiff.

"The rest of you, clear this room, now!" Keasling yelled. Thirty seconds later, the rec room was emptied except for the five Delta operators, the general, and the woman, who was now fidgeting nervously.

King stood and greeted the perfectly uniformed general with a casual salute, which garnered a strange look from the woman. "General, what can I do for you?" King said. "As you can see, we were in the middle of something." King motioned to Rook, who was still holding on to Knight's shirt, a phlegm wad in his mouth.

"You're shipping out in two hours," Keasling said.

King squinted, assuming there was a miscommunication. "Actually, we're not heading out until tonight."

"Not anymore you're not."

King crossed his arms over Elvis's face. "General, pardon me for being a dick, but unless your trip involves a barbeque with the commander-in-chief, you're going to have to find—"

A large hand came to rest on King's shoulder. It was Bishop. His next words were the first he'd spoken all day, and they stopped King in his tracks. "Jack, something's wrong. Listen to him."

King turned to Keasling. "What is it?"

"The president died yesterday," Keasling said matter-of-factly.

Rook let go of Knight and all five faces around the table fell. King's mind raced. If the president was dead, and the government's reaction was to mobilize his crew, that meant only one thing: the President had been assassinated. With that assumption in mind, he had only one question left. "Who's the target?"

SIX

Keasling sighed, took off his hat, and wiped his arm across his forehead. He sat on the back of one of the nearby couches and said, "That's the thing, Jack. There isn't anyone to kill. Not yet, anyway."

"Then what's the deal?" King asked.

Keasling motioned to the woman, who was chewing on her lip and looking around the room. "She is."

King turned to the woman. "And you are?"

The woman said nothing in return. She was still scanning the room with her deep brown eyes, absorbing every detail, sound, and color.

"Hello," King said loudly. "Miss?"

The woman snapped out of her distracted state and met King's eyes. For a moment her brown eyes fluttered, but not in some kind, flirtatious way. She looked more like an android recalling some bit of information. And it wasn't far from the truth. Her mind had heard what her consciousness had missed and was quickly replaying the words for her. "Sorry," she said, shaking King's offered hand. "Sara Fogg. CDC."

"The CDC?" King said.

"Centers for Disease Control and Prevention," Sara added.

"I know what it stands for." He hid his amusement with a serious voice. Fogg was beautiful, poised, *and* extremely distracted. Out of her element. Then again, he had no idea exactly what element she'd call home. She didn't look like the rugged type—styled short hair, face made up—but her short fingernails held chipped polish and what appeared to be a layer of trapped dirt. She wasn't afraid to get her hands dirty. "What I don't understand is why you are here."

"I'm a disease detective," Sara said.

Rook raised an eyebrow.

Sara noticed his skepticism. "I'm sure you all think that you're saving the world by killing terrorists. But statistically you're only saving a few thousand lives every year. What I do saves *millions* of lives. Terrorists are not the real killers on planet Earth. Disease is."

Keasling held up his hand, silencing her. "Let me explain. You're making a bad first impression."

King stayed silent. Most people shared Sara's opinion about what they did. But disease couldn't fire bullets and it didn't plot the demise of civilization. Disease was a fact of life, not the enemy. Not an assassin. "Let's get back to the president. How did he die?"

"Actually, he's not dead," Keasling said. "*Died*. The Secret Service with him at the time were able to bring him back. He's resting comfortably in a hospital right now, though he'll be under constant observation for the next few days. But, for thirty seconds yesterday, the president *was* dead."

"And?" Knight asked.

"The president had a heart attack. He—"

"I thought the president was a health freak," Queen said.

"He is," Keasling replied.

"How does a health nut have his ticker stop?" Rook asked.

"Genetic defect?" Knight offered.

Keasling tried to respond, but Rook beat him to the punch. "A secret addiction to fast food?"

"*Rook,*" Queen said with the tone of a high school Latin teacher.

Rook shrugged. "Hey, the guy lived."

Sara's frustration built. This was going nowhere fast. She grunted and spoke. "It *wasn't* a heart attack. The president died from a genetic disorder known as the Brugada syndrome. He's perfectly healthy. His cholesterol is better than average. His heart rate is like a metronome. He's in his forties but has the body of a thirty-year-old. And his heart is structurally normal."

Sara found five sets of eyes on her. They were listening.

"But when he was given an electrocardiograph, a characteristic pattern emerged—one that belongs to people with Brugada. Sudden death is caused by fast polymorphic ventricular tachycardia or ventricular fibrillation. Either one of these arrhythmias can occur in an instant, with no warning at all. Sensations commonly warning of a heart attack—pain in the left arm, shortness of breath—do not occur with Brugada; your heart simply stops and you fall over dead. The president was conscious for only a few moments after his heart stopped. He felt a pain in his chest. Then a wave of nausea. That's it. He doesn't remember hitting the ground.

"There are no outward signs that any one person has the disease until they fall over dead, unless of course you think to test yourself, which is ridiculous because only point zero five percent of the world's population has the gene and out of that number only a tiny fraction become active, mostly in men. It's so rare that most doctors don't even know about it."

Sara finished and ran her fingers through her spiky black hair. "Questions?"

Rook gave a flick of his fingers, as though shooing a fly. "So the president was born with some kind of stealth disease. How does this involve us?"

"When a new president takes office, he's given a gamut of physicals, screened for diseases and genetic disorders that might pose a risk. This includes an electrocardiograph. He was cleared of Brugada two weeks after he took office. The Brugada syndrome is a germ cell mutation, meaning it's inherited from parents at birth. Tom Duncan did not have

Brugada when he took office . . . he *contracted* the disease one week ago, when he was unknowingly exposed to a new strain of avian influenza—bird flu."

King felt the hair on his arms rising. He sensed there was more news and that it was dire. Why else would you need the world's most effective Delta team to deal with a disease? It's not like you could shoot something microscopic.

Sara rolled her neck. She had explained this more than ten times in the past day, and it was getting old. She'd been shuttled from one facility to another as the backbone of a plan was formulated with her at its core. "Bird flu is not typically contagious to people, but there are cases of it jumping species, and this strain looks like nothing we've seen before. It's mutated in a way that it is just as contagious as any other flu, but it also carries genes, which it adds to the host's DNA."

"The gene for Brugada," King said.

Sara nodded. "Turning a typical nasty flu into a guaranteed killer, at least to men. It's airborne, so a cough or sneeze will do the trick in spreading it to the people around you. It spreads like the common cold, but kills as surely as a bullet to the back of your head. What was once passed down through birth is now contagious and the whole world is at risk. Several of the president's aides who came down with the flu have also tested positive for Brugada, as have the Secret Service men who revived him and the doctors who treated him. The White House is now under quarantine. No one comes or goes. But that's just the beginning. We had to track down everyone who visited the White House, and everyone they came into close contact with for the past week. Hundreds of people have been quietly quarantined in their own homes until we can have everyone tested, but many are showing flulike symptoms already."

Sara paused to make sure all eyes of the stone-faced team were on her, and then continued, "The president *caught* the disease from someone else, so we knew there was a source. We traced all of the president's meetings over the past few weeks, backtracking the itineraries of anyone he came into

contact with. We got a red flag one week back. Daniel Brentwood, owner of Elysian Games, met with the president after
spending some time in Asia, incubator for most of the world's
emerging bird flus."

"*And* Brugada," King added.

"Yes."

"So this is what? A new bioterror weapon?" Rook asked.

"That's possible, but we have yet to determine a motive or
goal and no one has claimed responsibility. But we know one
thing for sure: if someone gave Brentwood Brugada, they
took a huge risk. If this had gotten out in the open it would
have been a pandemic that would make the Black Plague
look a light shade of gray."

"Was this created in a lab?" Queen asked.

"We don't think so, but it seems likely someone is now
weaponizing it."

"Have you warned anyone?" Knight asked.

"Warning people would only complicate things at this
point."

"Are you saying," King said, "that the majority of people
in the United States . . . in the world, could contract this
genetic-disease-carrying bird flu, which could kill them at
any time, and you're not telling anyone about it?"

"You need to understand that there is no cure for this.
And we believe the new strain is contained for the time being. Telling people would be counterproductive. Picture a
world where every person might just drop dead at any moment. Can you imagine what kind of chaos revealing this
threat would create? We'd see more people being murdered
than actually dying from the disease. There is no quick fix
here. It's more than a simple virus. The disease alters genetic code. *Permanently.*"

"I didn't think that was possible," Knight said.

"Under normal circumstances, it's not. Most of us die with
the genetic code we were born with, and if we're not hit by a
truck or struck by lightning, it's the same genetic code that
determines the time and method of our death. But mutations

do occur. Overexposure to radiation, the sun, or ingestion of certain chemicals can alter our genetic code."

"You're talking about cancer," Queen said.

Sara nodded. "That's the typical manifestation, yes. When a mutation occurs in a cell and it's not repaired, and the cell divides, that mutation will be carried on so that all cells duplicated from the one will contain the DNA change. This is an acquired mutation, and is generally not passed on to our children, but that doesn't hold true with Brugada, which is typically passed down through generations.

"To find a cure, we need to find the source, or a person near the source with an immunity. Even then, our chances are slim, but if we don't succeed, within a week, people—mostly men—are going to start dropping dead. The president's aides, Secret Service agents, senators, most of the White House staff. They're all going to die, very soon. Never mind the possibility that this has already been deployed in other parts of the world. Half the world could have contracted the disease and no one would be the wiser."

"So the disease doesn't affect women?" Knight asked.

Sara shook her head no. "It does, but not nearly as frequently. We're not sure yet how this new strain will act, but we believe it will hold true. All that has changed from the original disease is the time frame in which it kills—the president and Brentwood both died within a week of contracting flu symptoms. Women, for the most part, are unaffected."

"Which is why you need the Chess Team," Queen said.

Keasling cleared his throat. "You're the only woman in the Special Forces, Queen. If all these guys drop dead, you'll still be around to finish the job."

"But she won't be alone," King said, eyeing Sara. "Will she?"

"No," Sara said. "I'm going with you."

Rook frowned. "No offense, but I think that's a really bad idea."

That was just the kind of macho garbage Sara had expected. And she wasn't going to take it. There was too much at stake. "Just because I'm not a soldier—"

"I'm not trying to bust your chops," Rook said. "I just don't like—"

Sara raised her voice. "I can watch out for myself."

"But you don't have to watch out for yourself," King said. He looked back at Rook. "Because that's *our* job."

Rook shrugged and leaned back. "Just don't want her getting hurt is all."

"And you won't let her get hurt," Keasling said. "*She's* your mission. Keep her alive long enough to complete *her* mission."

"To find the cure," King said.

"Yes," Sara said.

Knight squinted his almond-shaped eyes. "But why just her? Why not a team of scientists?"

"The first reason," Keasling started, "is that we need to keep as low a profile as possible. A whole team of scientists would be hard to miss. And Miss Fogg is—"

"Better than any team of scientists you'll find. I have two doctorates. One in molecular biology. Another in genetics. And an undergrad in biochemistry. I've published on molecular evolution and analytical morphometry. When I got bored with the research labs I joined the CDC and pursued fieldwork. I've been in outbreak hot zones around the world. Kenya. Congo. India. I've handled cases of bluetongue, malaria, cholera, dengue fever, and leishmaniasis. *And* I've spent the last week studying Brugada, which is more time than anyone else physically capable of joining this mission."

"Been shot at?" Rook asked.

Sara sucked in a quick breath. "No. But you won't find anyone with my credentials who has been."

"You're probably right about that," King said, then flashed an honest grin. "And what you deal with is more deadly than bullets, anyway, right?"

Sara's lips curled in a slight smile. "Right." She composed herself, stepped forward, and opened the top of her blouse, revealing her sternum and a small stitched-up incision. "If we're just about finished with my interview, you all need to have some minor surgery. Each of you will have a cardioverter defibrillator implanted on your heart. Without getting technical, if your heart stops beating it will deliver a shock that should bring you back."

"Should?" said Knight.

"Mortality rates in Brugada patients with cardioverters has been zero percent for the past ten years, but this new strain may affect the body in different ways. We haven't had long to study it, so I can't make any promises."

Keasling stood. Time was short. "Wheels up in two hours. Get squared away and to the Pope airfield by . . ." Keasling checked his watch. "Thirteen hundred hours. We'll debrief in detail there."

"What about the surgery?" Queen asked.

Keasling smiled. "It's a long flight."

"Where are we headed?" King asked.

Keasling's smile fell. "Brugada's birthplace. Annamite Mountains . . . Vietnam."

SEVEN

Pope Airfield

The beast roared and surged forward, gaining speed and tensing the muscles of the two people clinging to its back. The Harley-Davidson Night Rod Special not only looked badass with its straight-shot dual exhaust, all black-and-chrome body and sleek design, but it moved like a fighter jet, or at least as close as you could get with wheels touching the ground.

With the throttle opened up, King and Queen tore down the black tarred road that led to the Pope Air Force Base. King had saved for five years and had bought the 2009 motorcycle just three months previous. Since he'd bought it, Queen had become a regular occupant at the back, holding King's waist loosely, her blond hair rippling in the wind. In the first week they'd suffered a barrage of jokes inferring the deadly duo were now a couple, but a few bloodied noses and broken fingers put that rumor to bed long before King and Queen would ever share one.

The two were close friends, perhaps closer than many lovers, as they'd saved each other's lives on numerous occasions, but the bond between them was closer to brother and sister than anything else. They fought together as King and Queen, he outsmarting while she moved in for the checkmate. They couldn't be stopped.

But they could be late. Which they were now.

Late to saving the world. And for what? A quick stop at 7-Eleven. But King knew the supplies he bought there would come in handy.

Rook, Knight, and Bishop had gone ahead, taking King's and Queen's gear with them, so they'd be prepped to depart, but Sara's briefing was scheduled to start five minutes ago. There might be hell to pay, but it was *her* best interests he was looking out for. She'd thank him later.

They pulled up to the security gate five minutes later, having covered the distance to the base at an average speed of ninety miles per hour. Queen was all smiles. The guard checked their IDs and opened the gate. "They're waiting for you in Decon," the guard said with a salute.

Decon was a room inside hangar 12, Delta's personal spot on the airfield, which housed their classified transport. Though the room had been deemed "Decon" by the less-than-creative powers that be, Rook had renamed the room Limbo, the place between Heaven and Hell where missions began and ended.

King offered a slight salute in return and pulled into the 2,194-acre base, home to the 43rd Airlift Wing, the 23rd Fighter Group, and the 18th Air Support Operations Group. It served as a launchpad for many major U.S. military mobilizations, but more frequently was utilized by the mass of Special Forces units based at Fort Bragg.

They drove into the open hangar toward Limbo, which was little more than a glorified conference room featuring potted plants (fake), a long conference table, and a ring of executive chairs. The room's technology lay hidden behind the walls and beneath the surface of the table. King pulled up in front of the open door and found Sara, arms crossed, waiting in front of the high-def flat screen that not only fit seamlessly into the wall, but when turned off faded to the color and pattern of the wall, making it effectively disappear. He and Queen entered Limbo without a word and took their seats at the oval table. Keasling stood at the back of the room, waiting with his patented scowl.

Sara quietly closed the door and dimmed the lights. She wiggled the mouse attached to her laptop. The screen came to life, as did the flat screen embedded in the wall. Two horizontal squiggly lines appeared on the screen. The first image, labeled NORMAL, featured a small hill, a deep valley, and then another hill.

normal

The second image, labeled RBBB, featured three peaks, each taller than the previous.

rbbb

"These images are from President Duncan's echocardiogram," Sara said. "The image labeled normal is just that. This is what his QRS complex—the visual representation of his echocardiogram—looked like when he took office."

Sara pointed to the second image. "This is what the president's QRS complex looks like now. RBBB typically represents a variety of common medical conditions affecting the right side of the heart or lungs. This includes blood clots, chronic lung disease, atrial and ventricular septal defects, and cardiomyopathy. But that's not all. When RBBB is detected in an individual who suffers from none of the above, it is seen as having no medical significance, is labeled a "normal variant," and discarded. The point is that even when an echocardiogram is employed to detect health risks, Brugada slips through the net."

Sara clicked the mouse. The screen showed an image they all recognized. A double helix. "DNA. Home to our genetic code, and birthplace of the mutations that sometimes create adaptations that help a species thrive. It's also the home of countless genetic disorders that kill and disable more people every year, and with far more efficiency, than all of history's wars. Brugada is even worse. It has the potential to be an undetectable pandemic. It could wipe out most of the male population within a single year. Without a male population, the human race will cease to exist shortly after . . . even with the judicious use of sperm banks."

The image zoomed in to a specific strand of code. It was labeled SCN5A. "This gene, SCN5A, is an encoder for human cardiac sodium channel on chromosome 3p21. You don't need to understand that, you just need to know that this is your enemy. This is the cause of Brugada. But most of us aren't born with this gene. This new strain of bird flu is delivering the gene to our DNA, then flipping the 'on' switch. We're after the 'off' switch. If we can find the source of this new strain, perhaps in a female carrier, we might be able to understand it better, and in turn, learn how to shut it off. Even better would be discovering a male carrier living with the new strain, but not succumbing to it. Studying *his* immunity would provide the solution we're after.

"But it won't be easy to find. Brugada first emerged in the modern world in Asia. Joseph Brugada discovered the symptom in 1992, but it's been around for a long time. In the Philippines it's known as Bangungut, translated as "scream followed by sudden death during sleep." The Japanese called it Pokkuri. In Thailand, Lai Tai. And in Vietnam, *cái chết bất thình lình*. The Sudden Death. Its roots have been traced to the Annamite Mountain region where deaths from Brugada have been common enough that it is part of the local folklore.

"Vietnam is also one of the most active breeding grounds for avian influenza. It's likely that a villager in the region carrying the SCN5A gene was infected by the virus, which picked up the gene as it mutated within the host's body. When the infection was passed on, the gene went with it. Five years ago, a scientific expedition to the region described one village in particular that reported a far larger occurrence of Brugada in its history. This is where we're going."

Sara advanced to the next slide. A satellite image of a small village surrounded by vast jungle appeared on the screen. "This is Anh Dung. The village we think might be the birthplace of the Brugada syndrome and quite possibly the source of this new strain."

Sara glanced at each of the stone-faced Chess Team. They were attentive, she'd give them that. She advanced to the next slide. A photo of Daniel Brentwood in his younger days, looking youthful, very nerdy, and full of mischief, filled the upper right portion of the screen. The rest was a world map.

"Daniel Brentwood was exposed to the new strain of bird flu, we believe, in Hong Kong. But, thank God, symptoms didn't present until after he returned to the States. Had Brentwood been hacking away in the tight confines of a 747 cabin that pandemic I mentioned would already be under way. With a nasty habit of sneezing into his hands, Brentwood was the perfect way to spread the disease."

Keasling cleared his throat. "Which is why we believe that the disease has been weaponized. It was no coincidence that a man publicly scheduled to meet the president was exposed at the perfect time to transmit the disease to the president, but *not* a plane full of people. The odds of this being random are slim. This took intelligent planning. Military planning."

"You're saying this was a hit on the president?" King asked.

Keasling nodded. "Most likely."

Sara continued. "Everyone else infected so far is an unlikely target surrounding the president, or a part of Brentwood's personal life. We believe everyone he came into contact with is now under quarantine."

Sara's last sentence was followed by an uncomfortable twitch of her cheek. She wasn't positive and Queen noticed. "You *believe?*"

"It is *possible* someone was unaccounted for. A bank teller. The mailman. Girl Scouts delivering cookies. Only God knows for sure."

"Assuming the worst," King said, "how long do we have before Girl Scouts start dropping dead?"

"A week."

"From now?"

"From two days ago. Which brings us to the scenario I would like you all to consider. This is not only what could have happened if Brentwood had been sneezing on that plane, but also what could be happening right now if someone was missed. Brentwood is the blue dot." The world map came to life. The blue dot representing Brentwood bounced around Asia, producing flowering red dots as it went. Some moved to other countries where other red spots appeared, those moving onward as well.

"Brentwood took a flight to London, with two hundred fellow passengers. It's likely that a large number of them, if not all of them, could have been infected. We've confirmed that they're not."

The blue dot streaked across the map, stopping in London, where a mass of red dots appeared, some moving around the small island countries, others moving to more distant locations in Europe, some to Africa, and still others to South America. The blue dot, however, stretched across the Atlantic and came to a stop in Washington, D.C. A new bloom of red dots appeared. Then a green dot.

"The green dot is Duncan. Just seven days ago," Sara said.

The animation continued. The blue dot moved up to Boston, where new blooms began. Then from there, several red dots streaked to various parts of the country. Los Angeles, Houston, Miami, Denver. Others entered Canada. Some went to Mexico. Several large blooms emerged around most of the major cities in the United States and around the world. The animation paused.

"This would have been today. But we were lucky. Brentwood canceled most of his appointments when he got sick, seeing only family, a few friends, and the president. What we're dealing with is closer to this." Sara pushed a button revealing an altered map. Most of the red splotches faded, with the largest remaining flower of red being in Washington, D.C. "The president, feeling fine, kept his appointments throughout the week and his healthy immune system had fought off the flu. Again, we got lucky. Exposure was traceable and minimized.

"Now, back to the worst-case scenario, continuing from today." Sara clicked the mouse. The animation continued. Red spots spread and grew. No continent was untouched. Most major cities were completely red and several small towns had turned red as well.

"Two weeks," Sara said.

Red covered the majority of the country, except for the most rural spots. The same was true around the globe. Even Antarctica had some red spots.

"A month."

The world was coated in red. If there wasn't any red, people didn't live there.

"From what we've seen, this new strain of Brugada kills within a week. That means there would already be people dying."

King shifted in his chair. "Could this be happening now? Some other outbreak we don't know about yet?"

"Someone would notice all these people dying from the same disorder," Rook said.

"When a fat man dies of a heart attack, does it make the news?" Sara asked. "When a tired man falls asleep at the wheel and wrecks his car, do you read about it in *The New York Times*? When a woman commits suicide by falling off a bridge, does anyone care? People who die from Brugada often appear to have died from another cause and the flu is generally beat inside of a week. There are countless reasons why doctors would never suspect that people were dying from Brugada. More than that, the only method of testing for the disorder is through an electrocardiograph, which measures the electrical fluctuations of a *beating heart*."

"The victim has to survive," Knight said.

"Not survive," Sara corrected. "Be brought back. Brugada is one hundred percent fatal. Very few people are resuscitated unless they're in or near a medical facility. If this gets out . . . if this thing spreads, all hell will break loose. If we fail . . . this might be our future." Sara looked up at the image of the red-covered world and shook her head. A world without men loomed on the horizon. It might take a year for them all to contract Brugada and die, but if an outbreak occurred, accidental or as an attack, it *would* happen. The human race would die.

"Our goal is simple," Sara said, pushing past her fears and getting back on task. "Visit the village of Anh Dung, take blood samples from the women and any surviving men, and analyze them on the spot. If we get a match . . . if we find an immune male . . ." This was the one part of the plan Sara totally disagreed with. But she knew their options were scarce and it ensured success. ". . . we will . . . kidnap the individual and bring him back. We're confident a cure can be developed quickly at that point."

Sara took a deep breath. She was done and prayed to God she wouldn't have to explain all that, to anyone, ever again. She preferred to be working, not giving lectures. "Any more questions?"

Rook raised his hand. "Just one."

Sara cringed inwardly. She didn't even know why the team charged with her protection had to know anything about Brugada. Keasling said something about knowing their enemy. She thought that was a ridiculous answer, but the solemn faces around the room told her that the urgency of the mission had been impressed upon them. With the lives of six billion now dependent on six, the explanation had provided motivation in spades. But did they really understand or would they write it off as the fantasy of a CDC kook? "Go ahead," Sara replied.

"Why the hell are we still sitting here?" Rook said.

They understood perfectly. She raised her hand toward Keasling. "General?"

Keasling walked toward the front of the room. He took the laptop mouse and zoomed the satellite image out. As the image pulled back, border lines cut the land into three chunks. "Anh Dung is here, just inside the border of Vietnam. They will not take too kindly to our little raiding party, so we will touch down here . . ."

Keasling pointed on the other side of the border. ". . . in Laos, just north of Cambodia. The region is known as the Annamite Convergence Zone, where all three countries come together in a patch of mountainous land no one in their right mind would claim. It's a thick jungle, hotter than Los Angeles in August and more humid than Satan's sauna. The terrain is rugged, with mountain peaks and deep valleys. Right now the weather is calm, but the region is known for sudden monsoons. If it starts raining, take shelter and pray. On top of all of that, the region is home to the beloved Ho Chi Minh Trail and rife with old land mines. Scan any clearings or fields before jaunting across."

Keasling closed the laptop and flicked on the lights. While the others squinted at the sudden light change, he continued. "Now, for all intents and purposes, we are invading a foreign country. A country that is still licking wounds opened when you all were just pups. You will not only leave your

ANNAMITE MOUNTAIN RANGE CONVERGENCE ZONE

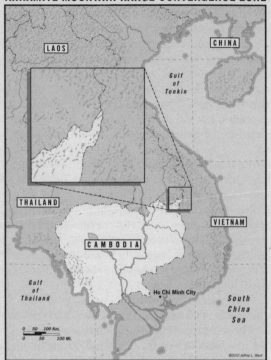

identification behind, but contact will be kept to a minimum. If you are captured, we cannot come for you. If you are killed, we will never know."

Sara blanched as she listened to Keasling. She'd been so focused on her mission that she hadn't given much thought to the physical danger she would soon face.

"The only time you will make contact is when your mission is complete and you are en route to the extraction zone. Any questions?"

"Yeah," King said. "Where is Deep Blue?"

The team's handler typically joined mission briefings—

and often delivered them himself—via a remote connection, remaining silhouetted to protect his identity.

"Blue will not be a part of this mission," Keasling replied.

Rook crossed his arms and tilted his head to the side. "Why the hell not?"

Keasling raised his voice a little. "Not only does satellite surveillance provide zero strategic advantage in a jungle too thick to penetrate, but he's dealing with another crisis at the moment. You don't have to like it. That's just the way it is."

Nods all around. They didn't like it, but there wasn't much they did like about most missions. Other than finishing them successfully. Being one of the world's most elite special ops teams meant getting the hardest jobs in the worst-case scenarios. Not one of them would complain.

Keasling reached into his pocket and removed what looked like six wristwatches. He slid them, one at a time, to each member of the team. King slapped his hand over the device, then looked at the screen. It was blank save for a green bar of color stretching across the bottom of the small digital display. "These are?"

"In case you need inspiration. Essentially an outbreak meter. While we can't have direct communication, these can receive signals that can't be deciphered or interpreted. They're based on the terror threat meter. Green means everything is hunky-dory. Red means the world is screwed."

"Pandemic," Sara said.

"Or the start of one," Keasling corrected. "We're technically at yellow now. Lewis will send a test signal while you're in flight and upgrade the threat level from green to yellow."

All six slipped the devices onto their wrists.

Keasling leaned forward, hands on the table. "We've picked up a slight increase in local chatter, but nothing to be concerned with. While we're not expecting any hostiles, that doesn't mean there won't be any. Whoever sent the attack on President Duncan is familiar with Brugada. They might be in the area."

"The Vietnamese?" King asked.

"They'd be brazen little shits, if it was them. It's unlikely, but we're looking into it. The fact is, we have no idea where this thing came from, who sent it, or why. Frankly, we don't give a damn about the *why* right now. We just want to stop the end of human civilization if someone decides our time on the planet is up."

He stood up straight. "You have five days."

EIGHT

Thirty Thousand Feet above the South China Sea

While in development, the sleek plane carrying the Chess Team to their destination halfway around the world was code named Senior Citizen. Now in active service, yet still classified top secret, the stealth transport had been dubbed Crescent for its half-moon shape. Its two turbo fan engines pushed the black specter through the night sky at speeds up to Mach 2, but held a casual Mach 1 speed as it approached the target area. The Crescent could haul up to twenty-five thousand pounds, including tanks, but this one had been converted for Special Ops HALO (High Altitude-Low Opening) drops and, as a result, featured several private rooms complete with bunks, closets, and heads. It had a price tag of five hundred million dollars, not including the billions in research and development, but it did its job, which right now was to transport two pilots, two doctors, the five members of the Chess Team, plus their newest addition, Pawn, halfway around the world—undetected.

"You're serious?" Sara said, arms crossed over her small chest. "Pawn?"

King nodded as the incision over his heart was stitched up. He winced as Dr. Mark Byers gave the wire a few tugs, pulling the cut flesh together. He'd been given local anesthesia, but because they were jumping right into a mission, the dosage had been low and the effects long since diminished. Luckily, Byers announced he was done, with a quick snip. "Thanks, Mark."

The balding doctor winked and began wiping down the scalpel he'd used to open King's chest. "Just try to avoid any physical activity for the next few days. Wouldn't want it to reopen."

As King laughed, Byers, who'd given King more than a few stitches in the past few years, patted his shoulder and added, "I put in a few extras. It should hold. Just make sure I don't have to give you more when you return, eh?"

"No kidding. You do a terrible job. I've got scars in places no other man has seen."

Byers guffawed as he placed the scalpel in an alcohol solution. "With that birthmark of yours you'd be lucky to find anyone, man or woman, willing to find all your scars. You're just lucky I get paid so well."

King smiled while inspecting his freshly sewn wound. "You get paid well?"

"Better than you."

King shook his head. "I'm the one taking the bullets."

"And I'm the one pulling them out of your ugly ass. Which do you think is harder?"

As the banter continued, Sara tuned out the rest. Her impatience mounted. She'd asked him a question and he outright ignored her. She'd been told that the "Chess Team" was supposed to be the best—smarter and tougher—but she was beginning to have doubts. She knew that Delta operators were more casual than their Special Forces counterparts like the Navy SEALs or Army Rangers. She knew they received stipends to purchase their own weapons. They had to blend. They had to look normal, fit in with a crowd. But that didn't mean they had to be unprofessional.

And King, their leader—she had no idea what his rank actually was, as Delta had done away with ranks—was more casual than the rest. His blue jeans, Elvis T-shirt, and scruffy black hair wasn't a cover. It was him. Who he was.

But the positively most annoying aspect of the mission thus far was the plane. If it was stealth, why was it so loud? Not to mention the smell of ordnance, oil, and human sweat that assaulted her nose and brought on a headache that had taken four ibuprofen to tame. And the shaking . . . the dipping up and down . . . the consoles with blinking lights . . . the—

Sara focused her mind back on King to avoid descending into sensory overload anxiety. She'd been diagnosed with Sensory Processing Disorder a few years back, which at the time had been a relief because it removed the guilt she'd carried for being so picky and demanding about her environment, but it didn't ease the effects of the disorder. Her senses were not only hypersensitive, they would get mixed up. Smells could give her blinding headaches. She could feel sounds. Rain, cursed with manmade chemicals, caused her to break out in hives. The sun, which most people felt as a blunt warmth, felt as a thousand pinpricks on her skin.

She'd managed to find her own coping mechanisms for most of the everyday challenges, and much of her work as a disease detective for the CDC kept her in familiar territory, even while in the field. But this mission, with its vast numbers of unknowns, new people, new experiences, and totally new surroundings was wreaking havoc with her senses faster than her mind could keep up. Her only defense was distraction . . . and that was hard to come by when she was being ignored.

While lost in her frustration, Sara hadn't noticed her clenching hands, her reddening cheeks, or her pulsating jaw muscles. But King had. He was quite aware that Sara was about to lose her cool, and all it took was a few seconds of ignoring her. She needed some work. A lot of work. He hopped off the operating table, picked up some clothes from a nearby stool, and said, "Did you say something?"

Sara felt close to popping, but swallowed her words upon seeing King's back. Not only was the musculature perfectly sculpted, but it was covered by a large, purple . . . something. A tattoo?

"It's called a port-wine stain. It's a birthmark."

"A vascular malformation."

King chuckled.

"They're genetic. Connected to the RASA-one protein activator. You probably had a grandparent with one. They're caused by dilated capillaries, usually on the face."

"Not this one. It runs down my ass and around to my inner thighs." King turned around with a smile as he donned a black, moisture-wicking long-sleeve shirt. Sara caught a glimpse of his chiseled stomach and blinked as the words that had been on the tip of her tongue dissolved into the recess of her mind. "Wanna see?"

"What? No. Absolutely not." Sara continued to blink as her mind began to catch up with her distracted senses. Then she remembered: Pawn. "My code name—"

"You'd like something else?"

Sara began to respond, but was quickly cut off.

"Like it or not, you're part of the Chess Team now, and the other names are already taken. Any time we take someone else on, they become Pawn. That's just the way it is. If you want to rename yourself RASA-one, go for it, but from now until we debrief in Limbo, you're Pawn."

The room fell silent except for the wind rushing by the aircraft and the roar of its engines. Sara sighed with the realization that she was picking the fight to vent the anxiety caused in part because of the impending thirty-thousand-foot jump, but also from her assaulted senses. It was a stupid fight to pick. "Fine." She turned to walk away and added, "At least I know I'm the expendable piece."

King snatched her shoulder and spun her around. He glared into her eyes and said, "*No one* is expendable on this team. Including you. *Especially* you."

He held her gaze and in that moment she felt the powerful

sincerity of his words. His voice carried the passion of a man in love—though he was not. Still, his words stirred something in her and kept her from replying.

He noticed her forehead and shoulders relax. She'd be okay. "Of course, you're working for the military now. We're all expendable."

Sara's laugh was cut short as the door to the makeshift operating room swung open. Rook's head poked in. "Hey, quit dry humpin' and get your shit together. We're an hour and fifteen out. Time to get geared up and start prebreathing."

King smiled at Sara as Rook ducked out. Despite his insistence on designating her Pawn, he couldn't stop thinking of her as Sara. And he felt it important he didn't. Just a second's worth of believing she could take care of herself might be enough for her to wind up dead. They might call her Pawn . . . one of the team . . . but she was really Sara, the sitting duck. "You heard the man, quit dry humpin' me and get ready to jump."

Sara began to respond, but a flicker of color on King's wrist caught her attention. He saw her frown and looked at his arm. The outbreak meter had gone from green to yellow. Lewis's test signal had transmitted. It was a simple change in color, but carried dire implications.

"It'll be okay," he said, placing his hand gently on her shoulder.

Her stomach knotted at his touch. She wondered if this is how it felt; going into battle with strangers. They knew nothing about each other, but every gesture, touch, and word snuck past her personal defenses. In that moment she noticed King's presence in full. The thin scar on his neck. The confidence of his stance. Even his smell—metallic. And for a moment, until he spoke again, she felt safe.

"Time to go." He nodded to the door and followed her out.

In the hurried fifteen minutes to follow there was little time to think. They quickly donned their jumpsuits, harnesses, bailout bottles, gear, and weapons, all of which had been triple checked during the flight over the Pacific. Then they sat, placed oxygen masks over their faces, and breathed 100 percent O_2 for the next hour, which flushed nitrogen from their bloodstreams. The air pressure outside the Crescent was one-third that of sea level's. Jumping at thirty thousand feet with too much nitrogen in your body would give you the bends, akin to what SCUBA divers experience if they surface too fast. Nausea, headaches, and, in worst-case scenarios, death could occur. Not a good way to start an operation.

For the next thirty minutes, while prebreathing, Sara read and reread their mission profile. They were meeting up with a CIA operative out of Laos who'd spent a lot of time in the Annamite range. She knew nothing about this person other than they held the code name Pawn Two. How original. Then they would head for Anh Dung, a village smack dab in the middle of a mountainous nowhere.

The side benefit was that the mountain range had become a modern Noah's Ark. Before the war, only local villagers ventured into the massif. It was the same for generation upon generation, going back thousands of years. And now even the villagers were afraid to tread on the explosive soil. Only a few biologists and cryptozoologists had braved the region. It was a gold mine of unclassified mammals the likes of which the world had not yet seen. Sometimes the scientists went in and never came back out, but the draw continued to that day.

A red flashing light took attention away from the dossier in her gloved hands. She put it aside and heard King's voice loud and clear in her earpiece. "Two minutes, people. Pawn, get over here."

As the seconds ticked by, King fastened himself to her back. While Sara had been skydiving several times before, she'd never done a HALO jump and even if she had, she had a feeling King would still insist they jumped tandem.

Thirty seconds until jump time, she felt the Crescent slow significantly. Then the hydraulic bay door hissed open, exposing them to the freezing thirty-thousand-foot night air.

She felt the temperature change even through her protective jumpsuit.

"Switch to your bailout bottles," King said. "On my mark . . . jump!"

One by one, the Delta team jumped from the back, commencing a free fall that would take them rocketing toward the earth's surface only to be yanked up by their chutes at an extremely low altitude. King and Sara jumped last.

Cast out of the nearly invisible Crescent, the team, all wearing black, disappeared into the night. If not for small glow-in-the-dark diamonds on the back of their helmets, the team would find staying together impossible. King found the four diamonds below and tilted himself and Sara forward. They glided through the air and joined the rest of the team, who'd already taken up formation.

As the thirty-below wind whipped past, Sara was amazed at how different this was from low-altitude skydiving. A typical drop might last only seconds before chutes deployed, but they'd already free fallen ten thousand feet and had another nineteen to go before they'd open their chutes. The downside, of course, was that at one thousand feet, descending at terminal velocity, there was no time to open a reserve if the main failed. For that reason, none of them even had reserves.

But Sara's mind wasn't on becoming a stain on the ground. She was enjoying the freedom of the moment. Not only was she free of earth, but her senses were free as well. The wind generated pressure on her body like a heavy blanket. The white noise of rushing air blocked out everything else. And the darkness above and below let her eyes relax. It was as though she were in a wonderful bed.

King noticed Sara's body go slightly limp beneath him. If she passed out it would make for a rough landing. Hell, it was going to be rough already. But if she were unconscious, someone would most likely get hurt. He knocked on her helmet with his fist. "You okay?"

"Never better," came Sara's reply through his earpiece. "I'm—"

"King, LZ is compromised," Knight said coolly.

King looked past Sara's helmet and saw crisscrossing patterns of tracer fire slicing across the field that was supposed to be their deserted landing zone. King had no idea who the combatants were and had no time to ponder about it. *Damnit, where are you, Deep Blue,* King thought. They could have used him now. But he wasn't there, and King would have to trust what he could see with his own two eyes.

The field was surrounded by miles of thick jungle and uneven terrain. There was nowhere else to go.

"Land at the edge of the northern jungle and hump it inside as soon as you hit. Protect Pawn. Shoot to kill."

Sara's body went rigid and her breathing became frantic. She'd never been in a firefight and they were dropping straight into a war zone! She felt a second knock on her helmet.

"Sorry, Pawn," King said in her ear. "This is gonna hurt."

NINE

Annamite Convergence Zone—Laos

Chaos reigned as the Chess Team hit the thousand-foot mark and deployed their chutes. Their parachutes snapped open loudly, but the sound was drowned out by the staccato machine gun fire being traded by the opposing forces below. With their one-hundred-twenty-mile-per-hour descent slowed significantly, the odds of surviving a normal landing improved greatly, but they were far from traveling at a safe speed . . . and this was no normal landing.

With ten seconds to impact, there was no time to issue orders, change plans, or even hope for the best. From the moment the tracers were first seen and King's initial orders were given the team had been relying on their single greatest asset: instinct. It told them to come in fast. To roll, cut loose, and make for the trees. To stay together.

Only one of them lacked these instincts.

Pawn.

"Oh, God. Oh, God. Oh, God!" The words issued forth as if she were a stutterer on speed. Sara whipped her head from side to side, taking in the crisscrossing bolts of light that revealed the path of thousands of invisible bullets. Her subconscious told her to pray. Death loomed and her maker would soon greet her, but she couldn't get past "Oh, God." Perhaps it would be enough?

Then a voice penetrated her mania. "Go loose, Pawn!"

Without fully registering the statement, her body obeyed and went slack. She heard the sound of tearing fabric, a grunt, and then met the ground. The world went dizzy as she was turned over, cut loose, and shoved away. She fell face-first into soft, muddy earth, surrounded on all sides by four-foot-tall reeds.

"King, this place is crawling," came Rook's voice in her ear. "The forest is a no-go for now." She looked to the side, expecting to see Rook beside her, but she couldn't see anything but reeds in all directions, lit from above by the angry fireflies flitting back and forth.

Not fireflies. Bullets.

"How many?" King replied.

"I'm seeing ten to fifteen," Knight said as he scanned the reeds with a pair of night vision goggles. "From each side. These guys are looking to engage at close range and we're at ground zero."

Sara felt a hand wrap around her mouth and tried to scream, but her voice was muffled. She was yanked around and found King's face only inches from hers. He put his finger to his lips, shushing her.

"Bishop," King said. "Waist level. Full spread."

"I'm ready," Bishop said. It was unusual for him to be called into action at the outset of a mission, but his skills were obviously called for.

King pushed Sara down, lying on top of her so that the side of her face squished into the mud and the chaos finally got to her. She breathed deep as the tracer fire left purple streaks in her vision, the ceaseless pop of gunfire pricked her skin like hot needles, and the wet mud itched her face. Something in her mind snapped, almost audibly, like a breaking branch. She screamed like a banshee, but no one heard.

Not over the staccato roar of Bishop's machine gun.

With each fired round, he loosed the pure rage built up inside him—a product of childhood abandonment and a side effect of the regenerative formula coursing through his veins. For a moment, the advancing soldiers on either side paused. Bishop stood tall above the reeds, his new, XM312 .50-caliber machine gun loaded and ready. The weapon, normally only usable from atop a tripod, had been lightened and modified to hold a drum magazine, rather than a chain of bullets, which also allowed for a faster, eight-hundred-round-per-minute firing rate. The portable killing machine was one of a kind and dubbed the XM312-*B* by the designer. He pulled the trigger with no delay and laid down a swath of waist-height lead. Men gurgled and fell. Reeds exploded into the air. In fifteen seconds, Bishop's weapon had belched two hundred .50-caliber rounds in a 360-degree area. A jagged thirty-foot clearing, with Bishop at its center, had been mowed down when he took his finger off the trigger. Writhing bodies of injured combatants lined the east and west of the new clearing. King and crew, now visible, were arranged single file down the middle from north to south, with Knight in the lead and King at the back end.

For a moment, silence returned to the field as both sides tried to determine what had happened and who was left alive.

In that blessed silence, Sara's mind returned and took in the world. King rose off her and pulled her up. With both ears free to hear and the night returned to an obsidian fog, sounds that most people tune out as background noise—the gentle northward breeze, the rubbing of reeds—entered her ears and through some neurological crosswire became physical sensation. She felt the attacker coming and reacted.

"King, behind you!" Her voice ripped through the silence like tearing flesh, violent and shrill.

King reacted fast, spinning and firing a three-round burst with his M4 assault rifle. A body stumbled out of the reeds and crumpled to the ground close enough for them to see in the moonlight . . . close enough for them to make out the red and white checkered scarf covering his head. King recognized it as the calling card for one of the region's most notorious fighting forces, but they were supposed to be relics of a bloody past.

"That's just great," King said before jumping to his feet, grabbing Sara by the arm, and yanking her violently behind him. The others were already charging for the forest and they were lagging behind. Sara felt positive that King could easily catch up to the others, but his obligation to protect her kept him rooted to her side. She focused on the task and picked up her pace.

King noticed Sara had found her footing and let go of her arm. They'd move faster separately. He hoped she knew enough to stay close and keep her head down. The moment both sides of this confrontation discovered their men were dead, they would assume that the other side had won and unleash hell on their position, and King did not want to be around when that happened. The new clearing would become a very large target. As King and Sara entered the reeds and made for the trees, a barrage of bullets fired from both forces descended on the clearing. The injured men left in the reeds began shouting for their forces to cease fire, but were soon reduced to pulp.

The rain of bullets widened as both forces sought to cut down any fleeing survivors. The bullets hissed in pursuit as they ate through the reeds, seeking flesh. But the hiss of bullets through vegetation turned to woody clunks as she and King entered the dense forest, leaving the killing field behind.

King's hand on her chest told her to stop moving. Panicked beyond comprehension, Sara froze. Her mind spun, trying to catch up with her senses, which had been pounded during the battle. In that still moment, she thought about her parents, her friends, and the children she wanted to have someday. She wondered if her body somehow knew it was about to die and was instinctually flashing her life before her eyes. She ducked without realizing it, but King took her arm and pulled her back up straight.

"Settle down. You're safe." Moving quickly, King opened her backpack, extricated her night vision goggles, and put them on her head.

"Can you see?" he asked.

The world came into high-contrast green focus as the goggles absorbed what tiny fraction of light entered the forest through the thick canopy and amplified it.

"Yes," she said, surprised at how shaky her voice sounded. It was then that she noticed her knees were equally as shaky. She moved to sit.

King's firm grip on her arm held her up. "Uh-uh," he said. "Time to go."

Sara looked up and saw Knight, Rook, and Bishop bunny hopping into the forest. A sob almost escaped her as she realized the night's action—and danger—were far from over. She stood to run and felt a clap on her shoulder. She saw Queen's bright smile lined by green lips.

"Don't worry, Pawn, I got your back."

With that Sara was yanked into the darkness and began running through the night. With each step her body felt worse, racked with pain from physical and emotional stress, not to mention that running in full-body military garb in eighty-degree heat with ninety percent humidity was like strapping wet sandpaper between her legs. At the same time, she became more relieved as each passing moment took them farther away from the two factions in the field. She had no idea who they were, but King's reaction to the red and white checkered scarf told her he recognized at least one side of the battle. Still, she doubted the fight had anything to do with them.

A local conflict of some kind, she thought. *It is a volatile region.*

The Chess Team pushed forward through the dark, each confused by the hot LZ, each remaining silent as Knight led them forward through the night, toward their rendezvous point with Pawn Two. Though the mission had started out with a resounding bang, the team had come through unscathed and on course. Just a bump in the road, Rook would later say.

But not one of them, with their instincts and training, was aware that they were being followed by one who knew the forest infinitely well and stalked them with ease. She'd been following them since their dramatic escape from the killing fields and had been observing them since.

The skinny woman will undo them, she thought.

She would fall first.

TEN

The sun rose, bringing with it the hope of full-color vision and the chance to rest. The Chess Team had been moving since their landing. They'd traveled in silence, save for Sara's heavy breathing. She was in good shape for the average person, but due to the level of activity combined with the sudden extreme stress of the battle, Sara moved like the walking dead.

An hour ago, as the sun first began to cut through the canopy and they removed their night vision goggles, Rook had surprised Sara by coming back to help her walk. He claimed her slow pace was going to get them all killed, but after a while he started chatting about his family. Turned out he was a real mama's boy. Went on and on about her homemade whoopie pies. And he had sisters. Three. She reminded him of the youngest. Hence his chivalry and premission concerns.

But Sara was grateful for the help and conversation, which kept her mind occupied enough to forget her overactive senses. He kept her moving when she slowed. As her legs grew wobbly from the weight of the thirty-pound pack on her back, he took it and carried it along with his own forty-pound pack. He seemed giant. Surreal. Like God had sent a superhuman big brother to watch out for her.

The terrain, which had been blessedly level for the past

two miles, began to slant uphill, gradually at first, but the grade grew steep as they ascended the Annamite foothills. Sara did her best to keep moving, but the slippery coating of leaves on the forest floor kept the ground shifting beneath her feet. Upon falling a third time, her muscles gave up and she slouched to the ground, a prone figure in black.

Rook paused. "Knight, hold up a sec. Pawn's done."

A half mile ahead, Knight stopped moving, pulled out his canteen, and took a swig. Queen joined him a moment later. Then Bishop. They shared drinks and energy bars, waiting patiently for those lagging behind. They felt secure in the fact that they were in the middle of nowhere and hadn't seen or heard signs of danger since the previous night.

But they were wrong.

They weren't alone.

King backtracked to Rook and found Sara nearly unconscious at his feet. He shook his head. *Not good,* he thought. More than any of them, she had to keep moving or everyone on the planet could be at the mercy of whoever had control of the new Brugada strain. He felt the jagged edges of the stitches in his chest rubbing against his moisture-wicking undershirt and felt a measure of comfort. If *he* died from Brugada, at least he'd come back.

"Catch up with the others," King said to Rook. "I want an ETA when we reach you."

"You got it," Rook said before heading out.

King knelt down, lifted Sara's head, and smacked her lightly on the cheek. Her eyes fluttered. "Drink this," he said, holding a small container to her lips.

She sipped, coughed, sipped again. A moment later she was sitting up chugging the bittersweet mystery liquid. With the small thermos empty, she looked at King with wide, alert eyes. "Oh God, I can't believe you brought coffee."

"Espresso, actually. You just drank about five servings."

Sara's forehead scrunched. "Is that normal for you to carry?"

King stood and shook his head. "Made a pit stop before we shipped out. Thought you might need it. Make sure you drink a lot of water now or you'll get dehydrated."

Sara noticed they were alone. "Where are the others?"

"Waiting."

"Shouldn't they be here? In case something happens?"

"I wanted a moment with you."

A twinge of fear squeezed Sara's stomach. What was he up to? "Why?"

"Because I'm about to be a bastard and I didn't want an audience." He squatted down and faced her. "Listen. It makes total sense that you're the core of this mission. We're all here for you. But you've got to start carrying your own weight. Push yourself beyond what you believe you're capable of. The pain doesn't matter. Physical injury doesn't matter. You can spend the rest of the year, hell, the rest of your life healing mind and body, but the mission comes first. Your survival is my mission, but that doesn't mean your experience has to be a good one."

Sara nodded, her jaw slightly agape. She had yet to consider what the lasting effects of this mission, aside from death, would be. Flashes of limbless veterans filled her mind. Victims of post-traumatic stress—shell shock. Night terrors. Would she become like that?

She looked at King, thinking, *Why isn't he like that?*

Then she screamed.

"In the tree!"

The black shadow descended as King dove, rolled, and took aim with his M4. But even his honed reflexes weren't fast enough. The black figure crouched behind Sara, using her as an effective shield from any bullets King might unleash. A knife was placed against Sara's throat. The attacker was steady. Practiced.

"Lower your weapon," the figure said with an accented feminine voice.

King followed her order.

He didn't move, ask questions, or make threats. He waited.

The silence continued for twenty seconds. Sara sensed that these were predators sizing each other up.

"Pawn Two," King said. "Let her go."

"She's going to get you all killed," Pawn Two said. "If you can't protect her, she has no business out here."

"Who said we can't protect her?" It was Rook. The muzzle of his .50-caliber Desert Eagle hovered an inch from the back of Pawn Two's skull. One shot would make her head simply cease to exist.

King stepped forward. "Pawn Two. If you do not remove your knife—"

With a quick twist the knife was removed from Sara's throat and sheathed in Pawn Two's sleeve. Sara scrambled away and turned to face her attacker. If she hadn't nearly been killed by the woman, she would have found her almost comical. She was dressed in black, like they were, but wore a mask over her face like some kind of ninja. And she wasn't imposing at all. Her five-foot height was balanced by a spindly build. She looked like an overgrown ant, but her gleaming green eyes revealed her to be a praying mantis.

As the Chess Team took up positions around her, keeping their weapons trained on all parts of her body, Pawn Two removed her hood. Her oval eyes squinted when she smiled. "Consider it an object lesson."

"You could have been killed," King said.

"And she would have been," Pawn Two said, motioning to Sara. "If she hadn't warned you, it would have been you with the knife to your throat."

Not only did King not have the time or energy to have this discussion, but he also knew she was right. Sara was a liability. But he had no choice. She was the mission.

The woman finished tying her spaghetti-straight black hair in a ponytail and extended her hand to Sara. "They'll keep calling me Pawn Two, I'm sure, but you can call me Somi, short for Sommalina. Sommalina Syha. Sorry about the neck."

Sara took her hand and was pulled to her feet. The woman

was a mystery. Not only was she small, exotic, and dangerous (not in that order) but she was also charming. She walked to a tree, reached around, and picked up a Franchi SPAS-12 shotgun. Its dual design allowed the shooter to fire both single pump-action shots and gas-powered automatic shots of up to four rounds a second.

Rook raised an eyebrow. "That's all you got?"

"Born and raised in the jungle. This is all I need, G.I. Joe."

"Just call me Gung Ho," Rook said.

Somi smiled and started off into the forest.

"What's the hurry?" Queen said, her voice cut with tension and distrust.

Somi paused and looked at each of them. "I've been following you since you touched down. One of the two factions you found fighting has been following you as well. The others were Khmer Rouge remnants defending their turf. They stayed put."

King tensed. This was bad news. Why would someone follow them?

"Well, that's just shitabulous," Rook said. "How many men are we talking about here?"

Somi shrugged.

"You don't know?" Rook said.

"It was dark."

"Then how do you know they're following us?"

Somi put her hand on Rook's mouth. It appeared more an act of seduction than of covering his voice, but the effect was the same. Rook held his breath.

"Listen to the wind," Somi said.

They listened. All of them. And each heard nothing but Somi's lingering sarcasm. But in the still silence of the jungle, Sara felt them as her senses turned the distant shuffle of feet through leaves and the odors of men caught on the wind into a physical sensation. She couldn't hear them. But she could *feel* them like a gentle tickle on her skin.

Strange, she thought. In the city, her senses were so

overwhelmed that she rarely fully understood the world. She just focused on her destination and moved, doing her best to ignore her senses. But in this natural setting she seemed to be more aware of what she felt. She spoke without thinking. "They're coming from the southeast."

Sara blinked and looked at the others. They were all staring at her as though she had two heads. "What?"

"I was joking," Somi said.

"But you said—"

Somi held up a small PDA. "Motion sensors. I spent all day yesterday lining the game trails with them."

King squinted. Twice now Sara had warned him of danger long before he knew it was coming. In the reed field she may very well have saved his life. He turned to Somi. "Is she right?"

Somi was already looking at the PDA, her lips pursed, her forehead crisscrossed with confusion. "Dead on."

Bishop walked up to the group, leaving the tree he'd been leaning on throughout the interchange. "We better go." He turned and began ascending the foothill. Queen and Knight followed.

"No more object lessons," King said to Somi.

She nodded. "The next lesson you get won't be from me, and it won't be an object lesson."

She said it with such confidence, King realized she knew more than she'd revealed. "Pawn, stay with the others. We'll bring up the rear."

Sara nodded slowly. Her muscles, tight with tension, fought against her as she moved. The introduction to Somi had been so unnerving that it had exhausted her. The caffeine seemed to be wearing off already. She remembered King's reprimand and pushed against the pain in her legs. The mission would be completed, no matter the cost to their bodies or psyches. They just had to succeed and survive. She left with Rook, moving fast to catch up with the others.

When the group was out of earshot, King turned to Somi. "Who are they? Who is following us?"

"I wasn't sure at first, but after last night's battle ended I had a chance to inspect the dead men's uniforms. VPLA. The Death Volunteers," Somi said with a frown. "Vietnamese special forces."

ELEVEN

Seven sets of lungs heaved wet air in and out as the newly expanded Chess Team ran for their lives. King hadn't made the decision to run lightly. He knew the team was tired. He knew several preferred to stand their ground. But that wasn't their mission. If they could get in and out without facing the VPLA hot on their heels, so much the better. They posed a direct threat to his mission: to protect Pawn One.

Sara.

It was highly unlikely that even the Chess Team could protect her against such overwhelming odds, even if they themselves survived. So his only option was run like a bastard and stay ahead.

For Sara, a mixture of caffeine and adrenaline reawakened her muscles and kept her moving at a pace she'd never have believed possible. She knew if they stopped, she'd never get started again. But she didn't think King would give her a chance to stop. The man was a machine. He hadn't told her why they were hauling ass up the steep grades of the Annamite foothills, but she recognized a twinge of fear in his voice when he gave the order to run. And in that fear she saw a twinkle of hope. His fear gave her confidence. She didn't know if he feared for his life or simply feared failing the mission, but his trepidation let her know that he wasn't cocky to a fault. He knew when to fight and knew when to run.

Only she hoped the running would end soon.

It did. Thirty minutes later, after running four miles and ascending eight hundred feet, they broke out of the jungle's shadow and into a clearing. The late-day sun beat down on them, making them squint, but it also freed them from the moisture of the jungle and clouds of mosquitoes.

"We can stop here," Somi said between gulps of air. Even the stealthy jungle veteran was out of breath. "Anh Dung is a half mile to the north, through the field."

"Anh Dung?" Sara asked.

Somi nodded. "Our target, yes."

"I thought it was in Vietnam?"

"There are no 'Welcome to Vietnam' signs in the bush," Somi said, shaking her head with a sarcastic smile. "Or on the roads, for that matter."

"We've been in Vietnam for about an hour," King said. "We're almost there."

Sara felt rejuvenated. This nightmare was nearly half over. "Then we need to keep moving," Sara said. This drew odd looks from the exhausted team. "We're not going to be able to walk in there, say 'Aha! Here's the cure!' and walk out again. I don't know how long this will take."

King took a deep breath and nodded.

"You're sure?" Somi asked. "You're not going to be able to think well if you're exhausted."

Sara took a drink of water, screwed the cap back on, and wiped her mouth. "We don't want to be caught, do we? No more object lessons."

King grinned. Sara was more resilient than he expected. He turned to Somi. "Do you have any more motion sensors?"

"A few," Somi said.

"I want them placed at the most likely entry points to this field. If they're still following us, I want to know about it before they're knocking on our front door. Rook, you're with Pawn Two. Knight, Queen, I want trip wires set wherever there isn't a motion sensor. Make them loud. Bishop, you're with me. We need to sweep a clean path through this field."

Rook handed Sara her backpack. "You'll be needing this."

Sara took the pack and slung it on her back. The weight of the world seemed to land on her shoulders, not only because of the pack's thirty-pound load, but because the instruments it contained, combined with her mind, were all that stood between the human race and extinction.

The team split up without another word. Somi, Rook, Knight, and Queen headed back into the sultry jungle without complaint and disappeared into the darkness. Bishop slung his FN over his back and then quickly assembled a portable metal detector. He began sweeping the device back and forth as he entered the tall brown grass.

King motioned for Sara to follow and she did. He brought up the rear, his M4 ever at the ready.

Tension racked King's back. The mission was turning into a disaster and it seemed the seven of them, six really, would have to hold off a superior force long enough for Sara to finish her job, however long that might take.

King watched Sara as she walked in front of him, keeping in tight formation behind Bishop, only pausing when Bishop stuck small orange flags in the ground, marking the location of land mines, which turned out to be an easy job as the locals had already marked the mines with stones. Though from the height and withered condition of the field, it was clear they still avoided its deadly soil. She seemed to be comforted by the wall Bishop's large body created, or perhaps she was simply hiding from the sun in his shadow. She seemed to avoid direct sunlight whenever possible. But she had come a long way from the distractible woman he'd met at Fort Bragg. Hell, they'd landed in a war zone and she had actually warned *him* of danger.

He didn't know what to call it. A sixth sense? Women's intuition?

King watched as Sara turned her head from side to side, her nostrils flaring, as she walked through the field in Bishop's wake. She was smelling the air . . . like a dog. *Exactly like a dog.* Three quick sniffs. Turn. Three more sniffs. She winced, held her hand to her nose in a classic "I have a headache" gesture, shook it off and kept sniffing. When he passed through the area that caused her apparent pain, something fragrant tickled his nose, but just for a moment. The subtle odor was a hint of something. Maybe a flower. But she'd reacted to it strongly.

She continued on like this for a minute, then her breaths became deeper. But the only thing King could smell was the— Wait. There *was* something. Hidden behind the odor of dry grass. Barely perceptible, it hid from his mind, making it impossible to identify. If he hadn't been paying attention to Sara's sniffing he'd have never noticed it.

He breathed deep through his nose, seeking to capture the smell like a perfumer studying a new scent. Nothing.

Sara turned to King. "You smell it, too?"

"I only noticed it because I saw you smelling the air. But it's faint. I can't I.D. it."

"But it's so strong." A shiver ran through Sara's body and King noticed. She was freaked out. Spooked. Something she smelled had her on edge, which meant she recognized it.

"Bishop, you smell anything?" King asked.

Bishop shook his head no.

"Pawn," King said. "What do you smell?"

It was the question that Sara dreaded from the moment she first picked up the odor, when the breeze shifted south and brought the new scent along for the ride. She'd experienced it several times before, always associated with being called to the scene of an outbreak. The smell of the dead and the dying drifted with the air and always assaulted her nostrils long before she saw the lines of bodies. She wept for the dead then, knowing that simple and cheap inoculations would have saved countless lives, but now . . . now she had to find a cure for a totally new disease before someone decided to commit worldwide genocide. They might not intend to, but every outbreak of the new Brugada strain could mean the end of the human race. There would be no weeping for the source of the smell on this trip. There was no time.

Sara answered the question with a whisper. "People, but they're dead."

Sara stumbled and looked down. A mound of dirt was hidden in the grass, six feet long, two wide.

King noticed it. "A grave."

"There's more up here," Bishop said. "A lot more."

King and Sara entered a clearing cut into the grass field. Twenty unmarked graves filled the space. Dry soil covered them, powdery and untouched by rain. Short grass surrounded each grave. The graveyard was new. Twenty people had been buried there in the last week.

A breeze bristled the tall grass surrounding the graveyard, flowing from the north, from the village, and brought a fresh wave of stench. The stench wasn't from the graveyard. And the others smelled it now, too. King grimaced and lofted his M4. "Let's go."

With Bishop in the lead, they reentered the grass and headed for the odor's source.

TWELVE

Anh Dung—Vietnam

Sara gagged as she exited the tall grass and entered the village proper. The odor of decaying human flesh had been filtered by grass, but here in the open, the stench overpowered the senses—hypersensitive or not. Sara covered her nose with her arm, working hard not to retch.

Bishop scrunched his nose in revolt, but said nothing and kept his weapon at the ready. King held his breath, removed his backpack, and dug inside. He removed three surgical masks and passed them out. After putting on his own, he said, "They're not perfect, but they'll help."

With the smell partly blocked, they turned their attention to the village. Fifteen huts standing upon two-foot stilts lined the small dirt path that wound down the middle of the small village. They were simple, yet effective. The stilts protected from the monsoon floods. The thatch roofs, made from tightly coiled reeds, kept the rains at bay. And the wooden plank walls held each structure firmly together while providing some protection from the elements. But they weren't designed to survive an attack. Sara could picture what the village must have looked like, but now it was in shambles.

Walls had been torn apart. Roofs had crumbled or burned.

The village looked like a howitzer had used it for target practice. But the structural damage to the village paled in comparison to the devastation wrought upon its occupants. Bodies were strewn throughout the village. Hanging out of doorways. Twisted over rocks. Lying in mud. Most of the dead had gaping wounds, exposing marbled flesh, glints of white bone, and skin torn like weak fabric. They'd been slaughtered. And not one body was seen outside the village. Whatever force had struck the village came so fast that not one villager had a chance to run.

"Brugada didn't do this," Sara said.

"I'd say so," King said as he approached a woman's headless body crumpled against a hut. Her head was in her lap, stained brown with blood. A swarm of flies dispersed at his approach, forming a wary, buzzing cloud above. He knelt down next to the woman. Her eyes were white and moving. Maggots. He looked at her neck. The skin, muscles, and veins were stretched and jagged. Her head had been torn off, not cut. King shot up, M4 at the ready.

With Bishop keeping watch in all directions, King went about quickly inspecting bodies. Some had been pummeled to death. Heads and chests bore indentations the size of his fist. Others had been torn apart, limbs removed, jaws snapped wide open, heads crushed. After inspecting the sixth victim he headed for the path. Footprints of all sizes had been pressed into the damp earth. King knelt and ran his hand through his hair, which was messier than usual thanks to the humidity.

Sara stood next to him, unsettled by the carnage. "What happened here?"

"Doesn't make sense," King said, his voice nearly a whisper.

Sara realized he was spooked.

King pointed to the last body he'd inspected. She looked at it. A young woman, perhaps still in her teens, lay gutted. Her organs displayed next to her in the short grass. Her face a petrified mask of horror. Sara looked away quickly.

She'd only seen a flash of the carnage, but it was more than enough.

"You need to see it for yourself," King said. "Look again. At her chest."

Sara brought her eyes back up and looked at the girl, avoiding the trail of intestines hanging from the cavity below her ribs. On her chest were four lacerations stretching from shoulder to ribs. She'd been mauled by something. Some kind of animal.

"And her head, at the temple," King instructed.

Sara looked. Two thick puncture wounds had been gouged in the side of her head where something large had bitten down.

"A tiger?" she said. Vietnam had as few as two hundred tigers left. The species was on the brink of extinction. But she couldn't think of any other possibility.

"Tigers are man-eaters, but not like this."

Sara's thoughts drifted to the Noah's Ark theory of the Annamites; to the large mammals still being discovered in the Asian wilderness and the external pressures placed on the region during the Vietnam War. "Maybe the tigers in the Annamites are different? Hyperevolved."

He waited for the explanation.

"When species are as isolated as they are here, they tend to evolve differently. In places like Australia, where evolution took its own path over millions of years, we see a totally unique group of mammal species."

"Galapagos Islands. Darwin. I'm with you."

"But in certain situations—when food is short, or even overly abundant—we see rapid evolution. We've been able to artificially boost the speed of evolution by three hundred percent in the lab, but in the wild, in extreme cases, the change can take place over a single generation. If food is abundant we find a process called plasticity. The evolving species eats more food, matures more quickly, and reproduces at earlier and earlier ages, creating a perfect recipe for evolution to occur quickly between generations."

"Like rabbits."

"Exactly. When food is plentiful, rabbit populations explode."

"Rabbits didn't do this."

"Not plasticity . . . Hyperevolution caused by food shortage or extreme competition tends to happen most frequently when humanity encroaches on a habitat. These kinds of changes are taking place all over the world at a *slightly* increased evolutionary pace. As the human race hunts Kodiak bears, their size continues to decrease, making them faster and harder to find. Squirrels, raccoons, and hawks have adapted to living in cities. There are more than five thousand coyotes living in Los Angeles. They've become more cunning. Faster. Smaller."

"Seems like you could just as easily end up with a superpredator. Fear and running away may let you live to fight another day, but eventually you *do* need to fight to survive."

Sara looked at him. "It's possible."

"Even so, *this* makes no sense." King shook his head. "Tigers kill to eat. They'd have no reason to kill an entire village. Even a hyperevolved tiger."

"Sometimes evolution is more of a psychological change, making a population more fearful or secretive. But it can also lead to extreme territoriality and violent behavior. A tiger forced into a new territory by a more dominant specimen might see the human population as competition and—"

"Do this."

"In theory. But hyperevolution requires an actual change in the genetic code, which certainly takes more time—even hyperevolution caused in accelerated breeding scenarios. We're assuming that tigers don't already have this instinct built in. It's not inconceivable that tigers have latent abilities and instincts that could be triggered in certain situations."

"That's possible?"

Sara gave a slight nod, trying to stay focused on her thoughts rather than the gore surrounding her. "Genetic assimilation. Basically, the genetics of a creature, whether it be tiger, human, or shark, remain unchanged despite phenotypic changes—appearance—or behavior. The genetic code remains intact, but the expression of that code is affected by the environment."

"Like playing the same song through different sets of speakers."

"Exactly. All the music is there, but some speakers have more bass than others, so a vocal track might get drowned out. Let's say there's an island populated by ground-dwelling squirrels typically preyed upon by birds. They stay close to the ground, seeking shelter in brush and subterranean dens. But introduce a land predator and the squirrels are suddenly climbing trees. The instinct and ability to climb trees have always been there, but weren't triggered until the introduction of a predator. The predator is basically a barrier to the continuing success and survival of the squirrel. Same as an ice age or food shortage might be. The genetic assimilation is a hard-wired method of overcoming evolutionary barriers without having to evolve over several generations, which often takes too long to be useful. It's much faster than evolution and requires only a few generations to perfect the change . . . sometimes no generations."

"Like flipping a switch."

"Yes."

"Can the switch be flipped off?"

She shrugged. "It's all theory. No way to know for sure."

"So this could be an average, run-of-the-mill tiger reacting to a unique situation the way any other tiger would."

"It's possible."

"Except . . ." He pointed up and down the path. "There isn't a single cat print."

Sara knelt, looking at the footprints. Then one stood out among the others. "What about that one?"

The single print looked human, but too wide and too deep. While overweight people with wide feet weren't unheard of, it didn't make sense in this part of the world. "Have you ever se—"

Debris from inside one of the huts spilled out. Clay pots and clumps of reed thatching tumbled down the hut's ramp to the ground. King and Bishop stood between Sara and the hut and took aim, ready to reduce the already ailing structure to toothpicks. An old woman stumbled down the ramp and fell to the earth as gravity proved too much for her brittle bones and aging muscles.

They rushed to her and found her mumbling incoherently through her white, dehydrated lips. Her hair was straight and completely gray. Not a hint of youth remained. Her wrinkled face, etched with years, softened at seeing them. She saw their guns and sighed.

Sara frowned upon seeing the old woman. She was someone's grandmother . . . perhaps great-grandmother. Had she seen them all die? Her daughters? Her sons? Were their bodies lying around the village? Sara remembered what it was like attending her grandmother's funeral, seeing the open casket. Death seemed so well preserved then, like an illusion of life. Her grandmother looked more alive in death than this woman did alive.

Sara's heart went out to her. She shared some water from her canteen. The woman gagged and the liquid dribbled from her mouth. She was too exhausted to drink.

"Nguoi Rung," the woman said. "Nguoi Rung. Nguoi Rung."

King could see she was fading fast. "She's not going to make it."

A battle raged in Sara. She wanted to save the woman. And she might even be able to. She had everything she needed to start an IV liquid drip in her pack . . . but there was still a chance the woman would die before Sara had a chance to draw her blood. And that was a risk she couldn't take. Sara opened her backpack and removed her medical kit. She popped open the green case and riffled through the supplies. She took out the IV kit and set it aside. Her hands shook as she removed the syringe from its sterile packaging and attached the needle.

The old woman stopped repeating the words when she

saw Sara turn to her, needle in hand. Her face twisted into a mask of concern, as though she were asking, "Are you no better?"

Sara fought the tears growing in her eyes. Her emotions would undo her if she let them. "Hold her down," she said to the two Delta operators, who looked just as confused as the dying old woman.

"Hey . . . ," King said, obviously perplexed.

"I don't want to do this. I really don't. But look around you. Everyone in this village is dead or gone. And look at the bodies. They're all women! The men are buried out there, in the field. If they all died from Brugada, and the women didn't, then her blood is the last chance we have. Getting her healthy enough to survive this might take days. We don't have days." Tears broke free and ran down her cheeks.

King and Bishop laid down their weapons and held the woman tight. King propped the woman up so that her head was against his chest. He wrapped his left arm under and around the woman's arm and squeezed. With his right hand he gently rubbed her head. "It's okay," he whispered. Though he knew she had no idea what he was saying, he felt sure she'd understand the gesture.

Sara pushed the woman's dirty sleeve up away from her forearm. The veins were easy to see against her malnourished skin as they filled with blood from King's tight grasp. She struggled only a moment and then became resigned to her fate.

"I'm sorry," Sara said as she worked the needle into the woman's vein. Sara sniffled as the woman's very life-force seemed to drain away with the blood filling the syringe.

Fifteen seconds later, the syringe was full. Sara removed the needle from the woman's arm and capped it. The future of mankind now depended on a syringe full of an old woman's blood. Sara instinctually picked up a cloth to put against the puncture wound created by the needle, but the sludge-like blood left in the woman's body lacked the force to exit the wound. Her slowing heart was trying to pump mud.

"Nguoi Rung," the woman said once again. Then her eyes closed and she was gone. Dead as the rest of the women left rotting in the village. But unlike the other women, her body remained unbroken and her death, while not of her choosing, was for a far more noble cause.

"There's nothing left for us here," Sara said. "We can set up camp somewhere else. Somewhere safe. And I can analyze her blood."

"And if you don't find what you're looking for?" King asked.

"We're going to be here for a while. If someone else survived this mess, we'll need to find them."

Rook and Somi had placed the remaining four motion sensors along the most likely routes into the village. Rook paused at the top of the slope, searching for any movement in the jungle below.

"See anything, Gung Ho?" Somi asked.

"Not a thing." Rook looked back at her. "You're in intelligence, right?"

Somi nodded. "What are you thinking?"

"I'm thinking that someone should have known the LZ was hot." He stood and headed toward the village. "More than that, I'm wondering how they knew we were coming at all."

"Coincidence?"

Rook shook his head. "You think we should chalk it up to dumb luck?"

Somi clapped him on the shoulder. "Sometimes that's exactly what intelligence is."

He smiled as they crossed through the field, watching for the little orange flags Bishop had placed in the grass marking the clear path.

"Seems like your opinion of the intelligence community isn't that great," Rook said.

"You could say that."

"How'd you get into it?"

"My father."

"Seems kind of old-world."

"This *is* the old world."

"Right . . . But you must have a choice now?"

Somi's momentary frown wasn't lost on Rook. "Not everything is a choice. Not when it comes to family. Or honor."

The field cleared and they entered the village. The stench of thirty rotting corpses filled his nose, but not even that could foul his mood. He saw King, Bishop, and Sara standing over a body. "Man, now I know why they named this place Anh *Dung*. It smells like shit."

Sara whirled on him like a tornado. "What did you just say? Look around you! Do you have any idea what—"

Rook didn't hear the rest of the sentence. A wave of nausea took his breath away. He felt his eyes roll back and sensed gravity pulling on his body. Then nothing.

Rook was dead.

THIRTEEN

Mud splattered as the girth of Rook hit the path. His face sank in to the ears. If his lungs were working, he would have drowned in the ooze. But Rook was already dead.

Somi placed her shotgun on the ground and struggled to roll Rook onto his back and out of the mud. King arrived a second later, dropping his M4.

"We need to get his pack off," he said.

Somi held Rook on his side while King yanked off the backpack. He tossed it aside and rolled Rook onto his back. He felt for a pulse. Nothing. He positioned his hands over Rook's chest to begin CPR. Before he could push, a hand on his shoulder stopped him.

"Don't," Sara said, "you'll break his ribs."

"You're damn right," King said. "You want me to let him die?"

Rook's body jolted. King flinched back.

Rook coughed mud into the air, sat up, and wiped his face. He looked at the mud on his hands. "Son of a bitch! Someone please tell me I did not just fucking die from Brugada."

King smiled and slapped Rook on the shoulder. "Good to have you back." He pulled Rook to his feet. "Are the motion sensors in place?"

Sara shook her head. Rook had *died*. He was dead at their

feet. If not for the cardioverter defibrillator in his chest he would have stayed dead. And now, just moments after his return from the dead, King was back to business as though nothing had happened. She didn't know what to think. Had they seen so much death that a fallen teammate had no emotional toll?

As he removed a handkerchief from his vest and began wiping off his face, Rook said, "They're all up and running. Queen and Knight were setting up the last trip wire when we headed back."

Sara couldn't stand that no one was addressing Rook's near-death experience. "Are you okay, Rook? You were *dead*."

Rook thumped his chest and gave a weak smile. "Feels like bad heartburn. If you've got a glass of milk, let's talk. Otherwise, drop it."

It was then that Sara realized their silence wasn't about not caring, or being immune to death. They were terrified of it. They didn't even want to speak of it. She watched as Bishop, who hadn't moved or stopped keeping watch during the whole ordeal, shared a brief smile with King. Their relief at Rook's survival shone clearly in their eyes. These guys were family. They were—

Sara froze. Something felt different. So small she couldn't pinpoint it. The environment had changed, but with the distraction of Rook's death and the constant reek of decomposition, she'd failed to notice it before. "King, something's not right."

King felt hokey issuing the order based on Sara's intuition, but her ability to sense things had been uncanny thus far. "Form a circle. Cover all sides. Pawn, get in the middle."

Sara found herself wedged at the center of three massive bodies and one small one wielding a shotgun.

Silence returned to the ravaged village. Sara concentrated on blocking out the smell, focusing her attention on her hearing. No good. The stench overpowered her senses. She held her breath and closed her eyes.

She ignored the brewing headache caused by the foreign

smells, the sun pinching her exposed skin, and the severe itch behind her ears. Through it all, she felt something. Running. Breathing.

Then they all heard it. A man screamed, his voice a high-pitched staccato. The group collectively turned toward the shriek. The stranger burst from the tall grass and entered the clearing, fear etched onto his face. He carried an AK-47. His green uniform was emblazoned with a red badge that held a single gold star at its center. Vietnamese People's Army. Not a Death Volunteer. Without pause he barreled across the clearing, heading for the tall grass on the other side and the forest beyond.

King took aim and prepared to fire, but paused. The man was terrified. Not just terrified. He was scared shitless, screaming like some B-movie horror bimbo. Then the man saw them. He didn't have time to register whether they were friend or foe. He just saw them standing there and opened fire.

The grass in front of the man exploded as a human-sized blur struck him head-on. The soldier's feet came out from under him as he flipped back. A moment later, he lay still on the path, as dead as Rook had been only minutes before. His attacker stood over him.

Queen.

Faster than anyone had seen, she'd launched her fist into the man's throat, crushing his windpipe. If he were conscious, he'd be struggling to breathe, but the impact robbed him of any fighting chance he had. He was dead by the time the others reached her.

"Damn, Queen. You put the fear of God in that guy."

"He wasn't running from me."

"Then who?" King asked.

"Or what," Sara added.

Her lips twitched. "Someone else."

King didn't like that answer, but if Queen didn't know, she didn't know. "Any more?"

"He was a scout. Got past us before we set up the perimeter. There were three of them. Knight followed the other two." Queen looked at each of them. "He's not back yet?"

"Up here." Knight's voice came as a whisper. If not for the comm systems they were all wearing, no one would have heard him. They looked up, though no one knew exactly where to look.

Rook found him first. "You sneaky monkey. How the hell did you get up there?"

Knight lay on a hut roof, his legs splayed wide, dispersing his weight over the thatch. Focused on what he saw through the scope of his PSG-1 semiautomatic sniper rifle, he quietly shushed Rook. "Two in the field, coming this way."

The muzzle of the PSG moved slowly and steadily as Knight adjusted his aim, following the two figures. He couldn't see the short men in the grass, only their wake as they moved through it. The grass on either side of the men began moving.

"Hold on," Knight said. "Two more targets . . . make that four. They're heading for the first two."

Knight watched as the four new shapes moving through the grass converged on the two scouts. It was like watching lions stalk gazelle—unseen predators. They were only ten feet apart now. Thirty seconds more and they'd meet, just a few yards from the edge of the field. "Take cover. These guys are going to go at it."

King took Sara by the shoulder and started pulling her away. But as he did, she got a whiff of something pungent. A mix of urine and feces, as foul as the rancid smell of death all around them, but totally different. It smelled . . . wild.

She shook free of King's grasp and ran to the man that Queen had killed.

"Damnit, Pawn. Get your ass back here." He charged after her.

Sara knelt next to the man and rolled him over. She jumped away upon seeing his back. The man had been half dead when Queen got to him. Four bloody tears in the man's shirt revealed matching half-inch-deep lacerations.

King stopped before launching himself on top of Pawn. He saw the man's back.

Sara looked up at him. "Whatever killed everyone in this village is still here."

"King, *get down*." It was Knight. A whispered warning. King jumped on top of Sara, pinning her to the ground, shielding her, and the vial of blood in her backpack, with his body.

The tall grass at the edge of the field burst with a fury of motion. Knight's four new targets had just engaged the two remaining scouts. Grass danced madly as the sounds of battle filtered through—fists pounding bodies, tearing flesh, breaking bones.

The two men had been attacked and killed so quickly that neither had had time to run, fight, or even scream. King fought the urge to shudder. He'd never seen anything like it. Not that he saw anything. The clear mental image created by the sounds told him everything he needed to know.

A body fell half out of the grass. The man's black scarf covered what little of his face remained. The rest looked like it'd been gouged out by a jagged-edged ice-cream scoop. The body was yanked back into the grass and a new sound emerged.

Chewing.

"Knight, what do you see?"

"A lot of bloody grass," Knight replied. "Wait. Something brown is . . . shit!" King looked up at Knight and saw him duck as a detached arm flew over his head.

His quick movement shifted his weight on the roof and the thatch gave way. He fell through and landed on the hut floor.

Rook ran to the hut, his FN SCAR-L assault rifle at the ready. He squatted next to one of the hut's stilts and covered the area. "Knight?" he whispered.

Knight grunted and slid himself to the hut's entrance. "Here." His ribs throbbed, probably bruised, but he wouldn't complain. He slid down the hut's ramp and took up position, aiming at the field where the feast was still going on. "Guess they didn't like me watching them eat."

"What are they?"

Knight shrugged. "No clue."

King watched in silence as the grass swayed and the symphony of snapping sinew and grinding bones played out. "Bishop, if you wouldn't mind?"

Bishop approached without answer, his hand on the trigger of the modified machine gun that had already claimed more than twenty lives on this mission. King pulled himself off Sara and took aim at the field. He took the safety off his M4's grenade launcher and waited for Bishop. "Pawn, stay down."

Sara wasn't about to move. She'd heard what happened to the men in the grass and her superpredator theory seemed more plausible than before. She'd seen the man's brutalized head and the limb thrown at Knight. She would cling to King's back like a baby baboon if he'd let her.

Bishop arrived and steadied himself next to King. "Unleash hell on my mark."

Bishop nodded.

King's finger came to rest on the trigger, nanoseconds away from pulling it and decimating the animals in the field. Then he felt the tug on his pant leg.

Sara.

King knew it wouldn't be good. She had a knack for delivering bad news. He looked down. Their eyes met. And then she shifted her eyes twice, quickly, motioning to the field of tall grass . . . behind them.

King spun, and flinched at what he saw. But he didn't have time to fire, shout, or move. A massive explosion shook the ground. Then the thing was gone. He spun back toward the other side of the field and saw a cloud of smoke rising in the distance.

The grass around them fell silent. Bishop lowered his weapon. "They're gone."

"What the hell was that?" Rook said, looking at the rising plume of smoke.

"That was our perimeter being breached." Queen smiled at Rook. "The man said to make them loud."

King yanked Sara to her feet and the team met at the center of the village. He turned to Somi. "How many?"

Somi looked at her PDA and pushed a few buttons. The display showed a counter of how many times the motion sensors had been tripped. "Thirty . . . and climbing. Fast."

"We've got what we need here," Rook said. "Right? We can bug out."

They looked at Sara. "It's the best we can do, though I'm not sure it's enough."

"It had better be," King said. "We need to circle around and get back to Laos for pickup or we might not make it out at all."

"Where to, boss?" Rook said.

King looked up at the Annamite Mountains, towering above the village. The terrain would be steep and rough, but tracking them would be difficult. "Up. Double time."

The team set out at a fast pace, heading for the mountains.

As they moved, King tried to ignore his fears. They were being pursued by ruthless, highly trained Death Volunteers and a contingent of the regular Vietnamese army, the VPA. Neither frightened him. He'd been trained to fight overwhelming odds and had successfully done so countless times. But he was accustomed to fighting *men*. Whatever had killed those scouts were *not* men. They were something else. Something worse. He knew it the instant he looked back into the grass and saw those eyes.

Those red-rimmed, yellow eyes.

EVOLUTION

FOURTEEN

King did his best to forget the inhuman eyes that he'd seen staring at him from the grass. But they were ingrained in his mind, as though he'd stared at a bright light before entering a dark room. He could see them, fixed on him. Thinking. Plotting. He knew what it was to stare into the eyes of a predator. That was his job. But somehow, this was different. More primal. Almost evil. Malevolence for its own sake.

A bullet ripped into the tree next to his head and pulled him from his thoughts.

The Chess Team ran for their lives. The traps they had set had gone off, one by one, no doubt inflicting massive casualties. But it only seemed to incense the surviving soldiers. Rather than regroup and come up with a strategy, they'd plowed ahead as though their lives lacked any meaning. They fired chaotically. They screamed. They jeered.

As it turned out, it was a brilliant strategy. The Chess Team was completely unprepared to fend off a large-scale attack. They had just started up the mountainside when the main force of VPA soldiers swarmed into the village, shooting at huts and the already dead. Then, like hounds chasing a fox, they followed the Chess Team's footprints toward the mountain and up it. They continued to fire their weapons as they gave chase. King doubted any were taking aim, but eventually, one of them would get lucky.

"Knight," King said. "Find us a place to pin these bastards down."

Knight, being the fastest member on the team, bounded up the mountainside. He scanned left and right as he ascended, looking for cover. Sparse tree trunks rose up and fanned out into thick-leaved trees, creating a canopy that all but blocked the sun. The forest floor held a thick mat of detritus and little else. They needed something big and bulletproof and they needed it now.

Knight's pulse quickened as he ran farther and higher. With each step he felt failure looming closer. His teammates' lives depended on his success. He'd been in similar situations before. Every member of the team had depended on Knight taking a perfect shot at least once. But this was different. His skill with a sniper rifle wouldn't help them now, just his speed and Mother Nature providing a boulder or crevice or . . .

There! The gray stone stood out in stark contrast compared to the brown litter on the forest floor. A smile crept onto his face. He paused and looked back. He could see the heads of the others bobbing back and forth as they ran to catch up.

Farther down he saw the first of the pursuing force. There were more olive green uniforms than he could count. He wondered if this would be their Alamo. Then he shook his head. If the Chess Team had been at the Alamo, things would have turned out differently.

"King, straight up from your position. About a minute at your current pace. Plenty of cover."

"Copy that, Knight. Mind giving us some breathing room?"

"One dose of 'fear of God,' coming up." Knight covered the remaining distance to the stone in three strides. It wasn't until he was on top of it that he realized this wasn't some kind of natural formation. It was a wall. Or what remained of one—thirty feet long, five feet tall, and two thick. Ancient by the looks of it, but sturdy as hell. You couldn't ask for a better defensive position.

He jumped behind the wall, leaned on the top for balance, and dropped down the bipod supporting the front end of his German-made Heckler & Koch PSG-1 semiautomatic sniper rifle. Looking through the scope he saw Somi in the lead, followed by Queen, Bishop, Rook, and Pawn. King brought up the rear and as a result, became the primary target for the pursuing soldiers.

Knight adjusted his aim slightly. A fleet-footed soldier had gained on King. He was only twenty feet back and about to unload a clip from his assault rifle into King's back. The shot was tricky; King was bobbing back and forth as he ran, his head coming and going in the sight. Before he could tell King to duck, the soldier took aim. Knight pulled the trigger. The man's head disappeared.

"Damnit, Knight," came King's surprised voice. "You almost took off my ear . . . nice shot."

Knight smiled. *You haven't seen anything yet.* He moved through his targets quickly, not going for head shots every time, just trying to make contact. A single shot from a PSG-1 to any part of the body was enough to take an assailant out. And out here, with no hospital, every shot would eventually lead to death. The team was thirty seconds away now.

After the tenth soldier dropped, his arm severed at the shoulder, his scream inhuman, the rising tide of men stayed close to the trees, snaking in and out of sight. Knight had a harder time finding targets, but their ascent had slowed. Knight squeezed the trigger for the seventeenth time and the seventeenth enemy fell, clutching a hand over a fresh hole in his chest. But where one man fell, five took his place. They were fighting an army.

One by one the team jumped over the wall and took up position. Sara slumped over the barrier and collapsed behind the others, heaving one breath after the next. Her lungs and legs burned. Her mind swirled with overloaded senses brought on by the close-range gunfire. She covered her ears and scuttled back away from the wall, watching as her protectors prepared to make a final stand for her sake.

King hopped the wall and landed next to Knight. He tapped his shoulder.

"One second," Knight said. "I've got three more rounds in this magazine."

Three shots rang out in quick succession. Three more soldiers fell. Knight ejected and discarded the clip before slapping in a new one. He turned to King. "Yeah?"

King smiled. "Nice shooting."

"You were expecting anything less?"

Sara was amazed at the team's levity given their situation. She watched as Queen readied her UMP and placed some grenades against the wall, ready to throw. Was there a smile on her face? Bishop held a stoic expression as he propped his machine gun up on the wall. She'd seen what that could do. Then there was Rook. He was all smiles and had the craftiest look in his eyes, like he was in on a practical joke about to be played.

The truth wasn't too far off.

Rook saw Sara watching. "You want to see how to make your enemy soil themselves?"

"On my mark," King said.

At least he is still being serious, Sara thought.

"Now!"

Rook fired a grenade from his FN SCAR assault rifle, then tossed two more, while King, Queen, and Knight lobbed three each, in various directions and distances. Sara's eyes widened. The mountainside was about to be lit up like the Fourth of July in Washington, D.C. She covered her ears and closed her eyes.

The screams of the soldiers couldn't be heard over the echoing booms of the grenades exploding, one after another. The ground shook and smoke wafted through the air. For a moment, everything went silent.

Rook leaned up over the wall. A swath of mountainside had been cleared of trees. The ground was covered in fallen trunks, smoldering earth, and remnants of human bodies.

Anyone approaching from below would be slowed by the fallen trees, slick with blood, exposed by the clearing, lit by the freed sunlight.

The silence ceased as the coughing and groaning of the still living began to filter out from the debris. A battle cry came next. Then a hundred men charged out of the dark forest and up the cleared mountainside. Their fire was concentrated on the Chess Team's position, but the stone wall and steep angle protected them.

The Chess Team responded in kind, though much more efficiently. Bishop held down his trigger and swept the machine gun back and forth, chewing up earth and bodies alike. Queen, King, and Rook fired their weapons in quick bursts, catching the few who made it past Bishop's storm cloud of bullets. Knight swiveled back and forth, firing occasionally at the men staying in the trees, attempting to circumvent the battlefield. Somi, on the other hand, held her fire. Her shotgun would only be useful for up-close and personal combat, which would come soon enough.

In that moment of pure pandemonium Sara felt safe. She could see that the Chess Team really was the best. They could handle this, and more, if need be.

A sudden pressure around her chest and blackening vision tore her away from the action. *Brugada!* Sara thought before losing consciousness.

But Brugada was not to blame.

The VPLA Death Volunteers had the most complete map of Vietcong tunnels, which crisscrossed the region from North to South Vietnam and into portions of Laos and Cambodia. This was their backyard, after all. And they trained in jungle warfare and tunnel attacks more than any other special forces unit on the planet. For them, desert warfare, trench warfare, even urban warfare were unlikely. Vietnam wasn't about to invade another country or take part in a NATO mission. If they fought a war again, it would be like the last, on their home turf—in the jungle. And they were more prepared for it now than they had been during the Vietnam War, when they had held off a superpower. *The* superpower.

And Trung was determined to ensure they would have the power to do it again, and more. With the key to Brugada in Trung's possession, their status in the world order would change. The few nations who had the ability to decide the fate of the world with a push of a button held the most power—were respected. Vietnam would soon earn that respect, and power, as well. The success of their current task was a testament to that.

Though they had failed to capture the U.S. team when they touched down in the field, contingency plans, including the one now in action, had been planned in advance. Every movement the Americans made had been tracked. They knew the U.S. team would reach the village first. They knew the massive number of regular soldiers thrown at the Americans would force them to higher ground. And they knew, thanks to their maps, that there were only three locations on the mountainside suitable for making a stand. Three portions of an ancient wall, built long before modern Vietnam existed, still stood along the mountainside. No one knew who had built them. No one cared. But they'd been important strategic points for the builders and Vietcong alike. As such, hatches hidden beneath the ground litter led to a network of ancient tunnels—tunnels that could be used for retreat from the wall, or approach to it from behind.

Teams of four had been dispatched to each tunnel, two men to enter the tunnel, two to guard the other end. They had beaten the Americans there and lain in wait. With the battle under way and a spotter on the mountain above keeping them apprised of the woman's whereabouts, they simply had to wait for the right moment to strike.

Thanks to an informant they knew exactly where the U.S. team would touch down. Smartly, the Americans had chosen an LZ in Laos rather than Vietnam, limiting the size of the force Trung was able to mobilize without starting a war between the two nations. What they hadn't expected was the arrival of the Neo Khmer Rouge the previous night, whose presence provided the distraction that allowed the Americans to slip through.

Ultimately, it didn't matter. The Neos were routed quickly and the mission continued unabated.

Scouts hiding in the trees around Anh Dung had identified the tall woman as their primary target. She was the Americans' expert. Their scientist. Their hope for a cure to the Brugada sent to them by the major general. The others were soldiers.

The initial American assault had almost brought the tunnel down, but its ancient stone walls managed to hold out through yet another battle. While many of the other Vietcong tunnels had since collapsed, this tunnel had been constructed of sturdier stuff long ago. The two VPLA men in the tunnel received word to strike. The hiss of shifting leaves and squeak of old hinges might normally have given away their exit from the tunnel, but the ceaseless gunfire of the U.S. team concealed their approach. Though they could have easily killed a few of the Americans from behind, that was not their mission. It didn't matter whether or not the U.S. team lived or died. All that mattered was their target.

The two men approached her from behind as the battle raged. One crouched low while the other reached up with the drug-laden rag and held it over her mouth. As she collapsed, the men caught her body, preventing it from making an impact one of the American soldiers might feel, and then carried her back to the tunnel. Like trap-door spiders, they were only exposed for seconds before returning underground with their prey.

As they entered the tunnel, one of the VPLA soldiers turned back. His eyes met Somi's, who had turned around, shotgun in hand. One pull of her shotgun's trigger could have fired a volley of shells, tearing the man apart and sounding the alarm. But no shot was fired. Instead, she nodded.

The VPLA soldier responded in kind, offering a brief smile.

Mission accomplished.

But then a twitch of his wrist and a flash of metal told another story.

Mission accomplished? Almost.

The flung knife crossed the distance and buried silently into Somi's chest.

She dropped her shotgun and fell to the ground. The hatch closed above the two Death Volunteers and together, they dragged Sara into the network of tunnels.

Somi fell to the ground and felt the blade shift, slicing through muscle and veins. The skin hugging the knife grew warm with her blood. As she lay there, behind the backs of the Chess Team, she realized her loyalty to the VPLA had been misplaced. Before his death, her father, a diplomat, had been close friends with Major General Trung. Over time he'd become personally and financially linked to Trung and the pair aligned their political and military agendas. But with her father's death, Somi learned that her father had become indebted to Trung, who transferred her father's debt to his one and only child—sixteen-year-old Somi. Every step she had taken since, including enlisting in the CIA, had been at his request. She served him well over the years, fulfilling her father's debts, but that didn't seem to matter now. It seemed she would finish paying her father's debts with her life.

For the first time in her life she found herself unwilling to follow the wishes of Uncle Trung. She had already given him her life. She would not die for him, too. Not willingly.

She leaned her head onto her arm. Blood seeped over and dripped from the knife hilt. As she watched her life fade, drop by drop, she became filled with a need for vengeance. King had to be told. Pawn was gone. She breathed deep, intending to shout a warning over the gunfire, but the knife stole her breath as it cut deeper. She tried to move, but found the pain overbearing.

There was nothing she could do.

Somi rolled onto her back and watched as the occasional sliver of blue sky peeked through the thick canopy above.

FIFTEEN

Rook's cheek shook as he fired the last three shots in his clip. He jammed in his fourth and final clip and took careful aim. A three-shot burst ripped through the air and into the body of another fleeing soldier. The VPA regular army had been brutalized. At least one hundred of them lay dead and dying on the cleared mountain slope. But they kept on coming, though more slowly and carefully now. Their initial enthusiasm brought on by superior numbers had faded after encountering the Chess Team's lethal aim and devastating tactics.

The gunfire had died down on both sides to sporadic bursts, allowing the team to talk again.

"Like pigeons in front of a 747," Rook said, before firing three more shots. "Splat."

Knight fired a shot. The bullet blasted through the chest of a VPA soldier, splattering those around him in blood. They turned and fled. Others across the field followed suit. Knight pulled away from his sniper scope, which he'd been staring through for the past five minutes. "They're bugging out."

They'd succeeded in holding off a small army, but no one hooted a victory cheer. They weren't done until they were back at Fort Bragg sharing a case of Sam Adams.

"Anybody hit?" King asked.

No one answered.

"I think a mosquito bit me," Rook said. Then he felt something on his leg, squeezing. He turned and instinctively raised his weapon. He dropped it a second later. "Pawn Two is down!"

He knelt next to Somi. Her eyes were glossy and her lips were purple. But her chest rose and fell. She was alive. Then he saw the knife in her chest. "How did—"

"Bishop, Knight, keep an eye on our friends down there," King said as he and Queen joined Rook by Somi's side.

"Cut her shirt off," Queen said. She shrugged out of her backpack and opened it up. A medical kit sat on top. She removed it and popped it open. She set aside a roll of gauze, two gauze pads, and a package of QuikClot. Then she began assembling a needle and syringe.

Knight untucked Somi's long-sleeve black shirt. It was like a second skin on her and getting his KA-BAR knife underneath proved a challenge. He didn't want to stab her again. Once the knife slid in, he moved with confidence, slicing her shirt up the middle. A second slice from her collar to the knife sticking out of her chest freed the shirt, which fell away. Somi's tattooed stomach and black bra were revealed. The knife stuck out of her chest like a skyscraper in the middle of Arkansas, just to the inside of her right-side shoulder strap.

A near-lethal strike, it had missed her lungs by inches. Instead it had chipped bone and sliced through muscle. Normally, the wound wouldn't be fatal, but in the field, where operating tables and surgeons were in short order, a variety of wounds could slowly take a life.

Knight fired twice. The blast cut through the momentary silence. "They're regrouping just out of sight. I'm catching a few stragglers, but they're up to something."

"Rook," King said, "call it in. Get us an armed evac over this clearing. Get it yesterday."

"You do remember that we're not supposed to be here, right?" Rook said as he opened his backpack where his secure satellite phone was hidden beneath a cache of equipment.

Their orders had been to remain silent and only make contact when they had completed their mission and returned to the designated EZ . . . in Laos. But that plan didn't include two hostile forces and a reenactment of the Vietnam War.

"Screw it," King said. "We need to get out of here now. We have what we came for."

Somi suddenly reached up and grabbed King's arm. Her lips moved slowly, parting and closing like those of a dying fish. Then her eyes closed and she fell back. Her eyelids twitched. She fought to stay conscious.

Rook shuffled through the backpack in search of the phone. "This was a lot easier with Deep Blue in our ears."

Queen returned to the scene. Without pausing to explain or give warning she plunged the syringe deep into Somi's leg. She depressed the stopper, sending the clear liquid into Somi's leg.

Queen looked into Somi's eyes. "Morphine. For what comes next."

Somi nodded and gritted her teeth in determination, though her quivering lips revealed her fear.

Queen waited for a count of five, giving the opium-derived drug time to massage her nervous system, then grasped the knife handle and yanked it out. Somi didn't scream, but a sound like a tortured rodent squeaked through her clenched teeth. A fresh flow of blood pulsed from the now-open wound on her chest.

"Queen . . . ," Rook said.

"We don't have time to be gentle." Queen ripped open the pack of QuikClot and removed the four-inch pouch filled with 3-mm-diameter zeolite beads that absorb blood and rapidly promote coagulation. "Now hold her wound open."

Rook abandoned his search for the phone and knelt down. Saving Somi's life would have to come first. He pried the wound open with his fingers, ignoring the blood flowing over his hands and under his fingernails.

Somi sobbed for a moment, trying to speak, but unable to catch a breath. Unconsciousness loomed.

Using her index finger, Queen shoved the flexible pouch into the wound.

Somi groaned and struggled only for a moment. The morphine was working. "Give me the knife."

He handed it to her. She looked at its blood-soaked blade then slid it beneath her belt. "Mine now."

With the wound packed with QuikClot, Rook sat Somi up as Queen wrapped gauze around her chest and shoulder, pulling it tight to keep pressure on the wound. As Somi leaned back in Rook's arms, feeling a mix of morphine and blood loss pulling her mind away, she reached out for King.

King leaned in close. "You'll be—"

She grasped his arm. "Th— This is not . . . an object lesson." She let go and succumbed to the drugs and pain. She slumped in Rook's arms, unconscious.

King nearly fell over when he spun around. He searched in every direction.

Nothing.

Sara had disappeared right out from under their noses. "No one move!"

King searched the area, taking in every depression in the earth, every disturbed leaf, every hidden clue. He found the flattened area where Sara had been lying. The leaves behind it were disturbed in a four-foot area. King pounded the butt of his M4 on the earth. A dull thud revealed a hollow space beneath.

Rook was by his side, aiming his assault rifle toward the earth. He nodded to King, who dug in, pulled up the hidden hatch, and opened it. Rook swept the area, looking for a target, and found nothing but a dark tunnel descending into the heart of the mountain.

"Knight, get as high as you can," King said. "If we're being watched, I want you to find out. Take out anything you see living and breathing that's not one of us."

Knight nodded and bolted up the mountainside.

King unslung his backpack and dropped it at his feet. "Queen, you're with me."

Queen tied off the gauze. "Try to keep her still," she said to Rook.

Rook stood up. "Do I look like a nurse to you? I'm coming."

Bishop fired a ten-second burst down the hill. "Rook."

Rook pointed his FN SCAR over the wall and fired a grenade. It exploded seconds later, followed by screams. He turned to King for an answer.

King knew that Rook wanted to come because he and Sara had bonded. You didn't carry someone's thirty-pound pack for miles and not develop some kind of connection. But there wasn't time to debate or pull punches. "Sorry, Rook. You're too big and too slow."

Bishop fired another volley down the mountainside. *"Rook . . ."*

"Besides . . ." King clapped him on the shoulder. "It sounds like you'll be doing more than nursing."

King jumped into the tunnel and hurried in. Queen followed and pulled the hatch down behind her.

Rook looked down at Somi. Unconscious, she lay still next to her shotgun.

"Rook!" The urgency in Bishop's voice came through loud and clear. Bishop speaking at all was unusual. Bishop sounding worried was unheard of. Rook looked over the wall. His eyes went wide.

"Holy shit."

SIXTEEN

Swirling green dust glowed in the pair's night vision, choking the view and their lungs. But King and Queen plunged forward through the dry fog without pause or complaint. A member of their team had been captured by the enemy—the *only* member of the team who needed to survive this mission. But what was worse was that she had the only blood sample from Anh Dung. A blood sample that might hold the answer to the question the whole world might soon be asking: Is there a cure for Brugada?

The tunnel was four feet tall and equally wide; large enough for them to move about, but too short to stand and a little too short to crouch-run. King had tried when he first entered and found himself smashing his head and the assault rifle slung over his back—a soldier's two most important weapons—into the stone ceiling again and again. He couldn't afford damaging either so he tried the hands-and-knees approach. Crawling proved to be faster and far less painful—though still painful enough to make them long for the tunnel's exit. The padding built into the knees of their black, Delta-issued fatigues took the brunt of each impact, but their legs and arms were jarred nonetheless.

As they continued on, King took note of the tunnel's solid construction. The walls, floor, and ceiling were nearly smooth and lacked any joints where slabs had been fitted

together. It was almost as though the tunnel had been burrowed straight through the mountain. The slight downward
slope confirmed it. They were traveling into the mountain's
core, not along its outer edge.

Through the dust, which had been kicked up by those they
were pursuing, King saw the tunnel branch in three different
directions. He stopped quickly and Queen bumped into him
from behind.

"What is it?" she asked.

"The tunnel splits."

"Then we'll split up."

"That won't help."

Queen crawled up next to King and saw the three tunnels.
"Which way . . ."

The branching tunnels split like a trident, two angling off
to the left and right while the tunnel they were in now continued straight on. King removed his night vision goggles
and clicked on a small Maglite flashlight. The tunnel filled
with yellow light. The dust became brown. The walls gray.
He moved forward slowly, shining his light at the floor of
each tunnel. He was hoping to find the floor of only one tunnel disturbed, but whoever took Sara knew what they were
doing. All three tunnels showed signs of movement.

"King, look." Queen pointed at the inside wall of the left-
side tunnel.

There was an inscription carved into the stone. Just a few
mixed lines. Some kind of Asian script, though King couldn't
place it to any specific country, not even Vietnam. He looked
at the other tunnels. Each held a different inscription. He realized they were signposts, like exit signs on a freeway. But
which exit to take?

King returned his scrutiny to the dust-covered tunnel
floor. They could split up and then turn back when the dust
disturbance ran flat, but that would take too much time, and
both of their first guesses could be wrong. There had to be a
sign. No one could conceal themselves perfectly.

Then he found the flaw. Two tunnels had been disturbed

by at least one person crawling and making a mess. The third had been disturbed in a very similar fashion, probably by a man bringing up the rear, but he'd failed to completely conceal the two parallel lines carved into the grit by Sara's dragging heels.

"This way," King said as he extinguished the flashlight, donned his night vision goggles, and lunged into the right-side tunnel.

Queen took one last look at the carved symbols and pounded after him, unaware that a pair of eyes was watching her retreat.

SEVENTEEN

Knight reached the top of the mountain without incident. He'd seen no sign of man or beast. He believed anything living with half a mind or a speck of instinct would have taken off after the battle that raged below. He took up position on a rocky outcrop overlooking the jungle below. The high perch provided a view to the horizon, but he'd need Superman's X-ray vision to see anything moving beneath the canopy. What he could see clearly was a range of mountains—the Annamites. The forest thinned out and then ceased to exist near the top of each mountain, which provided him with a view of anything moving on them. But the most important view was down the slope. The jungle was dark with shade provided by the canopy, and much of the slope was concealed behind layers of tree trunks. For amateur snipers, it would prove an impenetrable shield behind which enemies could move freely. For Knight, it was just the kind of challenge he excelled at solving.

Knight felt secure in his hiding spot, surrounded by large rocks and clumps of tall grass. His backside was hidden from view, even from those who might look down from the mountain's peak. And below him . . . well, anyone below him would be dead before realizing he was there.

Plunging his hand into one of the many pockets of his pants, Knight found his custom-made silencer. The barrel of the PSG-1 lacked threads that a silencer would normally need to screw onto a weapon, so he'd had one made for it. Confusion and stealth were the compatriots of all good snipers, especially when you wanted no survivors. A shot echoing from above would let the target know from which angle to hide. Seeing the man next to you suddenly lose his head without any indication of direction was enough to freeze any soldier in his tracks. Knight slid the silencer into place and tightened the clamps that held it.

He quickly detached his optical sniper scope and replaced it with a heat-sensitive infrared scope. Unlike his night vision scope, the infrared scope didn't magnify visible light—he'd be blinded in the bright daylight pounding the mountaintop—rather it detected heat variations against the ambient temperature. Typically a living creature would show up as red, orange, and yellow blobs against a blue/green background, but with the air reaching one hundred degrees beneath the broiling canopy, which held the heat in, a human being would appear as a slightly cooler spot. Hard to detect, but easier than using the naked eye to pierce through darkness.

With the scope attached he lay down, propped open the rifle's bipod, and searched for targets. He didn't have to look for long. Running from his position were two men. Trees momentarily blocked his view of them, but he tracked them smoothly as they descended. He looked for their weapons and found a distinctive, cold blue shape—AK-47, the staple weapon of the world's poorest armies. The gas-operated assault rifle, being the most numerous weapon of its kind on the planet, was cheap, compact, and powerful. But at this range, they didn't stand a chance against Knight's rifle.

The two men moved quickly—nearly running. Either they knew he was watching, which he doubted, or their mission was complete and they were heading home.

Not so fast, Knight thought. If he could stop these two, the rest of their squad might wait around for a minute longer before leaving. And that might be just enough time to let King and Queen catch up.

Knight slowed his breathing and closed his left eye while he looked through the scope with his right. His finger stroked the trigger gently—foreplay before the kill. He tracked the first man's head, bobbing up and down and shrinking slowly as he moved farther away.

His finger twitched and a bullet was sent noiselessly through the air. A second later, the man in front pitched forward and tumbled. The second man didn't miss a beat, though. He jumped over the first man's body and quickened his pace. These men were highly trained. They didn't react to death, which meant they didn't fear death. *Death Volunteers,* Knight thought.

"Who wants to volunteer next?" Knight said. "Go on, you can raise your hand."

Knight pulled the trigger again and the second man went down, his head hanging from his shoulders. Knight scoured the area for more targets and found none.

Realizing he hadn't seen where the first man had been hit and not wanting him to radio a warning, Knight began pushing himself up. He'd have to make sure they were both dead.

Then he heard the grass rustle behind him. He focused on his surroundings without moving a muscle.

It wasn't windy. Not even a breeze.

Knight rolled onto his back without taking his eye off the scope. He saw a massive red shape fill the scope. He pulled the trigger.

His weapon was knocked aside as a tremendous weight slammed into his chest. But then it was gone, tumbling down the rocks behind him. He'd hit it.

It screamed in pain. But the noise wasn't fearful. It was angry.

Knight realized he'd shot one of the creatures from the field—one of the things that had torn the VPA scouts apart and thrown a human limb at him.

Brush exploded below as the creature ran. Knight tried to find it again through the infrared scope, but it was gone. He looked with his naked eyes and saw a wave of brush bashing left and right as the creature retreated. But he couldn't see it through the scope. Its body heat matched the surrounding air.

Definitely not human, Knight thought.

Then he noticed a change in the movement of the brush. The swath of moving foliage grew wider, spreading out into a V. A loud hooting and breaking of branches rose up from the mountainside below.

The beast was coming back.

With friends.

EIGHTEEN

The mountain was alive.

Or at least it appeared that way. Brush, ferns, and tree limbs all converged on the wall defended by Rook, Bishop, and the still unconscious Somi. It was as though the mountain had come to life and decided to attack. Rook aimed down the incline, but had no idea where to shoot. With limited ammo he had to make sure his shots were true. Firing at a bush swaying in the wind would be a waste.

But what was bush and what was camouflage?

Rook guessed and fired a three-round burst. Foliage exploded from the assailed brush, but nothing else. He grunted with disappointment.

He tried again. This time he was rewarded by a yelp of pain. But the hillside continued its advance, slow and inexorable. At least the attackers didn't know it was just the two of them. If they had, Rook felt certain they would have already charged en masse.

Rook ducked behind the wall and looked at Bishop, who was lining up targets, but not firing. "How much ammo you have left?"

Bishop squatted behind the wall and shook his head slowly, clearly annoyed. "Not enough."

"You know we're screwed, right?"

Bishop nodded slowly.

"Any ideas?"

Bishop smiled. "Shoot 'em up and run like hell?"

Rook grinned fiendishly. "You should talk more often, Bishop. I like your style."

Bishop chuckled.

"One shot per target," Rook said as he switched his assault rifle to single-round firing. "Hit as many as possible. Kills or not, it will take them out of the fight."

Rook took several deep breaths like a swimmer preparing to dive. "I'll go first."

Bishop nodded.

Rook rose up over the wall, found a target, and squeezed off a single shot. He moved on, sighting new targets, and fired again. And again. And again. Still, the hillside rose up toward them. Some shots were rewarded by grunts of pain, or a body toppling over, but just as many struck nothing but earth, wood, or the already dead.

Click. Rook pulled the trigger and nothing happened. He was out of ammo. He tossed the assault rifle aside. He'd had it for five years. One of his favorites. But now it was a dead weight.

"Your turn, big guy."

Bishop stood, lowering his machine gun onto the wall and taking aim. But before he pulled the trigger a shot rang out from below.

Rook flinched back as the meat on Bishop's shoulder exploded. Bishop shouted in pain and fell to his knees, breathing hard. He gritted his teeth, eyes burning with rage.

After wiping the blood from his eyes, Rook watched as something he'd heard about, but never seen, took place. The baseball-size wound on Bishop's shoulder began to heal, slowly at first, then the flaps of skin on either side stretched out, as though reaching for each other, and sealed the wound perfectly, like it never existed. QuikClot had nothing on Bishop's regenerative ability. But it took its toll on his mind.

Rook reached to his hips and felt his dual Desert Eagles still resting in their holsters. They all knew what would have to be done if Bishop lost control—a .50-caliber round to the head was the only cure.

Bishop looked at him. "Not yet." He stood, taking hold of his machine gun again, then pulled the trigger and held it tight. Rounds and tracers streaked down the incline for ten full seconds, tearing the hillside to pieces.

Click.

"So much for one shot at a time, eh?"

Three pops sounded out in the distance. The two men held their breath and locked eyes. Both recognized the noise. They looked up and saw three small projectiles arcing towards them. No . . . *over* them.

"They're bringing the mountain down on top of us!"

Bishop abandoned his machine gun and lunged for the tunnel hatch. There was nowhere else to go. An army waited below and the mountain would soon crumble down above them. Bishop yanked the hatch open as Rook hoisted Somi into his arms, and placed her by the open hole.

Rook jumped into the tunnel, took Somi under the shoulders, and dragged her into the hole. Somi's feet disappeared from view as Rook dragged her away. Bishop jumped in a moment later and closed the tunnel entrance over him.

Darkness consumed the tunnel.

There was no time to turn on a flashlight. They simply charged into the darkness, waiting for the mortars to strike. Unlike shells fired by howitzers or field guns, mortars sailed through the air without a hiss or whistle. They were deadly silent until the first boom rang out.

Boom.

The ceiling of the tunnel shook. A cascade of dust poured from freshly formed cracks.

Boom.

Bishop and Rook, both large men, bruised and battered their bodies as they surged through the tunnel, smashing their heads, knees, and elbows into the surrounding stone surfaces.

Boom.

The third mortar struck. Rumbling echoed through the tunnel as the mountainside above gave way and rolled down the slope, covering the wall they'd so futilely defended. Then the hatch gave in to the sudden weight. It split and allowed the mountain to reclaim the space as its own.

A plume of dust rocketed down the tunnel, enveloping Rook, Bishop, and Somi. They stopped moving and covered their mouths, coughing and wheezing as the air fouled. Rook, who had been shuffling backward and dragging Somi with one arm, pulled her lithe frame up close to his body. He wrapped his sleeve around her nose and mouth, though he wasn't sure how much good it would do.

In fact, until the dust settled, they were as good as trapped. They couldn't breathe and Rook was sure they couldn't see a lick, even if he'd turned on his flashlight. He did the only thing he could think of: call the others. After activating his throat microphone, he spoke through wheezes. "King . . . Queen. This is—Rook. Do you copy?"

Nothing. No response. He didn't bother trying again. If they didn't respond it meant they were indisposed, the signal was being blocked, or they were dead. "Knight. Tell me . . . you're there, little man."

The signal came through fuzzy, but it was there. "Sorry, big guy," came Knight's voice. Rook could tell he was out of breath. A loud hooting sound filled Rook's ears, making Knight's voice hard to make out. But he was there. "Can't talk right now. Running for my life."

"You and me both," Rook said. He knew not to try talking further. If Knight said he was running for his life, then he was. "Good luck."

"You too."

The signal cut out. Knight was gone. Rook hacked as he breathed in a mouthful of dust. His head spun. Bright spots of color danced in the dark tunnel, lulling him to sleep. He fought the urge, knowing that he was close to passing out. Then he stopped fighting and gave in as his lungs filled with more dust than oxygen.

NINETEEN

Washington, D.C.

Tom Duncan sat in silence, looking at the Rose Garden on the other side of the window. He leaned his head back against his leather executive chair and immediately felt annoyed at how well the headrest's contour fit his head. He'd been sitting too much over the past three years. It was the hardest thing about being president. Sit-down meetings, dinners, and debates. Life on the campaign trail had been all action, moving from one place to the next, exciting, energetic. And while being the president of the United States was hardly boring, Duncan craved mobility.

Instead, he sat in the Oval Office, waiting for Domenick Boucher, the CIA director, to bring news on the Chess Team's mission. He regretted that Deep Blue was not able to be part of the mission, but the team's handler wouldn't have been much help on this mission. With the thick jungle canopy blocking visual and infrared satellite images, the team was as good as invisible. And since Deep Blue had been otherwise occupied, he'd put the team in Boucher's hands.

A knock on the door pulled his attention away from the roses and the Chess Team. He turned as the door opened. Boucher entered, a grimace pulled down below his white mustache. Something had gone wrong.

Boucher sat on one of the couches positioned in the center of the Oval Office. It faced another couch on the other side of the presidential seal that had been hand sewn into a deep olive green carpet of Duncan's choosing. He wasn't big on decorating, but it was something he had to do when he took office. Not every president did so, but the previous president had an eye for Texas tan and cowboys that made his skin crawl. The decorator he brought in had been told one thing: make it strong. When Duncan had seen the green rug, he nodded and smiled. The decorator had done his homework and chosen the same green that graced the uniform of the U.S. Army Rangers. It helped Duncan feel more comfortable in the office, but did nothing to reduce his craving for the good old days.

Duncan sat on the opposite couch from Boucher and leaned forward. "You don't look happy, old man."

"Nor will you be," Boucher said as he opened a small, ultrathin laptop. The screen blinked to life and requested a password. He typed as he spoke. "You know, your doctors would pitch a fit if they knew I was showing you this stuff. You're not supposed to get worked up."

"My doctors can go to hell," Duncan said. "I didn't have a heart attack. I'm still in perfect shape."

"Except that you could fall over dead any second."

Duncan smirked. "As could you."

Boucher had been one of the first men to visit the president after his near-death experience. Thanks to a moist handshake he'd also been one of the first to be passed the disease. As a result, he was now under quarantine in the White House with about two hundred others, who had remained on duty despite sleeping at their desks or taking turns in Lincoln's bedroom. To the outside world, the White House and government were still fully functional. Employing a cadre of phony commuters coming to work in the morning and leaving in the evening, but never entering the White House proper, they hoped to keep the current situation under wraps for as long as possible.

Boucher scratched the still-healing wound where his own cardioverter defibrillator had been installed. "Don't remind me." He turned the laptop around and handed it to Duncan.

A satellite image showing endless amounts of green canopy came into view. Several light spots represented clearings in the trees. "What am I looking at, Dom?"

"Vietnam. Annamite Mountains. We knew there wouldn't be much to see, but we took a gamble, recorded the region surrounding the coordinates. This is a compilation of several images taken over a half hour. The small clearing at the center of the image is Anh Dung, the village we believe contained the source of Brugada's new strain. You'll have to zoom in quite a bit to make out the details."

The president used the laptop's touch screen to zoom in on what was a small brown speck in a sea of dark green. Pixels cleared and an image resolved. The village of Anh Dung, as seen from Earth orbit. The president held his breath when he saw the bodies. He zoomed in closer and sighed with relief. The bodies didn't belong to his team. They were villagers . . . a lot of villagers. Something had gone terribly wrong. He could tell by the color of the bloodstains and the hollowed-out faces of the villagers that the carnage had taken place a few days previous. "What happened?"

Boucher scratched his stubble-coated cheek. "Our forensics people say that it was an animal attack. They pointed out several claw and puncture wounds as evidence. Seems damn suspicious to me, though."

Duncan nodded. Animals didn't exterminate entire villages. People did.

"We don't know if the team came through here, but—"

"They did."

Boucher's large nose twitched. "How do you know?"

"The mud." Duncan zoomed in farther. The image was crystal clear. A benefit of having the most expensive and expansive satellite network in the world. A boot print had been captured by the mud. "That's a U.S. military–issue boot print."

Boucher put on a pair of thin spectacles. He looked at the

image with raised eyebrows. "Well, I'll be damned." He sat back. "When you're done running the country, maybe you could come work for me?"

Duncan smiled. "It's bad enough sitting in here, let alone some windowless room with fluorescent lighting."

"You could increase our budget before you leave office."

Duncan chuckled, though he knew they were both cutting the tension with humor. Boucher had more to show him. "What's next?"

Boucher cleared his throat. "Zoom out and scroll northeast. You'll find a clearing that wasn't there a year ago. Hell, it wasn't there yesterday."

Duncan found the clearing. From a height it appeared to be a clear-cut swath of jungle. He zoomed in. At first the scene was impossible to discern, then it came together as his eyes picked out individual details. Trees had fallen, some in pieces. Among the trees lay bodies. A lot of bodies. The wounds of the dead, unlike those of the villagers, were vibrant red—fresh. Then he noted several prone bodies, but they didn't appear injured. In fact, they looked to be crawling through the clearing, up the mountainside. Their heads were covered with brush and leaves. Camouflage. He counted quickly now that he knew what to look for.

Boucher saw him counting. "There are at least fifty advancing. We think there are more in the trees below."

"Who are they?"

"No idea. The brush they're covered with conceals anything that might tell us who they are."

"What are they doing?"

"Note the fellow in the upper left. The one holding a tree branch. He was our first clue."

Duncan found the man. He looked like the others, but a splash of red made him stand out. After zooming in farther, Duncan could see it was the man's brains exploding from the back of his skull. He'd been shot. A bullet had poked through the front of his head and punched out the back. A bullet fired from above.

He didn't wait for Boucher's instructions. He followed an imaginary line, tracing the bullet back to its origin. He stopped when he reached the trees. "Damn."

"There's a gap in the tree cover," Boucher said.

Duncan found it and zoomed in closer. The gap filled the screen. He'd never been good at guessing objects based on macro photographs. "What is it?"

"Muzzle flash."

The image came clear to him. He could make out the front end of the weapon—a long slender barrel hosting a tall sight. An explosion of light flared from the front of the weapon. He recognized its custom shape. He'd never held the weapon, but had seen pictures. The XM312-B.

Bishop.

The president sighed. They were alive. And fighting. He looked up at Boucher feeling hopeful and then realized there was more.

Boucher stood up, stepped over the presidential seal, and sat down next to Duncan. He pushed a button on the laptop's keyboard. The image changed. A mound of fresh dirt and debris filled the image. Dust still clung to the air. The tops of trees poked out.

Duncan looked into Boucher's pale blue eyes. "Is this . . . ?"

Boucher nodded. "Taken five minutes after the previous image. Looks like they brought the mountain down on top of them. We don't know exactly what happened, but it doesn't look good."

"When were these taken?" Duncan asked, his voice nearly a whisper.

"An hour ago."

"Keep watching the area. Get me images of anything and everything that changes, even if it's a tree falling over."

Boucher stood and collected the laptop. "Yes, sir."

"Expand the search area, too. Use as many resources as you need. I don't need to tell you what's at stake if the mission has failed."

Boucher pursed his lips and shook his head. "No, sir. You don't."

"Thanks, Dom."

Boucher turned to leave, but paused. He'd been the CIA director when Duncan took office. He'd overseen the Chess Team's creation at Duncan's request and arranged for Deep Blue's insertion into the team. He knew what those five lives in Vietnam meant to him. He put his hand on Duncan's shoulder. "We'll get them back, Tom."

Duncan just nodded as Boucher left through the northwest door that led to the main hallway of the West Wing. A plan began to take shape in his mind. He wouldn't just sit back and let the Chess Team die.

Before his thoughts could get any farther a knock came from the northeast door. "What is it, Judy?" He realized he sounded angry. But Judy, his secretary, who was used to his moods, took no offense. She strode across the room, picked up the remote, and turned on the wall-mounted flat screen. She switched the channel to CNN. "Trouble's brewing."

An image of a bombshell reporter filled the screen. The volume was turned down. As Judy turned it up, Duncan read the woman's lips. It was easy to recognize his name. With the volume up, he only needed to hear the next two words. "Heart attack."

The cat was clawing its way out of the bag.

He turned to Judy. "Better turn on the coffeepots downstairs."

Judy nodded and rushed out, closing the door behind her. Duncan always referred to the White House Situation Room as "downstairs." He'd probably be spending the rest of the day there as the press descended on the White House, expecting to be given access to the press room only to be turned away at the door. Then would come the phone calls. But they couldn't be told the truth. That the entire White House was under quarantine. That the disease contained within could wipe out the human race. Chaos would ensue.

Tom slid back into the couch and rubbed his temples.

His plans to help the Chess Team would have to wait. They might be fending off attacks from unknown assailants, but he would soon find himself up against a more cunning adversary—reporters. Until they were dealt with, the Chess Team was on its own.

TWENTY

Annamite Mountains—Vietnam

After ten minutes of crawling on hands and knees, King wondered if he'd picked the right tunnel after all. They had paused for only a moment when the whole mountain shook and a blast of air shot through the tunnel. Despite being concerned about the cause and whether or not the others were in trouble, there was no time to waste on finding out—or even wondering about—what happened. Whoever took Sara had only a minute or two head start, and they were dragging a prisoner. They should have caught them by now. King stopped and turned back to Queen. He was about to have her backtrack and follow one of the other tunnels when he heard a noise.

No, a voice.

The words were impossible to discern. They weren't English or any of the other four languages King and Queen spoke—they were Vietnamese. King recognized the tangy sound of the language. He also recognized the hurried tones of the two men speaking. They knew they were being followed.

A new sound filled the tunnel. A loud swooshing sound that faded into the distance. Then another. And finally a third. They were sliding. Sara and two others. King rushed forward through the darkness until he reached the source of the swooshing sound. The tunnel turned downward at a forty-degree angle. The bottom was nowhere in sight and the sound of their quarry faded as they descended the tunnel.

Queen's hand gripped his shoulder. He looked back at her. She pointed to the floor next to the drop-off. Through his green-tinged night vision goggles, King saw a block of C4 and a timer counting down. He barely had time to register the number on the display—00:15—when Queen shoved him from behind.

"Go!"

King dove into the tunnel alongside her. He counted down the seconds in his mind while he formulated a plan. The two men carrying Sara were probably not alone. They'd leave one or two men behind to make sure no one escaped the tunnel after its destruction, but wouldn't hang around to risk losing Sara.

Ten seconds.

King looked ahead as he continued gaining speed down the smooth tunnel. A tiny speck of light revealed the tunnel's exit far ahead. "Lose the goggles," King said as he took his off and discarded them. They were about to be plunged into daylight. The goggles would blind them and seal their fate.

Queen took off her goggles and tossed them behind her. "Any ideas?"

Five seconds.

The exit grew larger quickly. They were going to be spewed from the earth a second too soon.

Three seconds.

"Play possum!" King shouted before going limp.

Their bodies slid out of the tunnel, fell four feet, and tumbled to a stop on top of a bed of leafy ferns. By all accounts, the pair appeared dead. A quick roll would have spared them a jarring landing, but their bodies simply crashed to the forest floor, contorted and still. The two men left guarding the exit approached slowly, weapons raised. They weren't fearful, but they weren't stupid, either.

A muffled whoop sounded from deep inside the tunnel and a light vibration rolled out through the forest floor.

The two guards stood over King and Queen. They cocked their weapons. King fought the urge to grimace. These guys weren't taking any chances. *C'mon,* King thought, *just another second.*

Then it happened.

A plume of dust rocketed out of the tunnel, filling the air and the guard's lungs. The men gagged and choked, waving their hands in front of their faces and stepping back out of the cloud. When they saw the two apparitions emerging from the brown haze it was too late.

King buried his KA-BAR knife into the throat of the first man, while the other faced Queen's arms. His neck snapped a moment later. The two bodies slumped to the forest floor. It would have been easier to shoot the guards, but the men carrying Sara would have heard the reports and doubled their efforts.

King withdrew his knife from the man's neck. As he wiped the blade off on a fern, he looked at the uniforms of the dead men. Dark brown and black tiger-striped camouflage patterns were printed on the uniforms, perfect for blending in with the rotting forest floor. But a red patch sewn onto the men's shoulders, featuring a skull inside a large golden star, revealed them as Death Volunteers.

King sheathed his knife and searched for tracks. He found them leading into the jungle. He readied his M4 while Queen slid her UMP off her back. They looked each other in the eyes. Both knew they were about to face a special forces unit of unknown size with only two weapons and a heap of guts to help them win the day.

"Let's make this a fast-food run," King said. "Grab and go. I don't want to be around when the rest of them show up."

She nodded and started off into the jungle. King stopped her.

"Queen, if Sara is K.I.A., our objective becomes her backpack." He hated himself for saying it. But getting the job done sometimes meant being a cold, heartless bastard.

She could see he didn't like issuing the order, but she knew it was the right thing to do. They both did. Queen flashed a smile. "Don't worry, King, we'll get your girl back." She took off into the jungle, running fast. King followed close behind.

"What do you mean, 'my girl'?"

Queen looked over her shoulder as she ran. "You stopped calling her Pawn."

"Shit." King realized she was right and picked up the pace. Not knowing the size or skill level of the force they'd be up against when they caught up with Sara's captors didn't bother him. He was used to that. This new unknown that had snuck up on him like an assassin bothered him most. Sara. He didn't know a damn thing about her. Hell, Rook knew her better. But Queen pegged him. Something about Sara had caught his eye and he'd be damned before letting her become another missing American in the jungles of Vietnam.

Two minutes later King saw the head of the first Death Volunteer as he carried Sara through the jungle. He raised his M4 and took aim.

TWENTY-ONE

Being an American born to Korean immigrants never bothered Knight. He had a traditional Korean name, Shin Daejung, but that's where his connection to his Korean roots ended. He had visited Korea once, on a mission. The team flew into South Korea, crossed the demilitarized zone, saw to some nasty business involving a Sudanese terrorist being hidden, and hopped back over the border in time to share beers with some soldiers at the most laid-back military base he'd ever been to. For military personnel looking for a slow pace, South Korea was the place to be. Knight's only other true Korean cultural experience had come at age ten, when his mother decided he needed to experience the cuisine of his homeland. The roast squid didn't go over too well. In fact, the one time Knight truly appreciated the country of his parents' birth was when he saw the brilliant movie *The Host*. He'd always been a fan of monster movies. Bold heroes. Guns blazing. Running for your life.

The real thing, he knew, was no fun at all. Having survived an encounter with the mythical Hydra reborn had taught him that much. It seemed God, or someone, thought he was due for another lesson.

Vegetation slapped his body as he careened down the mountainside. Trees whipped by in a blur. His breath pulsed in time with his rapidly beating heart.

He'd been running for two minutes straight. Flat out. Top speed. He'd learned to run as a teenager when it seemed like every jock in high school wanted to pick on the small Korean kid. They never could catch him.

But these weren't jocks. Knight wasn't even sure they were human. The din they were creating sounded almost chimpanzee-like, but there were no chimps in Vietnam. The only thing he knew for sure was that the things were fast. Damn fast. And relentless. They'd been steadily gaining on him since the chase started atop the mountain. He dropped his sniper rifle and shed his backpack to lose weight, but still they gained.

And now they were twenty feet back. He could hear trees shaking. Branches breaking. Feet slapping earth. And over it all, their chorus of hoots and hollers. These were the creatures from the village. And he had witnessed the carnage they could wreak on a human body. The two soldiers they'd caught were torn apart and crushed like they were nothing more than rotten vegetables. To be caught meant death.

To evade the predators he had to risk another kind of death. He placed his odds squarely against his own survival, but not trying, lying back and taking it like the Grim Reaper's whore, just wouldn't do.

Knight nearly tripped and fell when he saw what was left of the wall they'd so staunchly defended. A mass of earth and tree had come loose from above and crashed down on the position. He had heard the three explosions that must have brought the mountain down before he heard from Rook, so he knew they'd survived.

A glitter of sunlight from above revealed the swaying of trees. The trees, with their tall trunks and thick leaves, swayed from a weight high above.

My God, Knight thought, *they're in the trees!*

Knight leaped over what was left of the ancient wall and sprinted into the clearing the team had made. The VPA soldiers were nowhere to be seen. Not yet, anyway. Hurdling fallen trees and bloody bodies, Knight hopped like a fleeing bunny through the clearing. Out in the open, the predators hunting him down would lose the use of the trees, but they'd also be out in the open. He could look them in the eye.

Upon reaching a ten-foot plot of earth that was free of fallen limbs, both tree and human, Knight chanced a look back. He nearly shouted in fear at what he saw, but maintained his composure, though he nearly lost his balance. The things behind him were . . . primal . . . and they looked at him through yellow eyes with a hatred he'd never before experienced. They ran like men, bipedal, but carried the gait of an ape, low and short. Their faces, surrounded by a blossom of orange-brown fur, were almost human—and that frightened Knight the most. One of the beasts roared at him, revealing twin two-inch canines. The hair on their backs rose like a pissed-off dog's, bouncing wildly as they charged. With every movement, grunt, and breath, they emoted rage. Power. Death. It wasn't an anger born of revenge for the one he'd shot. They simply hated him for existing.

Shadows swept around Knight as he reentered the forest. After his eyes readjusted, he spotted what he'd been looking for since reaching the clearing—green uniforms. A lot of them. The large Vietnamese company hadn't gone far.

They had yet to spot him, but they were on guard. The sound of the war cries of the beasts giving chase flowed through the forest like a living thing, its source impossible to identify.

Knight broke through their ranks at full speed. He shouted in fear, eyes wide with exaggerated horror, and pointed behind him. He doubted any of them could understand English, but he shouted, "Run for your lives!"

His blatant and honest fear coupled with the fact that Knight held no weapon and took no action against them made the Vietnamese men pause. A moment later they realized his warning should have been heeded.

Men screamed as they were tackled from behind. Skulls cracked. Spines were yanked from backs. One soldier was beaten with the limb of the man standing next to him. The carnage swept through the VPA ranks as Knight continued running and the pack of hunters kept on chasing, killing everyone in their path.

A few smart men near the back of the group abandoned their mortars and fled. Knight ran with them.

The man next to Knight couldn't have been a day over eighteen. He was in shape and fast. The men were neck and neck. Screams rang out from all around them as men on either side were taken down. Leaves and earth shot into the air. Flesh exploded. Guns fired hopelessly, popping at random and then silenced. Knight's running partner glanced over and his eyes went wide. Evidently he'd taken Knight for one of his own. Realizing the truth, the man reached for his French MAT-49 submachine gun, which bounced on his back.

As the man brought the weapon around, Knight pulled out his handgun and took aim. The red bead of the laser-aiming module appeared on the man's forehead a second before a single .45-caliber bullet pierced his skull and rup-tured out the back. As the man fell, the whole scene took on a surreal feel. The flash and sound of the bullet leaving the gun were hidden by the weapon's suppressor. Full of life and fury one moment, the man was still and lifeless the next. But as his body fell to the ground, another filled the void.

It lunged over the falling body, arms outstretched and claws extended. Knight dove, turned toward the creatures, whose red-rimmed eyes bore into his, and unloaded the en-tire clip. They fell together, landing in a heap of entwined limbs.

But only one of them stood again.

TWENTY-TWO

Rook woke to find the air cleared and his head throbbing. He pulled his small Maglite flashlight from his vest and twisted it on. A small amount of dust flitted through the air, but it was breathable. He examined the tunnel, solid stone on all sides. As claustrophobia threatened to take root in Rook's mind, he turned his attention to the others.

Bishop sat up and rubbed his forehead. He looked Rook in the eyes and slowly shook his head.

"We need to get out of here," Rook said. He pointed the light toward Somi's shirtless, supine body. She showed no sign of consciousness, but her red-stained, gauze-wrapped chest rose and fell. "She's alive."

Rook stood and bent down to avoid hitting his head on the low ceiling. "You manage to grab one of our packs?"

"No," Bishop said. "I got this, though." He held up Somi's shotgun.

"Well, that's something," Rook said. He took Somi's hands and pulled up. Her head hung down, but cleared the floor by a few inches. Bent over and holding half of Somi's weight, Rook pulled her through the tunnel. There was no discussion about which way to go and no debate over whether or not they should go at all. If they stayed still they would die, and there was only one direction they could go.

Ten minutes later they reached the three-pronged fork in

the road. Rook set Somi down with a grunt. He lay flat on his back, which throbbed from the constant bending. His head ached from bumping it several times while pulling Somi. He reached into a vest pocket, pulled out a small packet of pain-killers, tore it open, and swallowed four dry. "Which way, big guy?"

Bishop inspected each of the three tunnels. He noted the scripted symbols etched into the walls but couldn't make sense of them. He turned to Rook. "No idea."

Rook sat up and groaned as blood rushed from his head, bringing a new wash of pain. He looked at the tunnel floors. Each showed signs of movement, one more than the other two. "Look there," he said, pointing at the right-hand tunnel. "I'm guessing King and Queen went that way."

Bishop nodded and leaned into the tunnel. "I think we should—"

A muffled whump sounded in the distance and the tunnel shook. A rushing hiss of air and dirt grew louder from the right-side tunnel.

"Don't we have all the luck," Rook said. He took Somi under the arms and charged into the left-side tunnel as a breeze began to swirl the dust in the small crossroad section of tunnel. Bishop followed close behind.

They'd covered fifty feet of tunnel when the shock wave hit the four-way junction. Dust exploded through the three open shafts.

Rook charged on, banging his head, pulling Somi, determined to not lose consciousness a third time in the same day. Then the tunnel disappeared beneath his feet. He fell and took Somi with him.

As he fell, Rook pulled Somi close and kept his back facing down, cushioning Somi's body with his own. He landed hard and the sound of snapping bones filled his ears. He expected a jolt of pain, but none came. His senses returned. He twisted Somi off of him. A second later Bishop came down on top of him like a wrestler from the top rope.

Rook coughed as air escaped his lungs. After a deep

breath he laughed, then groaned and shoved Bishop off of him. "You're not my type, big guy."

With Bishop's weight off of him, Rook turned his flashlight on and pointed it up, just in time to see a plume of dust explode from the tunnel, ten feet above. It spread into a cloud and drifted down around them. Rook could taste the grit, but it wasn't enough to make him gag.

Bishop picked up his flashlight, which he'd dropped upon colliding with Rook, and shined it around the room. Rook followed suit. The two beams cut through the dust-filled darkness, revealing a cavern fifteen feet tall and thirty wide. But the details were obscured by dust.

Rook shivered. "Hey, it's cold in here."

"We're under the mountain," Bishop said. "Ambient underground temperature is fifty-four degrees."

"Cold enough to chill a beer," Rook said.

"Or something else."

Rook turned toward Bishop and found him staring at the side of the cavern. The air had cleared enough for them to see the far wall. Three bodies, bound at the feet, hung upside down from the wall. Ropes tied to their ankles rose up and over the edge of the rise and disappeared into a tunnel above.

Rook's memory recalled the sound of breaking bones when he'd fallen into the cavern. He shined his light down.

Human bones lay scattered around the room like discarded trash. They weren't complete skeletons, just a mix of body parts casually dumped into the space.

Rook shuffled through the bones and stood next to Bishop, who was inspecting the bodies. Two were men, one a woman. All Vietnamese. All naked. Strips of flesh had been peeled off the meaty portions of their bodies—thighs, calves, shoulders—like they were giant sticks of string cheese. "Bishop, what the hell?"

"Villagers from Anh Dung." Bishop looked Rook in the eye, his face deep in shadow. "You were right about the beer, Rook. This is someone's refrigerator."

Distant noise echoed from the tunnel above, like a foghorn, only more organic. Rook and Bishop quickly stepped through the field of bones, knelt next to Somi, and turned off their flashlights. But the darkness didn't fade completely. Flickering light poured out of the tunnel.

Bishop raised the shotgun up. Rook snapped his wrist guards into a locked position, allowing him to fire his two Desert Eagle handguns with one hand each. He raised them up, ready to unload a volley of .50-caliber rounds.

"What's going on?"

Both men jumped as Somi's voice cut the silence.

Rook looked down and put the barrel of his handgun in front of his lips. He shushed her quietly, shaking his head. *Of all the times to regain consciousness.* He refocused on the tunnel as a figure stepped into view. His eyes went wide. He had no clue what the thing holding the torch was, but he recognized the limp body over its shoulder.

Knight.

TWENTY-THREE

Washington, D.C.

The president stood in front of a massive rectangular screen comprised of eight smaller screens that merged to form one. A single large image could be shown on all eight or an individual image could be viewed on each independently. This was the back wall of the White House Situation Room, which featured multiple flat-screen TVs mounted on every wall of the room. In this room the powers that be could keep watch on the entire world, receiving data from eyes on the ground, satellites, and the media. It was the media that held Tom Duncan's attention now.

All eight screens were dedicated to the image, blowing it up to life-size proportions. It was the White House. Just outside. A line of reporters speaking into microphones dominated the view. They were polluting the airwaves with theories about what was going on inside the White House. Why weren't they being given a press conference? Did the president have a heart attack? Was he dead?

What was most frustrating was that they couldn't tell the truth. Not yet. Not until there was a cure. But if they lied, and Brugada got out . . . well, then they would be lynched. Silence, for now, was Duncan's only option.

"Shut it off," Duncan said.

The Situation Room hiding beneath the West Wing of the White House was full of infected advisors, a few generals, and a number of officers from various intelligence agencies—all confined within the walls of the White House. Those who were not infected, but integral to the conversation, joined them via Webcam.

Duncan looked away from the TV screen and focused on the American flag standing next to it. He wasn't sure whether he should lower it to half staff or turn it upside down. While most people thought the upside-down flag to be an act of disrespect, those in the military knew it signified extreme distress—to be wary of a lurking enemy. Extreme distress didn't begin to describe the state of the White House.

He turned and faced the group sitting around the long conference table. His seat at the head of the table, opposite the massive screen, was empty, but he didn't feel like sitting. Hell, he didn't feel like talking. He wanted action and he wanted it now. "Give it to me straight. What are we dealing with?"

Stephen Harrison, head of the FBI, filled the screen of a laptop on the desk. He was communicating with them from the safety of FBI headquarters. "We were able to trace everyone who came in contact with you and with Brentwood, from family members to security guards at the airport. They've all been quietly quarantined, but friends and family are getting vocal. If this was just one or two people we could keep it quiet, but the total number is . . ." He looked at his laptop screen. "Five hundred thirty-three."

Silence.

Duncan took a deep breath and felt repulsed by the mixture of colognes and perfumes assaulting his nose. He let the air out of his lungs slowly and stared at the cherry oak conference table. "What are our options?"

"Lie," Harrison said. "Well, a half truth. Food poisoning. You passed out. But you're fine. We have everything we need in house for you to address the nation, show them you're in good health. It will quiet the media."

"For a day or two," Boucher said, "but they're going to want a press conference. We could be holed up in here for weeks, months! Until a cure is found."

"And if a cure isn't found?" Harrison said.

"It *will* be," Duncan said, his voice confident. He couldn't lie to the American people, but he could lie to the men and women in this room, even if they saw through it.

"Look, sooner or later, the press is going to catch wind of the quarantines on the East Coast. They're going to figure out that the White House is in the same situation. We need a contingency plan."

"Oh my God," someone on the opposite side of the room whispered.

Duncan saw an aide cover her mouth with her hand. She was looking at a small screen in front of her, an earbud in one ear. She was paying attention to the conversation *and* something else.

"What is it?" Boucher asked.

The woman's head snapped toward him. "The news."

Someone had the forethought to switch the big screen on before being asked. News reports from CNN, MSNBC, and Fox News appeared side by side. Each featured a news reporter speaking into a microphone, but they were clearly agitated, and ignoring the crew from other stations dashing back and forth through the shot.

"Let's hear Fox," Boucher said.

The volume was turned up.

"Again, this has just come in. More than five hundred U.S. citizens have been placed under quarantine with no reason given to their families. A source *within* the White House, who spoke on the condition of anonymity, told the Associated Press that the White House is also under quarantine, that several staff members are being held against their will, and that a disease, something called Brugada syndrome, is responsible. While we have yet to discover what Brugada is, we will keep you up to date as our researchers—"

"Enough," Duncan said. He stood and placed his hands

on the tabletop, leaning toward the group around him. "Stephen, how is that contingency plan coming?"

Harrison blanched on camera. "On it." The screen went blank.

"The rest of you, go do your jobs. Do *not* contact the press. I want radio silence, people, understood? The only outside contact you can have is to government and military agencies. No family. No friends. No press." He turned to Judy, who was standing behind him to the right. "Let the press know that I will address the nation soon."

Mumbled conversations broke out around the room.

"Just do it," Duncan said, his voice bordering on anger. "Now get to work."

The group set about doing their part. Several rushed out, others got on cell phones. General Keasling, who'd waited in silence through the meeting, spoke to Boucher via Webcam. The president sat down next to Boucher and spoke into the Webcam. "Have we heard anything yet?"

"Not a peep," Keasling said. "We're watching the area with five satellites and endless spy plane passes."

Duncan scrunched his lips and shook his head. "Not good enough. The solution to all this is in that jungle."

"What are you thinking?" Boucher asked.

Duncan set his eyes on Keasling. "How many troops can we have on Vietnamese soil in three days?"

Keasling thought for a moment and then asked, "Just troops? No tanks, jeeps, or other equipment?"

Duncan nodded. "Just troops."

"A full brigade, five thousand men. I think that would do the job."

Boucher's forehead scrunched up. They were talking presidential suicide. An aggressive, invading president rarely got reelected, not without someone crashing planes into buildings. "Tom, you don't really want to invade Vietnam?"

"As a last resort, yes. A sudden overwhelming force will give us the time and security to solve this problem. Then we'll evacuate."

"The region's unstable as it is," Boucher said. "Other Asian countries—scratch that—every other nation on Earth that isn't a pal is going to feel very threatened. It could provoke a world war."

"That's why it's Plan B. I want to be ready the moment we catch wind of Brugada spreading. Worldwide genocide is not something I am willing to risk, even if it makes me unpopular. I want our forces in the region on high alert and ready to go at a moment's notice, just in case."

"I'll see to it," Keasling said before closing the connection.

Duncan turned to Boucher. "Dom, you're a spook. Find out who our White House snitch is and fire them, Trump style."

Boucher nodded. "Gladly. But . . ." He raised his eyebrows, further wrinkling his age-etched forehead. "Tom, just curious, what is Plan A?"

Duncan grinned. "If you need something done right . . ."

TWENTY-FOUR

Annamite Mountains—Vietnam

Though all of his instincts told him to rush in, guns blazing, King held back. Jumping into a fight half cocked always got someone killed. With odds stacked to alpine heights against them, success would come only with a solid plan. Communicating through their throat microphones, Queen and King split up and encircled the VPLA camp they'd found.

Twenty large, olive green tents arranged in a squared formation revealed a sizable force, yet few were present in the camp. The VPLA had cleared the area of brush and scrub but had left the tall trees unscathed. Far from being environmentalists, they were well aware that the trees' thick canopy provided cover from prying eyes in orbit. They were invisible to the world here in the jungle, free to do whatever they pleased, without consequence.

Not today, King thought as he crouched behind the exposed roots of a moss-covered tree, watching the men in the camp and assessing the situation. The two Death Volunteers carrying Sara set her down in the center of the camp and were greeted by three others. None seemed to carry any kind of authority or rank, which was strange, but he could not hear or see another living thing inside the camp. Unguarded and lax, the site would make easy picking. Even the men who'd taken Sara seemed at ease—like they knew he and Queen had been killed in the tunnel.

"Queen," King whispered into his throat mic. "What's your take?"

Queen looked down from the canopy. She'd shimmied up a tree far from camp and then made her way through the twisting branches of the canopy. It was like another world in the canopy, like a second layer of jungle through which movement was almost as easy as it was on the ground. Concealed by overlapping layers of large leaves, Queen watched without fear of being spotted.

"I count five," Queen said. "Nobody else is home. Might be our best chance."

King knew she was right, but couldn't shake the feeling that something looked off. The men were too relaxed, too sure of themselves. The VPLA might be special forces, but they weren't Delta, and you'd never find a Delta operator looking so relaxed when enemies were on their doorstep.

"King . . ." Queen's voice sounded hesitant. Distracted.

"What?"

"Your watch."

King looked at the outbreak meter on his wrist. He'd all but forgotten the thing. It demanded his attention now. Three of five bars were full. The third was orange. Something in the world had changed. Something bad.

Time was running out.

The five VPLA men laughed, snapping King's attention back to them. Though he couldn't understand a word, he could tell the men were telling jokes. All the while, Sara's unconscious form lay still at their feet. One of the men rolled her onto her back with his boot. She lay propped up on her backpack looking as though she'd fallen asleep tanning by the pool. The man who pushed her over knelt down next to her. His hand gestures and laughs told King all he needed to know about what would take place next.

"I'm moving now, Queen," King said. "Cover my ass, but only fire if you need to."

King moved toward the camp, crouching low behind the brush that clung to the outer fringe of the site. He came in low behind one of the long green tents. The men standing had their backs to him, blocking the view of the man kneeling down next to Sara. As the man undid Sara's backpack straps and protective vest, all eyes were on her.

As King came within twenty feet of the men, Queen's voice filled his ear. "King, I don't like this. It's too damn fishy. Shred them, grab her, and get the hell out."

King agreed, but wanted to get as close to his targets as possible. He didn't want to risk hitting Sara and wanted to scoop her onto his shoulder before the last Death Volunteer hit the ground. This speed would only come with being close. Any VPLA in the area would hear the gunshots and rush to inspect. The time between firing at least five shots, grabbing Sara, and exiting the camp had to be minuscule. Efficiency was key. Fifteen feet would have to be close enough. He raised his M4 and took aim.

The soldier on the ground next to Sara rolled her over and began tugging off her backpack. Sara's eyes popped open and locked on King's. She'd been awake the whole time. He read her lips as she mouthed a single word to him. "Run."

But it was too late. Four fifteen-foot-long hatches sprang open in front of each row of tents. From each leaped ten VPLA soldiers, their weapons trained on King. None fired.

Queen's barely discernable whisper entered King's ear. "Clear your throat if you want me to hold off."

King cleared his throat and lowered his M4 to the forest floor. He raised his hands and looked in the eyes of the men surrounding them, turning slowly. He saw anger in the eyes of each and every one of the men. Except one. He was shorter than the others, yet carried more confidence . . . and no weapon. A single yellow star adorned the right shoulder of the man's black and brown tiger-striped camouflage uniform.

"Major General," King said with a nod.

Trung grinned and glanced at the gold star. "Major General Trung." He walked around King, looking him up and down. Then he leaned in close, removing King's KA-BAR knife and holstered pistol. He shouted an order to the five men still standing over Sara. They yanked her up, all of their casual aura vanished. An act.

Sara shrieked as she was pulled up. Her arms were twisted back by one man while a second pulled her up by her hair. With wide eyes, she began to whimper as the general approached. He held the razor-sharp KA-BAR knife up to her face and allowed Sara to see her own horrified expression in the blade's reflection.

He drew the blade slowly across her cheek.

It felt like little more than a pen being dragged over her skin, cool and hard. But when the intense sting set in, Sara realized he'd actually cut her! Warm blood seeped from the four-inch slice and ran down her cheek. Sara's chin shook as tears filled her eyes.

Trung moved the knife from Sara's cheek to her neck.

"Please," Sara said, as the first of her tears mixed with the blood on her cheek, burning in the open wound. "Don't . . ."

King's fists were clenched tight. His breath lodged in his chest. His eyes locked on the knife approaching Sara's throat. He believed the VPLA general was testing his nerve. They wouldn't kill Sara. She might have answers. It would be a strategic blunder, and from what he'd experienced this day, the VPLA had their shit together. They wouldn't screw up something as elementary as killing their most useful captive.

Blood began to drip from Sara's neck. He looked in her eyes, which were trusting him to keep her alive at all costs. That was the mission.

The knife stopped moving, though its blade remained buried in a few layers of skin. Blood ran down the gleaming metal and gathered around the hilt before dripping and slapping onto the dried leaves below. The general looked back at King. "Your female partner. She has thirty seconds to show herself."

King's jaw muscles bulged as he bit down in frustration. This backwater major general and his squad of men who'd never seen action outside their own country had them pegged. Trung's perfect English was icing on the cake. His few spoken words, lacking any kind of accent, said, "I know you better than you know me."

And *that* was the truth.

King shook his head. "Queen."

Several of the VPLA soldiers jerked their weapons up as the canopy shook. They knew she was hiding. They didn't know where. Bark shredded from the tree as Queen slid down to the forest floor. She turned her UMP around and handed it to the nearest soldier. She raised her arms as the man took her knife and sidearm. The man shoved her from behind, pushing her toward King.

"Watch it, buddy," she said with a growl. They might have taken her firearms but she still possessed her most lethal weapons. To remove those would require several amputations.

The knife came away from Sara's throat and the men dropped her to the ground. She held her hands to her wounds and found the blood flow to be minor. They were superficial cuts.

Trung spoke to the men in rapid-fire Vietnamese. They sprang into action. King, Queen, and Sara were bound, hands behind backs with zip-tie handcuffs, then shoved into the largest of the tents.

King's eyes widened upon entering the tent. The odd collection of devices, tools, and tables told him more about the tent's purpose than he wanted to know.

Trung walked in front of his three prisoners and grinned upon seeing the expressions on their faces.

King's concern.

Queen's rage.

Sara's fear.

He stepped in front of King and spoke quietly. "Today

you will learn to speak your first Vietnamese word, *sụ' tra tấn.*"

King didn't need a translator to understand the word. It would be one he remembered for the rest of his life.

Torture.

TWENTY-FIVE

Rook's body shook with rage as he tried to launch himself at the dark figure lowering Knight's limp form into the pit. Bishop's bulging arms held him in place while his whispered warning kept the silence. "Know your enemy, Rook. It's too soon for revenge."

Rook stopped and watched without speaking as Knight slid down the wall, head first. His arms were free, dangling down below his head. With his feet bound together by a rope that led up and over the edge of the pit, Knight looked like a fresh version of the dead villagers hung next to him. Just another side of beef in the meat locker.

The thick figure set the torch down, further obscuring itself from view, but in the dim flickering light its orange hair could be seen. The hair struck Rook as odd because everything else about the figure looked human . . . though hunched, like an old man . . . or an ape. As the figure bent down and tied off the rope Rook knew he wasn't watching an ape. Apes weren't intelligent enough to tie knots. And they sure as hell couldn't get the jump on Knight.

Before they could see it clearly, the form turned and walked away. The torchlight faded in the tunnel.

When it was no longer visible, and the chamber descended once again into darkness, Rook switched on his flashlight and dashed to Knight's side.

A wreath of light hung on Knight's body. His protective flak jacket had been removed. Tatters of black fabric dangled from his shredded fatigues. The small screen of the outbreak monitor on his wrist had been shattered, though the device still functioned. Wounds cut across his chest. Yet his body, his limbs, seemed mostly hale. As Bishop arrived, Rook lowered his light, illuminating Knight's face.

Rook stepped back and covered his mouth. Not so much from the sight of Knight's limp body, but more to remind himself not to shout a string of curses. What little of Knight's face wasn't caked in blood was pale. Rook leaned forward. It wasn't his skin that was pale, it was dust. He'd been dragged through the forest and caves, and dust had clung to his face. Rook reached up to check for a pulse, but Knight confirmed his physical state before Rook's hand reached his throat.

He coughed.

Knight was alive!

Rook dropped the flashlight and fell to his knees. He placed one hand under Knight's blood-soaked head and the other under his back. Bishop reached up and cut the rope binding Knight's ankles. In a flurry of motion, not caring who heard, Rook kicked the bones at their feet away until a small clearing had been formed. He gently placed Knight on the floor. "Hang on, buddy."

Bones clattered behind Rook as Somi stumbled over for a look. She paused, supporting her weight on the wall, the knife wound stabbing pain into her body with every breath. "Keep quiet."

Rook glared at her.

"They'll come back," she said.

Rook stood while Bishop began inspecting Knight's wounds. "Look, lady. I don't give a damn about how you might do things out here in the magic forest. We take care of our own."

Somi pursed her lips and nodded. She'd never worked with Delta operators before, but she could see they had different standards when it came to living—and dying. She found it . . .

inspiring. Thinking about her betrayal, she winced inwardly. Her loyalty to the VPLA had never faltered before.

But she had experienced firsthand how Trung rewarded loyalty. These men were different. They had earned her respect. Her goal now was to escape these tunnels and then disappear. Let Trung think her dead. Vengeance would be easier that way. For now, Rook and Bishop were her allies. She watched from her spot on the wall as Rook rejoined Bishop over their half-dead comrade.

"Can you hear me, Knight?" Bishop said, his voice nearly a whisper. "Knight . . ."

Knight's eyes blinked and then opened.

"Bish . . . Rook . . ." Knight reached out and took Rook's arm. Knight's words were slurred and wet as he spoke with tired lips. He glanced around the cave. "So much for pearly gates."

"You little death-cheating bastard," Rook said with a grin. "What, it's not enough to cheat at Go Fish? You have to cheat death, too?"

Knight chuckled, then winced. "Broken ribs. Sprained ankle, too. Maybe broken. Concussion for sure. Got something to drink?"

Bishop and Rook helped Knight sit up. He took painkillers from his pocket, popped them in his mouth, and drank from Rook's canteen. "I caught a few glimpses of the caves," he said between drinks. "They're huge. Tunnels everywhere."

Bishop leaned in close. "Knight. What are they?"

Knight closed his eyes.

"Knight?"

"I'm . . . thinking," Knight said. His eyes opened. "They're not . . . human."

"Apes?" Rook said.

Knight shook his head, almost imperceptibly. "Too intelligent. Cunning. But they're apelike in some ways."

Knight winced as pain throbbed in his chest. He fought past it and continued. "Fur like orangutans. Muscles like silverback gorillas. They're not apes, but they're not human.

They're something else. Something . . . ancient. You can see it in their eyes."

Knight coughed, spit a blood-red glob from his mouth, and sighed. He rolled his head toward Rook. "We need to get out of here." He nodded toward the cave tunnel where they'd watched the creature exit. "That way."

"We can't fight them," Somi said.

"Not a chance," Knight said. "But the tunnels are wide and I saw daylight a few times. We can make it."

Rook nodded. "We can't stay here and wait for someone to get hungry for Korean." He turned his flashlight to the wall covered in upside-down cadavers. "Any ideas?"

"Yeah," said Somi. She reached up with her good arm and grabbed hold of one of the body's pant legs. She jumped up with a quick pull, placed her foot on the body's crotch, and pushed off. She landed on her uninjured side in front of the tunnel where Knight had been lowered from. She grunted and then looked at the three surprised Delta operators. "We do what he said. We get out. Now."

TWENTY-SIX

The backyard held green grass and four flower gardens. Yet in dire contrast to this lush beauty stood two warriors. Each held a bow and arrow, notched, aimed, and drawn. Both let fly. The first, belonging to the girl, struck the target dead center. The second flew off to the side, ricocheting off a stone and striking the wooden fence that enclosed the yard. "Nice shot, Siggy."

"Kiss my ass, Jules," the young man countered.

At sixteen Jack Sigler spent more time on a skateboard than anything else. School had long since become unimportant, and family . . . well, they were family. But when his sister asked if he'd like to shoot some arrows in the backyard, he couldn't pass it up, even if it meant spending time with his dork of a sister.

A bookworm to the core, Julie had a secret side she let out only when their parents were away. Bows and arrows, throwing knives, library books on the military. He figured she was working on some kind of paper, but she'd been doing it for a while. Not that he cared enough to figure out what she was up to. He just wanted to shoot some arrows. He knew their parents would put the kibosh on the activity if they ever found out, so he kept his mouth shut. In fact, he guessed the invitation to shoot with Julie was more of a bribe than an attempt at brother-sister bonding.

"Just keep your left arm straight and look down the shaft."

Jack took aim again and let the arrow fly. This time Julie just watched. The arrow skimmed off the top of the target and buried into the fence.

"Hold your breath before you shoot again."

"You got it, Master Yoda."

"I don't care if you're a crappy shot," Julie said with a smile. "I just don't want Dad to find the fence chewed to shreds."

Jack took aim again. He found the target with his eyes and begrudgingly held his breath. Adjusting slightly, he felt a sense of peace for a moment. Just a moment. And in that fraction of time, he enjoyed being with his sister. He let go of the wire and felt it slap against his bare arm. "Son of a bitch!"

Jack dropped the bow and held his arm. He expected to see a deep gash when he lifted his hand away but found only a wide red mark where the wire had hit his skin and slid across his arm. Insignificant compared to many of his skateboarding injuries, the red welt embarrassed him more than it stung. He stormed toward the house.

"Jack," Julie called, her voice full of humor.

"Leave me alone," he shouted back.

"But look!"

It wasn't the reply he expected. He looked over his shoulder and paused. His arrow sat in the center of the target, next to his sister's.

"You see," Julie said. "Big sisters are good for something."

The faintest of smiles crept onto Jack's hardened face. "Yeah, guess so."

He rejoined her on the improvised archery range, and for the rest of the week while his parents were on vacation, he and Julie forged a temporary truce. By the end of the week his aim was keen. Things went back to normal with the return of their parents, but it had been one of the first times in his life he appreciated his sister. He remembered her with fondness.

She gave him strength.

He needed it now.

The memory faded, replaced by seizing pain. Trained to reduce the agony of torture by escaping from the body and entering the often parodied "happy place," King turned to his sister for help.

It didn't work.

King's involuntary scream ripped through the tent's thin green fabric and met a wall of trees and foliage that muffled the noise and sent the sound waves back to the earth where they were absorbed and silenced. No one outside of the small VPLA camp would hear his anguish. Bound tight, hands over head, to a tall stake stretching toward the tent's ceiling, King could do nothing to ease the pain. Not much could.

Eight hundred thousand volts of electricity coursing into a human body tended to have that effect. That the general was placing the stun gun against King's temple increased the agony tenfold. A three- to five-second charge could bring a man to his knees, causing loss of muscle control and disorientation. King had received eight separate jolts in the past three minutes . . . to the side of his head, his chest, and the back of his neck. All from a handheld, battery-operated stun gun any jerk could pick up on eBay for minimal cash. Cheap, affordable torture.

With deep breaths, King fought to regain control of his spasming muscles. Hot sweat poured down his shirtless chest and back. They'd stripped him from the waist up and confiscated his outbreak meter before binding him to the stake. The carved muscles beneath his skin bounced to an unheard rhythm, slowing after a few seconds. The port-wine stain reaching up his back glistened deep purple. After his muscles stopped twitching madly, the tight pain subsided. But it would be ten minutes before full control returned. And Trung would be back before then. He fell forward. With his hands bound above his head, his weight pulled his arms back at a painful angle. Having no strength left he could do nothing to right himself.

King had been trained in withstanding torture. To keep his mouth shut under duress. To die if need be. And he knew he would. The problem with his training was that it didn't cover this scenario, because he wasn't being asked any questions. Trung was like a kid with a magnifying glass over a hill of ants. The smile on his face confirmed it. He was enjoying himself.

"You got a hard-on yet?" Queen noticed, too. She was strapped to a stake next to King's, also shirtless, her breasts exposed, her six-pack abs even more impressive than King's. Like King, her outbreak meter had been taken, no doubt being inspected in another tent. Her chin and clavicle were stained red from blood. But it was not her own. The man who'd removed her clothing attempted to fondle her breasts. She nearly took his nose clean off with her teeth.

Trung had the undisciplined man shot for his actions. Their torture began shortly after.

Not a word had been spoken since.

Other than King's screams the only sound in the tent was Sara's weeping. She'd been tied to a chair. Her clothes remained on. Her body untouched. As King used what little energy that remained to look up and meet Sara's trembling eyes, he realized the torture was not meant to loosen his or Queen's tongues. Intimidation was the goal, and it was directed at Sara.

After finishing with King and Queen they would turn their attention to her. She would tell them anything they needed to save herself . . . and if not that, then to spare King and Queen any more pain. King's cheeks twitched.

It would work.

Trung walked around Queen with the stun gun, flicking it off and on. A blue arc of electricity pulsed across two metal prongs, buzzing like a giant angry wasp.

Hardly intimidated, Queen flashed him a smile, her lips still encrusted with the dried blood of Trung's dead man. She'd been shocked, the same as King, but had not screamed. With nothing more than a grunt, she'd endured the electric torture. He'd shocked her head, her breasts, her armpits and stomach. But she didn't give in.

All her life, her expression of pain had always been delayed . . . and violent, like her father's. If she stubbed a toe, she remained silent until the pain dissipated. Then she put her fist through the wall. If that hurt, she did it again, and again, until she couldn't feel the pain anymore. She stored pain like a battery and only unleashed it when ready. Trung's stun gun had filled her battery long ago. She just needed an outlet to free the charge.

The glare in Trung's eyes said he wouldn't give up. He clicked the stun gun off and dropped it onto a table that had been tied together from tree branches. He turned to the guard at the door and spoke briefly. The man nodded and exited quickly.

Trung paced, a grin ever-present on his face.

Things were going to go from bad to worse.

Sara's shaky voice broke the silence of the waiting torturer and the tortured. "S-sir. If you need my help. I'll do whatever you need. You don't need to—"

"You would have done whatever I needed you to long ago," Trung said without breaking stride. "But I am not finished here." He glanced at Queen.

She met his eyes, fearless.

Trung grinned. "You are too eager for pain. It is not fitting for a woman of your . . ." He looked her up and down. ". . . form. Of course, beauty fades. Or can be remade. Perhaps you will lose your fight after you've lost your allure?"

The guard returned holding a long metal rod and a torch. The tip of the rod was hidden inside the flame. Trung undid his shirt and opened it up over his chest, revealing a brand in the shape of a star. A skull grinned evilly at its core. The symbol of the VPLA Death Volunteers.

"We all have them," Trung said. "Only yours will be much more visible."

Trung reached out and took the brand from the guard.

King lifted his head. Sara gasped. Queen's eyes twitched with rage. But she didn't shrink back.

The glowing yellow star-and-skull brand rose up in front of Trung's face. He inched forward holding it out straight. "Try not to move," he said. "We want it to look nice."

Outside the tent, men flinched at the sound of a bestial growl that emerged from the tent. It rose in volume and then turned into a roar, louder than any they'd heard before and more horrible than the ones they'd been hearing in the night-time jungle. Like the ocean being forced through a three-inch hole, a volume of rage had been unleashed through Queen's open mouth. The thick canopy, endless trees, and distance of miles could not hold it back.

Every living thing in the area heard the primal cry.

But Queen did not move. Her eyes remained fixed on Trung's while the brand singed her skin, scorching a symbol that would never fade. When Trung removed the brand and stepped back, fear filled his eyes. He'd never met such a warrior. Like a tiger, she was to be respected . . . and feared. And now she bore the Death Volunteer symbol where every-one would see it. She could have been a goddess. He bowed to her, then exited, giving his men orders to shoot her when morning arrived.

TWENTY-SEVEN

Rook locked arms with Bishop up above and scrambled out of the pit, joining Somi and Knight. While Knight lay with his back against the wall, the others squatted in front of the entrance to the tunnel through which Knight's captor had exited. They gazed into the dark tunnel. No sign of light. No sounds of movement. The smell of death never left the chamber. They'd almost grown accustomed to it.

Rook looked at his watch, its Day-Glo feature casting his face in a faint green light. 10 P.M. "Maybe they're sleeping."

Bishop nodded. "Let's hope so."

Looking at his watch, Rook's eyes moved to the outbreak meter strapped next to it. The small screen displayed three bars, green, yellow . . . and orange. He held it up for the others to see. "We need to get a move on." He motioned to Somi's knife wound. "How's that feeling?"

She sneered. "Like I got stabbed in the chest, you prick." Then she grinned. Despite the pain in her chest, it was clear to her that she would survive the wound, and she was feeling some of her normal feistiness returning.

"Ahh, quit your whining," Knight said. "At least you can walk." Knight spit some more blood. His feistiness was all for show.

Bishop inspected the tunnel. Like the one they'd come

through it was marked with an intricate symbol. Yet something was different about the tunnel. Bishop got on his hands and knees and moved forward. As the tunnel closed in around him, he realized the difference. This tunnel was smaller, perhaps three feet tall and nearly as wide. It would be tight, but not too tight. He turned to Somi. "There are symbols marking the entrances to the tunnels. Do you recognize the script?"

He moved aside and directed his flashlight toward the symbol, allowing her to get a clear view. She moved closer and ran her fingers over the symbol's swooping and crisscrossing lines. "It's not Vietnamese."

Of that much she was sure. Before her father's death, Somi had been in love with the region's history, and had planned to become a historian. Trung changed all that, but she used her training, both in Asia and the United States, as an excuse to pursue her passion. Knowledge was power. History repeated. Those were the justifications. But she knew she couldn't always be a spy and hoped to retire to a quiet museum someday. Not only was her knowledge of the region's history expansive, but as a CIA double agent in Asia, she was expected to speak and read multiple languages, making her knowledge of various scripts above average. But what she saw here defied logic.

"Vietnamese, Korean, Japanese. All were derived from Chinese. The oldest Chinese writing goes back to the Shang Dynasty, 1500 B.C. Archaic Chinese. But this looks . . . older."

Somi stared at the symbol as though in a trance. "Over the years, ancient bones dated to nearly 5000 B.C. have been found in China featuring a previously unknown script. I haven't seen the script, but read it was primarily pictorial—representational images. Modern Chinese is only about four percent pictograph. For a long time, experts thought the Chinese language developed on its own, without a precursor language. The bones hinted at something more, but no one has been able to trace the text to an origin."

Knight leaned in and looked at the symbol. As an Asian

man in covert operations, he, like Somi, had been tasked with speaking as many Asian languages as possible. He could speak and read Mandarin Chinese, Korean, Japanese, and Thai. Similarly, Rook was an expert in Germanic languages, Queen in Western European, Bishop in Arabic, and King in South American. Altogether the team could communicate in most parts of the world.

"What's a precursor language?" Rook asked.

"Japanese is basically Chinese reworked to fit their culture and pronunciations," Knight said. "Just like English, French, and Spanish are all derived from Latin. Most languages on Earth today evolved from something that came before."

Somi nodded. "Chinese has always been thought of as an original language. But if these symbols are as old as this place seems to be . . . this may be the precursor language for Chinese. Proto-Chinese. The calligraphy is similar in style to Chinese, but the symbols are totally different, and much more basic."

Rook raised an eyebrow. He didn't care about ancient languages. Not right now. He was more interested in getting the hell out of there. "Pretty intelligent for someone in intelligence, but can you read it or not?"

Somi shook her head. "No."

Rook looked at Knight. "You?"

"Nope."

"Well, it better say 'exit,' because I'm out the door." Rook knelt down and climbed into the tunnel, holding his small flashlight between his teeth and a Desert Eagle in each hand.

Knight rolled onto his hands and knees, careful not to hit his swollen ankle, and crawled after him.

Bishop gave Somi a lopsided grin. "You next."

She glanced at the wrapped wound on her chest, then at the tunnel. Crawling would not be easy. "Great." Using her good arm, Somi limp-crawled into the tunnel behind Knight.

Bishop took one last look at the chamber of bones. They glowed brightly in the flashlight's beam. He brought the light back to the center of the chamber. A shadow shifted, leaping back out of the light, then up.

Bishop's eyes went wide. Something was in there. It had been right behind them. And they hadn't heard a thing. He brought the flashlight up and directed it down the opposite tunnel, the one through which they'd entered the chamber. Deep in the recesses of the tunnel, two eyes reflected the yellow light back at him. Then they blinked, and were gone.

The eyes opened again a moment later. Larger. More menacing.

Closer.

Bishop fired two shots at the opposite tunnel, knowing most of the pellets would hit the wall, but hoped enough would enter the tunnel and strike the creature to make it think twice.

The shadowed creature howled. Hit. But now it was charging.

"What the hell's going on back there?" Rook's voice echoed from the tunnel.

Bishop dove into the tunnel, the sound of scattering bones clacking behind him as the creature crossed the chamber. "Rook, move! As fast as you can! They're right behind me."

Bishop rolled onto his back and leaned up, pointing the shotgun toward the tunnel's exit, right between his legs. He nearly dropped the flashlight from his mouth when the ruddy brown creature leaped up and surged toward the tunnel. He caught only a glimpse of it before he pulled the trigger. The shotgun blasted loudly in the enclosed space. Bishop bit down on the flashlight, his shout of pain mixing with the creature's. He'd hit it, but it still lived. He found it with the flashlight again. The bloodied beast was still advancing.

Ignoring the pain and ringing in his ears, Bishop took aim again. For a moment he wondered if the blasts would ruin his hearing. Then he remembered his ears would heal in seconds. And his mind would drift farther toward madness. But there was little choice. He pulled the trigger.

The shot echoed off the tightly enclosed space, the sound

waves striking Bishop's ears again and again, faster than he could perceive. What his senses *could* confirm was that his aim had been true. The creature, now faceless, slumped to the cave floor.

Bishop dropped the shotgun, its four shells spent. He glanced back at the opposite tunnel as he began moving. What he saw made him slip back over and crawl like a manic mole.

Glowing eyes, more sets than he cared to count, watched him from the opposite tunnel. As Bishop fled, a loud whooping, more terrifying than his contained shotgun blasts, filled the tunnels.

TWENTY-EIGHT

When it came time for Julie to head out to college and make the family proud, she didn't do exactly what everyone expected—medical school. She did the exact opposite. She enrolled in the air force. Turned out his sister wanted to be a pilot. Not just any pilot. A fighter pilot. Two years later she had earned her wings.

"Hang on, Siggy!" she shouted back to Jack, who was in the backseat of the F-14 Tomcat, a dual-engine supersonic fighter jet. She had the wings folded back and they were hauling ass across a clear sky, twenty thousand feet above a deep blue ocean.

The plane slowed suddenly and Jack felt himself tighten against the seatbelt. He saw the wings opening up on either side. He knew what that meant and clung to the leather seat beneath him with both hands. Then they were upside down, twisting and turning through the sky.

He felt his stomach lurch.

Julie was cheering. "Don't lose your lunch on me, Sig! You know how hard it is to get the smell of puke out of these things?"

The twisting stopped, but a new sensation took over. His stomach was no longer lurching, it was still a thousand feet above him. Jack peered around Julie's helmet and saw a sparkling swath of blue. A vertical dive.

He opened his mouth to shout, but nothing came out. He pounded on her seat. In his mind he begged her to pull up. Pull up!

The endless sparkling blue resolved into cresting waves, rising and falling. A loud hiss filled the cockpit. All around him the sound grew louder, dominant. Then the blue ocean reached up and grabbed them.

King opened his eyes. Darkness surrounded him. The hiss persisted. His body ached.

During times of intense stress, King dreamed of his sister's death. The event had been the catalyst for him joining the military, but it still unnerved him to think about. And this time, the wave of pain rolling through his body made it feel like the dream was real, like he'd really been in that plane when it crashed. As the memory of his previous torture came back, he almost preferred the dream.

For a moment King wondered if he was still inside the nightmare. All around him, the incessant hissing continued and reminded him of when his grandfather would fall asleep in front of the TV at night. He'd sit through Carson, the national anthem, and then six hours of static. On long visits King could hear the TV all night. It annoyed the hell out of him, but when his grandfather died, he missed the sound and occasionally left his TV on at night. After his grandfather died, and then Julie, he was out of family members that he liked. That was, until the Chess Team came together. They'd become his surrogate family, and he was the father figure. The head of the proverbial household.

He was failing his family.

He lifted his head and grunted. His muscles spasmed as he pulled, slowing only after he stood straight against the pole he was tied to.

"It's raining." Queen's voice sounded as strong as ever. Mentally, King pictured her, beautiful and tough. But he knew she was topless and bearing a brand that would never fade.

"I'm sorry," he said.

"King . . ." Her voice was soft, gentle even. "Shut up."

King managed to chuckle, but it hurt like hell.

"Guys?" The new voice was shaky and quiet. Sara.

"We're here, Sara."

"I can't see you."

"That happens in the middle of the night," Queen said. "It's dark."

A table shook, its contents jingling as they rolled back and forth.

What the hell? King strained to see through the darkness. Someone was in the tent with them.

"Keep talking," Sara said.

"Sara, stay quiet," King said, his voice managing to sound harsh though it was only a whisper. He was about to speak again when a hand grasped his face. He flinched back as a second hand found his other cheek. Both quickly fell and wrapped around his body.

He expected to be crushed or stabbed, but he felt no pain. Only a shaking body. Sara's voice was right next to his ear now, her head resting on his shoulder. "Thank God. Are you okay?"

King was speechless. He had to still be dreaming. How could Sara be free?

"How?" he managed to say.

Sara sniffled and wiped her tear-coated cheeks. "I've read enough books and watched enough movies to know that if you get tied up to flex your muscles so that the ropes are loose."

King's chest shook as he quietly laughed. A jolt of pain took the humor right back out of the situation. "They usually check for that," he said.

"Maybe with soldiers, but not with CDC lab rats."

Queen's voice cut through the banter. "Damnit woman, untie us already!"

"Sorry," Sara said, and then began frantically untying King and Queen. Five minutes later, they had located their discarded clothing and redressed. The only articles of clothing missing were the outbreak meters and Queen's bra. One of the soldiers had pilfered it as a souvenir. They then set about finding weapons. While their firearms had most likely been claimed by the VPLA soldiers, King was pleased to find his KA-BAR knife on one of the tables. He couldn't see it, but he knew what it felt like. He also found the stun gun that had caused, and continued to cause him, so much pain. He put the device in his pocket.

Queen found an assortment of torture devices that made worthy weapons—three ice picks, a metal hook, and a now-cold branding iron. Sara took a knife from King, but felt sure her shaky hands could do nothing with it. Still, she put it in her pocket, pretending it gave her some kind of reassurance.

With the rain pounding down around them, their hushed voices were drowned out and their movement through the tent was concealed. It would make excellent cover for their escape as well. As the three crouched by the tent's exit, they peered out into the campsite. A fire at the center of the small compound fought against the rain, but it was a losing battle. Though the firelight shone weakly, King's wide-open pupils could clearly see the surrounding area. There were two guards patrolling. Both had their heads down, keeping the rain out of their faces. They didn't appear to be alert, but he had learned his lesson about doubting the VPLA.

He turned to the others. "We'll make a run for the forest when both have their backs to us. The rain should conceal our . . ."

Before King could finish his sentence the hiss grew quiet and then stopped. He wanted to shout curses at God. One minute more and they would have been gone. One minute more! King peeked through the exit again. The guards were shaking the water from their waterproof ponchos. Then they met next to the fire and lit cigarettes in the lingering flames. They'd have to risk it when the men were looking the other way. Waiting until morning, when Queen was to be executed, was hardly an option.

King looked back at Sara and Queen. "Get ready," he said, and then pointed to the left. "Head that way and don't stop until I tell you—"

He saw Sara tense. But she wasn't preparing to spring from the tent. She was confused. Hearing something, maybe. He'd learned to trust her sense of the world around her and focused on tuning out the jungle noise. Then he heard a distant explosion that instantly registered. Mortar! Sara looked at him with wide eyes. Only then did he realize he'd spoken the word aloud.

Queen had heard it, too, and acted without pause. She pushed between them and pounded from the tent. She held two ice picks, one in each hand.

King followed, but stopped when Sara stayed behind. He turned back to her and reached out his hand. "We only have a few seconds at best."

She took his hand and felt his strength despite all he'd endured. She'd been ready to give Trung anything he asked for and she hadn't been touched. But King had endured hell. On her behalf. As she raced beside him, hand in hand, she thanked God for the man and then prayed this wouldn't be the end.

The guards, now on alert after hearing the sound of a mortar being fired, saw Queen as soon as she exited the tent. But the ice picks had already flown from her hands. One man was struck in the eye. He went down screaming. The other caught the pick with his Adam's apple and toppled over holding his throat.

As soldiers woke and exited from tents, half dressed, half asleep, but armed with assault rifles, Queen, King, and Sara bolted through the center of the camp in plain sight. Queen veered toward the two fallen guards, intent on taking their weapons. She was knocked down when the two men exploded, burst like water balloons, struck by an exploding mortar round. King hoisted her up as the sound of continuous mortar fire sounded in the distance.

"Run!" King shouted. He knew some of the VPLA were

already in pursuit. He could see the trees at the edge of the forest being pelted by bullets. If not for the recently awakened state of the VPLA men, he was sure they'd already be dead. But with the camp under attack, only a small force would pursue them.

As they entered the jungle, mortars exploded all around the camp. The explosions were followed by loud voices, inhuman shouting, and very human screams. Intense gunfire followed—a full-blown battle between the Death Volunteers and someone else was being waged. Had the Khmers followed after all? For a moment, King thought he heard a voice shouting in English, but not Trung's. He listened, but the sound of violence consumed the night. Pulling an individual voice from the chaos was impossible.

Fire blossomed as some of the tents took mortar rounds. The light lit the first few layers of forest. King saw Sara just in front of him, scrambling over a massive tree root. But Queen was nowhere to be seen.

But he knew she was there. She just wasn't running.

"You'll follow us?" he asked the darkness.

"Yes," came Queen's voice. "When I'm done."

TWENTY-NINE

Making sense of the network of tunnels became impossible as Rook charged ahead, no longer caring about finding a way out. Losing the cadre of attackers following them was his top priority. With the penlight between his teeth doing little to illuminate the three-foot-square tunnels, Rook often bumped into walls where he thought an open tunnel was, or crashed through unseen debris that felt and sounded like loose bones.

Knight and Somi managed to stay close behind him, despite their wounds. Fear of monsters in the dark tended to make even the severely injured forget their pain.

Bishop brought up the rear, charging like a bull on hands and knees, slowly catching up to the others, who had a head start. For a large man in a small tunnel, he was fast, but the calls and growls of the creatures giving chase were growing in volume. He wasn't nearly fast enough. He risked smacking his head on the tunnel's ceiling again and looked up. Rook's light veered sharply to the left.

Rook's voice followed the move. "Left!" He'd been shouting directions in case Bishop lost sight of the light, which was the tunnel's only source of illumination.

Knight's silhouette dove into the side tunnel, followed by Somi's. Bishop prepared to follow, but was snagged from behind. He looked back and saw the faintest outline of a savage face biting down on his boot. The pressure compressing the boot was immense. If not for the steel toe, his foot would have been crushed.

Yellow eyes blinked at him and a growl rose from the beast's unseen chest. Bishop kicked out with his snagged leg and smashed the creature's head into the tunnel wall. It shrieked, but held on tight. Putting all of his considerable leg muscle into his actions, Bishop smashed the creature's head two more times. As he did he saw several pairs of eyes bobbing and weaving behind the flailing creature, waiting for their turn at him, but stuck behind the first in line. With a final desperate grunt, Bishop brought his other foot down, smashing it into the face of the creature holding his foot.

His foot came free and the creature's eyes closed. He heard its body fall unconscious to the tunnel floor. Just as he spun to crawl away, he saw the eyes of the creature next in line above the fallen beast. It was squeezing past.

Bishop launched himself into the tunnel, following Rook. But he was far behind now and could barely make out the light ahead. Rook shouted something, possibly a new direction, but Bishop was too far away to hear, and the racket behind him grew louder all the time.

Bishop continued crawling as fast as he could, moving in a straight line, praying the tunnel didn't suddenly come to an end and knock him out cold. But it didn't come to an end. It dropped away. Bishop shouted as he tumbled forward. For a moment he caught sight of Rook's light, but it was fading fast. Gravity suddenly took hold and Bishop slid down a steep grade. His hands brushed the smooth tunnel floor that had been designed to function like a slide. His speed grew when he pulled his boots off the floor and stretched his arms out straight. He wanted to put as much distance as he could between himself and the things giving chase.

Then the tunnel spat him out. He fell four feet to a stone floor. He rolled with the impact and got back on his feet. Rook's hand clasped his shoulder.

"We'll stop them here," Rook said.

Bishop looked at Rook. He could see him clearly, cast in a dull green light that had nothing to do with the penlight that was still in his mouth. Somi sat on the stone floor next to Rook, breathing heavily and wincing with each breath. Knight was fighting to stand. He didn't want to die on his back.

Rook moved to the tunnel exit, holding his two Desert Eagles. He looked to Bishop. "Shotgun?"

Bishop shook his head. No.

A growing howl escaped the tunnel.

"Here they come," Rook said. He tossed Bishop one of the handguns and took up position in front of the tunnel. "Take them as they come out."

Bishop understood the plan. They couldn't miss. He took up position next to Rook and aimed at the tunnel.

When the first creature launched out of the tunnel, it appeared so ghastly in the green light of the chamber that both highly trained men flinched. It hit the floor, landing on its feet, and sprang back up without missing a beat. Rook and Bishop opened fire with two of the world's most powerful handguns. Rook fired three shots, Bishop two.

The creature, now headless and full of gaping holes, fell at Rook's feet.

Then a second fell from the slide, hooting and baring its teeth.

Better prepared, Rook and Bishop fired one shot apiece, again removing the majority of the creature's face and skull. It fell at the feet of the first.

A scraping sound slid from the tunnel. Then it stopped. Hoots, different than before, boomed from the tunnel, but these were less aggressive.

"They're running away," Rook said. He stepped over the two dead bodies and aimed up into the dark tunnel. He fired his remaining four rounds. Sparks flew as the bullets bounced off the walls, moving up the tunnel. Then Rook heard the sound he was hoping for. A grunt of pain followed by sliding. Wet sliding.

The third creature fell from the tunnel moments later, its back and left leg shredded by Rook's bullets.

Rook pushed it over with his boot, looking into its dead eyes.

A distant roar stopped Rook in his tracks. They'd killed three and sent the rest packing. But these things were smart. They'd be back. Probably with reinforcements. He slapped a new cartridge into his Desert Eagle and handed two more to Bishop. "I've got two more for myself, but that's it."

Bishop nodded and pocketed the cartridges.

Somi spoke, but neither man understood the language. They turned around and found her standing, leaning against what appeared to be a stone statue.

"What'd you say?" Rook asked.

Somi looked back, her eyes wide. "I said, 'good God.'" She turned away from them again. "Look."

Throughout the action at the base of the tunnel neither Rook nor Bishop had taken in their surroundings or wondered much about the green glow that allowed them to see. The penlight fell from Rook's mouth as he took in the vast grotto.

Seventy feet across, twenty feet tall, and hundreds of feet long, the chamber was immense, but that was its least impressive aspect. Lining the walls and forming structures throughout, like a city, were layers of bones—glowing green. The crumbled statue supporting Somi's weight represented one of a few nonbone structures in the subterranean cavern. The rest looked like a scene from Dante's *Inferno*, a metropolis built from the dead.

Rook moved slowly toward the nearest structure. He focused his attention on a skull, noting its size, structure, and teeth. "It's not human." He looked back to the others and motioned to the dead creatures. "I think it's one of them. Or something like it, at least. The canines are smaller."

Reaching out, Rook slid his finger across the forehead of the skull. Its cool surface was coated with a thin layer of what felt like damp dust. The line he traced with his finger ceased glowing, like a scar across the skull's forehead. His finger came up glowing like the rest of the bones.

"Fungus," Knight said. "Bioluminescent." He hopped toward the entrance of a nearby structure and peeked inside. Two steps, built from rows of skulls, led to a five-foot door frame. The dark interior was also entirely constructed from rended skeletons and some kind of mortar. Built into the walls were what looked like long benches with femur tops, almost the size of twin beds. Knight eyed the flat space longingly as his body pulsed with pain. He sat on the top step, leaning his head against the skull-lined doorframe.

"Think it's dangerous?" Rook asked.

"Probably not," Knight said. "But I wouldn't eat it."

Rook wiped his finger off on his flak jacket, smearing the green glow all over his chest. He shook his head in frustration. This place was more like an alien world than the underside of a mountain in Vietnam.

"It's a catacomb," Bishop said. He'd crawled on top of the stone base Somi still leaned on and had a view of the entire emerald chamber. "Generations of their dead must be buried here."

"Catacombs . . . ," Rook said. "Like in Rome?"

Bishop nodded.

"But that would make them . . ."

"Civilized," Somi finished. "And intelligent."

She reached out for Rook and held on to his arm for support. As he braced her weight against his body a pang of guilt surged through her. She had betrayed this man, who now shared her weight. Worse, she knew they would probably die to save her. She pushed her conscience away, choosing to focus on the dilemma at hand. "But not now . . ."

"Frankly, I don't give a rat's ass," Rook said. "I say we jump ship now."

"Running blind might not be the best idea," Somi said. "Understanding them might help us—"

"Knowing is half the battle. I get it. That doesn't change the fact that we're being hunted."

"But look," Somi said, pointing out the green skull's canine teeth. "These are small. Almost human in size." Somi pointed at the three dead bodies. "Those things have huge canines. They're not the same. And the symbols. What if these creatures created them? What if the Chinese language originated from these creatures? We might be able to communicate with them."

Rook sighed. He left Somi standing on her own and walked to the three dead bodies. He took the only one that still had a head by the wrist and dragged its body across the floor, laying it at Somi's feet. "Okay, Mr. Wizard, you've got two minutes to tell me something new, other than that these things smell like ground beef in the sun. Then we're finding a way out of here."

Somi nodded and fell to her knees. "Your flashlight," she said, raising a hand to Rook. He picked his flashlight up from where he'd dropped it and handed it to her. She started by looking at the creature's eyes, shining the light in them. They were yellow and highly reflective, which graced the beast with amazing night vision. Otherwise they looked human. Facial features were a cross between human and ape. Short nose. Domed forehead. Thick cheekbones. But the canines—they looked more like a lion's.

Reddish-orange, three-inch-long fur surrounded the face and coated much of the rest of the body. Stiff and coarse, the fur felt more like pine needles than anything else. A clearing in the thick body hair caught Somi's attention and she moved toward it. She pushed away a tuft of hair from the creature's chest, revealing a tan, smooth-skinned breast.

"It's a woman," Somi said.

"Female," Rook corrected. "That's no woman."

Bishop hopped down from his perch. He inspected the other two bodies. "These are as well."

Somi moved on, feeling the creature's arms and inspecting its hands. The arms were full of thick muscle. The hands bore hard and sharp fingernails. Not exactly claws, but no doubt deadly. Then she moved on to the bones making up

the nearby structure that looked like a small hut. The bones
were longer and thinner than she imagined those of the
dead females to be. If they were the same species, they'd
changed a lot since the catacombs were built. Evolution on
that scale took time, even in extreme conditions, which
meant that this place was old . . . ancient . . . perhaps older
than modern humanity. *Making these things what? Our
ancestors?*

Somi's thoughts were interrupted by Rook's voice. "I think
we're going to have to cut your two minutes short. I know why
they're leaving us alone in here." Rook stood at the small entrance to the structure next to the one Knight sat in. Somi and
Bishop joined him.

The inside of the bone-built structure looked like a
simple hut. A fire pit had been carved into the stone floor.
The bone ceiling above lacked any green coloration, as it
was coated in thick black soot. A long pile of leaves and forest debris lay to one side—a bed of sorts. On the other side
lay a pile of fresh bones, rotting meat still clinging. Green
uniforms littered the area. The remains of a VPA dinner.

"They live here," Bishop said.

"Time to go," Rook said.

"I'll be staying," Knight said. "For now."

"Bullshit."

"I'm not trying to be a martyr," Knight said. "But I need to
rest or I'm not going to make it far. You know me. You know
that I can get out of here quicker, faster, and more quietly by
myself than with you. No offense."

Rook wanted to argue, but knew he couldn't. He and Bishop
were big, sometimes clumsy, and often loud. They *would* attract attention. Being apart from them may actually be safer.
And he had no doubt Knight could get out on his own.

"Besides, this one doesn't look lived in." Knight scooted
back into the building.

Rook looked at Somi. "You want to stay, too?"

She shook her head. "I'll stay with the big men carrying

fifty-calibers, thank you." She grinned at Knight. "No offense."

"You want one of the girls?" Rook said, offering Knight
his handgun.

"Keep it," Knight said. "You'll need it."

"See you on the outside, then." Rook sighed, then quickly
grabbed Somi and threw her lithe body over his shoulder.
Holding his Desert Eagle in one hand and Somi with the
other, Rook set out toward the opposite end of the catacombs.
Bishop nodded to Knight and followed.

Knight slid inside the bone structure, crawled to the bed,
and rolled up onto his back. He was asleep on the bed of
femurs before Rook and Bishop were out of earshot.

Rook, Bishop, and Somi passed by a variety of buildings
all built from bones, like some city of the dead. Different
styles of architecture could be seen in the buildings, which
all glowed green with microorganisms, yet were blessedly
free of the larger and much more deadly forms of life that
called the cavern home.

After five minutes, the opposite end of the cavern came
into view. A full-size tunnel awaited them. Rook smiled. No
more crawling like mice in a maze. Then he saw the eyes.
Two pairs. Staring at him from the darkened exit.

Somi and Bishop saw them, too.

"Put me down," Somi said.

Rook didn't argue. His aim would be better. He put her
down and pointed his weapon.

Somi stepped in front of them. "Wait." She held out her
hands, showing her palms. She shouted a quick phrase in a
language Rook recognized but didn't understand.

"What did you say?" Rook asked in a whisper.

"Peace, in Chinese."

The eyes remained unblinking.

Rook inched forward, holding his Desert Eagle in front
of his body. "Flashlight," he said, and held his hand out to
Somi. She handed him the small light. He turned it on and

aimed it at the eyes. An awful-looking, hair-covered face emerged from the darkness. But its gray color revealed it as nothing more than a statue. Perhaps identical to the ruined statue they'd found at the opposite end of the grotto.

Rook turned the light toward the other set of eyes. But before he got to them they disappeared. Rook fired without pause. He knew the eyes hadn't simply disappeared. They'd blinked. The creature leaped into the green-lit chamber, hollering and pounding toward them. For its five-foot size it was a monstrous sight. Its orange hair, dull brown in the green glow, rose up like porcupine barbs. The vertical hair bounced wildly, making its body hard to target and its motion a blur. Its bared teeth glowed light green. Its breasts bounced madly on its chest. Another female.

The creature's sex didn't stop Rook. He pulled the trigger, firing one shot, confident in his aim. But the beast lunged and the bullet passed harmlessly through its tall hair. Rook fired again and missed as the creature came within ten feet.

Three shots rang out. The beast fell and slid to a stop at Rook's feet.

Rook looked at Bishop. "Took you damn long enough."

Bishop shrugged. "Thought you had it."

"Yeah," Rook said, unnerved that he'd missed the creature twice. "So did I."

A swooshing sound filled the chamber all around them. All three recognized the sound. Slides. Lots of them. The creatures were entering the catacombs through slides, just like the one they had used, but they were coming from all directions.

They were surrounded.

THIRTY

The rain came again as storm clouds blocked out the moon, casting the already shaded jungle floor in absolute darkness. The downpour pelted the jungle canopy with more water every ten minutes than Los Angeles received in an average year. Rainwater pooled in the largest leaves at the highest points of the canopy, then spilled down, joining other streams of water, until it fell to the jungle floor as small waterfalls. The hiss and splash of water falling from above blocked any noise Queen made as she backtracked toward the VPLA camp.

But the sharp voices of the Death Volunteers pursuing them cut through the din. As did their flashlights.

Easy targets.

In the confusion of the mortar attack and their haste to chase down their escaped prisoners, the soldiers were forgetting nighttime strategies. Stay quiet. Stay dark. Strike hard. Queen, on the other hand, recited the mantra in her head as she climbed up a tree and mounted a branch.

A cascade of water fell from above, splashing over Queen's head and spraying out around her body. Even if one of the VPLA soldiers thought to point his flashlight up, which they had yet to do, the water would obscure her shape. The cool water stung her blistered skin as rivulets followed the course set by the raised and ruined flesh at the center of her forehead.

She could feel the star-and-skull brand throb in time with her quickening pulse—a reminder of what had been done to her. Forgetting wasn't an option. Never would be. She would see the torture-stain every time she looked in the mirror. She wouldn't fret upon seeing it. She wouldn't cry for her ruined good looks. She would use it. She would become it. Not a death volunteer. Death incarnate. She drank in the pain as the cool water caused the burnt flesh to contract.

It fueled her.

The men moved through the jungle, using their flashlights to follow King and Pawn's escape route. But the wet jungle floor made their footing unsure. Queen counted the flashlights. Four. She felt for the weapons she'd taken from the tent.

The ice pick. The hook. The branding iron.

She dropped the ice pick and hook to the jungle floor. The implement of her torture would be her weapon. The dropped items would serve a different purpose.

Queen waited.

The men approached, almost at a run.

Then a flashlight glinted on metal. The men stopped, bent, and inspected the ice pick.

Queen descended.

She brought the branding iron down on the man standing behind the others that were crouching. He didn't see her coming, and his consciousness barely registered his death. The wet splat of the man's body hitting sodden soil couldn't be heard over the torrent of water falling from above.

She rounded on the other three men like a lion, roaring as she dove into them, swinging the brand like a sword, aiming for their foreheads, leaving a brand of her own, in blood. The men were well trained, but her ferocity made them shout and cringe. For a moment she wondered if they thought she was one of the creatures waging war against their camp. She could hear them in the distance, hooting like savages. But before she had time to ask, all three men were dead, bloody star-and-skull brands beaten into their skulls.

Queen collected their flashlights and firearms, hiding them behind the tree. She would collect them later, but the rest of her vengeance would be carried out using only the brand. Leaving the weapons and dead men behind, Queen set out for the camp.

Staying low, she emerged from the jungle into the dull glow of the burning camp. Her blond hair hung around her shoulders, matted with water and blood. The star-and-skull wound on her forehead shone red in contrast to her wet, white skin. She took in the chaos of the camp, looking for her target.

The VPLA fired into the forest at the other end of the camp. Mortars occasionally exploded in and around the camp, claiming more trees than soldiers, but the shouting and rapid gunfire revealed the enemy's approach. Her chance to strike, perhaps her only chance, was now.

She broke from the jungle and ran past one of the burning tents. As she rounded the tent into the camp proper, she wound up and clubbed a VPLA soldier in the back of the head. He landed facedown in the mud, unmoving. Queen shook a hair-covered chunk of flesh out of the brand and ran across the camp, clubbing soldiers from behind as she moved. They were so distracted by the booming battle being waged between their compatriots and some unseen, but very loud force, they never thought to look behind them. It wasn't a noble attack, but when the odds are against you, fight dirty. Better to lose face than your head. And she felt no guilt about slaughtering the lot of them. Not after what they'd done to her.

Queen stopped in the center of the camp. Five soldiers lay dead in her wake. Then she saw him. *Trung.* He stood near the front lines. A brave soldier. Shouting orders, working things out. No doubt defeating his enemy.

Flamethrowers lit up the forest beyond, followed by in-human shrieks, confirming the turn of events.

Not if I can help it, Queen thought.

She charged, heading straight for Trung. He stood between two men, who repeated his orders to the others fighting in the jungle. The two soldiers would go first, then the major general. She would do him special.

A mortar exploded behind Queen. The shock wave nearly knocked her over, but she remained upright and moving. But Trung had glanced in her direction and saw her coming. He shouted to the men standing next to him. Queen hurled the branding iron, striking one man in the face. As the other brought his weapon up, Queen dove, rolled, and came up with a fistful of mud. She launched the mud into the man's face and dove left as he fired.

Pockets of mud exploded as the bullets ripped through the earth at Queen's feet. Leaping up, she shot the heel of her hand into the nose of the muddied soldier, shattering his face and sending bone fragments into his brain, killing him. Blood sprayed from the man's ruined face and coated Queen's. She looked for Trung, but the camp was now empty. Gunfire faded in the distance.

The VPLA had fled.

The soldier knocked down by the branding iron grasped her ankle. Queen shouted and kicked him in the throat. The man flopped over like a dying fish, gurgling for breath. She bent down and picked up the branding iron. It wouldn't go to waste. She clubbed the man's head once, putting him out of his misery. An act of mercy. More than they would have done for her.

Through the hiss of rain, Queen heard shouts and wet footfalls. She turned back toward the camp and found twenty terrified regular VPA soldiers staring at her. Queen stepped into the clearing, hair in clumps, face coated in blood, branding iron in hand, and seven dead VPLA Death Volunteers lying behind her on the ground bearing bloody brands matching the one on her forehead.

The men lowered their weapons and stepped back, their faces showing a terror that only comes upon seeing the supernatural. To them, Queen appeared as a vengeful spirit. The dead returned in search of reprisal.

They neither ran nor met her hate-filled glare. They simply stepped aside and allowed her to enter the jungle on the other side of the camp. Right now, her anger was directed toward the Death Volunteers. They seemed to understand that much, and wanted to keep it that way.

As Queen walked through the camp, past the VPA soldiers and the dead men, she noticed that one of the men she had killed clung to a backpack. Sara's backpack. She bent and took it, and an AK-47, from the man's hand as she walked past. She glanced inside the pack briefly and saw everything, including the blood sample, still secure inside. Quickening her pace, she disappeared into the jungle like the apparition the soldiers believed her to be.

Thirty feet into the jungle, the VPLA camp behind her blossomed bright orange and let out a demon's roar. Fire had spread despite the heavy rain and reached an ammo depot or fuel tank. Whatever it was, the resulting explosion was massive. A wall of heat washed through the jungle, creating a loud hiss as the falling rain and saturated leaves, trees, and forest floor flashed into steam. Queen fell as the shock wave rushed over her body. Out of range of the heat, she quickly recovered and looked back at the camp. Through a copse of burning trees she saw a crater where the camp had been.

In the wake of the explosion, the jungle fell silent. Both forces were either dead or in hiding.

In the silence, the breaking branch behind her was like a warning klaxon.

She spun around wielding the AK-47. But before she could pull the trigger a strong hand caught the barrel and pointed the weapon up. Queen's shot ripped through the canopy above and disappeared into the sky, falling back to earth miles away.

It was the only round she got a chance to fire.

THIRTY-ONE

It fell from above, lashing out with its strong, thick-fingernailed hands, and ripped open a gash in Somi's right leg. As she shouted in pain and fell, Rook spun and fired three shots, opening a jagged six-inch hole in the creature's chest.

"What the hell are these things?" Rook shouted as he twisted around, searching for more targets. But the creatures were staying low, out of sight. Rook realized they were smart—smarter than anyone would believe after one look at their ugly mugs. The first to attack from the doorway had been a diversion while the other snuck up from the side. A simple tactic, but it had almost succeeded. Now the others were up to something.

For a moment Bishop wondered if the creatures had found Knight. As hoots and growls echoed around the grotto, bouncing off the walls, emerging from the bone huts, or above them, he realized all of their attention was on him, Rook, and Somi. As long as they were trying to escape, Knight would be safe. But how long they could hold out . . . well, he didn't want to think about that. He would survive, of that there was little doubt. Short of having his head taken off, his body would regenerate back to full health. But not his mind. It would descend into a madness that might frighten even these creatures. Since death was preferable, he hoped a confrontation could be avoided altogether.

Bishop helped Somi to her feet, listening to the intricate variations of the animal voices sounding out around them. "They're talking."

The language was unlike anything any of them had heard before.

"Great," Rook said, heading for the open doorway, keeping watch in all directions. He could see them now, faintly in the green glow of the chamber, moving in and out between bone huts: climbing roofs, scaling walls, advancing like a horde of mutant ninjas. But he held his fire. Missing was not an option. The killing would be up close and personal. *Damn, I wish Queen were here,* he thought.

Rook reached the darkened doorway and cast his penlight inside, moving it side to side. The hallway stretched on beyond the reach of his light but two positive things stuck out. First, the grade of the hallway moved up. Up was good. Second, he didn't see any yellow eyes or orange fur.

A roar turned Rook around. The creatures emerged into the open one by one; their bodies, short but massive, made them look like hellish imps in the green glow.

Bishop leaned Somi against the edge of the doorway and joined Rook. Twenty of the creatures stood around them in a semicircle, rocking on their heels, waiting. "Not good."

Rook looked back at Somi. "Go ahead. Get the hell out of here. We'll catch up."

"No," Somi said, standing. With her energy flowing from her body along with her blood from the deep leg wound, she wasn't going anywhere . . . not fast enough, anyway. She hobbled up next to Rook and looked at the waiting gang. "Give me your gun and go."

Rook scoffed. "First Knight and now you? *He* will get out of here in one piece. You'll be torn to shreds. Now get—"

Somi began pulling down her pants on one side.

"What the hell, Somi, you—"

Rook froze when he saw a brand marking her thigh, a star with a skull at its center.

"I led them to you," Somi said. "I let them take Sara."

Somi looked down at the knife wound. "This was my reward. They bought me with my father's love, then my silence with a knife."

Rook's face turned bright red. Few things stung a soldier more than betrayal.

"Rook," Bishop said, his voice tinged with concern. "They're coming."

The half circle closed in slowly. The creatures meant to overwhelm them, give them too many targets . . . but they were still wary of the guns. They had to know some of them would die. What were they after that they would risk their lives to get? It couldn't be food. They had plenty hanging in their meat locker.

Then it occurred to Rook. The one that had attacked from above and torn open Somi's leg could have easily taken off his head instead. But it chose to attack her first. Looking at their bodies closely, Rook saw that they were *all* females.

Oh, hell, Rook thought. They were after him and Bishop. And they wanted them *alive.*

He stepped back, away from Somi. "Bish, time to fall back." Bishop stepped back and the creatures started growling loudly. Some began to hoot.

Somi stood limply in front of them, facing off against twenty of the creatures. She looked back at Rook, guilt washing over her. He'd kept his gun, and for good reason. Why would he trust her after what she'd revealed? She was his enemy. As Rook's and Bishop's bodies slid into the darkness, Somi said, "You're a good soldier, Rook."

Rook didn't reply, but a moment later a single Desert Eagle slid out of the dark and bumped against her foot. She reached down to pick it up as the creatures flew into a flurry of activity. Some beat their chests, angered by the men's disappearance. Others paced anxiously. And then, as Somi stood again, Desert Eagle in hand, one of them charged. Somi fired two shots. It fell at her feet. Two more charged, their screams issuing forth as much spittle as volume. Somi dropped the first and jumped to the side as the second at-

tacked. It bit into her leg before Somi shot a point-blank
.50-caliber bullet into the side of its head. The creature's
skull exploded, but its teeth remained buried in her leg.

Somi didn't wait for any more attacks. The creatures were
close enough. She opened fire, squeezing the trigger four
more times, killing two more of the creatures, leaving fifteen
very pissed, very unsure beasts left standing. Then came the
click.

Out of ammo.

The creatures were smart enough to realize this, too. All
at once they raised their hackles, roared, and pounded toward her. Somi waited for them, standing still, clutching the
handle of the knife in her belt—the source of her pain. *Just
a few more seconds,* Somi thought, *and then the pain will be
gone.*

As the first creature came close, its jaws open wide, heading for her head, she gripped the knife handle tight and
yanked the blade from her belt. She ducked down as the
beast dove for her. She twisted the knife up and thrust.

The blade hit sternum, slicing skin. Nothing more. But as
the creature's forward momentum carried it over Somi and the
still-thrust knife, the blade slipped up as the sternum ended.
A sound like leather being cut was followed by a wet splat.

Somi stood, ignoring the fact that she was covered in the
creature's disemboweled internal organs. There was no time
to feel disgust. The others were upon her.

She swept her arm in an arc, holding the knife out straight.
The blade ripped through throat and windpipe, killing another. In the same motion she swung the knife at a third
attacker, intending to shove it through the eye socket and into
the brain. But the creature flinched back and twisted, taking
the blade in the meat of its thick shoulder.

The creature spun away. Somi tried to retrieve the knife
from its shoulder but the bulging muscles and thick fur held
on tight. The knife was gone.

A screech filled the chamber, bouncing off the walls as
though the thousands of glowing green skulls were screaming

all at once. Then a shadow fell. Somi looked up and saw a pair of red-rimmed yellow eyes descending toward her.

Red.

There would be no defense against this one. Even if Somi had the knife, she knew a killer when she saw one.

Red planted her feet on Somi's chest and pounded her to the stone floor of the chamber. A resonant crunch signified the breaking of several ribs.

With the wind knocked out of her, Somi couldn't even scream as Red took hold of her arms and yanked. With a sickening wet tear, both arms came away from Somi's body as though she were a plastic doll in the hands of a weight lifter.

Red leaned down to Somi's face as blood drained onto the stone floor.

Somi's vision faded, but she could still smell and taste the creature's rancid breath. As shock set in she wondered if the creatures would eat her alive. Would they tear off her legs too? Gorge on her guts? The creature leaned in closer, moving its lips, searching for something.

Somi felt her head turn to the side as darkness totally replaced her vision. Hot breath touched her ears. Just before Somi's heart beat her last, a deep and primal voice spoke. "Big men, ours."

THIRTY-TWO

As dawn crested over the jungle, streaks of orange light snuck through the foliage and shot to the ground like laser beams. One of the beams struck King's closed eye. He twitched. Both eyes opened and darted back and forth. They were alone. The three of them. Huddled together between two large tree roots, covered with large palm leaves, both for camouflage and for fending off the rain, which had stopped only an hour before.

After backtracking through the dark to Queen and narrowly avoiding being shot by her, the three had taken the weapons, backpack, and flashlights and fled from the VPLA camp without a word spoken about what they'd endured. They walked through the dark and rain for three hours, heading ever up, deeper into the Annamite range, where they finally decided to stop and rest. All three fell asleep within minutes, even Sara, whose mixed-up senses usually made sleep under the best conditions a challenge.

King looked to his right and found Queen facing the other way, her sleeping body curled up away from him like an angry lover. From this perspective she was the same Queen he'd grown to love like his now-dead sister . . . but he knew she'd changed. Become a darker version of her former self. He had yet to see the brand on her forehead, but he knew it was there. And he would have to be careful of how he reacted to it. Had this happened to his actual sister, King might have felt a deep sadness. It was an appropriate response to such a horrible act. But this was Queen. Compassion wouldn't go over well and might earn him a swift kick in the groin. He made a mental note to not even glance at it when she finally let him see. Better to ignore its existence. Treat her the same.

Weight shifted against his body to the left. Glancing over, he saw Sara's sweet face resting against his shoulder. She had long dark lashes he hadn't noticed before, but they were offset by the dirt on her cheeks and her normally spiky hair lying matted against her head. She'd gone from sophisticated scientist to dirty tomboy. *Still beautiful, though,* he thought. He wondered what it would be like waking up next to that face under more . . . comfortable circumstances.

For a moment he wondered what *he* looked like. Though he'd been tortured, like Queen, the remaining pain from his ordeal resided in his muscles. No one would see it. But his shaggy hair felt heavier than normal. *Probably filled with mud,* he thought. His clothing clung wetly to his body. He rubbed his cheeks. The stubble on his face was longer than usual, almost a thin beard, and his goatee itched to be trimmed.

King almost laughed when he realized that for the first time in his career as a Delta operator, he was concerned about his physical appearance while in the middle of a mission. But then he saw a backpack lying next to Sara and remembered that she was more than a pretty face. She was Pawn. And the cure to Brugada—possibly the fate of the world—depended on her success.

He leaned over and gently tapped his hand against her cheek, ignoring how soft she felt, and refocused on his job. "Pawn, wake up."

Sara groaned. He took her shoulder and squeezed. "Ouch. I'm awake, I'm awake."

Sara sat up, rubbing her eyes, and issuing a grunt that sounded like "yug."

"You can complain later," King said. "You need to analyze the blood sample in the pack."

Sara groaned as her body ached. She looked at King, his hair messy and clumped with dirt. She grinned. "Got any more espresso?"

"I think the major general drank it all."

King watched Sara smile. Times like this, despite the insanity surrounding them and her mind-boggling intellect, she seemed like a normal person. But she wasn't. Not quite. "So what is it with you?"

"What do you mean?"

"The sniffing. The listening. You sense things before I do."

"Intimidated?"

Truth was, he did find her a little unnerving. He'd made a career from his fast reflexes, keen senses, and sharp mind. She seemed to have him beat on all counts. She just didn't know how to use a gun.

She brushed aside the hair stuck to her forehead. "Sensory Processing Disorder. Or Sensory Integration Dysfunction. Depends on who you're talking to. It's a neurological disorder, which means no one understands it yet."

Her hair fell back onto her forehead. Losing patience, she shook it with her hand and pushed it aside again. "The brain and nervous system are made up of billions of neurons—excitable nerve cells. They communicate with each other through synaptic transmission. Chemical and electrical impulses—electrochemical signaling. Sensory neurons are how the body dialogues with the mind, relaying information on stimuli experienced by our bodies. When a sense, say hearing, detects something, neurons send these signals to the brain following paths that are hard-wired when we're young. Picture a train track. When we're children the branches can be shifted back and forth, but as we age the tracks rust into place. Sometimes they rust in the wrong direction and some of the information running from the ears reaches the part of the mind that processes and translates physical touch to our mind. A lot of the information still gets to the right place—I *can* hear—but I often feel sound too.

"Sounds interesting, but you wouldn't think so if you got a headache every time you smelled perfume, or when it rains. I hear distant noises like they're right next to me. A honking horn is like a punch in the chest. When I see a cute dog, or baby, my gums hurt."

"That's . . . weird."

"It's annoying is what it is."

"Whatever it is, it's kept us alive a few times."

Sara brightened. Was that a compliment? Before she could ask, King changed the subject.

"When she wakes up," he said, motioning to Queen and then at his forehead, "don't mention her—"

King's sentence stopped short as a fist struck him hard on the left shoulder. He grunted in pain. Queen stood up next to him. "Don't treat me like I'm some sissy crybaby, King. And don't ignore it."

Ignoring it turned out to be impossible. The brand, still fresh, stood out bright red against her white skin.

"How's it look?" Queen asked.

King and Sara couldn't help but be curious. They stood and looked closely. King wanted to say something about how it looked painful. How it needed antibiotics. Maybe some aloe. Something to . . . make it better. Turned out Sara knew exactly what to say.

"Looks pretty badass."

Queen reached up and touched it. She winced as her fingers brushed against the singed flesh. "Hurts like a bastard." Then she was done. "What's the game plan?"

King looked at Sara. They both looked at Sara.

"I'll test the blood sample."

"And then?" King asked.

"If it's good . . . If it's good we'll get out of Dodge."

Queen picked up one of the AK-47s stolen from the VPLA soldiers she'd killed. She inspected it as she spoke. "And if it's not?"

"We stay. Until we find a solution." Sara looked at them. "Or we die."

Queen laughed. "Watch out, Pawn. You hang around us too much longer; you might just grow a set of balls. Then King won't want anything to do with you." She chuckled and walked away. "I'll keep watch."

After a quick, uncomfortable shared glance with King, Sara set to work. She opened her backpack and removed her equipment. The vial of blood. Her laptop. And a small battery-powered VFT, or virus field test. Just one of the handy devices the CDC utilized in the field that most hospitals didn't yet know existed.

Sara powered up the laptop. When the screen blinked to life, the Linux penguin appeared, and a digital chime rang out. A surreal quiet descended in the jungle. Birds stopped calling and insects ceased humming. The foreign noise of the laptop cycling to life sounded more unusual in the jungle than the explosions or gunshots routinely ignored by the wildlife. Sara disregarded the sudden silence and continued working. After plugging the analyzer into the USB port, Sara turned it on. Using a small dropper, Sara took a drop of blood from the vial and squirted it into the analyzer's cylindrical sample tube. After resealing the vial of blood, she closed the VFT top and flipped a switch. A gentle hum filled the air as the VFT went to work.

"So what does that do?" King asked. "Look for viruses?"

"It looks for the antibodies created by the human body when it defends itself from a virus. This one has been updated to find the antibodies for our new bird flu, but it will still find anything else this woman might have been exposed to."

"How long will it take?"

"Just a few minutes."

Results began coming in. Sara looked at the scrolling text, which listed every antibody in the woman's system, giving a comprehensive breakdown of the bugs she'd been exposed to before her death. The list was extensive, and refreshing quickly. Sara would have to go through them one by one, looking for the new flu. The results from the test came fast, but analyzing them might take some time. The last remnants of sleep faded as her eyes opened wide. She thought she'd seen the something and fought to scroll up the screen as the list refreshed again and again. But she couldn't find it.

Not before all hell broke loose.

Queen barreled back into camp, her AK-47 missing and her eyes wide. The jungle shook behind her.

Sara stood. What the hell could have disarmed Queen and sent her running?

The answer came from above. All at once, bodies fell from the trees. They moved so fast, Sara couldn't make them out. Blurs of motion, like a net of bodies, fell over King and Queen, driving them to the forest floor. She saw tan skin. Orange hair. And then nothing. Still conscious, Sara realized something had been placed over her head. The attack, for the most part, had been nonviolent. She wasn't hurt. Just subdued.

Her mind spun with fear, but not for her life. She was becoming numb to the sensation of being near death. She felt afraid for the sample. The laptop had been so close to delivering an answer. The mission was almost over. And now she had no idea what would happen to the sample and her equipment. Would it be stolen? Destroyed? Taken with them? What she knew for sure was that time was running out. If they didn't succeed, millions of people could die—or worse, *everyone* could die. And right now, with the sample gone and the three of them once again in bonds, the latter, more terrifying option seemed more likely.

King and Queen suffered the same humiliating fate: captured without a fight or a shot being fired. If word of this debacle ever got out at Bragg there would be no end to the teasing. If they survived.

As King and Queen stopped struggling, accepting their fate and waiting to see what came next, the three were lifted off the ground and carried through the jungle. Their captors' movements were silent and swift. In the silence, Sara's senses took in the faint noise of feet on earth. There was something odd about the way they moved . . . about the way they breathed. She slowly reached out with her hands and felt the one carrying her. She felt skin, soft and damp. Then hair. Thick. Dirty. Like a German shepherd. The hair covered most of her captor's back.

Sara's eyes went wide beneath the hood that had taken her sight. *Oh God,* she thought, *they're monsters!*

THIRTY-THREE

The shots fired by Somi rang in Bishop's ears as he charged up the tunnel with Rook at his heels. Neither man was a fast runner. Both relied on superior firepower, accurate aim, and brute strength in combat. Speedy retreats didn't sit well with either of them. But they'd been caught with their pants down in a subterranean necropolis by a horde of superhuman she-things. Running like hell made perfect sense.

As the green glow of the bioluminescent fungi–laden chamber faded, darkness returned with a vengeance and slowed their progress as they began moving by penlight. The one thing that gave them hope and allowed them to keep charging at near top speed was that the tunnel, which was wide enough and tall enough for them to run upright, side by side, also stretched onward and upward at a blessedly straight and steady grade. The question nagging both of them: Could they outrun the savage she-tribe?

A wet hooting rolled up the tunnel, issued from below.

"I swear I can smell their shit-eating breath all the way up here," Rook said as he ran with one hand against the smooth tunnel wall and the other stretched out straight in front of him. "Back off, you nasty bitches!"

His shout echoed down the tunnel and before it had fully faded was interrupted by a voice somehow deeper than his own, yet feminine. It roared, "Big man, rude!" followed by, "Big man, mine!"

"Holy . . ." Rook took his hand off the wall and willed his feet to tread faster. He could barely make out Bishop in front of him, but could tell he'd picked up the pace, too. They'd both be doubled over in a minute, or knocked out cold from running into a dead end, if they didn't find a way out soon. But letting those things catch them in the tunnel . . . that just couldn't happen.

Thirty seconds later, Rook felt as though he would collapse. His legs were heavy. His head pounded from exertion. Though he still moved like a runner, a speed-walking soccer mom could have passed him without effort. Bishop fared better. He was winded, but his regenerative body kept the strain to a minimum. Both men paused, sucking in breath. While the creatures behind them had stopped hooting, their furious footfalls and heaving breath filled the tunnel behind them.

"How many rounds?" Rook asked.

Bishop ejected the Desert Eagle's magazine and frowned. "One." He handed the gun to Rook. "I can stay."

"What is this, a Martyr Gras parade?"

"I'll survive."

"And be turned into a mindless killing machine. I don't think so."

Bishop nodded. They would fight together.

"Good, now shut up and get ready for a fight." Rook turned to face the mass of beast-women charging like 1960s school-girls after the Beatles.

"Rook," Bishop said. "Your flashlight."

Rook looked at the light in his hand. It was out. Dead.

"I can still see you," Bishop said.

Both men turned. Weak light poured into the tunnel from not far away. It was dim—filtered—but promised daylight and escape. They ran despite the pain in their lungs, hoping that clear sight might improve their odds of survival.

Of course, it seemed more likely they'd simply get the pleasure of seeing each other die.

The grade flattened out and both men sped up. The source of the light, a large exit overgrown with vines and brush, loomed before them. Afraid the overgrowth might take time to hack or climb through, both men surged at the wall, leaping into it like cannonballs.

Vines snapped. Brush exploded. The two men shot from the exit as though birthed from the mountain. Week and disoriented, they rolled down the mountainside, cushioned by leaf litter. Thirty feet below the exit, they slid to a stop.

Bishop stood quickly and pulled Rook to his feet. "Run!"

Rook complied immediately.

The beasts descended the mountainside after them. Rook pictured Knight in this same scenario, running from the creatures. If he hadn't been too small to make the cut he could have been the fastest running back in the NFL. The man was living lightning. And these things had caught *him*. Rook began to holler as he ran, keenly aware that the creatures were at his back. He could hear their breathing. He could see the trees moving around him as they gave chase above. For a moment he felt a small sense of respect for the highly effective hunting party. Then he heard a deep and steady roar over the sound of his own shout. Looking ahead he saw the jungle drop away—a cliff lay ahead. The unmistakable sound of flowing water rose up from the widening gorge.

A river. But they couldn't see it. It could be a one-hundred-foot drop into raging white water. There was no way to tell. It didn't matter. Anything was preferable to being eaten alive or torn apart. Without a word shared between them, Rook and Bishop leaped from the precipice and soared out into the open air.

The river, fifty feet below, looked deep and fairly placid. They would survive the fall. But would the creatures give chase? Rook turned as he fell and saw the beasts line up along the cliff's edge. The biggest of the bunch, the one with red-rimmed eyes, pounded her chest with each syllable. "Big man, mine!"

Rook extended his middle finger toward her just before crashing into the river.

Bishop came to the surface, gasping for air. Rook's limp body surfaced a few feet away, facedown in the water. Bishop swam to him, looped an arm around his chest, and pulled him back. Rook thrashed and then coughed before collecting himself and treading water under his own power.

"Think I hit the bottom," Rook said, rubbing the back of his head.

Bishop nodded. He had felt the river bottom graze past him, but he'd curved his body upon entering the water feet first. His entry into the river had been controlled. Rook landed nearly headfirst and struck like a mortar round.

Bishop motioned to the boulder-covered shoreline opposite the cliff they'd jumped from. It would make for excellent cover while they rested, and if they were lucky would provide a natural barrier between them and the creatures, who seemed afraid of the water. They might be smart enough to speak, Rook thought, but there was no YMCA around to teach them how to swim. That was for damn sure.

They crawled onto the bank and worked their way deeper into the tall boulders. Hidden from view, they felt safe enough to stop, but not just to catch their breath. That was the least of their concerns. Rook summed up their situation. "Okay, we've got a pack of crazed beast-women after us. Somi is a turncoat, and K.I.A. Knight is M.I.A. The VPLA took Pawn. We have no way to contact King and Queen. And to top this all off, I dropped my magnum in the river."

Bishop took his shirt off, revealing his sculpted body, and laid it on a rock to dry.

"Did I miss anything?" Rook asked.

A woman's voice hollered in response. Both men tensed. It didn't sound like one of the creatures chasing them . . . but it didn't sound quite right, either.

She shouted again.

Crouching, they crept through the rocks toward the sound of the eerie voice.

The next vocal blast made them both jump.

The voice was feminine for sure, but carried an inhuman volume to it—enough to make it clearly audible, even over the roar of the river, which picked up speed as they moved along its shore.

The woman's high-pitched voice came again, and then became a deep pulsing sound. Was she being tortured? Or giving birth? Either way, she sounded in need of help. Rook prepared to bolt clear of the rocks and rescue the damsel in distress, but Bishop's strong hand on his shoulder stopped his valiant charge.

Bishop pointed at his eyes with his index and middle fingers, and then pointed to a space in the rocks where a long boulder had long ago come to rest atop two others, forming a small window. As the woman's shrieks ebbed and flowed over the rocks, they became even louder and more frantic. Rook fought the urge to safeguard those in need and peeked through the small portal.

"What the . . ." Rook watched, mesmerized by the surreal sight. Slowly, he reached into his pant leg pocket and found his small binoculars. He raised them to his eyes, ignoring the spots of water in his vision, and took a close-up look at one of the oddest sights he'd seen in his life. He looked away from the binoculars, eyes wide, and handed them to Bishop. "Bishop, what the hell?"

THIRTY-FOUR

Washington, D.C.

Jeff Ayers yanked the wheel left, passing by yet another vehicle whose operator was either elderly, listening to loud music, or a moron. That the ambulance's flashing red lights hadn't caught the driver's attention was one thing, but the blaring siren and honking horn he had at his disposal usually sent most drivers to the side of the road.

Not so with this joker.

The ambulance cut to the left of the black SUV. Ayers gunned the vehicle and cut back into the right-hand lane. The suddenness of his appearance must have shocked the SUV's driver. The brakes locked and the vehicle spun twice. It stopped when its back end struck and decimated a small sports car.

Glancing in his side mirror, Ayers saw the driver get out of the SUV, fist shaking in the early evening air. The man would live. The woman lying on the sidewalk two blocks up with no pulse, she was another story.

The sun had yet to fully descend behind the Capitol building and he'd already been called out to three deaths. The first two were found by strangers. Long since dead. Reviving them had not been an option, and the cause of death had been a mystery. Aside from the wounds caused by falling to the ground, neither showed any signs of injury. And both had been young.

The current call had come in just minutes ago. A woman, gray haired and varicose veined, had fallen down in front of a drug store. Three people called 911. Ayers had just been leaving the morgue, where he'd dropped off the body of a previous victim, and, determined to not lose another race with Death, hit the sirens and the gas.

A blur of small shops and parked cars filled the windows. His eyes scanned everything for movement . . . and for a crowd. There was always a crowd.

The shops cleared and a parking lot opened up on the right. He saw the CVS sign, and a small group of people gathered below, looking down. It was a smaller group than usual. Then he remembered the victim was old. The aged always drew smaller numbers of onlookers.

"Get ready," Ayers called out to his partner, David Montgomery, who sat in the back of the ambulance. They had been a team for five years and had saved, and lost, a lot of lives during that time. He turned into the parking lot, applied the brakes gently, and came to a stop ten feet from the group.

No sooner had the ambulance been put in park than the back doors and driver's door burst open. Ayers, being the closest to the action, arrived first. "Move aside," he shouted.

Several stunned and wide-eyed people stepped slowly aside, as though in a dream. He recognized the look. They had seen a person die. Perhaps they'd stood in line with her, waiting as she slowly counted out exact change. Or helped her find the right shade of lipstick. Or filled her prescription. And now she was dead and they saw their own mortality, and weakness, reflected in the final event of this woman's life. It was a feeling that Ayers had long ago abandoned, because unlike these people, he could bring the dead back.

When there was time.

He fell to his knees and checked the old woman for a pulse. She had none.

"Paddles!" he yelled to Montgomery, who was rolling a stretcher toward him.

Abandoning the stretcher, Montgomery dove inside the ambulance. He reappeared with a portable defibrillator.

Ayers tore open the woman's light blue blouse, sending buttons flying into the circle of onlookers. With unflinching fingers he unhooked her front-clipped bra and exposed her flaccid chest. He reached up without looking and closed his hands around the two handles he knew would be waiting.

"Charging," Montgomery said.

Ayers held the paddles above the woman's chest, listening to the group around him.

"Can they really bring her back?"

"No way."

"It's been too long."

"What happened to her, anyway?"

"Charged!" Montgomery's voice, louder than the rest, acted like a trigger for Ayers.

"Clear!" he shouted, then placed the paddles against the woman's skin, one to the left and above her heart, the other to the right and below. The shock came fast and hit hard. The old woman's body arched and lifted off the ground. Then she was back down and still.

With no heart monitor attached to the woman yet, Ayers had to hand the paddles back to Montgomery and check the woman's pulse.

The faint rise and fall of the woman's heart tickled his fingertips.

Someone in the crowd saw his smile and shouted, "He did it!"

A light cheer and scattered clapping sounded around him and woke the woman.

She opened her eyes. "What happened?"

Ayers closed her blouse for her. "We're not sure, ma'am, but we're going to take you to the hospital now and find out."

THIRTY-FIVE

Annamite Mountains—Vietnam

Bishop handed the binoculars back to Rook, the slightest of frowns showing on his normally placid face. Rook returned the binoculars to his eyes, needing to see the sight again, not to confirm its reality, but out of curiosity. The scene on the other side was what Norman Rockwell might have painted while on acid.

Rook adjusted the binoculars, bringing the scene into crystal clear, close-up focus. He said, "Ugh" as he took in the hairy, nearly naked man standing atop a rock with a home-made fishing rod. All that covered his blazing-white ass cheeks was a swatch of cloth wrapped around his waist and between his legs, like a sumo wrestler's mawashi loincloth.

The man's clearly Caucasian face caught Rook's attention. *What the hell is a white guy doing in the Vietnamese jungle?* Thick and crudely cut brown hair hung in oily clumps just above his shoulders. A pair of glasses slowly slipped down his nose. He adjusted them, pointed to the river, and called out, "There! Do you see it?"

American.

His smiling face and occasional chuckle stood in stark contrast to the horrendous shouts of his still-unseen companion— the source of the tortured screams. But she wasn't in pain. Far

from it. The horrid sound was laughter. Though he had yet to
see the woman as she stood on the other side of the rock the
man stood on, it was clear these two were enjoying a nice day
of fishing by the river . . . in Vietnam.

Moving slowly—gracefully—the man's companion walked
forward and into the river.

Rook flinched back so quickly he almost fell over.

Bishop steadied him. "What is it?"

"He's . . . he's fishing with Cha-Ka!" Rook's voice was a
loud whisper, still concealed by the roaring river and gleeful
cheers of the woman.

"Cha-Ka?" Bishop asked.

"Sid and Marty Krofft," Rook said. "*Land of the Lost*?
Rick, Will, and Holly Marshall? Cha-Ka was a little caveman."

Bishop shrugged.

"What, you didn't watch TV on Saturday mornings?" Rook
shook his head and handed Bishop the binoculars. "Look for
yourself."

Bishop did.

The woman squatted in the shallows. Her face, while
smooth and pretty, was surrounded by a mane of brown hair
that flowed from her head, cheeks, and chin like an ape's.
Her muscular chest was concealed by loose-fitting rags tied
like a bikini. The flesh underneath appeared hairless. As
was her midriff, backside, and thighs. But the rest of her . . .
Rook was right; she looked like a tall cavewoman. Not quite
as primal as the beasts that had mauled Knight and pursued
them to the river, but not quite human, either. Her muscular
build confirmed it. If not for the clearly feminine curves of
her body, Bishop might have mistaken her for a lower primate, but she was clearly something more.

Bishop put the binoculars down and looked Rook in the
eyes. "I think we should avoid them. She doesn't look like
the others . . ."

"But she's related," Rook said. "That's what I was thinking, too. Someone's been tinkering with Mother Nature."

Bishop nodded and motioned toward the fishing duo.

Rook nodded.

That guy.

The woman's screams reached a rapid crescendo. Rook peeked through the space in the rocks. A large fish was hooked on the line. With no reel, the man had to back up to pull the fish in. As the fish approached the shore, the girl splashed deeper into the water and pulled the line in. She dragged a large catfish out of the water, its shiny black body flapping madly. The girl then lifted the great fish up, clutched its tail, and brought it down like a club. With a wet splat, the fish struck stone. The wiggling stopped.

For a moment Rook wondered if they'd stumbled upon some kind of lost world; a place untouched by modern man for so long that ancient creatures still stalked and primitive tribes fought for survival. But there were no dinosaurs here and this cavewoman couldn't hold a candle to Edgar Rice Burroughs's barbarian queen. Burroughs's heroes never fell in love with something so . . . primal. They would have shot it on the spot.

But the man. The enigma. His presence complicated things. Were there others like him? Would they have been safer on the other side of the river with the hulking hairy midgets? He couldn't be sure. All he really wanted was to get the hell out of Vietnam.

Screw the rest of the world, Rook thought, *I already died from Brugada once. I can do it again. Let the rest of the world here figure it out on their own and let Cha-Ka and Rick Marshall live happily ever after.*

As he thought it, he knew it was a passing fancy, the whim of a normal person. But that wasn't him. At his core he was Delta, and his mission was far from complete. And it wouldn't be until they got away from these two and figured out what to do next.

But a shifting breeze ruined any chance of going undetected.

Cha-Ka lifted her head and sniffed, her very slender,

very human nose crinkling with each breath. Then she casually leaned over and spoke into the man's ear.

Neither Rook nor Bishop could hear the woman's words,
but they knew they'd been detected. Before either could slip
away, the man's voice boomed over the river's roar. "Come
on out. We know you're there."

Both men froze. Neither wanted anything to do with the
man and his hairy counterpart. But they were caught like a
pair of Peeping Toms. The man didn't sound angry or nervous, just in control. Master of his domain.

Bishop spoke in a whisper. "I'll go out. You stay down. They
may not know there are two of us."

"I'll go," Rook said.

Bishop shook his head. "You'll do something rash and
get yourself killed."

"And you won't?"

"You know me," Bishop said. "I'll hardly say a word."

Bishop stood up, his six-foot-tall body clearing the thick
stones. He leaped up and over the boulders, landing like the
Incredible Hulk on the other side.

The man and strange woman took a step back. They were
clearly expecting a local, perhaps a five-foot, half-starved
man or woman. A gigantic Middle Eastern who looked like
a professional wrestler was a rare sight in the Annamite
Mountains.

Then the man's confidence returned. "My, my, aren't you
a strapping young man."

Bishop stood still, trying to glean what he could from
the stranger's face. His confidence seemed genuine. He
wasn't afraid of Bishop at all. Bishop remembered the raw,
physical strength of the creatures they'd encountered in the
tunnels and the way the woman here had smashed the catfish. If the woman standing before him now had the same
strength as her more feral neighbors, the man had good
reason to be confident. Judging by his use of "young man"
and the crow's-feet around his eyes, Bishop placed him

around forty-five years old, but his muscle tone looked like an athlete's. Bishop realized the man lived in this jungle, probably had for years.

"You speak English," Bishop said.

The man's eyebrows rose in surprise. "As do you."

"I do, too," said the woman, though her voice sounded more like a young woman's. Closer now, Bishop could see that while her body was like that of an adult, her face appeared younger, no more than twelve years old. "Father, tell him I do, too."

Bishop's muscles tensed.

Father.

"He can hear you just fine, my dear," the man said. He stepped forward. "My name is Anthony Weston. Dr. Anthony Weston. You'll have to forgive her. She's just a child."

It was Bishop's turn to be surprised. "This is your . . . *child?*"

"Yes." Weston appeared confused for a moment. Then his face brightened. "This must be terribly confusing for you."

Weston turned his back to Bishop, walked past the girl, and sat on a rock behind her. She stood motionless between them. "She is not my daughter. She is my son's, son's, son's daughter. My great-great-granddaughter. They all call me father, as I am the originator of their race. I am their Adam. Isn't that right, Lucy?"

The girl smiled.

Bishop tensed. The man's story was more twisted than he could have guessed. But it didn't match up. This girl had to be at least a teenager. Then two generations before her . . . That would make Weston far older than he appeared.

"How much do you weigh?" Weston asked.

"How could she be your great-great-granddaughter?" Bishop asked, ignoring Weston's question. "You're not that old."

"Very observant of you. You're U.S. military, right? But no ordinary soldier . . . Too smart . . . and too big for that."

The man thought for a moment and then voiced his conclusion. "You're after the same thing those insidious Vietnamese soldiers are searching for, is that it?"

Weston saw Bishop's serious gaze hadn't faltered. "Right, right. My age. I must be in my forties now. I stopped keeping track years ago. But this one here . . ." Weston tussled the girl's hair, messing it up like a bona fide grandfather might do. "Lucy here is three years old."

Blood drained from Bishop's face.

Three . . . years . . . old.

Weston scoffed at Bishop's grimace. "Come now, you're smart enough to see she's not entirely human. They walk within two weeks of birth. Can climb trees at six months. Hunt at one year. They're fully mature by two years. Most give birth *before* they are three. Lucy is my descendent, so she is part Homo sapien, but she is also something else, too."

Bishop looked across the river. "One of them?"

Weston's face showed true surprise. "You've seen them?"

Bishop nodded.

"And have they seen you?"

Bishop nodded again.

Weston pursed his lips and nodded his head, mulling something over.

Bishop interrupted his interlude. "What are they?"

Weston looked up as though startled. "Huh? Oh. The wenches. That's what I like to call them. Though I suppose they are responsible for everything good in my life now." Weston leaned back and crossed his arms. "I came here in 1995. I'm a cryptozoologist and came to the Annamites in search of new species. I expected to find wild pigs or antelope, but I found *them,* the Nguoi Rung. The forest people. Even I had written them off as the creations of superstitious villagers before I stumbled upon them here in the mountains. After discovering their group, I watched them for a week, observing their hunts, tool usage, and customs. I knew from the beginning that they were something more than apes. They were unique in the world. Intelligent, but not human. Then they found me out. Chased me down."

Weston shifted slightly at the memory. "I thought they were going to kill me, and they nearly did. But that was not their intent. One after another, those in heat . . . had their way with me, starting with Red, the dominant female. Then they left. Two days later they returned for me. I had a fever and a foot in the grave. It seemed odd to me at the time, but they brought me back to their cave and restored my health. When the fever abated, two more had a go. But as I struggled less, their bites became more gentle, and drew less blood." Weston motioned to several scars on his shoulders.

"Over time I discerned that all of their males had died inexplicably. They were simply carrying out their genetic urge to mate and propagate the species. Being the right size and appearing as close to one of their males as any creature they had ever seen, they took me as one of their own. I became their alpha male, studying them as I lived among them. When my first daughter was born I realized we shared a common heritage. How else could they bear my children?"

Weston stood and stretched. The story was coming to an end. "I began exploring the cave systems and came upon the most incredible find."

"The bone city," Bishop said.

Weston again looked surprised. "You're quite lucky to have made it out of the necropolis. They've taken residency there since their banishment."

"Banishment?" Bishop asked.

"They're old and unintelligent. What they did to me was unthinkable. Unforgivable. I can't stand the sight of them. And they were holding the kids back." Weston picked up a stone and skipped it on the river. "But where were we? Ah, yes. The necropolis is the tip of the iceberg. What I discovered was nothing short of a miracle. The Annamite Mountain range has been described as a modern-day Noah's Ark. In a way, that couldn't be truer. You see, the Nguoi Rung are the ancestors of a civilization that developed here hundreds of thousands of years ago. Homo sapiens evolved and lived among the Nguoi for thousands of years, interbreeding and peacefully coexisting. But humanity became violent and warlike. Pushed the Nguoi east. They fled as far as they could and settled here. For thousands of years their civilization blossomed. When humanity reached the East, into Asia, the Ngoui retreated to the mountains, lived in seclusion, and slowly died out for lack of resources as humanity encroached. What remains of them, some twenty-five females, are what natural selection has left us with after so many generations of hiding and hunting. Savages with a spark of intelligence. A spark that is much brighter in their offspring. But they are all that are left. They are the last . . ." Weston looked into Bishop's eyes. ". . . of the Neanderthals."

Neanderthals? Bishop's stunned expression was impossible to mask.

Weston smiled with delight that his revelation had made an impression. "But with my help the species is making a comeback and is reclaiming the land that had been theirs long before the first human learned to speak. Which, I'm afraid, is bad news for you . . . especially given your size."

Just as Bishop's mind began to pull back the curtain of the veiled threat, Weston's voice issued a quiet order to Lucy. She sprang up from the rock in an instant, bouncing off a second rock, and dove toward Bishop. She moved like lightning and Bishop's broad body made an easy target. He managed to bring his fist around, catching the girl in the gut, but not before she swept her outstretched, sharp-clawed fingers deep into his throat, cutting through arteries, windpipe, Adam's apple, and spine.

As the girl fell to the rocky shoreline, gasping for breath, chunks of Bishop's destroyed throat splashed into the river. Bishop fell to his knees. His head tilted back and then fell to the side, connected only by a thin wisp of flesh and spine. As his body fell back, his hand stretched out an open palm, then fell limp. With a splash, Bishop's big body landed in the shallows of the river.

Weston stood above the body and petted the girl's head.

Lucy looked up at Weston. "Why, Father?" she asked, more curious than remorseful.

"He was too big."

"Red?"

Weston nodded. "We can't let her have children again." He pushed Bishop's body out into the river, which swept him away. Blood plumed into the water from Bishop's open neck. Weston looked down at Lucy. "The fish will thank us."

With that the two turned and left, Lucy carrying the dead fish, Weston the fishing pole. They didn't give Bishop's body a second glance.

Behind the rock wall that hid him from view, Rook's body shook with rage. He'd heard everything . . . seen everything. Only Bishop's final act—his outstretched palm, which could have just as easily been an involuntary death twitch—had kept him firmly rooted in his hiding spot.

He clenched his fists as the image of Bishop's throat being ripped apart replayed in his mind. No one could recover from that. Not even Bishop. Rook crept back into the shadows of the boulders that lined the river.

He waited in silence, controlling his breathing, his anger, like he'd seen Bishop do so often.

When he was sure no one was watching, he began scaling the cliff wall, all the while making a mental checklist of everyone he needed to introduce to a bullet, or any other sharp object he could find. Hell, blunt objects would work just as well. Whether or not Rook would get his revenge was uncertain. The mission still took precedence and he wouldn't let Bishop's death be in vain. Reconnecting with the team and getting Pawn and the blood sample out of the jungle and back to the States were still the priority. If Weston, or Cha-Ka, or any of the "old wenches" happened to get in the way—or remotely close to the way—Rook wouldn't back down.

THIRTY-SIX

Queen's eyes opened and saw nothing but black. She'd been knocked unconscious during the brutally efficient attack. She could see specks of light filtering through holes in the hood over her head. The smell of rotting fish filled her nose with each breath. She wasn't sure if it was from the hood or her captor's body—a body she was now inspecting without moving a muscle.

The shoulder beneath her was broad. The gait felt long and the steps were heavy, punishing her stomach with every jolt. The back was interesting—covered in thick hair.

A man, Queen thought.

But something was off. First, there was too much hair. Even the hairiest Italian didn't sport a back patch that thick. Second was the attack itself. She'd done battle with the best the world had to offer and always came out on top. These guys had not only subdued her, but King as well. Killing them with a firearm would have been impressive enough, but capturing them without firing a single shot—she found it hard to believe possible. Yet here she was, being carted around on the shoulder of a fish-smelling monster of a man. She had infinite respect for the way they'd done it, though. The sheer audacity of attacking armed soldiers with nothing but bare hands had been her solo claim to fame for years. But these guys . . . they made her look bad.

Queen's competitive nature kicked in. If these guys thought they could beat her at her own game, let them try again. She wouldn't hide behind a gun next time. That had been her mistake. That's what allowed them to take her so quickly she never got a chance to see them.

Keeping her body loose like a rag doll, Queen listened. She could hear the footfalls of several others up ahead, but none behind. They were at the back of the pack. Somehow calling them a pack seemed more appropriate. While she recognized the body holding her as part human, its animal quality was hard to ignore. Her mind returned to the village of Anh Dung, remembering the creatures they encountered there. Then the attack on the VPLA camp, the hoots and cries echoing through the forest. Definitely not human. A rare twang of nervousness filled Queen as she considered the idea that they were not dealing with human beings . . . *again*.

Then one of them spoke and erased her fears. "Hurry. We are far behind."

The voice was feminine . . . and to the left.

"Father will be pleased with our find," said the man holding her, his voice deep and strong. "They know our speak."

Queen came to three very quick conclusions.

First, this was some kind of backwoods tribe.

Second, they must have been fathered by a Vietnam vet who stayed behind and taught them English. That or some Vietcong who learned the language and stayed in the bush after the war ended.

Third, now was the time to strike. She knew there were only two of them present and the others were far ahead.

It was the perfect time to unleash some of that anger stored in her internal batteries—quietly. No need to attract the others' attention.

Her strike came like a cobra's. She snapped straight up, shot her hands out, and twisted. The man carrying her managed a "Huh?" before his neck snapped. Big and strong as he was, his bones were still breakable. Queen fell to her feet as the man carrying her slumped to the forest floor. She jerked the hood off of her head and saw a wide mouth ready to scream a warning. She lunged and cupped her hands over the mouth, pinning the smaller body against a tree.

Then Queen hesitated. Beneath a heavy brow, the eyes staring back into hers were young . . . wide, childlike, and fearful. But the face . . . Though feminine, only the eyes, nose, mouth, and upper cheeks lacked hair. Queen frowned. *What the hell?* This was no doubt a child. A little girl. But she looked like a red-haired version of the X-Men's Beast on a bad hair day.

She fought like him, too.

The girl knocked Queen's arms away, then leaped into the air. She took hold of the tree above her and flipped upside down against it. She clung there, looking down at the stunned Queen like a rabid squirrel. The reddish hair that covered her face and head covered portions of her body as well. A long V of hair tapered from her shoulders toward her waist, where a tied rag hung like a loincloth. Her thighs were nearly hairless, but her calves and feet were coated in fur, as were her forearms and triceps. Her biceps and upper torso were lightly covered in hair as well. Her chest, which seemed too ample for a young girl, was clothed in a rag similar to the one tied around her waist. Primal, but modest. She looked more cavegirl than ape . . . or human.

The girl growled and pounced. She landed on Queen's chest with a surprising weight that knocked her off her feet. The girl jumped away from Queen just after the two hit the ground.

Queen lay still on the forest floor, watching as the ferocious child scaled the trees, leaping from one to the next, and finally disappeared from view high in the canopy.

Quick to her feet, Queen ran, knowing the girl would return with others. She would have liked to inspect the dead male, but couldn't risk getting caught again. She followed a diagonal course in the same general direction as the girl. She wouldn't leave King and Pawn behind. Circling around toward the enemy would give her a chance to follow, but would also confuse those trying to track her. They might not expect her to give chase, especially when even the little girl could have killed her. Surprise had allowed her to kill the larger male. She had to be sure surprise remained on her side.

A loud hooting filled the forest. The others were returning.

Queen caught a glimpse of five large males moving through the trees faster than she could run on land. She ducked behind a fallen palm and watched, afraid to move lest she be heard. The five males' vocalizations reached a crescendo when they discovered their dead counterpart. If Queen were caught again, they would do much more than knock her out. The inhuman shouts continued as the five pounded down the path, back the way they'd come.

Queen smiled. They might be stronger, faster, and more agile than her, but they weren't the smartest primates in the jungle. Of course, she had no idea how long they would follow the path before realizing Queen had not taken it. They might not be strategists, but they weren't exactly dopes, either. They could talk, after all.

Not eager to test their IQs, Queen watched the five males vanish into the jungle, then set out after the others. What had started as a noble mission to save the world from some new bioweapon had descended into a dirty fight for survival. First Delta versus VPLA Death Volunteers. Now man versus beast.

THIRTY-SEVEN

Knight dreamed of his mother, calling him in for lunch, and then woke to silence. He had slept through the wailing calls of the Nguoi Rung, through the echoed reports of Rook's powerful handgun, through the gruesome death suffered by Somi, and lastly, through the shouts issued in Rook's direction from Red, in plain English. Had he heard any of this he might have not lingered upon waking. And as a result he would not have made the mistake that carried him deeper into the ancient layers built by inhuman hands.

He sat on the bed of bones and rubbed his head. Though his slumber had been sound, his body ached after lying on a bed of knobby limbs. He stretched his back, breathed deep, stretching his battered rib cage. Relief came as a pop in his sternum signified a realignment—of what he couldn't tell, but he felt better.

In the darkness created by the bone structure, he had a clear view of the space outside. He could see the wall of the cavern, glowing green, and the skeletal structures at its base. The view was just a sliver of the interior, but the cavern's light was steady. He looked for movement. A shifting shadow. A flicker of light. Anything that would betray the presence of somebody, or something, waiting for him. He slowed his breathing so that he could no longer hear his own breath, and listened.

He saw nothing.

Heard nothing.

Then stood.

His ankle throbbed, sending him back down onto the bone bed, which rattled under the sudden return of weight.

Knight froze, watching and listening again. When no one approached he was even more sure that he was alone. In the quiet cavern his rattling bed would have been like an alarm bell. Or dinner bell.

Leaning over, he took hold of a conjoined radius and ulna that made up a decorative pattern running the length of the bed and yanked them free. He then separated them from each other with a quick pull. Though the bones were solid, the tissue holding them together turned to powder in his hands. Using duct tape kept in his cargo pants he lashed the forearm bones to the sides of his wounded foot and lower leg.

Not exactly a gel cast, Knight thought, *but it will have to do.*

He stood with a grunt, but the pain was bearable. The makeshift splint would serve its purpose, to help take the weight off the ankle and distribute it to his calf. Limping, he moved to the doorway and took a peek outside. Nothing but the emerald sheen of ancient bones.

He slid silently from the doorway and rounded the side of the building that had provided his refuge. He peeked around the corner and saw a long, straight passage, what could only really be called a street, stretching straight away for a distance that looked greater than several football fields. Both sides of the street were lined by more buildings ranging in size and intricacy. There was no way to know the original purpose of the place, but the design, the craftsmanship, that went into each building was impressive, if not hauntingly beautiful.

After a quick listen, Knight whisked across the street, to the far side, where buildings rose up into the bone-covered stone wall. He hoped to find a tunnel that would take him out of this place and into the bright yellow light of day. Hell, even the dull filtered light of the jungle's canopy-covered day would be an improvement. Even the humidity and heat of the jungle, which could not be found in the cool, dry caves, held greater appeal than the necropolis. It was the air that bothered him. He could feel the dusty air clogging his nose, dust created by the bones and bodies that were left to rot in this cave. He was breathing the dead.

Doing his best to stay in the shadows, Knight moved as swiftly as possible on his injured leg, but the glowing green moss that covered every external surface filled the cavern with ambient light. If one of the creatures that lived in this cave happened to look in his direction, he would stand out like a black meteorite on an arctic ice shelf.

So it was, when he heard the steady slap of broad bare feet approaching from a side corridor, he ducked into the first dark tunnel he found. Before disappearing into the darkness he removed a bandanna from his pocket and wiped several bones clean of their green moss. He pocketed the glowing rag and moved away from the necropolis.

When the footfalls came closer he had no choice but to follow the tunnel. It ran straight for fifty feet, and as Knight covered the distance he hoped to find it turning upward, but it didn't. It descended, deeper into the mountain. Deeper into the lair of the Nguoi Rung.

THIRTY-EIGHT

Waves of heat caressed Sara's body. She still couldn't see, but she knew from the dry warmth and the occasional pop that she was sitting in front of a fire. The cold stone against her hands, which were tied tight behind her back, coupled with the occasional echoed voice, revealed she was in a cave. She tried to focus on her other senses, her odd senses, but something about the enclosed space and constant heat of the fire kept her from "feeling" anything more than her immediate surroundings.

She couldn't even tell if King was with her. She had sensed a struggle behind them when they were still on the path and wondered if Queen had escaped. A group of their captors gave chase to something, but there was no way to really know what had happened. Queen might have escaped, but Sara held out little hope that she could make it far, never mind return to free them.

"Sara, you there?"

A wave of emotion, both joy and dread, swept through Sara. "King," she said, his name infused in a sigh of relief. "You're alive."

"Given my current condition and the pain in my head, I'm starting to wish I wasn't."

"Are you injured?"

"Nothing that won't heal, but they've got me hog-tied

upside down. Don't suppose you managed your loose-rope trick again?"

Sara fought with her bindings but quickly gave up. "Not a chance."

King sighed. This mission had been one humiliation after another. Landing in a battlefield. Sara's abduction. Being captured and tortured by the VPLA. And now, after rescuing Sara, they had been captured *again*.

The question nagging him was *who* had captured them. He couldn't remember a thing up until a minute ago when he woke to a pounding headache. At least they were still together. Or were they? "Queen?"

"She's not with us," Sara said. "I think she escaped."

King didn't know if that was a good thing or not. They'd already been separated from Knight, Rook, and Bishop. The team found strength together. Each represented a part of the whole. King the head, cunning and cool. Bishop and Rook the arms, strong and steady. Knight and Queen the legs, mobile and deadly. Still, with Queen on the loose, a rescue attempt would be no doubt forthcoming—if she was still alive.

Sara waited for an answer, but King remained silent. She couldn't handle the silence. Not now. With her senses shut down and her vision blocked, his voice helped ground her. But what to ask him? She knew so little about him. His childhood? Did he have a family? A girlfriend? The man was hardly an open book. "King," she said, "why do you do what you do?"

"What do you mean?" King asked, hoping she wasn't planning on a long conversation. His head pounded with every utterance.

"Delta. Most kids want to be a fireman or paleontologist or . . ."

"Or a doctor," King said.

"Yeah, or a doctor."

"I wanted to be a farmer. Corn. I loved corn on the cob. Wanted to eat it all the time."

"So what happened?"

"Other than becoming a teenager, discovering girls had boobs, and deciding a skateboard was better for me than vegetables?" As King's attention turned inward, the pulsing pain in his head ebbed.

"That's hardly far from normal. What made you . . . I don't know . . ."

"Into a soldier?"

"I guess."

"My sister."

"Must have been some awful teasing." Sara managed to smile beneath her hood. The idea of anyone teasing King to some kind of breaking point seemed impossible. Like trying to freeze the ocean's tide or stop the rotation of the planet. The man had deep, strong roots. Her impression of him being an over-casual grunt had been replaced by a deep respect for the man. His easygoing demeanor hid a calculating, efficient soldier. But he was more than that. After all he'd seen and done, King still had a heart. And a heart like that, one that could endure through the worst horrors the world had to offer, and keep on beating . . . keep on caring . . . that heart belonged to a man worth getting to know better.

"Julie, my sister. We hated each other for a while. I suppose most siblings do at one time or another. Then things changed. We got older and closer. Then she left for the air force. Wanted to be a fighter pilot."

"Did she make it?"

"Yeah. She was amazing."

Sara waited for King to continue. She doubted he opened up like this to anyone, probably not even to the Chess Team, and didn't want to pressure him. Maybe the blood in his head made him loopy. Or maybe the connection she felt growing between them was mutual. But she couldn't take the silence anymore. "And?"

"She crashed."

Sara kicked herself for pushing it, but then King continued.

"It was a training accident. She never did see combat. I enlisted that year. A tribute to her, I suppose. Pretty dumb, looking back at it now. Turns out I was good with a gun."

"And a knife."

King chuckled, then grunted as pain jolted through his blood-filled skull. "And a knife. Of course, everything changed when Deep Blue . . ."

King fell silent.

"What is it?"

"Deep Blue sat this mission out."

"Why?"

"I'm not sure anymore . . ." King faded into his thoughts, putting pieces together. Why wouldn't Deep Blue take part in a mission? Death or severe injury. His identity had been kept a secret, so he was most likely a man with a position of power. A busy man. Another mission? What could be more important than theirs, and if so, why hide that from the team? And that had never stopped him before. *Brugada*. The word came to King in a flash. It had something to do with Brugada. Had to. Before his mind could finish the puzzle, his concentration faded with Sara's voice.

"King . . ." Sara sensed movement to her side. The new arrival was close enough to feel despite the fire. "Someone's here."

"You're quite perceptive," said a friendly sounding male voice. It wasn't Bishop, Rook, or Knight. The hood came off her head and all at once she could see. The fire, five feet away, blazed brightly. She squinted and tried to see the man standing above her. But her blurry vision couldn't make out the details of his backlit form.

King felt himself lifted up and then placed gently on the stone floor of the cave. Then his hood came away as well. King blinked as his eyes adjusted to the flickering light. He could see Sara across the cave, squinting. A fire danced between them. And to his right, a man squatted. King looked at the man's spectacled eyes. They were electric blue and friendly. Then he glanced down and noticed the man was clothed in only a loincloth. A spectacled, hairy, not-so-handsome Tarzan.

Great, King thought.

The man smiled. "Sorry for your discomfort. My name is Dr. Anthony Weston."

THIRTY-NINE

Wet.

It seemed the whole world was wet.

The bark of the trees felt slick to the touch. The earth underfoot sank with each step. And the air, once breathed, coated the lungs with a viscous layer of sludge. The jungle felt like this all the time, but Rook had only just taken notice. As fatigue and despair set in, the wetness closed in around him. Rage filled his body like never before. His team . . . his friends . . . were missing or dead. *All of them.* He might see some of them soon, he thought, in the halls of Valhalla, or wherever warriors went to when they died. They'd all be there. Whether his passing would result from violence or simply succumbing to the elements, he wasn't sure.

He struggled to escape from his wet and clingy clothing. The tight, waterlogged fabric slowed him down, made him clumsy and noisy. He slid out of his heavy flak jacket. There wouldn't be any bullets flying from the group he hunted now. His shirt went next, peeling off him like the skin off a rotisserie chicken. Shirtless now, his taut, white skin breathed and his body relaxed. He removed the outbreak monitor from his wrist. The gentle glow of its digital screen, no longer covered by his sleeve, would give away his position. He noted the orange level and pocketed the device.

After a quick peek over the semicircle of exposed tree roots he had been hiding behind, he lay down on a muddy patch of earth and wallowed in the mud like a great white pig. From his blond hair to his boots, the dark, wet earth covered him. Satisfied with his handiwork, Rook stood and leaned against the tree. While not a perfect camouflage, the dark gray coloration more closely matched the jungle floor than his jet-black uniform. With so many people . . . so many *things* . . . against him, stealth would be key. He smiled for a moment, remembering the scene in *Predator* when Arnold Schwarzenegger covered his body in mud to escape the heat-sensing sight of the alien hunter. "Up there . . . in them trees," he quoted one of his favorite lines with a whisper, "I see you." The movie had been one of many teenage favorites that inspired his trip to the army recruiter. Arnold had it lucky. Just one alien to fight. Rook had a whole tribe of bona fide Neanderthals.

Rook tossed his removed clothing into the mud and stomped it down with his bare feet, creating a wet slurping sound as the ooze held on to his foot. With the clothing—and its scent—hidden, he was ready to go.

Then a sound stopped him cold. The barely perceptible scrape of tree bark. Something approached from behind.

With a roar, Rook spun around and caught the attacker midleap. The dark form roared back, feminine and savage.

Lucy, he thought.

Rook brought a roundhouse around and caught the beast in the side of the head, which brought about a satisfying grunt. But before he could follow up, a knee crushed into his crotch. A fist to his sternum followed it and sent him onto his back in the mud. Lucy wasted no time, pouncing from above and pounding his gut with a savage punch.

Rook grunted and shouted, "That's it, time for a beat-down!" He brought both fists up, intending to crush the shadowed head looming above him. But a single word stopped him.

"Rook?"

The face lowered, too coated in mud to recognize. Rook found a pair of eyes, as blue as his, looking back. "Queen?"

A flash of white cut through the dark wraith's face. A smile. "Rook!" With mud-coated lips, Queen leaned down and planted a deep kiss on Rook's mouth.

When she pulled away, Rook grinned from ear to ear. "Good to see you, too."

Queen stood. Like Rook, she had shed her clothing from the waist up, including her outbreak monitor. The rest of her was coated in a layer of mud. She looked more like a swim-suit model in body paint than a lethal killer, but Rook knew better. So he tried not to look at her body. He told himself to picture her as one of his sisters. Ignore her curves. Ignore the kiss she'd just planted. She was *Queen*.

But she was—

Queen noticed his distraction and then reminded him who she was. "If you get a hard-on, I swear I'll cut it off, Rook. Now get off your ass. I was just happy to see you alive."

Rook took Queen's offered hand and stood, rubbing his stomach, another reminder that the beauty standing next to him caged a beast inside. With Queen by his side, Rook's thoughts turned back to the mission. "Where's King? Did you find Pawn?"

They crouched together in the nook of the tree. "We got her back, but then . . . something attacked us. Captured all three of us without a fight. We didn't stand a chance."

Rook nodded, eyes filling with fury. "Dr. Weston and his spawn."

"Weston?"

"Picture Doctor Dolittle, but with a hankering for animal love, and you're on the right track. He's got a whole village of freaks. They're faster than Knight. Stronger than Bishop."

"I saw them," Queen said, "when I escaped. How do you know what they are?"

Rook took a deep breath. He wasn't ready to tell the story, so he turned it into an ugly little pill for Queen to swallow. "He explained everything to Bishop right before his hairy little bastard child took off Bishop's head. Somi's dead, too."

Her eyes flared with intensity, neither widening or squinting. "Knight?"

"Injured, but alive. Hiding for now. He'll make it." Rook shook his head, remembering the things he'd seen. "There's more. The mothers of Weston's people . . . fully Neanderthal. Before we found him, they'd captured Knight. Hung him in a meat locker. Saving him for an afternoon snack. They're more monster than any kind of man, Neanderthal or otherwise. The first generation of Weston's group was born to them. I don't know how many of them there are now, but they mature quickly, like animals, so I'm guessing there are a lot."

Queen nodded after taking it all in. "You have a plan?"

"I was going to cover myself in mud, recon the area, find Weston and Cha-Ka, and then kick some ass . . . but with King and Pawn captured . . ."

"We need to rescue them and complete the mission."

He ground his teeth, remembering Bishop's death.

"And if we run into Weston on the way," she said, "well then, we'll just see what happens."

He could live with that. "Have a direction?"

She pointed. "North. Probably at the base of that mountain."

A tall green mountain with a clear rocky peak could be seen through the small holes in the canopy. A layer of fog drifted around the uppermost peak.

"In the tunnels, the ones you and King took. Did you see the symbols on the walls?" Rook asked.

Queen remembered them well. "Every time the tunnels branched."

Rook nodded. "Like road signs. Well, there was more . . . a lot more. A whole city of the dead. Buildings built from bones. Neanderthal bones. The place glowed with green algae. It was creepy as hell and huge. If it had been made by man, it would easily qualify as a world wonder. But Weston shrugged it off as no big deal. Said it was the tip of the iceberg. I'll bet my left nut that we won't find them *on* that mountain."

Rook met Queen's eyes, glowing blue, surrounded by mud. "They'll be *in* it."

FORTY

Weston squatted on his toes, elbows resting on knees. He appeared to have reverted back to some sort of savage state, the kind you see in 1970s caveman movies—hairy hippies dressed in cloth diapers and smelling of raw meat. The one flaw to his caveman appearance was his thick glasses that enlarged his blue eyes.

Sara found the man's scent repulsive and focused on breathing through her mouth instead of her nose.

"Don't suppose you could untie us?" King asked, squirming to get comfortable.

Weston frowned. "I'm sorry, but we've learned to not trust people from the outside world."

"There were three of us," King said, knowing the statement would ask the question he'd been wondering since his hood was removed: Where was Queen?

"Your friend aptly demonstrated why we trust you so little," Weston said, his frown becoming a scowl.

"She escaped?" Sara asked.

"Indeed," Weston said. "Just after killing one of our guards and nearly killing a little girl. She'll be found soon enough, though. And if the others can keep themselves from exacting their revenge, she'll be joining you here."

Hearing Queen had escaped and was still at large was good news, but knowing Weston was overestimating his odds of capturing her a second time was excellent. He had no idea whom he was pursuing.

King looked Weston over. The man had a friendly face and demeanor, but he'd seen dangerous men put on a good show before. "You're American?"

"Once upon a time, that's what I called myself, yes."

"But not anymore?"

"You seem very confident for a man who's tied up," Weston said with a smile.

King grinned. "This isn't the first time."

Weston laughed and stretched out his arms as though to embrace the air. "And yet, here you are! Very good . . . very good . . . Do you mind me asking why it is *you* are here?"

King didn't speak. Sara followed his lead when Weston looked to her for the answer.

"This isn't an interrogation," Weston said. "I'm not a soldier."

The silence continued.

"Perhaps something is not right in the world?" Weston asked. "Perhaps you thought the solution could be found here? In the Annamites. We have listened to the Vietnamese soldiers. Heard them talking about a cure for something that originated here. And you are here for the same reason."

King directed a cold stare at Weston.

"Tell me," Weston said. "Which one of you is the scientist?"

Weston looked at King, amused by his harsh glare. "Certainly not you." He looked at Sara and shuffled over, never rising from his squat, like a lazy gorilla. He squeezed her arm gently.

Sara pulled away. "Get the hell away from me."

Weston laughed and hobbled back to his place by the crackling fire. "You're the scientist. Too soft and delicate for a soldier."

King never flinched and his voice held its typical cool tone. "What do you know about the Brugada syndrome?"

Weston's eyebrows rose and he smiled widely. "Is that what they're calling it? Sounds ominous."

"It is ominous," King said. There was obviously no reason to hold back. Weston knew something and it seemed only total honesty would pry it free.

Weston rocked on his feet. "How many are dead?"

King tried to shrug but his bound arms barely moved. "Not many."

"We became aware of it at an early stage," Sara chimed in.

Weston looked confused. "I'm not sure I understand. A few people die and the U.S. Special Forces invades a foreign country for the cure?"

"One of the first people to contract the disease is a public figure," Sara said.

"*Is* a public figure? Not *was?* This person survived?" Weston leaned forward, his interest rising. "Who was it?"

"The president," King said.

Weston nearly fell over with surprise. "Of the United States?"

King nodded. "Which is why we're here."

"Of course, it makes sense now." Weston calmed and said, "But how did it reach the president? Surely he doesn't moonlight in the jungles of Vietnam."

"Brugada has been weaponized," King said. "Someone tried to assassinate him."

"And it's contagious, piggybacking on a bird flu," Sara added. "We managed to contain the outbreak by quarantining hundreds of people, including the president and most of the White House staff. But next time we might not catch it in time."

"You know what it is, don't you?" King asked.

Weston looked at the stone floor of the cave and rubbed his bare foot across it. "People have been dying from the sudden death in this region for hundreds, perhaps thousands of years. It kills villagers every year. And it wiped out the male population of the Nguoi Rung. The old mothers are all that are left." He looked up. "What makes you think there is a cure?"

"We know the original strain of Brugada originated in this area. The new strain most likely did, too. Who are the Nguoi Rung?"

"You'll find out soon enough. What about this new strain?" Weston asked.

"The original strain is a genetic defect passed down through generations," Sara explained. "Thanks to a mutation, it is now contagious and death comes within a week. It could wipe out the entire human population on Earth. Including you. And whoever else lives here with you."

Weston pounded a fist against his chest, displaying his virility. "And yet, here I am. Exposed at the source, and alive and well. Perhaps you've come to the wrong place?"

Sara glared at him. "This is the right place, and you know that, don't you?"

Weston's smile faded some. "You may not understand my position. To you, I'm a freak. My people are monsters—animals you wouldn't think twice about destroying. Abominations. I see the fear in human eyes when they see them. And I am all that stands between them and the outside world. Between a culture older than humanity and destruction. You may be seeking to save human civilization, but I'm trying to save my . . ." His voice quivered with true emotion. ". . . my family. My children." He stood and walked behind a large rock. He bent down and came back up holding Sara's backpack.

She gasped.

Weston sat down and opened the backpack. He pulled out the laptop and set it down on the stone floor between himself and the fire. Then he removed the vial of blood and placed it next to the laptop. He opened the computer and pushed the power button. "You know, the laptop I brought must have weighed ten pounds. This can't be more than two. Technology is amazing, isn't it?"

"How long have you been here?" King asked.

"I arrived in 1995," Weston replied. Sara's eyes widened. "Fifteen years." The screen blinked on and chimed as the operating system resumed operations where they had been when the laptop had been closed. "Cute penguin." Weston spun the laptop around to Sara. "You were testing the blood?"

Sara ignored his question and looked at the test results. She did her best to show no reaction to what she was seeing. She scanned down the list of virus antibodies found in the woman's blood. The new strain of bird flu *had* been detected. That blood was their best chance at a cure.

"There's nothing there," Sara said.

Weston raised an eyebrow. "I was a cryptozoologist before finding my place here. I'm no fool. In fact, I know more about your Brugada syndrome than you do."

With a casual flick of the wrist, Weston tossed the vial into the fire. It shattered, sending a geyser of steam to the cave ceiling fifteen feet above. A breeze from deeper inside the cave carried the steam and smoke across the ceiling, removing all traces of the blood, and hope, with it.

Sara fought back a gag as she realized she smelled cooked human blood, but her repulsion became replaced by rage. "Why did you do that?" she shouted, fighting with her bonds, desperate to lunge at Weston and strangle the life from him.

"Because," King said, "he already has the cure."

Weston stood, picked up the laptop, and hurled it violently against the wall, shattering it. After its plastic body rattled to the stone floor, Weston calmly took his position by the fire.

His lack of denial was all the confirmation Sara needed. "Why don't you give it to us and let us go! With so much at stake how can you—"

"You have no idea what's at stake!" Weston shouted, his eyes wide and face reddening. "The civilization of the Nguoi Rung, the ancestors of my children, found refuge from humanity here. *My* children find refuge here. I cannot allow word of their existence to leave the jungle." His voice calmed. "It is an awful thing. I know. But I have done awful things to protect this hidden treasure and I will again if need be. You must remain here, with us. Whether you live among us or remain a prisoner is your choice, but you will not leave."

He rubbed his temple, closed his eyes, and sighed. "The rest of the world will just have to find a cure another way."

"And the VPLA," King said. "What will you do with them?"

"They will not leave the jungle, either." He met King's eyes. "I *have* done awful things, soldier. You of all people should understand that killing to protect your people, your home, is—"

"Noble," King said.

Weston smiled slightly. "Yes, noble."

"And the name is King."

A smirk returned to Weston's face. He picked up a stick and poked the fire. Sparks flew toward the ceiling. "Agent Orange, you've heard of it, yes?"

"An herbicide used in the Vietnam War to clear the forest," King said.

"It's still used as a defoliant for cotton before it's harvested," Sara added. "Traces of it can be found in cottonseed oil, which is ludicrous, considering it causes—"

Sara's eyes widened.

King snapped his head toward her. "Causes what?"

Sara met his eyes and then looked back at Weston. "Genetic mutation . . . soft tissue sarcoma, Hodgkin's disease, non-Hodgkin lymphoma, chronic lymphocytic leukemia . . . It's a carcinogen. Highly mutagenic."

"Impressive," Weston said. "It took me a few years to put all that together. Took another few to figure out why the children and I were immune."

"You experimented on the villagers," King said.

"Heavens, no. I *observed* them. Their deaths revealed the mechanisms the plague used to spread and how long it took to kill. The flu swept through the village. Days later, the sudden death claimed its first victim. Then a wave of death spread through the village. I watched as sometimes one man an hour would simply fall over dead.

"I hiked to a village to the north of here and spoke to them about what was happening. To my surprise this wasn't the first time. The village elder, an old man I had encountered several times in the jungle, told me about a time, thirty years ago, when a man in his home village, perhaps a carrier of Brugada, got very ill. They treated him with an herb found in the jungle, an herb I now know is resistant to the effects of Agent Orange, but retains traces of Agent Orange in its roots. Trace amounts of Agent Orange are still found in most local food sources, but they used a large amount of the highly contaminated herb, including its roots. They ground it up, boiled it, and gave it to the man as a broth. That's when things changed. A few days later the sudden death claimed him. Brugada and the flu had joined forces, so to speak. The flu continued spreading and the villagers began dying. The old man's mother wisely fled before she and her family caught the infection, but the majority of the village was wiped out. Somehow, the flu survived, perhaps in the local monkey population not affected by Brugada, and eventually reemerged in Anh Dung. I watched it all happen, exactly as the old man described it, the way I first observed the Ngoui Rung."

King fought with his bonds. He could kill Weston with his bare hands. Hell, he could do it with one hand. He growled as he spoke. "Everyone on the planet could die. Will you just observe that as well?"

Weston stood above King, a large stone suddenly in his hand. He raised the stone slowly, preparing to bring it down on King's head. "Sometimes a species goes extinct to make way for something better. It's been that way for millions of years."

"What race?" King shouted. "There won't be anyone left!"

"Oh my God," Sara said.

King stopped fighting his bonds and looked at her. So did Weston.

Sara's mind recalled the creatures at Anh Dung. Their inhuman captors. She'd sensed their bodies. She'd thought they weren't human. Now she realized the truth—they were half human. "His children," she whispered. "You might not be *causing* the extinction of the human race, but you don't mind it."

"Death is a repulsive thing. If the human race cannot find a cure for this awful disease then nature has deemed humanity unfit. It is the natural way of things. I'm sorry. I truly am. But we seek to preserve two civilizations at odds with each other." Weston's face brightened some. "That's right. I haven't introduced you yet!"

Weston put a hand to his mouth and called out in his best Ricky Ricardo impression, "Oh, Lucy!" He looked back at King and Sara. "I love doing that."

Lucy stepped into the room. King blinked at the sight of her, thinking the firelight was playing tricks with his vision. His face became as stone, frozen and unmoving, when he realized the half-human creature standing before him was real.

Sara gasped and shuffled back as best she could. For all of Lucy's attractive features—the face of a child and bright eyes—her more feral side—dirt-soiled hair on her face, back, lower torso, forearms, and lower legs coupled with long and dirty fingernails and toenails—revealed something ancient. Something children fear at night. Lucy smiled, revealing her inch-long canines.

"Lucy," Weston said as he motioned to King. "This is King and . . ." He motioned to Sara.

Sara sat still like a nervous rabbit, her heart beating wildly.

"Pawn," King answered. "She's Pawn."

"Chess pieces," Weston said, nodding. "How original. And here I thought you just had an enormous ego."

"Have that, too," King said, though his confidence was more an act now than ever.

"King and Pawn," Weston said, "this is my great-great-granddaughter Lucy. She is the most favored of all my children. My Neanderthal princess. The next generation of Nguoi Rung." He shook the hair on her head. Weston pulled away though Lucy seemed to want more.

Neanderthal? Sara's mind flashed to her earlier conversation with King. Plasticity. Genetic assimilation. Lucy seemed the likely product of both theories, but Weston had called her his granddaughter. A blood relation.

If Lucy is half human, Sara thought, *what does her mother look like?* She had seen the fossil remains of more than a handful of Neanderthals and Lucy looked *more* primitive. Thicker. Stronger. More predatory. Reconstructions of Neanderthals looked hunched and hairy, but overall not too dissimilar from modern man. Save for the keen eyes and language skills, Weston's granddaughter was a brute.

"How many?" she asked.

"Pardon?"

"How many . . . grandchildren do you have here?"

"Last time we counted, fifteen hundred." Weston rubbed his chin. "But that was three years ago. With the birth rate, taking into account the high infant mortality rate, we're probably close to two thousand now."

"Two thousand." Sara was astonished, but managed one more question. "From how many sets of parents?"

"Thirty Neanderthal mothers. One human father."

Sara fought the urge to place her hand over her mouth. Weston was the father of an entirely new species of primate—neither human nor Neanderthal. *Hybrids,* she thought.

Weston turned to Lucy. "I have an important task for you."

She brightened and clapped her hands.

Weston motioned to King. "Take him to a room. Watch over him and do not let him leave. But do not harm him . . ."

He looked at King, a twinkle of menace hidden beneath the intelligence in his eyes. ". . . yet."

Lucy hopped over to King.

"Stay away from me—" King grunted as he was flipped over. She took him by the waist of his pants and picked him up as though he were a briefcase. Then she was off, carrying him through the caves, hooting all the way.

Sara watched in renewed fear. In the hands of this *child,* King was helpless.

FORTY-ONE

Washington, D.C.

College seemed like a distant memory, with its late nights, early mornings, and copious amounts of caffeine to battle the extreme weariness that resulted. Today, Duncan felt like he'd returned to a more hellish version of college where failing a surprise exam resulted in death, as it had for several of his staff confined within the historic walls of the White House.

In each and every case, the implanted cardioverters had done their job, shocking the healthy hearts back to beating again. But the look of fear in the eyes of those who had succumbed to the weaponized disease broke his heart. They weren't soldiers. They were secretaries, cleaning staff, and chefs. Senators, congressmen, and aides. He doubted many of them would have joined the White House staff or chosen to serve their country if they perceived any risk of death.

Those who had fallen to Brugada only to be revived could be distinguished by the pallor of their skin, or wideness of their eyes. Those who had not yet fallen viewed those who had with a suspicious eye. Tension filled the halls, threatening to turn the people trapped inside the White House against each other.

The only group that had yet to fall at the hands of Brugada

was the one most prepared for its effect. The Secret Service hadn't suffered a man down. Domenick Boucher, too, had not tasted the temporary sting of Brugada, but his entry into the Oval Office was greeted as though he were Death himself, scythe in hand. He stepped inside the room, closed the door gently behind him, and leaned against it.

The man looked pale. In fact, he looked paler than the men and women who had risen from the dead.

Duncan sat up straight despite his fatigue. "Did it get you?"

"Not me."

"Who?"

Boucher sat on one of the two couches. "Beatrice Unzen. Age sixty-nine. At a downtown CVS."

"Here in D.C.?"

Boucher nodded. "She survived, which is how Brugada was able to be determined. We've managed to keep the doctors silent, primarily because, as far as they know, this is an isolated case."

"But . . ."

"It's not. There have been six deaths in the D.C. area. All healthy adults. Cause of death: unknown."

"How did this happen?"

"Seems Brentwood's driver forgot to mention he stopped at a convenience store for some scratch tickets. Security tapes show him sneezing while perusing the store, touching every damn Twinkie and Slim Jim he passed."

Duncan rubbed his temples.

"I've had analysts counting the number of visitors to the store since the driver's visit. At last check they were up to one hundred and thirty-one. Most can't be identified because the images are grainy and they paid in cash."

"Where does this leave us?"

"Honestly?"

Duncan nodded.

"We're screwed." Boucher sighed. "Our only saving grace at this point is that the press hasn't put two and two together.

They know about Brugada, but the cases appear to be innocuous among the average number of deaths seen in this city on a daily basis, so that no one has yet to notice. All eyes, thankfully, are still focused squarely on this office. With the White House locked down and the president apparently at risk of death, a few stiffs in the streets of D.C. aren't raising any eyebrows.

"But when the body count rises; when some smart young reporter digging for a new angle figures things out . . . well, Brugada will be just one of many worries."

Duncan nodded. They were facing a pandemic that spread, and killed, quickly with no respect for the healthy. He knew what such news would do to the nation. To the world. Many people would die at the hands of violence long before the Brugada seized their hearts. "How are my travel plans coming?"

"Everything has been arranged," Boucher said. "I recommend waiting until the last possible moment before leaving the White House."

Duncan stood. "I'll need to record something. Address the nation. No one can know I've left. If . . . *when* . . . word gets out, the world will want to hear from me. And they'll want to know I'm still here."

"I'll arrange it."

Boucher stood and opened the door for Duncan. The president stopped next to him and spoke in a whisper. "Update the team."

REVOLUTION

FORTY-TWO

Annamite Mountains—Vietnam

As darkness closed in around her, Sara wondered how Weston could see his way. Had his vision changed? Did he have senses like hers that allowed him to navigate in the dark? She tried to pay attention to her twisted senses, but they seemed to be nullified by the tight, echoing cave.

A gentle hiss, like a receding wave on a sandy beach, slid through the cave as Weston held his hand against the rock wall. He knew the cave well, but with a captive in tow, didn't want to risk losing his balance on one of the random outcrops where he often stubbed a toe.

The steady white noise of Weston's hand on the wall gave Sara something to focus on. Over the years, white noise had become her ally. It drowned out the sounds of the city, the pops of a house expanding and contracting with weather changes, and allowed her to sleep. Like a filter, it weeded out the noise and muffled the deluge of sensory overflow drowning her synapses. Her nerves calmed. She took a deep breath through her nose, but regretted it right away. His body odor struck her like a kick to the head. She stifled a gag, but before her nose was free of the scent, she picked up on another odor mingled with Weston's. Something fresh.

She moved farther to the side, hoping to walk outside of Weston's odorous wake. She sniffed again.

Weston's odor, now barely perceptible, faded as a new smell filled her nose . . . like ionized air after a thunderstorm. Sweet, clean, and refreshing. The air grew cooler and the tunnel grade rose and fell as they moved forward.

Sara tried to focus on the invigorating air, but couldn't help wondering what Weston had planned. He said there was something she needed to see. As a scientist, he believed she would understand what he was doing. Why it was so important. He had her pegged wrong, of course; she would do whatever it took to get the cure for Brugada back to the modern world, even if it meant exposing his tribe's existence. Spock had it right—the needs of the many did outweigh the needs of the few. Or the one. Who, at the moment, was Weston.

A sudden jolt struck Sara's left leg as she stubbed her foot hard against a rock jutting out from the wall. She stumbled, shouting in pain. She began to topple over, but was yanked up hard.

Weston's stench returned, now coupled with the vulgar odor of his breath up close. "Walk behind me. Wouldn't want you twisting an ankle, now, would we?"

Without reply, Sara continued behind Weston, breathing once again through her mouth and trying her best to ignore the throb of pain in her stubbed toe.

It seemed they had hiked a mile in the darkness, but it could have been a few hundred feet. Time and all sense of the world ceased to exist in the absolute subterranean gloom. What she did know was that they were headed toward the core of some mountain.

Or maybe not.

Faint light filtered into the tunnel from a source too far ahead to see clearly. Perhaps the size of a dime, the tunnel exit gleamed blue and green. The jungle? Had they passed *through* the mountain?

As they continued forward the light grew steadily brighter. She could see Weston now, his near-naked form

loping in front of her, cast in green and blue. The walls of
the cave emerged from the darkness. Sara was surprised to
see that the rough natural cave had become a buffed,
squared-out tunnel. She'd noticed the smooth footing earlier, but assumed it was a well-worn path through the cav-
erns. But this wasn't a natural cave. This was carved into the
earth. A massive undertaking and marvel of engineering.

She took the tunnel for a modern mine shaft at first, believing the Vietnamese must have worked these mountains
before the war and abandoned them when the region went to
hell. Then she saw the symbols on the wall. They meant
nothing to her, but they spoke of something ancient, something older than a mine shaft.

As the tunnel captured her attention she forgot about
Weston and his intentions. She focused on the walls. The
smooth surface sparkled with blue and green light. *Quartz,*
she thought, *reflecting the light ahead.*

Weston stopped, and she ran into him. The tickle of his
hairy back on her face snapped her to reality and sent a twist
of nausea through her core.

He turned to her. "Sit."

She complied. She wasn't sure what would happen if she
ran, but with King's fate uncertain and the rest of the Chess
Team missing, she didn't want to press her luck.

Not yet.

Weston moved to the tunnel wall and pushed. A slab of
stone slid in and then to the side. A five-foot-tall, three-foot-
wide hole opened up. Weston stepped inside and disappeared into the dark.

When he didn't immediately return, Sara considered escape. But where could she go? Back the way they came
wasn't an option. She would run into a village of Neanderthals. Or break her leg in the darkness. And forward . . . who
knew what awaited her there? Maybe something worse? She
bit her lip in frustration. *King would go,* she thought. *Think
like Delta. It would be better to go out trying—fighting—
than to not try at all.*

It wasn't exactly an official motto, but she could picture any member of the Chess Team saying the words. It was enough to spur her into action. Sara pushed to her feet and ran toward the light. She willed her feet to take shorter, faster strides. A sense of freedom filled her muscles and she covered the distance in twenty seconds. Just feet from the tunnel exit, she found herself squinting from the brightness of the shimmering aqua light.

Then she was free of the tunnel, facing the horrific reality of her situation.

Weston calmly walked up next to her and stopped. He had a knife in his hand and a gun holstered on his hip. "Beautiful, isn't it?" Without another word he grabbed her wrist firmly and yanked her toward him so their faces were only inches apart. Only Sara's bound hands on his chest kept them that way.

Weston grinned and glanced down. The tip of the knife poked her belly, threatening to slice through shirt and flesh all at once. Then, with a quick jerk, Weston lashed out with the knife.

A sickening tear sounded out as Sara screamed.

FORTY-THREE

Knight continued through the tunnel, his path dimly lit by the glowing bandanna laden with the phosphorescent algae. Despite his instincts telling him to turn back, that traveling deeper into the mountain was a bad idea, he pushed forward, driven by a desire to see where the tunnel led. That, and the tunnel had been blessedly free of savage ape-women. The smooth layer of dust on the floor gave him comfort as well. The tunnel hadn't been used for some time. Whatever was down here was no use to beasts, and that made it a welcome place for what they no doubt saw as a small Korean snack.

He did his best to tread lightly, hiding his footprints in the dust, but his injured and splinted leg, which clicked and echoed in the tunnel with every footfall, made stealth rather tricky. But he held on to hope. He'd escaped the necropolis without confrontation and, unless this tunnel was a dead end, felt confident he would make it back to the jungle.

When the tunnel leveled out, his hope grew. When a breeze tickled his nose, his hope soared. The *clack, clack, clack* of his bone splint sped up as he limped forward like a sprinting gimp.

Then the tunnel opened up and he froze.

Another chamber lay before him, but it was nothing like the necropolis. The floor dropped away, six feet down. The ceiling was eight feet above him and the space appeared to

be a baseball-diamond-sized square. A staircase carved into
the stone floor descended into a maze straight out of Greek
mythology. But this wasn't Greece and there was no Mino-
taur at the center of the labyrinth. Instead there was a large
crystal, taller than Knight, rising out of the floor like some
kind of Egyptian obelisk. The crystal held his gaze. Light
radiated from inside the polished monolithic object and
filled the space. Then the light shifted, shimmering like the
aurora borealis. As the glow moved about the space, he noticed twin streams of dusty radiance that appeared brighter
than the glow coming from the crystal. Knight followed the
light's path back to the source—two holes in the far wall.
But the holes were partially covered by circular hatches.

Rising from the base of each wooden shade was a thin
rope that attached to the ceiling through a series of stone
loops. The lines ended above the entrance and hung down,
weighted by two stones tied to the ends. The heavy stones
kept the hatches slightly open and allowed the sliver of light
into the chamber . . . a sliver of light that became amplified
by the crystal at the center of the hewn-out space.

Knight squinted at the hanging ropes, then glanced back
at the crystal. The whole contraption appeared to be a primitive light switch. "Can't be."

But it was. Knight pulled the cords down and, once in
motion, the weight of the stones pulled them to the floor.
The hatches sprang open, allowing the daylight beyond to
pour in, where it struck the crystal, refracted, split, and dispersed around the room as shimmering colors.

Details leaped out. The labyrinth was much more than a
simple maze. The one-foot-thick stone walls were covered,
front and back, by Somi's proto-Chinese. Each symbol took
up a four-inch-square space in a grid that was perfectly mea-
sured and even. It looked like an ancient Vietnam War Me-
morial, wrapped around and throughout the room instead of
a straight line. Knight descended the staircase and entered
the maze.

He imagined that with time he might even be able to figure

out what some of the symbols meant. If this really was the precursor language to Chinese, then the four percent Chinese that is pictorial might actually be found on these walls. And if that was true, he might be able to figure out more symbol meanings based on their surrounding context. But that would take years. With no understanding of the language, Knight made his way toward the center of the maze. He was tempted to climb on top of the maze and cheat his way through, but his memory of the view from above served him well. He reached the center, and the massive crystal, in just a few minutes.

As his gaze was drawn by the crystal he failed to notice the debris surrounding it, and tripped. He'd normally have turned the fall into a graceful leap followed by a roll and bounce back to his feet, but his bound ankle caused him to fall like a drunk squirrel. He landed facedown but softened the impact with his hands. Exhaustion claimed him as he lay there, annoyed by his clumsiness. He kept his eyes closed, listening to his breathing. It rattled.

No, not his breathing. Something else.

Knight opened his eyes. The top corner page of a red-ringed notepad fluttered with each of his breaths. He launched up into a sitting position. The notebook sat open with a pen dropped casually upon it. A slim coat of dust covered both. They'd been discarded long ago, but they belonged to modern man. Someone had been here before him. Someone knew about this place. The question on Knight's mind was: Did that person survive?

The area surrounding the notepad was covered in rubbings made from the maze walls. Smudges of charcoal filled large sheets of drawing paper. They littered the floor. Knight saw the now-empty sketchpad resting against a nearby wall. Whoever had been here spent a substantial time studying the language, but did they finish?

Knight picked up the notebook, flipped to the first page, and was surprised to see the college-ruled lines filled with English. The writing was chicken scratches, really, but readable. He started to read the first entry.

Dr. Anthony Weston
06/17/1995

The flight to Laos—awful. The food—abysmal. The
adventure—high! Despite my poor accommodations I
am nonetheless excited for my impending trip into the
Annamite range. The wonders that are just waiting to
be discovered in that deep, dark, and foreboding land
will change the way the scientific community (and my
ex-wife) view cryptozoology. To think that because we
inhabit the land means we have seen everything on it
is absurd! I may be fifty pounds lighter on my return
trip back to Oregon, but I will make up for it with the
weight of my discoveries. Discoveries that I hope will
heal the pain of the past and make those missing the
future proud of me. It is for this reason that I . . .

Knight stopped reading. It was clear that this Weston
guy was going to continue his rant for several pages. He

flipped through the notebook until he saw a drawing. He recognized the figure immediately as one of the primal woman, hunched in a mass of flattened reeds, as seen from a safe distance.

Knight read the text beneath the drawing.

In this, my fifth day of recording the activities of the Nguoi Rung, one of them sat still long enough for me to draw a picture. I have considered taking photos, but would most likely be detected. I have risked enough getting this close. If they find my perch high above them I fear they will flee.

Knight chuckled. The guy had no idea. Flee? They'd make a meal of him. Probably did.

He turned the pages, looking over more drawings and their accompanying notes. This Weston guy fancied himself as the next Jane Goodall, recording everything about the creatures he called the Nguoi Rung. When and how they hunted, which Knight had experienced firsthand. How they interacted with each other, what he believed to be a language. It was all there. He had chronicled everything about them that he could see without getting too close.

Knight turned the page and frowned. The wrinkled page lacked any text, but was covered in a mix of old mud and blood. He turned to the next page. Weston's writing returned, but there was no date and the man's written voice had changed.

Two months. God. I have been captive for two months and have only now retrieved my belongings. I have been humiliated, tortured, demoralized in unspeakable ways. The Nguoi are evil. God, please, kill me or save me.

He turned to the next page, expecting more of the same, but discovered something even more revolting.

A litter was born today. To the alpha female I have
named Red. A true litter. Six tiny babies. I witnessed
the birth, having gained some freedom of movement
throughout the group. The gentleness of the mothers
was impressive as they birthed the children one at a
time, pausing between each so that each new child
might have opportunity to suckle before the next
arrived. I was allowed to see them after much
complaining by the others, but Red allowed me
closer. They were my children after all, and by God,
they have my eyes!

Knight dropped the notebook. They had not only captured and raped Weston, but they had given birth to his
children. It was unthinkable. Unbelievable. Tense and disturbed, Knight held his breath and listened. Shaken by
what he'd read, he now feared that the Ngoui Rung would
recapture him. And then what? Would a similar fate await
him?

No, he thought, *they were going to eat me.*

And that was a preferable fate to what Weston described.
It wasn't just the things Weston had endured that disturbed
him, it was the new change in his voice. He no longer mentioned being saved or killed. The half-human spawn were
his children and had *his* eyes! Without needing to read any
further Knight knew that Weston had stayed with the Ngoui
Rung. Any good father would. With the notebook discarded
in the maze long ago, he might now be dead, but Knight was
positive that Weston had discovered the necropolis and this
maze. He had become part of the Nguoi Rung and father to
something inhuman.

Returning to the notebook, Knight skimmed through
the pages, glimpsing keywords like "children," "love," and
"happy." He'd really gone native. And had learned to enjoy
it. As he flipped through, Knight paused at another key-
word, "fucking," and read the entry.

The fucking old mothers beat me again today. They
are teaching the children to behave like savages.
Killing indiscriminately. Eating human flesh from
the nearby villages. It is vile. I cannot stand it much
longer. I must make a stand or flee this place . . . but I
cannot bear to leave the children behind, not now, not
with grandchildren being born.

Grandchildren? Knight thought. If this had been written
this year the oldest child would only be fifteen years old. But
the notebook had been discarded long ago, years ago. How
could there already be grandchildren?

Knight pushed the thought from his mind. Dwelling on
the twisted tale of Dr. Weston would have to wait. He was
more interested in what Weston had discovered about the
language filling this chamber. He flipped through the pages,
not reading the text, just looking for images. He stopped at a
page where a symbol had been drawn. The following pages
documented how Weston had found the symbols inside the
tunnels, his subsequent discovery of the necropolis and then
this room, which he called the Rosetta Chamber.

Skimming again, Knight marveled as, over the course of
one hundred notebook pages, Weston slowly worked out the
symbols' meanings. After what had to have been years of
work, the last ten pages of the notebook were filled with a
translation of the stones, which told a story starting on the
maze wall on the left side of the staircase and read all the way
through the maze until it ended back at the same staircase on
the right side. Knight read the first line of the translation:

This is the history of the Nguoi Rung—Note: I
cannot say what the name truly is, but I believe it was
a tribal designation of some kind. Note! Having read
further on I have deduced the Nguoi Rungs' ancestry!
Neanderthals!!!

FORTY-FOUR

Water gurgled past the body that lay half on the sandy shore and half in the lazy river. It had been pulled almost a mile downstream by the current before catching on a fallen tree, spinning out into a surge of rapids where it was shoved onto the beach. Fish inspected the body and found that the legs and feet were clothed and inedible. But had they been able to taste the man's flesh, they would have found it a replenishing food source; just as two rats on shore were helping themselves to a feast on the large open wound.

Despite the massive damage to his neck, Bishop lived. Though the near-fatal wound had slowed down his body's unnatural ability to heal, it hadn't stopped it. Rebuilding nerve bundles to a functional level took more time than rebuilding simple muscle. After several hours on the shore, the work on his spine was complete.

The muscles of Bishop's neck grew quickly and stretched out, finding and connecting with the muscles and skin of his head. His jugular vein grew, spraying blood as it lengthened and reunited with its other half. The inside of his throat reformed and had yet to finish when a new layer of skin grew over it.

The only remaining injury was on the side of his neck, where the two rats continued to munch on the regenerating meal.

Bishop sat up violently as his body expelled the water that filled his stomach and lungs. Three mighty heaves cleared the liquid from his system. He looked around. Eyes wide.

A breeze tickled his neck. He swatted at it.

A bubble popped on the river. He kicked at it.

One of the hungry rats, still thirsting for Bishop's blood, bit his finger. The wound healed quickly, but the pain registered even faster. Bishop roared and reached out, snagging the rat by a hind leg. It squealed and scratched. Unable to free itself, the rat leaned up and buried its incisors into Bishop's palm. Screaming, he brought the rat up and grabbed its chestnut-sized head. He yanked its head off his hand and then raised the body to his mouth like a corncob fresh off the grill. And he bit into it as if he could taste the dripping butter.

The rat squealed for just a moment before falling silent, before Bishop bit through its back, ribs, and spine, taking an apple-sized chunk out of its back. He devoured the flesh and bones, his insides healing quickly as the sharp ribs sliced his throat and stomach.

Movement caught his eye. Another rat. Rage filled him again and he discarded the dead rodent in his hands, giving chase to the second, pursuing it without cause, without thought, without hesitation—upstream.

FORTY-FIVE

King had never wanted to know what a piece of luggage felt like, but he knew now. He'd been carried recklessly through a network of tunnels, slammed into walls, dropped, picked back up, and sometimes dragged by a leg. But the humiliation of being so easily manhandled never found a firm grasp. The creatures, sights, and sounds he passed in the hallways were far too distracting.

The Nguoi Rung were everywhere, inhabiting the caves just below the mountain exterior. Some, like Lucy, were young women, performing what looked like ordinary household chores. But there were others. Happy children. Serious adults—young adults. The oldest, in human years, could only be as old as Weston had been here. Fifteen years. While the females all appeared to be wide-hipped and ready for child-bearing, the males ranged in size and stature. Some, skinny and diminutive, sat on logs, scratching with sharpened rocks on long smooth ones. *Writing.* Others, with bulging muscles and low brows, carved out cubbies in the cave walls or fashioned weapons.

Lucy dragged King up a winding stone staircase. With his hands still bound behind his back, he tried his best to hop up the stairs on his arms, but Lucy moved too quickly. More often than not, his back pounded into the next stair. As they passed by a row of circular windows that looked out over the jungle, King realized exactly how massive Weston's tribe, family, whatever he called them, had become. This wasn't a village. It was a city.

The staircase ended and the floor evened out. Apparently, Lucy's favored status granted her a room separate from the cubbyholes the others lived in below. They entered a room shaped like a slice of pie. Light streamed in from two large-hulahoop-sized, ten-foot-deep holes in the rock wall through which a blazing blue sky could be seen. And while moisture clung to the torrid air outside, the interior of the mountain felt cool and dry. If not for the smell of rotting flesh, he might have imagined this as a theme resort for the rich and bored.

Lucy casually discarded King onto a stone platform about the size and height of a coffee table. Its rough stone surface was scarred with a variety of scratches, like a cutting board, and smelled like an odd mix of every imaginable bodily fluid. What had taken place on this surface before his arrival, he couldn't say, and he didn't dare entertain the thought. Turning his attention back to the room, he watched Lucy walk toward a kind of stone table. It jutted from the wall, apparently part of the mountain itself. The five-foot-deep, six-foot-wide counter was simple enough, but something odd caught King's attention. A small rounded depression, perhaps an inch deep, surrounded the outside edge, coming together at a small hole in the center of the table. King glanced down. A hole had been drilled in the floor. A dark brown stain clung to the stone around the hole.

Lucy turned from the table, revealing a row of sharpened stones that had been hidden by her body, similarly stained. She opened a handmade wooden chest, covered in symbols similar to the ones he'd seen in the tunnels with Queen while in pursuit of the VPLA and Sara. At the time, the Death Volunteers had seemed like the largest danger he would face on this mission, and they'd almost killed him, Queen, and Sara. But the Death Volunteers would be like a holiday weekend compared to the hell in which he now found himself in. A hell that was about to get hotter.

Arms full of straw, sticks, and a few logs collected from the chest, Lucy set to work arranging them expertly in a fire pit built into the floor. Once she had a bottom layer of straw, covered by sticks, housed beneath a pyramid of four logs, Lucy struck a flint stone to the floor, sending up a cascade of sparks. After two more attempts and a lot of blowing, the blaze came to life.

"What's for dinner?" King asked.

"You," Lucy said casually as though talking to a head of lettuce about to be hacked into a salad. Lucy began testing the sharpness of her stone blade collection, rubbing them against her fingers.

King realized that the comparison to lettuce might not be far off the mark. He examined the scratches etched into the surface of the stone on which he sat. His eyes widened a bit more. He *was* sitting on a cutting board. A very large cutting board.

"I don't think eating me is what your father had in mind when he asked you to watch me," King said.

Lucy squinted at him like only an angry teenage girl can. "Father doesn't know everything. I have been taught by the old mothers, too."

"I thought they were banished."

"I see them when I want. Across the river. Father does not know."

In his heart, King didn't want to know, but had to ask. "And the old mothers have taught you . . . what?"

Lucy smiled. The little girl was gone, replaced by something feral. Though he had not seen them yet, King imagined the old mothers looked something like the girl in front of him now. "How to cook."

Lucy might be intelligent. She could speak, maybe even read or write. But any knowledge she had was taught to her by Weston *and* the old mothers, including morality. Her moral compass, so immature and tutored by inhuman minds, had been corrupted. He was sure that the Nguoi Rung, being intelligent ancestors of modern humanity, could be taught right and wrong. But like humans, they could also be taught to hate. To be evil.

"It doesn't bother you that I'm talking to you?" King asked.

Lucy stopped with a rock blade in hand. "Why should it?"

"Because I'm like you."

Lucy raised an eyebrow, which was more of a start to the hair on her head than an actual eyebrow. She smiled, revealing her sharp canines. "You're nothing like me." She squatted next to him, playing with the rock blade. "I'm strong. You're weak. I'm smart. You're dumb." She thumped her chest. "I'm Nguoi Rung. You're human."

"Weston is human."

"*Father* is alpha. Not human."

King sighed. She was totally brainwashed.

Lucy stood and hunched out a hip. "You're food. I'm hungry." Then she laughed. Her voice sounded like any other teenage girl's.

"How old are you, Lucy?"

Lucy sharpened the stone on another, chipping off flecks and creating a fresh sharpened edge. "Three."

"You're not three," King said.

Lucy spun on him. Angry. "Am too! Father explained it to the other man before I killed him."

King did his best to hide his growing concern. "What other man?"

"Big. Bigger than you. Dark skin."

Bishop.

"How did you kill him?" Bishop would be hard to kill. Short of—

"I took off his head."

King's shoulders fell, along with his resolve.

Bishop was dead.

King fought back his mix of despair and anger, focusing on the problem at hand like he'd been trained to do. Let her think she's three. Maybe they aged differently. She still acted like a teenager.

"Is this a kitchen? Do you know what a kitchen is?"

She huffed. "This is *my room. Not* a kitchen."

"Well, I like your room," he said quickly, fearing he'd offended her. "It's very pretty."

Lucy paused. The slightest of smiles shone on her face.

"Do you have a bed?"

A confused look slowly appeared on her face. Then she looked at him like he'd just pissed his pants. "You're sitting on my bed."

Despite King's internal revulsion at this Neanderthal girl sleeping on what undoubtedly served as both cutting board and bed, he managed to force out, "And your bed is very comfortable."

Lucy looked at him. "I don't like it. It's hard."

"Why don't you get a new one?"

Lucy scrunched her face. "A new one?"

King nodded. "A nice soft one."

"Father says this bed is good enough. Fit for a princess."

"My bed is soft," King said. "Like sleeping on a cloud."

Lucy sat at the edge of the stone bed. She rubbed her hand on the surface.

She's hooked, King thought. Now to reel her in. "You know if we got married, you could sleep on my bed."

"What is married?" Lucy asked.

"It's what people do when they love each other. You're not married?"

Lucy shook her head no. Her face grew serious.

"Father wears a wedding ring. He must be married to someone."

Lucy looked baffled. She wasn't bright enough to figure out she was being played, but she had enough sense to put together the puzzle pieces he'd laid out for her. Marriage equals love, which she apparently understood, and Weston was married. Ipso facto, Weston was loved, and she wanted what the father had. She wanted to be loved that way, despite having no idea what that meant. She looked in King's eyes. "And you would marry me?"

"Absolutely." The conviction in King's voice was convincing, but not quite enough.

"Why?"

King smiled. "You have pretty eyes, for one."

Lucy looked away, the faint bit of cheek not covered in fur revealing her blush.

"And like you said. You're smart. I'm dumb. You're strong. I'm weak. You're Nguoi Rung . . . and I want to be." Lucy looked at him again. "What's not to love?"

"But I am a princess here. A favored child."

"You listened to Weston speaking to me in the cave, right?"

Lucy nodded.

"You heard my name. What he called me?"

Lucy nodded, then whispered. "King . . ."

"You may be a princess here, but marrying me will make you—"

"A queen!" Lucy's smile was wide now. "How we get married?"

"An alpha has to do it."

Lucy bit her lip. "He won't."

"We can ask."

She looked unsure.

"The worst he can do is say no."

This seemed to resonate with Lucy. She nodded. "Okay." She headed for the door.

"Wait," King said.

Lucy turned.

"It's customary for the male to ask for the father's permission to marry," King said quickly. He tried to ignore how screwed up this conversation was. It was almost as though Weston were multiple people. Father. Alpha. Weston. What else was he to these people? God? "If he says yes to you, I still have to ask him. Then he can marry us right away."

Lucy stalked back into the room. She picked up the stone blade and leaned in close to King's face. She stared into his eyes, as though looking for some betrayal in his words. King returned her stare with a smile. She grunted and cut his bonds. "Stay with me."

King rubbed his wrists and stretched his arms. He had no intention of fleeing. Lucy could catch and kill him as easily as she no doubt did Bishop. While he would have liked nothing better than to escape into the jungle, Lucy was taking him to the one place he wanted to go more—to Sara. In the face of death he realized he would regret not getting the chance to get to know her without gunfights, explosions, ape-men, and bioweapons of mass destruction. But that could only be done if he first rescued her and then found some way to complete the mission.

As King walked he felt something solid in his pants pocket. He'd been unconscious when they took his weapons, but something had been missed. He searched his memory for what he kept in the pocket. The problem was, he didn't normally keep anything in that pocket. He slid his hand inside, feeling hard plastic and two metal points. His hand flinched out of the pocket as his body remembered the shock that normally followed a physical connection with the metal points. He didn't have to look to know it was Trung's taser. The Nguoi Rung who had searched him had either not noticed it or thought nothing of it. He wasn't sure if it would even work on the thick furred body of a Neanderthal hybrid, but it was something.

King stood and walked out of the room with Lucy. As they started down the curved staircase he'd been dragged up, Lucy stopped and turned to him, a gleam of teenage mischief in her eyes. "If he says no, I'm still going to eat you."

FORTY-SIX

Sara fell back and toppled to the stone floor. Her eyes stared in horror at the knife in Weston's hand. Then she realized she was leaning back on her hands. Her *freed* hands. He'd cut her bonds. Weston sheathed the knife on his belt and drew the pistol hanging on the other side. He pointed the weapon at Sara and waved it up and down.

"Go ahead. Stand," he said, "and feast your eyes on the wonders of Mount Meru."

Sensing Weston had no intention of killing her, she stood and did as he asked. The truth was, since her first glimpse of the otherworldly spectacle, she wanted nothing more than a chance to drink it all in. As she turned and faced perhaps the oldest and most magnificent wonder of the world, she nearly fell to her knees. The sight was dizzying—more overwhelming than staring into the Grand Canyon. Not only because of its beauty and size, but also because she stood on a precipice several hundred feet above the site.

A city, more beautiful than any she'd seen constructed by modern man, stretched out before her. It was clearly ancient in its arrangement, with smaller dwellings encircling the perimeter and more ominous structures growing in size toward the city's core. With each rise in structure size, a wall separated one part of the city from the next in true old-world galleried fashion. That the city had been founded on a hill beneath a mountain added to the upward rise of each gallery. The architecture had an Asian feel, but it was clearly the inspiration for the first Asian builders, who must have seen this city with their own eyes before setting to work. Everything was constructed from stone. Some structures appeared to have been seamlessly carved out of the very mountain itself. Others were built from large stone blocks, fit snugly together. The only sign of degradation was that several of the structures' roofs had rotted and caved in. But just as many appeared to have fresh roofs with newly hewn planks that glowed brightly in the aqua light.

And the light itself was perhaps the most exquisite attribute of the place. It glowed, as though conjured through some arcane magic, from massive crystals descending from the roof, three hundred feet high. Bundles of crystals clung to the ceiling, but a few, the largest of the bunch, stretched from ceiling to floor, putting the giant crystals discovered in Chihuahua Mexico's Naica Mine to shame. But the light did not generate from the crystals, it was merely amplified and cast out by them. The light source beaming itself onto the crystals was the same here as it was everywhere else in the world. Hundreds of small holes had been carved into the mountain above the tree line. Sun streaked through the holes, struck the crystals, and refracted throughout the chambers. A passing cloud caused the light to flicker. The most beautiful light display filled the chamber as the moving light split into colorful rainbows that danced across every surface.

Following one of the rainbow shards of light to the city below, Sara noticed several patches of green. Trees grew. Flower beds, too. All were manicured and stunning. But the city was not inhabited. It was a living ghost city.

And the city truly felt dead, despite the obvious new growth. At first Sara thought the otherworldly feel of the place was influencing her sense of undead dread. The growing feeling of unease peaked. Something inside her mind, like an elastic suddenly springing free from a snag, snapped back into place. She staggered, trying to make sense of the change.

Weston saw her stumble and took hold of her shoulder. "Are you all right?"

Sara held her hand up, but could not yet speak. She focused on standing. Then when she felt sure she wouldn't tumble over the edge, she tried to get a handle on her senses.

She breathed. She listened. She felt . . . less.

Sara's eyes went wide.

Smell was smell and sound was sound. She could feel nothing but the hand on her shoulder and ground beneath her feet. She sensed the world in five separate categories now, not a continuous mash-up.

"What is it?" Weston asked, sounding more interested than concerned.

"I have a neurological disorder. I feel and see sounds, sometimes smells."

"And now?"

"Gone."

Weston chuckled. "Amazing, isn't it?"

Sara's eyes widened as she surveyed the ancient natural structures. "It's the crystals."

"Indeed." Weston straightened his stance, proud like a child showing a new bike to friends. "Before I came to the Annamites, I was something of a postmodern hippie. I wore these crystals. Quartz. I'm not sure if I ever truly believed the crystals did what they were supposed to. I just thought they were pretty."

He took a deep breath, holding the air in his lungs, and then let it free with a smile. "Buddhism assigned quartz as one of their seven precious substances. Native Americans called them 'the brain cells of Grandmother Earth.' Ancient Indian Sanskrit reveres them as 'the gem that removes fear.' Throughout history, mankind has been—incorrectly— attributing power to regular quartz crystals. I believe the crystals of Mount Meru were the inspiration for the belief of crystal healing throughout human history. The difference is that these really work."

Sara's mind couldn't help but hypothesize. "Maybe it's the vibrations . . ."

"What was that?"

Sara's answer was more thinking aloud than an actual response. "All matter exists in three states. Gas, liquid, and solid. The atoms in a gas are loose. Free to shift and move about. In a liquid the atoms are condensed—squeezed together—but are still able to move about. But with solids the atoms are compressed—squeezed against each other and unable to move. In most structures, like stone, the collection of atoms is random. But with crystals, like quartz, the atoms are . . . organized. Motifs and lattices. It's like the atoms are trapped inside tiny boxes, bouncing off tightly enclosed walls. With trillions of atoms all following this same microscopic, unified pattern, they give off an imperceptible but powerful vibration.

"I doubt they're capable of healing disease or injuries, but the human mind is a network of neurons. Electrical impulses moving along paths crisscross the mind. But it's not orderly. People stutter. They forget. The mind can think, but it can't organize itself. Neurons collide. Get lost. Pathways break. How the mind really works is still a mystery. But we do know the mind can be a chaotic place. Perhaps these crystals align the neural pathways?"

"Like redesigning Boston in a grid."

"Exactly." Sara looked at Weston and immediately felt a surge of guilt. This man was her captor and threatened their mission. She glanced at her outbreak meter. Still orange. Despite her growing self-loathing, she had one more question. "Are they quartz?"

"They're part quartz, of that I'm sure," Weston said, "but they taste of salt if you lick them."

"That's why the air is so fresh. They're ionizing it."

Weston nodded and took another deep breath. "Invigorating."

Sara didn't think so. It was as though the crystals in the cave, having realigned her neural pathways, had corrected the way she sensed the world, making her whole and healthy. As the detachment from the sensory input she'd been born with grew more profound, nausea twisted in her gut. She had never experienced the world through normal senses. People suffering from a blocked ear often found themselves disoriented and dizzy. Sometimes sick. Sara thought this was far worse. And for the first time in her life she realized that having the mixed-up senses that caused her to lose sleep, appear spacey, and get annoyed at small things other people failed to notice, wasn't a curse. It was who she was.

How she'd been made.

And like a person switching abruptly from espresso to decaf, she didn't handle the transition with grace. The room swirled before her eyes, moving back and forth like the carriage of a typewriter in the hands of a frantic author. She fought the urge to fall to her knees. To puke. She couldn't show Weston her weakness.

She took a deep breath. The air, at least, was cool, clean, and well oxygenated. With each breath she felt her emotions level out. As her mind cleared, she realized that distraction had been her key to ignoring the world through her previously cross-wired senses. She would make it her key to ignoring a world experienced through normal senses, too.

She opened her eyes and looked down over the edge. A river flowed around the outskirts of the city. It entered through the far wall, flowing from a tunnel that had been arched with large stones fit perfectly together. The flow wrapped around the city, nearly all the way around, before exiting through a second tunnel, identical to the first. It was a moat, a fast-moving wall of water. It seemed more like a fortress than a city, and for a moment she wondered how the Neanderthal civilization had been wiped out.

Competition, she thought. They had been starved to death as humanity moved into the surrounding area, using up resources. Afraid of annihilation, the Neanderthals must have hunkered down while their population dwindled until just a few were left. And then . . . either a hyperevolution or genetic assimilation over a few short generations led to something different. Something capable of wiping out entire villages.

A superpredator.

But when Weston entered the picture, when he brought his human genetics and skills to the superpredator table, the small group of superpredators had entered a season of plasticity. The population boomed. And would continue to grow until conflict with the outside world, with humanity, brought the Neanderthal to the brink of extinction once again. *Of course, they'll have the run of the planet soon enough,* she thought.

Another flicker of rainbow light caught her attention and brought her eyes to the city's center where atop the peak of the hill, a tall temple stood. Five towers rose from the temple, each looking like a serrated stone spear tip. The design seemed familiar to Sara. She'd seen it before. On a postcard from a college roommate who'd traveled . . . where? Then it came to her. "Angkor Wat."

"Very good," Weston said.

She glanced at him and realized she might be able to heave him over the edge. Then she saw the gun in his crossed arms, still trained on her. He'd thought the same thing.

"Have you heard," Weston said, "that Angkor Wat was built to symbolically represent Mount Meru, home of the Hindu gods? That's actually incorrect. Most people think the spires represent mountains, but what they don't know is that Angkor Wat is a crude facsimile of the original temple constructed *here*. The first humans to reach this far into Asia were enslaved. Escapees spread the story of this place to humanity and a religion was born, or at least added to. *This* is the legendary Mount Meru. Revered by Hindu and Buddhist alike. The axis of all real and mythological universes. Surya the sun god is said to circumambulate Mount Meru daily.

"As you can see . . ." Weston motioned his arms at the array of circular holes cut into the mountain through which the sun spilled. "The sun does indeed walk around the mountain each and every day. This is the home of gods long forgotten, watered down, and driven nearly to extinction."

"Gods can be driven to extinction?" Sara said, surprised by the sarcasm in her voice. The last thing she wanted to do was antagonize Weston.

But he seemed unfazed. He merely grinned. Perhaps being separated from humanity for so long made him forget what certain tones of voice meant.

"All gods have low points," Weston said. "The Titans were defeated by Zeus. Set trapped Osiris in a coffin and sent him adrift in the sea. Jesus found himself nailed to a cross. There is, of course, one staggering difference between them and the gods residing here." He looked at Sara with excited eyes. "These are real. And I am their father."

"But no one lives here," Sara said, ignoring a fresh wave of nausea.

"Soon enough," Weston said. "I have forbidden the children to live here until the city is fully restored. With only a few remaining roofs to be replaced, it will not be long before this chamber echoes with the sounds of Nguoi Rung song again."

Sara pictured Lucy singing opera and nearly laughed. It was an absurd image. Even with her half-human parentage she seemed so brutal and savage that Sara doubted any of them could carry a tune. But they wouldn't be singing operas, they'd be cheering their newfound dominance over the planet. "How can you believe Neanderthals have more right to exist on Earth? You're human, too."

Weston grew angry. "Neanderthals and humans have *equal* rights to live. By setting you free I might save the human race, but I would damn theirs!"

"By choosing not to let us leave you might be damning the human race. More than six billion people." Sara sighed. She could see that Weston would never trust her to leave with the cure. The man was a stubborn fool too in love with his bastard children to care about anyone else. "You'll never be one of them."

Weston calmed, and for a moment, looked sad. "True. I have become as close as I can to being one of them. I have embraced their ways. I have learned to read and write their language. I have unlocked their buried history and mapped their world. In a way, I am more like the Neanderthals who built this place than the mothers of my children. What's important is that my children accept me . . . just as they will come to accept you." He motioned with the gun to the side of the cliff. "Move."

Sara nervously approached the edge. His last statement implied that he planned on keeping her alive and captive indefinitely, yet Weston's sanity had left him long ago, and he now had her walking toward a several-hundred-foot drop. Sara let out a small sigh of relief as she neared the edge. Descending along the wall of the massive cavern was a stone staircase cut into the interior mountain wall. All but invisible from the side, it came clearly into view from above. But if he wasn't going to kill her, what did he intend?

"What do you want with me?" she asked, starting down the staircase.

"I want to restore the Neanderthals to their former glory. They were an amazing people. A civilized people, far beyond the warring Homo sapiens of their time. But to do that, they need to learn."

Sara paused and looked back. "You want me to teach them?"

"Who better?"

"Umm, anyone."

"There is no one else here."

"King is—"

"—a killer," Weston said. "And I fear he will not give up the fight until *he* is killed."

Sara continued down the staircase without another word. Weston was right. She could do little to fight Weston, let alone his superstrong and superfast children. Escape, for her, was impossible.

Or was it? She hadn't seen any Nguoi Rung since being led into the cave system. And the city was abandoned. Alone with Weston, this might be her only real chance of escape.

But she needed to find out what his cure for Brugada was. She wouldn't leave without it.

She glanced back at Weston.

Given his size, strength, and no doubt, ferocity, coupled with the fact that he carried a knife and a gun, Sara's life was in Weston's hands, for now. She wondered if she'd see the outside world again. She longed for it now. She wanted her screwed-up senses back. She wanted to return to the noise and chaos of the city. And she wanted to see King again. Her thoughts lingered on King. Not on his body. Not on their mission. Not on his voice or his eyes or any of the other things women might think of when they thought about men. She focused on his uncanny ability to stay alive in the worst of situations, hoping to channel some of that confidence and cunning into herself.

If she didn't . . . she'd be a slave for the rest of her life.

Or dead within the hour.

FORTY-SEVEN

A lone hybrid Neanderthal crept through the jungle, avoiding twigs and dry leaves that might give away his position. As a sentry it was his duty to patrol the area directly surrounding the settlement. There were other sentries keeping watch, some on the ground, some in the trees, all keeping an eye out for dangerous animals or human military units that might pose a threat. He looked forward to the day when the renovations to Meru City were complete and their people could move out of the settlement and into the mountain itself. He had been chosen as chief lookout because of his keen eyesight. He would keep an eye on the city from high in the temple—the last line of defense against those who might manage to slip past their outer defenses. His days of sneaking around the jungle were almost at an end.

The hybrid stopped and sniffed at the air. Something unfamiliar had passed by recently. But he couldn't place it. Perhaps an animal, or even one of the old mothers? They often smelled foreign as they roamed the jungle, killing and eating whatever they could find. He envied the old mothers sometimes. They were free to hunt and eat what they wanted. Red had taken him to hunt once, when he was still young. They found two human women fetching water at the river. He'd tasted, and enjoyed, both, washing the blood from his hands and mouth before returning home. Father would have been upset because *he* was human, but he was not like the others. He was family.

He pushed thoughts of his parents from his mind. The internal battle between the old and new worlds of his people would distract him from his duty. His nose and ears lacked the sensitivity that his eyes possessed, so he stood perfectly still and observed the world around him. Light shimmered as the canopy overhead swayed in a light afternoon breeze. Branches groaned, leaves rustled, and the denizens of the forest sang out. Everything sounded normal. But the smell lingered.

Then he saw it. A piece of torn fabric hanging on a dead branch. He walked to the branch and picked up the cloth. With the fabric pressed against his nose, he breathed in deeply. The smell filled his nostrils. Someone had been here . . . someone *human* had made it past. Humans were really no threat; even armed with guns they rarely put up a fight. He never felt the need to carry a weapon of his own, though sometimes they used their enemies' weapons against them as they had during the attack on the VPLA camp. Of course, Father taught them that some human weapons were powerful enough to destroy entire mountains.

Even one human making it into the settlement could be disastrous.

He thought for a moment about hunting down the invader on his own. With no one around he could have his fill and bury the evidence, or throw the body in the river. But he decided against it. There was no way to know how many humans there were.

With his powerful lungs and broad chest, the guards back in the settlement would hear his call and know that someone had made it inside the perimeter. Their entire population would set out to find the humans and would no doubt round them up within minutes. He took a deep breath and then . . .

"Hey, buddy." It was just a whisper, but the sound spun the hybrid like a top.

Expecting to see his foe approaching by land, the hybrid

failed to see the figure descending from *above* until it was too late. Before any warning could be shouted, a spear fashioned from a straight branch sharpened to a point burst from his stomach, thrust through from behind. The hybrid's eyes went wide as the plummeting shadow resolved into a mud-covered, nearly naked human female. Her eyes showed bright white and blue from behind her darkened mud covering. And in her hands . . . another spear, thrust out toward his open mouth.

Queen's spear pierced the back of the hybrid's throat, severed vertebrae, and exited through the back of its neck. The creature fell back, convulsed, and then laid still. Queen pulled her spear from the hybrid's mouth as Rook stood from his hiding place behind the bush. He retrieved his spear from the hybrid's back, twisting and turning it to loosen the body's grip.

Without a word shared between them, they dragged the body behind the bush and covered it with leaves. The job done, they picked up their spears and began climbing. Queen went up quickly, stopping every now and then to give Rook a hand. After two minutes of hard climbing, they were in the canopy, invisible to the world below, but facing a new group of dangers.

Moving through the trees was slow and nerve-racking. A misstep might mean falling fifty feet to a very quick end or, at the least, a painful debilitation. They were also in unfamiliar territory. Fighting in the trees. Hiding in the trees. Queen had some experience, but given Rook's size, he hadn't spent much time climbing trees since he was a kid. They had considered going separate ways, but decided against it. They fought better together. They had also considered staying on the ground where they would have been more mobile, yet easier to spot. But recon was their goal at this point, not infiltration, so they opted for a high perch that would allow them a bird's-eye view. Perhaps they were too used to satellite imagery, but both could more easily assess a situation when seeing it from above.

They made their way, without incident, to the edge of the forest, where the hybrid settlement began. After working their way into the branches of a tree whose bark most closely matched the drying mud on their bodies, they turned their attention to the community below. Rook summed up *his* assessment in one word. "Shit."

They looked down on a large clearing at the base of the mountain. Perhaps fifty large huts filled the area. A line of caves pocked the side of the mountain. Fires glowed and cast off streams of smoke that billowed up and dispersed into the ominous rain clouds above. Animals paced in cages built from stone and wood—two tigers and four bears—and two crocodiles were fenced inside a small pond. But it wasn't the collection of predators that surprised Rook, it was the Neanderthal population.

"There must be more than a thousand of them," Rook said.

Queen nodded. She wouldn't bother counting. As the population moved about, some building, some foraging, some gathering, the total number would be impossible to discern. "You said Weston was here for only fifteen years, right?"

"Yeah . . . ," Rook said. "But he also said these guys matured and had kids by age three."

"So these . . . things . . . are all fifteen years old and under? A bunch of kids?"

Rook shook his head. "In our years they're kids. But they're not human. They're not kids. They're as adult as you and me, and much more deadly."

They watched in silence for several minutes as two elephants entered the camp, pulling fallen trees behind them. The trees were quickly cleared of limbs and then, using stone blades and raw strength, a group of large males began splitting the wood into long planks. Within fifteen minutes, the trees had been split into ten planks each. The elephants returned to the jungle with their keepers, and the hybrid males who had cut the wood carried it away. Two men carried each long stack of ten planks, nearly the equivalent weight of the trees they had been hacked from, one on each end.

"They're not even exerting themselves," he said.

"Look where they're going," she said. The male hybrids headed into the largest cave and disappeared into the darkness. "Why would they need all that wood *inside* a mountain?"

"I'm telling you," he said, looking at the mountain. "As many as we see out here, we'll find more in there. They're like ants. If they have King and Pawn, they'll be in there."

"If they're not dead already."

Rook cast a serious glance in Queen's direction. "Don't even think it."

She looked away from him and nodded. She could be a ruthless and efficient killer, but that didn't mean she didn't care about her teammates. It was hard to stay positive when the odds of survival, let alone rescue, seemed so insurmountable. Queen forced herself to look on the bright side; she'd already killed two of them. She could kill more.

"What's the plan?" he asked.

Queen looked up at the sky and then to Rook. The ferocious gleam in her eyes returned. "Wait until night, pray it doesn't rain, and then set the captives free."

FORTY-EIGHT

Knight read through the pages, enraptured by the text as though it were a good novel. The story, interpreted and annotated by Weston as he put the puzzle pieces together, was gripping.

It was an unknown history of both Homo sapiens and Neanderthal. The pages chronicled the rise of the human race, thousands of years of peaceful coexistence and commingling bloodlines, until something changed. Whether it was a leap in evolution or the will of a single human leader the story didn't say, but one thing was clear—humanity became violent. The Neanderthals had done their best to defend themselves, and despite their greater numbers and technological advances, they had little skill with war. Over generations, the Neanderthals were pushed north, out of Africa and into Asia, where they fled east.

They fled so fast, in fact, that the human race could not keep up. The Neanderthals chose to settle in the remote Annamite range because food and shelter were abundant, the terrain was easily defendable and . . . they found peace within the mountain. Mount Meru.

It spoke of giant crystals that healed the mind, of the construction of the necropolis from the bones of their dead, and of the building of a temple dedicated to the crystals and the god that provided them with this new home.

Three pages later, the story took on a new tone. Humans had been spotted. Scouts. Easily killed, but they knew more would come. The Neanderthals adopted a new form of leadership that Knight thought, despite their advanced civilization, was still quite primal . . . quite Neanderthal. The largest, most aggressive males would lead. Not the smartest. Not the most cunning. The warriors. They were preparing for war. The translation ended there. Knight read the last line.

> To the largest and fiercest among us we bestow the
> rights of leadership that we might survive what is to
> come. It is to be taught, throughout the generations,
> so that we might become warriors, so that we become
> what the humans fear most.
>   This is it!!

Knight turned the page, but Weston had stopped writing. It was his final entry and Knight realized it was most likely made the day he left everything on the floor of the cave and . . . then what?

The answer struck Knight, causing him to laugh. "The devil." Weston saw his chance to claim leadership. If his captors still lived by these rules, and Weston was a large man, he could assert his dominance and take control. But had he succeeded or was he dead? He hadn't returned to this place, that was for sure, but why was a mystery.

He placed the notebook back on the floor and shuffled through the large pages of wall rubbings. As he looked at the symbols he marveled at the ancient knowledge on display here. So much potential. If not for Homo sapiens, how high might the Neanderthal race have soared? They appeared on Earth long before modern humans and apparently got off to a good head start. But they hadn't developed a thirst for blood.

A folded piece of paper fell from the notebook. He picked up the page and opened it. Filling its surface was a detailed map of both the exterior and interior of Mount Meru. Knight longed for a YOU ARE HERE label, but even without one he was quickly able to locate the maze drawn on the map. An exit on the other side of the maze led up toward a chamber that didn't look possible. The drawing showed a city, with a familiar-looking temple at its core, surrounded by what looked like giant crystals hanging from the ceiling.

The crystals.

Knight looked at the giant crystal lighting the maze and remembered the Neanderthal account of crystals that healed the mind. "No way," he said, but it had to be true. Having seen the necropolis and read the Neanderthals' history, he believed they were indeed capable of such a thing. But what made the decision to head toward the city easiest was that it led further away from the old mothers, Neanderthal 2.0. He wanted nothing to do with them. Had he been a large man, he might try to assert his dominance, but he was a plaything in the hands of the savage women.

He certainly couldn't take charge, but Rook, or Bishop . . . they were just the men for the job.

Knight folded the map into a neat square and pocketed it. He limped his way through the second half of the maze and hobbled up the staircase that led to a tunnel opposite the one he had entered through. As he stepped into the tunnel, darkness surrounded him.

"Damnit." He'd left the bandanna saturated with glowing algae on the other side of the room . . . all the way back through the maze.

Screw it, he thought, then headed up into the darkness.

He stopped after only a few feet.

He'd heard something.

A squeak.

Then another. He held his breath and listened. The sound of tiny claws on stone filled the tunnel ahead.

A rodent.

Knight felt the thing hit his foot. It squeaked again, and then ran past. He saw it run down the staircase and enter the maze without hesitation. It was either out for a jog or something was chasing it. His fears were confirmed when a deep growl accompanied by heavy footfalls approached from the darkness beyond. Whatever was chasing the rat would find him first.

FORTY-NINE

Sara's footsteps echoed on the cobblestone street, bouncing off tall stone buildings and the mountain ceiling high above. Weston, being barefoot, walked in silence. His stride was confident and calm, the way a kid walks in his own house; every turn known, every contour familiar.

He really does belong here, Sara thought. She would have been happy to let Weston and his little clan live out their lives here, too, but she knew without a doubt that he could never be convinced of that.

Seeing the city up close, the architecture took on a new shape. Asian meets ancient Rome. Elegance amalgamated with power. Beautiful and chilling. The curved roofs sported long corner beams. The walls of the buildings were constructed from thick stones, perhaps once polished, but now rough. The larger buildings, with overhanging platforms, were supported by rows of columns that smacked of Rome's early Doric order. They had already passed through four of the five galleries, each one separated from the next by a large, gated stone wall.

Light shifted and rolled through the chamber, climbing buildings and sliding across streets. Weston had explained that clouds were moving by the mountain, shifting the sun's beams on the giant crystals. Sara's mother had hung crystals in the windows of her childhood home and the effect had been marvelous, but they were a joke compared to this. The cool, crisp air filled the nose like New England in the fall.

The walk had been long, yet after days of unsure footing in the jungle, Sara found the hard, smooth stone beneath her feet a welcome change. If not for the circumstances of her visit to Mount Meru she would have loved to explore. As it was, she was totally tuning out Weston's ongoing history lesson about the decline of the Neanderthal civilization. Apparently, the entire history of the species was recorded in another chamber, going back to a time before Homo sapiens existed. The temptation to become enraptured with the place was intense. The history, the mystery of it all. But Sara's mind remained preoccupied with something even more glorious—escape.

So far, she hadn't gotten beyond, "Take off my boots so he can't hear me running." The rest of her mental energy focused on learning the layout of the city. There could be no hesitation when she made her move, no delay in choosing a path. She felt confident she could find her way out through the gates, working through back alleys and avoiding open space, but once out of the city her plan fell flat. Climbing the stairs again wasn't an option. She'd be exposed. Weston could easily catch her. And she'd be headed straight back into the den of her enemies. The only other option she'd come up with had her jumping in the subterranean river and letting it sweep her away . . . wherever it went.

A sudden tap on her shoulder jolted her from her thoughts.

"Lost in thought, are we?" Weston asked, pushing the handgun against her shoulder. He could tell she wasn't listening to everything he said. Who could blame her? She had to be overwhelmed by the place, just as he was when he'd first stumbled upon it. And years of constant work had nearly returned Meru to its former glory—a city fit for gods. He pointed up. "We're almost there."

Sara looked up. She'd been so distracted by the buildings around her and plans of escape that she'd failed to notice the temple rising high above them. The fifth and final gate stood before them, open like the others. Sara took a step back. She had no desire to enter the temple. She knew it was the end of their trip and the beginning of her nightmare. But with the gun to her back, what choice did she have?

She walked through the open thirty-foot-tall arched gate, noticing the restoration work on its two massive doors had yet to be completed. No longer blocked by the fifth gallery wall, the temple stood boldly before her. Rows of balustrades surrounded the outer perimeter of the structure proper. Each vertical column featured a serpent wrapped around it, each different from the next. An entrance lay just beyond the balustrades. They walked through it, into a long courtyard featuring palm trees and flowering bushes. Lit by the colorful crystals above, the lush inner court erased the dire emotions brought on by the rows of snakes outside.

But Sara's sense of dread remained regardless of the inner temple's beauty. Weston had fallen silent when he should be talking the most. This place was no doubt home to a thousand stories worth telling. Yet, Weston simply pointed the way and kept his jaw clenched tight. Now *he* was distracted by his thoughts . . . by his plans. Was he simply hoping to change her heart by the power of the place, or was he taking her to a cell? There was no way to know.

She decided to see if the man could be softened, or at least understood. As they walked across the courtyard, she said, "Tell me about your family."

"They're here, with me."

"I mean before . . ." She waved her hands around at the city. ". . . all this. Before Vietnam. What were your parents like?"

Weston glanced at her, suspicion filling his eyes. He forced a grin. "My father was an alcoholic, abusive prick."

Strike one, Sara thought.

At the end of the courtyard, a steep staircase rose fifty feet up to where a massive rectangular entryway beckoned them into the temple's innards. Above the entryway, the five

towers—arranged in a quincunx, like five dots on a die—
jutted toward the chamber's ceiling, now only one hundred
feet above. The five layers of each tower curved up and in,
coming to a point. They looked more like serrated spear tips
now than they had from above. The place screamed of danger. Stunning to look at, but hiding an inner darkness. Perhaps
there was a reason humans had turned on their Neanderthal
counterparts?

"Up," Weston instructed when they reached the stairs.
Each step was a foot tall and a half foot deep. She took the
stairs slowly, using her hands and feet to keep from falling
back.

"What about a wife? You're wearing a wedding ring."

Weston stopped. She looked back at him. His frown said
it all: this topic was off-limits.

She quickly switched gears. "What about your mother?"

Weston's voice sounded lighter when he spoke. "My
mother . . . was an angel. And a good cook. Not at all concerned with health, though. Her cure-all for anything from
the common cold to the nastiest flu was apple pie, vanilla ice
cream, and a chocolate frappe. It's a wonder all that sugar
fueling the virus or killing my immune system didn't land
me in the hospital."

"Was she a stay-at-home mom?"

"At first, until my father left. Then she put her biology
degree to good use and became a zoo caretaker. She fos-
tered my love of the natural world."

At the top of the stairs Sara looked into the open maw of
the temple. The hallway stretched forward for fifty feet, where
it stopped under the central tower. Several skylights lit the
hall with cubes of light. She turned toward Weston as he finished ascending the stairs. "What species did she care for?"

"Gorillas, actually. Magnificent creatures."

"Huh," Sara said. "Ironic."

As soon as the word hit her own ears she realized the
implication and closed her eyes.

Strike two.

"What?" Weston blinked like he'd been slapped. His voice rose. "What did you just say?"

He stepped toward her, his face flushing. "Ironic? *Ironic!* You take my children for apes? They can speak. They can think. They have a *moral code*. That's more than you can say for most of the human race!"

"I didn't mean—"

"Yes . . ." He took her shoulder in his meaty hand and pushed her around. "You did."

With one more shove they entered the hallway. Two doors on either side of the hall led to square rooms arranged in a cruciform. Three steps staggered down the sides of each room's walls, plummeting into deep fishponds stocked with very large fish of a multitude of species.

Past the cruciform of rooms, at the end of the hallway, rose another set of stairs, this one leading out of the temple roof, into open air and the central tower itself. Again, Weston's instructions were simple but now punctuated with a shove. "Up."

Each step displayed a line of ancient pictorial text scrolling from one end to the other as though they were meant to be read as the steps were climbed. The Asian-style script was plain but artistic. Sara stopped on the fifth step up and traced the lines of the script with her finger. "Do you know what it means?"

Weston stopped next to her. "They're curses."

Sara looked up the stairs. The script seemed endless. "Curses on who?"

"On you. On me. On all of humanity." Weston waved the gun at her. "Keep moving."

A sick feeling burrowed into her stomach and made a home for itself. This whole temple, this whole city, had been founded on a hatred for humanity. And she was being led to its core. She didn't believe in ghosts, but she'd sensed the spirit of the place since passing through the first gallery gate. It wasn't just Weston that had her spooked. It was the entire city.

Homo sapiens were never meant to tread here.

They were not welcome.

Sara moved quickly up the stairs, not wanting to look at the script anymore and fearing the city might suddenly come to life and fling her down the steep incline. Reaching the top, she found herself out of breath and facing an average-sized wooden door. A relief had been carved into the wood, similar to the ones worn by many of the city's buildings and shrines. Yet this one was a recent addition. The wood of the door, like that of the newer roofs, shone brightly against the dull gray stone of the temple. The relief featured a single face—Weston's.

He stopped next to her, looking at the relief. "A bit crude, but effective, don't you think? They've only just begun to re-form their culture, yet their artistic skills—" Weston looked her in the eyes. "Their *artistic skills* seem to be intrinsic." Weston opened the door, motioned with the gun, and said, "In."

Sara complied.

The circular room she found herself in was one part holy temple and one part caveman bachelor pad—no doubt Weston's home away from home. Light poured in through circular holes that vented the ceiling. She realized this inner chamber was a miniature-sized version of the mountain above. It even had a crystal chandelier that reflected and amplified the light throughout the room.

At the center of the room, below the crystal lamp, was a fire pit. The surrounding walls were covered with several ancient carvings depicting scenes of human sacrifice, spirits, and strange rituals. Sara's eyes froze on a relief of several Neanderthal men holding a human woman down upon an altar. It became clear in that moment what the Neanderthals had done to offend the humans. Thousands of years ago, the Neanderthals would have been much more "human" than the group she'd seen. More hairy, maybe, but not nearly as strong. A hyperevolutionary leap had done that during their time in isolation. But they had been wicked, practicing what appeared to be magic of some kind, sacrificing humans, performing rituals. *Perhaps in secret at first,* she thought, *but they must have been found out.* And the Homo sapiens, horrified, did what they did best—exterminated.

She turned away from the relief and saw a modern-looking bed. Fashioned from wood and covered with a homemade mattress. Weston removed the belt holding his holster and knife and placed it on the bed. The red band of flesh on his waist revealed the belt was a smidge too snug. He sat next to the belt and scanned the walls of the room. "Before I got here, I thought the Neanderthals were victims of human ignorance and violence. But this room opened my eyes. They did awful things to humanity. True crimes. And they paid for it."

"Then why are you protecting them?"

"At the end of World War Two, did we kill all the Nazis? Did we continue dropping nukes on Japan? Of course not. We helped them rebuild. They were wrong and they got trounced. But the Neanderthals have never had a chance to make up for what they did wrong."

"And now they do, right? By allowing the human race to go extinct?"

"That's not my fault!" Weston was back on his feet, pacing and agitated. "Humanity is doing that to itself."

"How convenient for you." She shook her hands at him. "Just give me the damn cure and let me go!"

Weston paused his pacing, surprised by the tone and volume of her voice. For a moment he looked at her with different eyes, the same way he looked at King. Like a threat. "I'm afraid you would not enjoy receiving the cure the way I did."

Sara thought about the implications. About what she knew of Weston's time in the jungle. "From the old mothers . . ." Her hand went to her mouth as she realized the truth. "It's an STD?"

"A filthy way of saying it is transmitted through the blood, but essentially correct. That is one way it can be transferred. I have not, clearly, been able to study how it works in detail, but that is my best theory."

"Something is transferred," Sara said, her mind on the hunt for Brugada's cure and not on the rancid-smelling man beside her. "A virus, most likely, that modifies the DNA and disables whatever gene allows Brugada to become a killer. It's eloquent, really. An avian flu virus delivers the active gene and a second shuts it off. Viral competition."

"Interesting. The male Nguoi Rung population died off quite quickly. But the females survived. At some point, they contracted a virus—your competing virus—and it altered their genes, protecting them and future generations from Brugada. If not, the Neanderthal race would have ended with the deaths of the old mothers."

Sara's face brightened as she understood. "It makes sense. What were your symptoms?"

He thought for a moment. "Swollen glands. A slight fever. And a rash that eventually blistered, crusted over, scabbed, and healed. Really quite minor."

Sarah couldn't believe what she was hearing. It wasn't just like an STD, it *was* an STD. Weston had just described a classic case of herpes; granted, most likely a new strain, but herpes nonetheless. What made this even more believable was that herpes was frequently used in gene therapy, as it readily accessed and altered the genetic code. Several lab-engineered herpes-based cures were already in development for HIV, cancer, liver tumors—the list was extensive. In this case nature had done all the work, shutting down the SCN5A gene activated by the bird flu. "It's amazing."

"I'm tickled you think so, but you can wipe that look of hope from your face." Weston faced her. "I will not be sharing my blood with you and I am not a philistine, so do not think you can receive the cure from me through . . . other means."

Weston squinted suddenly, his eyes no longer meeting hers. She feared he was ogling her, but his expression was all wrong.

"What is that?" he asked. "On your wrist. It just changed color."

"It's a—" Sara froze as she looked at her outbreak meter. It glowed a deep, bloodlike red. Brugada was *out*.

The pandemic had begun.

She gasped. "No . . ."

Weston stepped forward, took her wrist, and looked at the rainbow of warm colors. "What kind of watch is this?"

Sara yanked her arm away. She held her wrist up in front of his face. "This means that the pandemic has begun. People are *dying*. You need to let me go."

Weston stared at her.

"Please," she said, her voice wavering with desperation.

"You know I can't."

Sara's fear turned to rage. "Not a philistine? You're allowing the human race to face the possibility of extinction!" She shook her head. It was useless. They'd had that conversation already. She looked at the wedding band on his finger. *Time to push his buttons,* she thought, before saying, "What about your wife? She's still out there, right?"

"I warned you not to talk about her."

"Did you love your wife? Did you ever?"

Veins appeared on Weston's forehead as he grew angry. "I said don't!" He raised the gun toward her.

The gun gave her pause, but Weston hadn't taken her all this way to shoot her. "What about children?"

Weston walked toward her, menace in his eyes.

"A daughter?"

No reaction. But she could see by the widening of his angry eyes that she was about to stumble on the truth.

"A son."

Weston paused, his eyes tearing.

"He'll be one of the first to die. Brugada affects mostly males. Let me go and I—"

"My son *is* dead. Drowned. I left him alone for ten minutes. *Ten* minutes. When I found him it was already too late.

I couldn't save him. My wife came to hate everything about me and divorced me six months later." He placed the gun's muzzle beneath her chin and raised her head so they were eye to eye. "But I found a *new* family. Everything I love is here, and I will be *damned* before I let another one of my children die when I have a chance to save them."

Strike three.

FIFTY

Pain shot up Knight's leg with every rushed step. He was in no condition to face a pissed-off Neanderthal. At full strength he didn't stand much of a chance, but in his current state it would be like a wingless fly standing up to a black widow spider. It would simply walk up to him, sink in its fangs, and be done with it. His only real chance at survival was to get lost in the maze before it found him, but that meant getting back to the middle, where all the different paths converged.

A scream reverberated through the room. As Knight reached a straightaway parallel with the entrance, he risked a quick glance back. What he saw increased his fear tenfold.

The shape was massive, more than twice his size.

The eyes blazed with raw hatred.

Bloody froth sprayed.

Muscles rippled.

The massive figure leaped from the entrance, clearing two walls and landing ten feet behind Knight.

Bishop.

But he was no longer Bishop. He was a regen.

And for Knight, unarmed and injured, that was a death sentence.

Knight didn't try to reason with Bishop. He didn't beg for mercy. He did the only thing he could do.

He ran.

But his run was closer to an awkward hop. He put more weight down on his injured leg. But as he rounded a corner, the splint struck the floor at an odd angle. The old bones wrapped around his ankle shattered. He went down hard.

He forced himself back onto his good foot. Just as he was up, Bishop came around the corner and lunged, arms outstretched for Knight's throat.

Knight dove to the side, landing with a roll, despite the shooting pains in his leg.

The speed of Bishop's charge carried him forward. In his madness he turned his face and arms toward Knight, never giving the approaching wall a second glance. He struck the foot-thick wall head-on. His neck bent at a crooked angle and *cracked*. He clenched his eyes and howled in pain for a moment. But his wounds healed quickly.

Wasting no time, Knight bolted around the next corner on his hands and knees, hoping to reach the center of the maze and duck into another channel before Bishop saw him again. If he could wait, silently, Bishop might continue his pursuit of the rat. Then again, he might stay and work the maze, as mindless as a rat. But there was no cheese treat at the end of this maze—only Knight.

The center of the maze loomed ahead, but before Knight's hopes could rise, pebbles began to fall all around him. Bishop had once again broken the rules of the maze. Knowing an attack was coming, Knight flipped onto his back.

Bishop leaped down and landed at Knight's feet, but the smaller and more skilled fighter was ready. He kicked hard against Bishop's tree trunk of a leg, and the practiced force of Knight's kick did the job. Bishop's knee bent backward with a sickening crack, toppling him forward. As he fell, Knight launched a second kick, this one connecting with Bishop's windpipe, which collapsed from the impact.

Bishop might be able to heal, but he still needed to breathe. And the wounds would take time to repair themselves.

As his regen teammate slumped to the floor, gurgling

madly, Knight crawled for the center of the room. But before he got three feet, his bad ankle was snagged. Then squeezed.

Knight screamed as the pain took hold of his body. Bishop's hand had him in a vice grip.

Fighting the pain from his tormented leg, he raised his good leg and crashed his heel down on Bishop's forearm. The impact caused Bishop's hand to open for a moment. It was all the time Knight needed. He yanked his leg free and frantically scrambled for the center of the maze.

As he crawled over Weston's charcoal rubbings, the pages slipped out from under him, slowing his progress. He wasn't going to make it.

Realizing this, Knight turned around and saw Bishop hopping out of the maze, while his twisted knee straightened and then popped into place. Knight held on to the large crystal, then pulled himself to his feet. He would make his last stand here. But there was no question as to the outcome. Knight had seen what regens did to their victims. They ate them. But it was worse than that. They didn't just kill and *then* eat. They killed *by* eating. There would be no suffocation. No killing strike. He would simply start gnawing on whatever piece of Knight's body reached his mouth first.

Knight braced himself as Bishop stepped forward on his newly healed knee. He growled and sneered, hunching as he prepared to pounce. He began his approach slowly, building speed as he stayed focused on Knight's throat.

Knight braced himself and prepared to throw a thumb into Bishop's eye, then attack his pressure points.

But the attack never finished.

Bishop's leg wobbled under him.

He fell to one knee, convulsing.

Then he retched. What looked like the spine, ribs, and flesh of a rat fell onto one of Weston's rubbings. A second heave coated everything in bile.

Bishop coughed, then sobbed, as though in agony. Then he calmed and looked at his hands. They shook. He looked up into Knight's frightened eyes. "Knight?"

"Bish?"

Bishop looked at the floor. The bile-covered rat flesh filled his gaze. "Did I do this?"

"Bishop, how—how are you okay? You were about to have me for dinner."

Bishop stood. "Sorry, I—" He stumbled backward, away from Knight. His face twisted with sudden fury, and he eyed Knight like a fat kid before a Happy Meal and stepped forward. He stopped, gagged, and held his head. "Knight . . ."

"Come closer!" Knight reached out and took Bishop's hand, pulling him to the center of the room. "Feel better?"

"Yeah . . . A lot better." Bishop shook his head and blinked his eyes. "What's happening?"

Knight placed his hand against the large crystal rising from the floor. "It's the crystal. Has to be. Weston—"

Bishop's eyes went wide. "You met Weston?"

"No . . . Did you? He's alive?" Knight looked at Bishop's haunted eyes. "Did he make you . . ."

Bishop nodded. "His granddaughter nearly took my head clean off. Wasn't quite clean enough, I guess. But she's not human. She's—"

"Neanderthal." Knight pointed out the notebook on the floor. "His journal. He wrote about the old mothers, his children, these crystals."

Bishop eyed the large chunk of partial quartz.

"The Neanderthals believed the crystals could heal the mind."

Bishop drew his knife and looked at Knight, who now looked a little concerned. Bishop smiled. "It's for the rock." He stabbed the knife hard into the crystal. It dented, but nothing more. He swung again, aiming for a crack. A chunk the size of his thumb fell to the stone floor. He reached down and picked it up. "Just stay there."

With the crystal clenched in his hand, Bishop walked backward, away from the crystal. He walked past the rat remains, where he'd first felt the crystal's effect. Seeing the rat again, Bishop wiped his hand across his mouth. It came away with goopy clumps of congealing blood. He scowled, then disappeared into the maze. Knight waited for the giant man to come barreling out, savage and hungry, but when he reappeared, he wore a broad smile, the kind of smile only those who had once been captive can wear.

He was free.

Bishop chuckled for a moment, rested his hands against the massive crystal, and shook his head.

His elation was contagious. Knight grinned, happy to see his friend not just alive, but well. He doubted any other member of the team would have had the inner strength to fight not only Bishop's deep-rooted personal demons, but the genetically altered ones as well.

Knight's smile vanished as he saw the orange glow on Bishop's outbreak meter jump to a dark pink and continue on to a deep red.

Bishop looked at the device and frowned, the joy he felt replaced by dread. "We need to find the others."

"Do you know where Rook is?" Knight asked.

Bishop shook his head slowly. "He saw what they did to me. I don't know if he'd go off mission to get Weston, but he's not going to try real hard to avoid him."

"Then we'll do the same."

"Know where he is?"

Knight held up Weston's map. "I have an idea."

FIFTY-ONE

"Then why are you still wearing your wedding ring?" Sara asked, trying to ignore the cold gun barrel pressed against the underside of her chin. Weston had it pushed so hard against the soft space between her jawbones that she could feel her rapid pulse pushing against the metal. For a moment she thought he would pull the trigger, but he eased up. His eyes were wet.

Wet eyes mean blurry vision, Sara thought. "You must still love her."

"For a time, yes. Her reaction was understandable." Weston wiped his arm against his nose, sniffled, and looked at his ring finger. The gold band glittered in the room's shimmering aqua light. "But now . . ." He laughed, a little too maniacally for Sara's peace of mind. "But now I just can't get the damn thing off."

The gun lowered some.

"You know, I wish she could see all this. What I've become. That my profession is valid. That I *am* a good father."

Water clung to his lower eyelids, ready to spill over.

"I know it wouldn't change anything . . ."

Weston's arms went slack for a moment. The gun pointed to the floor.

"It wouldn't bring him back."

Weston blinked. Tears fell. Eyes blurred.

Sara struck.

She stepped forward and kicked up like her father had taught her to in his ten years as her soccer coach. Kick with the laces! She did. And the connection with the small bit of fabric covering Weston's business was solid.

Weston cried out and fell to his knees. In his rage he reached out and pulled the trigger, but the pain rolling up through his gut and the wetness in his eyes threw off his aim. He didn't get a chance to fire again. Sara's second kick struck his wrist and sent the gun skidding across the room, sliding behind a stack of firewood.

Weston grunted and swung out wildly. His backhand caught her mouth and her bottom lip split. But she used the pain, along with knowledge of what she was doing to fuel the fire spurring her toward savage action. She needed the split lip and allowed Weston to strike her.

Sara lunged, grabbed Weston's scraggly beard with her left hand, pulling his head to the side. With her right hand, she grabbed hold of his left arm. And then, like a feral beast, she shot forward and buried her teeth into the meat of his shoulder. Though he howled and reeled, she held on like a vampire desperate for sustenance, letting the blood coursing from his body enter and mingle with the blood of her open lip. He would give her the cure whether he wanted to or not.

"Stop!" he shouted, his voice cracking and panicked. "Get off! Please!"

Sara let go and stood. Weston was on the floor, his torso a bloody mess, his face wet with tears. But it was his shoulder that held her attention. Old scars lay beneath the fresh wound she had delivered. Scars from his ordeal with the old mothers. For a moment she pitied the man. He had endured so many awful things, so much pain. *It's no wonder his psychology is skewed,* she thought.

But she wouldn't risk pitying him for long. She headed for the door, hopping as she slipped off her boots.

"You can't leave!" he shouted, spit flying from his mouth, collecting on his beard.

She focused her attention on escape and didn't bother responding. The cold stone of the temple was a shock to her feet, but she moved in total silence. She thought about looking for the gun, but he might be up and fighting before she found it. Instead, she took his belt and knife from the bed and discarded her boots as she ran out the door.

Weston's voice chased her. "You can't escape Mount Meru, Pawn! Whether it is from old age or violence, you will die here!"

For a moment she thought about rushing back and plunging the knife into his gut. It would solve a lot of problems. But she wasn't a killer and couldn't risk losing what she had taken from him.

She had the cure.

She *was* the cure.

She descended the steep staircase two steps at a time. All of the carefulness she'd put into climbing the stairs disappeared as she bounded down, free. She had to escape. She had to survive.

Upon reaching the bottom of the staircase, she tripped, rolled on the hard stone floor of the temple, then sprang back to her feet. But she didn't make it any farther. A moving wall blocked her path and sent her sprawling to the floor. Sara looked up into the face of the last . . . person she wanted to see.

Lucy.

FIFTY-TWO

Rook's leg shook, causing leaves to rustle and branches to sway.

"What are you doing?" Queen asked, her voice quiet but tinged with annoyance.

"Muscles in my leg are twitching," Rook replied. "I'm not built to spend an entire day clinging to tree branches like a frickin' monkey."

The day had worn on slowly. Conversation had been sparse because being discovered by the nation of monsters below, each strong enough to tear them to pieces—even the little ones—would be a very bad thing. As the sun moved through the sky, shifting its light behind the clouds that had continued to thicken with water, they had watched as the Neanderthals below went about their business as though nothing were out of the ordinary.

Wooden planks continued to be made. Pots cooked various stews. Animal limbs and torsos roasted over open fires. The hybrids picked at the food as they worked, never stopping for a full-fledged meal. They were industrious and dedicated workers producing stone carvings, ladders, tools, clay pots, and ropes. Not one of them sat idly by. Everyone worked. As each item the hybrids created was finished it was quickly hauled into the cave, and then work would begin anew. Something big was going on in that cave. Rook felt sure of it, and with every passing hour, the sheer amount of materials transported into the cave confirmed his suspicions.

Rook scratched at his arm where his mud covering had dried up and peeled back. A puff of dust fell from his body and mingled with the large leaves around him that shielded him from hybrid view. "I swear, the sun better go down soon; this crap is getting itchy."

Queen nodded. She wasn't one to complain, but she had itches to scratch all over her body and it took a phenomenal amount of willpower to keep from scraping off her dry earth camouflage. Worst of all was her forehead. When she'd first applied the mud to her forehead the cool dirt had eased the pain of the scorching VPLA brand. But now, with the water sapped and the dry earth constricting and scraping her skin, it burned with fresh pain. She scrunched her forehead in frustration. The resulting flash of pain from her mutilated skin squishing together in folds distracted her from the chafing skin all over her body, but it also loosened a dry sheet of mud so that it fell off in one large clump.

Feeling the mud fall from her forehead, Queen reached out and caught it before it could drop through the branches and create a billowing cloud of dust that might tip the hybrids off to their location. She looked at Rook and sighed with relief, a smile coming to her face after thwarting the close call.

But Rook did not return the smile. Shock, fury, and pity flashed across his face in waves, like the shifting colors of a cyanea octopus. "Queen . . . what the hell?"

She'd forgotten he hadn't seen it yet. "A gift from the VPLA."

They stared into each other's eyes for nearly a minute, neither changing expressions or shifting bodies. The communication bordered on spiritual, with both knowing and understanding what the other was thinking and feeling. Compassion. Anger. Sadness. Finally, Rook broke the silence. "Well, we're all going to have them. So we match."

Queen smiled. "You couldn't stand the pain, little man."

"Who did it?"

"Major General Trung."

"He dead?"

"Not yet."

"Will be?"

"Absolutely."

Rook agreed with a tilt of his head.

They returned their attention to the hybrid settlement. Everything looked the same. Rook sighed. "Ten more minutes of this and I swear I'm going to—"

Something tickled Rook's ear. He flicked at it and a drop of mud, wet and moist, struck a nearby branch. His eyes widened upon seeing it. They both looked up.

High above, the sky looked fuzzy, like TV static.

"What is that?" Rook asked. He'd never seen anything like it. The clouds had become speckled like a 1950s halftone comic book illustration. "That can't be rain. You can't see rain that high up . . ."

Then it hit. Raindrops the size of large grapes descended in an unceasing torrent. God had redirected Niagara Falls directly overhead. The hiss of the rain striking the jungle canopy was louder than a Super Bowl stadium filled to capacity. The feel of it, while refreshingly cool, was like being flicked from head to toe. And the mud covering that concealed their pale bodies melted away in seconds. Their gleaming white skin became a beacon to anyone who thought to look up.

Through the wet din a cry rose up. While there was no language to it, the tone and volume denoted urgency and warning. Had they been discovered? They peeked out through the leaves, more wary now that their white faces and blond hair could be easily spotted against the dark green foliage. The cry came again, louder and closer. A mass of hybrids dropped what they were doing, some picking up spears, and rushed into the jungle. Another large group ran inside the mountain, disappearing into the darkness. The clearing was empty.

Moments later, gunfire and explosions ripped through the forest some distance away. Both knew this might be their only chance. They slid down through the branches quickly, leaped to the jungle floor, and ran out into the open, their only cover being the blanket of large, glistening raindrops that blended nicely with their fair skin.

As they passed through the huts, workstations, and fires, they abandoned their crude wooden spears and upgraded to stone-tipped spears that leaned against hut walls. Queen noticed a KA-BAR knife stabbed into a fireside log. She wrenched it free as she ran past, and inspected it.

King's.

He had been here.

As they neared the large cave entrance, Queen saw a backlit monster of a hybrid approaching. The fight would be two on one, but Queen doubted they would stand a chance. Taking one out in a surprise attack was one thing. This was closer to jumping in front of a Mack truck. But they couldn't back down. Then she saw the string of cages containing pacing tigers and bears. Queen paused before the cages and, using King's knife, hacked away the handmade ropes that held the doors shut. The bears watched curiously. The tigers reacted instantaneously, throwing themselves at the gate.

Queen bolted and caught up with Rook, who had not stopped. In fact, he had sped up, ready to fight. Before she could shout a warning about the tigers approaching from behind, the large male hybrid stepped out in front of them. He had no weapon, but his six-foot-tall, broad-shouldered build, thick fingernails, and inch-long canines were all he needed on most days . . . except for today.

Rather than face the tigers or their new adversary, Queen dove and tackled Rook. They fell to the mud just as the two tigers launched into the air.

The three massive predators met with a flurry of crushing jaws and swiping claws. Blood flew. Savage voices roared. One of the tigers exploded from the fray, tossed through the air by the hybrid. But it twisted, landed on its feet, and attacked anew.

The hybrid fought amazingly in the face of a danger that would have most human beings weeping in a pile of their own feces, but the two giant cats proved too much. As one swiped at him wildly with extended claws, the other landed a killer bite on his thick throat. As the life was squeezed out of the hybrid, he pounded on the tiger, but it responded by increasing the pressure and holding on tight.

Before the tigers turned their attention away from their still-dying prey, Rook and Queen ran for the cave, entering without further incident and disappearing into the darkness.

FIFTY-THREE

"Lucy, stop!" King shouted as Lucy raised a fist and prepared to shove it straight through Sara's skull. He put his hand on Lucy's arm, not trying to hold her back—he knew he couldn't—but hoping his touch would distract her.

It did.

Her arm yanked away and then swung out, catching King across the chest. He careened back, slamming into a wall. The back of his head grew wet with blood. Stumbling forward, he felt the gash with his fingers, the salty sweat on them stinging the small wound. He would live.

At least for a few more seconds.

Lucy pounded toward him and slammed him back against the wall. "You may marry me, but you will never be above me."

King looked into Lucy's pretty brown eyes, so full of hate, and for the first time realized she stood at least a few inches taller than him. She'd inherited Weston's height. She was right. He never *would* be above her. He couldn't help but smile.

She pushed against him harder. "Why do you smile?"

Sara pushed herself to her feet, holding Weston's belt against her waist. The hard shape of the sheathed knife pushed against her belly. She reached for it. If Lucy intended on killing King, she might have to use it. But King defused the situation with the last grouping of words Sara would have ever expected him to say.

"Because you're right. And I'm happy to have found someone like you. Someone strong. Someone to protect me."

Lucy giggled, transforming from enraged killer to tween-age girl. Sara's eyes widened. He had her wrapped around his finger . . . already!

A pain-filled scream of anger sounded from the temple's top room. Weston. Still trying to stand up after the pounding Sara had delivered to his body and pride. He vented his anger and pain with a wild vocalization that barely sounded human.

Lucy let go of King. "Father?"

Sara saw an opportunity. Lucy, it seemed, was easily fooled. "He's hurt. Maybe even dying. I was going to get help."

"Father!" Panic filled Lucy's hairy face as she launched toward the steep stairs and took them in sets of four.

Sara ran to King. "C'mon!" she said, taking his wrist and pulling him through the hallway that ran through the cruciform fishpond rooms.

Still stunned by the blow to the back of his head, King staggered behind her. As they reached the last of the fishpond chambers, Sara abruptly stopped and turned to King. The loud clomping of his booted feet had caught her attention.

"What?" King said, his faculties starting to return.

"Lose the boots. They'll hear us."

King did as he was told without pause. He either realized she told the truth or trusted her enough to act on her word. The boots slid off quickly. Sara took them and tossed them into a fishpond. Large wet mouths opened and attacked the boots as they sank beneath the surface.

Side by side, they ran silently out of the hall and stopped. Standing high up on the cliff entrance was a group of hybrids, hooting and agitated. The humans hadn't been spotted yet, but would be when Lucy or Weston sounded the alarm.

King grabbed hold of Sara's arm and yanked her into the

tunnel. He glanced back the way they'd come and saw Lucy's and Weston's feet appear at the top of the doorway, descending the steps slowly.

A call rang out from the hybrids above. The noise sounded like a horn of some kind as it echoed throughout the city chamber. For a moment, King thought they'd been spotted, but heard Weston ask, "What's wrong? What's going on?"

Just before Lucy and Weston had a clear view down the tunnel, King grabbed hold of Sara and shoved her into one of the adjacent rooms. They were wide, empty alcoves, featuring nothing but three descending stairs that entered the fish pools. Nowhere to hide. Nowhere to go . . . but in.

"Get in the water," King whispered.

Sara looked down and saw the gleaming skin of several large fish reflecting the crystal light from above. "Are you crazy?"

Weston's grunts of pain grew louder as he was helped down the hall by Lucy.

"She will tear us apart if they catch us." King's eyes blazed with seriousness. "She killed Bishop. *Bishop.* You have no idea how hard that is. And she is more savage than even Weston knows."

Without another word, Sara slid into the water. King followed behind her, careful not to splash. Fish swarmed over their bodies, pressing their fish lips against them and sucking. Lacking proper teeth, the fish couldn't eat them, but their large bodies and fervent attempts at mauling the pair pushed them ever deeper. King wondered just how deep this well went. It could be hundreds of feet for all he knew.

As they continued to descend, King realized he might have traded a death at the hands of Lucy for a death at the fins of overzealous fish. He guessed they had descended thirty feet when they finally hit the bottom. He opened his eyes. Through the silhouettes of countless large fish swirling above his head, he saw the small square of light that marked the entrance. But here, far below the surface, he saw that the four fishponds connected underneath, forming one very wide, very deep pool.

Lucy helped Weston walk down the hallway. He could move, but leaned a lot of his weight on her body.

"Thank you, my dear," he said.

"Father, I—" Lucy stopped and sniffed.

"What is it?" Weston asked.

Lucy bent and smelled the floor. "They stopped here."

Weston's eyebrows rose. "They?"

Lucy ignored the question and entered the room where King and Sara had slid into the water. She smelled the perimeter of the pond. Fish roiled beneath her. Then she saw a different kind of movement and shot her hand into the water. Water coursed off her wet, matted arm hair as she pulled out the size-twelve military boot. "He took off his boots."

Weston snatched it from her hand. "*His* boots?" His eyes widened and his voice filled with anger. "You brought *King* down here?"

Lucy cringed. While physically superior to Weston, she still feared him. "He wanted to marry me. Wanted to ask your permission."

Weston's face contorted awfully. He bit his lower lip. Sneered. His eyes twitched. And then he went placid. He couldn't blame her. She knew nothing of modern men, charm, or lies. He should have known better than to leave her alone with a man like King.

Lucy pointed out his ring finger. "You are married. You are loved. And I am not!"

Weston shook his head sadly and rubbed her hair with his hand. He pulled her against his side and hugged her. "Everything he told you was a lie. No one could love you more than me."

A second loud call sounded from the top of the cliff entrance. As Weston headed for the temple exit, Lucy took his arm. "What about the human woman?"

"They won't make it past us, and the other exits are well concealed. We will find them both when we return."

Lucy held on. "And then?"

"I don't know."

"Can I kill them?"

He paused, looking in Lucy's eyes. "You are too eager for blood, Lucy. There is a time for such things, but not every problem can be solved through violence. They are trapped and sooner or later will expose themselves or starve to death."

Lucy pounded the stone floor. Weston felt the vibration beneath his feet. "The mothers would kill them. They are strong and fearless."

Weston did his best to hide his growing concern. Not just for his well-being—Lucy could kill him in seconds—but for the state of his family. What did Lucy know of the mothers? They were expelled long before she was born. All she knew was that they were to be shunned. But her knowledge of them went beyond the stories told to the Nguoi Rung children. She had either been told these things by someone else or had direct contact with the old mothers. And if that were the case, how many of the other children had been exposed to their primitive influence? If there was dissension growing, he would not be outdone by the vapid intellect of the mothers. "Kill them, then. Kill them both."

Lucy leaped and clapped, giggling with excitement. They exited the temple together.

As the fish came to realize that the new additions to the pond were not edible, they backed off, allowing King to tug on Sara's arm. She blinked her eyes open, clearly uncomfortable with the idea of being underwater, and perhaps nearly out of breath. She held her nose with one hand and pushed away fish with the other.

King pointed across the underwater chamber to a square of light that signified another exit above. They swam together toward the light and then arced slowly up; hoping Weston and Lucy had already left.

As they reached the halfway point, Sara began kicking wildly. Almost out of air, she was desperate to reach the top. King pulled her up and helped her rise more quickly. As they ascended through parting waves of fish, he held his finger up to his lips. The message was clear—no matter how badly you want to breathe, do it quietly.

They breached the water together, rising just above the surface. Sara did her best to suck air in quietly, but couldn't stop a gentle wheeze from escaping. King pulled himself slowly out of the water, taking care not to splash, and then pulled Sara out behind him. She fell to the cold stone floor, still clinging to her wad of now-saturated clothes, taking in mouthfuls of air like a dying fish stuck on the shore.

He glanced through the doorway and saw Weston and Lucy exiting the temple, hustling through the snake-shaped balustrades and moving toward the large exit.

He turned back to Sara, who had sat up. "They're gone."

She nodded and smiled. "You're not going to believe this," she said, enjoying his look of bewilderment. "I have the cure for Brugada."

King's face scrunched, but not in confusion. He stumbled, caught himself, and then fell to the floor. He landed on his back, one arm hanging over the top step toward Sara and the fish pool below. His face fell flat and still. His eyes open wide and unmoving.

Dead.

Brugada.

Sara knew what had happened, and like she did with Rook, she waited for the cardioverter defibrillator to do its thing. But nothing happened. Sara gasped as she realized that King wouldn't be coming back. The electric shock torture he'd endured at the hands of the VPLA had no doubt short-circuited the small device implanted in King's chest. He'd been shocked over the stitched-up incision more than once.

She'd discovered the cure too late to save him.

FIFTY-FOUR

Trusting that the large cave running straight into the core of the mountain was the right choice, Rook and Queen pushed forward through the darkness. An occasional fire pit with glowing embers provided the only light. The hiss of the rain and distant blasts of gunfire faded as they descended into the darkness.

They had passed several large rooms early on, each containing massive amounts of building materials. Spools of rope. Stacks of wooden planks. Everything they saw outside was being stored in the large rooms. They'd passed at least ten chambers on each side so far. Now they approached another pair of rooms, one on each side of the cave. With little light, they couldn't see what was inside these caves, but the darkness within warned of hidden dangers. They continued past the rooms without inspecting their contents.

The cave air felt cool and moist on their skin, clinging to their exposed bodies and chilling them. Rook shivered. "We need to find some clothes."

"What, now you don't like seeing me half naked?"

Rook chuckled. "I can't see anything. Besides, I—"

Queen came to a quick stop and slapped a hand over Rook's mouth. An orange glow filled the tunnel far ahead. Voices filtered to them from the shifting light. A group approached.

They crouched low and moved back to the short doorway on the left side of the tunnel, entering its dark interior without hesitation. They stepped back into the darkness, listening as the obscure voices grew louder. Suddenly, Rook tensed.

"Give me the knife," he whispered.

"Why?"

"Give me the knife." Rook's voice chilled the air further. "Now." He felt the handle bump his arm as Queen handed it to him, holding the blade in her hand. He took it and squeezed the handle.

"What do you hear?"

The voices came louder now, each distinct. At least two female hybrids. Three males. And someone else. "Weston," Rook growled.

Weston's voice echoed up the tunnel. "Check all the rooms. I want them found. Start here and work your way through the old and new cities. I want all of them found."

Rook shook his head. They would be searching this room. Despite his overwhelming desire to see Weston pay for what had happened to Bishop, he would have preferred avoiding this fight, especially with the odds stacked so high against him.

"How do you want to do this?" Queen asked.

"Alone," Rook said. "It's a fight we can't win, but at least one of us can survive. Find King and Pawn. Get the hell out. Complete the mission. They'll need you, and I need to do this for Bishop. He was my brother."

The light began spilling into the doorway. Rook looked back and saw Queen's face, her body crouched, ready to attack. She wasn't listening. Confident the loud, agitated voices of the hybrids explaining an ongoing attack to Weston would mask his voice, Rook spoke. "And you're my sister." Queen looked him in the eyes. "You know how I feel about my sisters, Queen."

Queen's jaw flexed as she bit down. Then she slid into the darkness.

He whispered, "Find King. Save Sara. That's the mission."

The voices outside rose in volume.

"It was a feeble attack, Father, easily defeated." The deep voice, clear and close, filled the room. "Their advance was paused. We have them surrounded."

"And yet we lost three sentries!" Weston's voice roared in the cave. "They're nearly on top of us and I promise you there are more. These are not simple soldiers. You would do well to remember that."

"The Americans were better, and where are they, Father?" The voice of the male hybrid grew arrogant as the group stopped in front of the doorway. The large male confronted Weston. "Two are trapped in Meru and the others are scattered!"

"I killed one by the river!" Lucy said, bouncing in a crouched position.

Weston's hand appeared on the large male's shoulder. "Shane, you are my oldest son, my bravest warrior. But you must trust me. You do not know the humans as I do. They outnumber us and have weapons that can destroy us all. Until they are gone from this jungle, we are not safe. Think of your people before you act, Shane, and do not underestimate your adversaries . . . ever."

As Weston finished speaking, he gave Shane a pat on the shoulder. Then the large male stepped to the side, revealing Weston to Rook . . . and Rook to Weston.

"Shane!" Weston cried out as Rook bolted forward, flinging the spear and diving out with the knife.

As Rook launched himself through the air, swiping the knife toward Weston's throat, a large force struck him in the side, sending him crashing into the cave wall. The knife fell from his hand and clattered to the cave floor.

Queen watched from the darkness as the four remaining hybrids surrounded Rook. He'd been hit by Shane as he'd twisted and struck out upon hearing Weston's fearful voice, but Shane had also taken Rook's flung spear in the chest. The large male hit the cave floor at the same time Rook did, except Shane no longer stirred.

Weston dove to his fallen son's side, feeling for a pulse on his thick, hairy neck. "No, no, no!" But there was no pulse. The sharp spear, flung by Rook's strong arm at point-blank range, had pierced the giant's clavicle and heart beneath. Weston stood, breathed deep, and choked back a sob. He turned toward Rook, took hold of the spear rising from Shane's chest, and yanked it out with a bloody slurp. He stormed toward Rook, who was nearly back to his feet.

Lucy lunged and swiped at Rook. He fell back in front of the doorway opposite Queen's hiding place. "Get the hell away from me, Cha-Ka!"

Weston made a sharp sipping noise with his mouth. The four hybrids instantly backed off, though they still surrounded Rook. Weston approached, spear in hand. "Cha-Ka. That's funny."

"Go to hell," Rook said.

"I used to love that show," Weston said. Then he screamed, raised the spear over his head, and brought it down.

Before the spear reached Rook's chest, a large hand swept out from the dark, striking the wood of the spear and snapping it in half. Everyone froze for a beat. Rook looked up at Weston's bewildered expression and realized they were thinking the same thing: What the fuck was that?

And then, all hell broke loose. Five-foot tall, fur-covered bodies flew from the cave. The hybrids roared as they were tackled by their grandmothers. Lucy squealed and dove away from the action. She cowered against the wall, farther down the tunnel. The others were quickly subdued, each being pinned down by two of the full-blood Neanderthals.

Then Red stepped from the darkness, her yellow eyes glowing in the firelight. She stepped over Rook, showing no fear of him, and approached Weston. Her head twitched as she spoke. "Big man. Mine. I find him first. He mine."

Weston stared into the red-rimmed eyes that had changed his world fifteen years ago. She had saved his life, albeit unknowingly, and had given him a family to replace the one he'd lost. That's why he'd let her live. In return he was bringing her people back from extinction—something she couldn't comprehend, but instinctually knew. That's why *she* let *him* live.

But if Red wanted Rook alive . . . the big man . . . she could only want him for one thing. The truce would be broken.

Competition, while good for business, never helped repopulate a species on the brink. But he had no choice at the moment. Red acted on instinct more than any kind of mental process. She was in heat and wanted to mate. She'd found an acceptable mate in this large and loud soldier and had pursued him into the very stronghold of her ancestors.

Weston looked at Rook and saw horror just beneath the surface. Whatever the old hags would do to him would be a fate far worse than death. "Take him," Weston said. "My gift to you."

He would take care of the old mothers later. Right now he just needed them out of his way.

Red huffed, spun around, and picked up Rook with little effort. She heaved him over her squat frame and carried him off into the darkness from which she had emerged. The others followed her. Rook's angry shouts and vile cursing faded into the distance as the group retreated through one of the many secret tunnels crisscrossing throughout the mountainside.

A distant shout sounded from the direction Queen and Rook had come. Queen couldn't make out the word, but the tone smacked of alarm.

"Come!" Weston said, and the band rushed toward the cave exit, carrying Shane's body and leaving behind a still-burning torch and King's knife.

Rook's last words rolled out of the darkness, incoherent and pained. Then he was gone, abducted into the heart of the mountain by a bunch of ancient monsters. Queen stood in the darkness. Her arms shook. Her breath was heavy. Bishop was dead. Rook would be soon. He would kill himself before letting those things do whatever they had planned. Or he'd fight until they had no choice but to kill him.

Her mind returned to the mission. The Nguoi Rung named Shane had talked about two humans being trapped in Mount Meru. She wasn't sure where that was, but suspected it was back the way they'd come. She scoured the tunnel for movement or signs of danger. The firelight and angry voices from Weston's crew faded as they hurried on their way. She picked up the torch left behind and retrieved King's KA-BAR knife. As she turned to start deeper into the cave a glitter of light caught her eye. It came from the room inside which she and Rook had hid inside.

She paused and stepped back into the room. Her eyes grew wide as a treasure beyond all comparison became revealed in the light of the torch.

"Son of a bitch." Queen's anger quickened her pulse to a point where she could feel it thumping bursts of pain across her branded forehead. If they'd only seen what this room contained a few minutes earlier, Rook wouldn't have been captured.

FIFTY-FIVE

Washington, D.C.

Secret Service lined the hallway in front of and behind him. They cleared the way, allowing for a quick departure and absolute secrecy. No one other than the man at his side, and the loyal protectors he would leave behind, would know the president of the United States had abandoned his post.

He felt awful for doing it, for the ruse, but some matters had to be attended to personally. And that meant leaving the White House. That meant breaking the quarantine. Not that the quarantine mattered anymore. Every major network was carrying the story now.

When the tenth victim, a second survivor, had been diagnosed, the doctors went to the press despite a warning from the FBI. The press coverage, as usual, was sensationalized. Not only was Brugada held responsible for the ten known victims in Washington, D.C, but also every death across the country with an unknown, unusual, or suspicious nature. According to the press, the current death toll was approaching five hundred.

Religious leaders, the more charismatic the better, were being interviewed about Armageddon, which provided an endless stream of "the end of the world is nigh" sound bites. Paranoia spread. People either locked themselves away or hit the streets. Those in their houses made the right choice, but more than a few became violent with anyone on their doorstep. Those in the streets adopted a carpe diem mentality.

Riots erupted in Los Angeles and Chicago.

And the press ate it up, fueling the end-of-days flames. Especially Fox, whose broadcasts took on a religious fervor. Acts of violence went uncensored. Journalists in the studio spoke with animated gesticulations, pitching voices, and wild eyes. Those on the streets cursed, shoved the drunk, and in Los Angeles, came under gunfire.

As Duncan passed by a now-empty office, he heard one such dramatic newscast come to a halt with, "We interrupt our continuing coverage of Pandemic Twenty-ten with a message from the president of these United States of America."

He paused at the door, looking at the wall-mounted TV. His face appeared, grim and serious, but with a practiced spark of hope. The words he had spoken an hour previous were still fresh in his mind. "Friends, we find ourselves in a difficult and troubling situation."

"Sir," Boucher's voice interrupted the TV as the recorded Duncan went on to explain the disease and provide a more accurate portrayal of the situation. Washington, D.C., was under quarantine. The airports had been shut down. And while neither a curfew or martial law had been ordered, they were options on the table in cities where looting had become rampant. And then he gave them hope. America's finest were on the task and he was confident—confident—a solution would be found.

"Sir," Boucher repeated.

Duncan looked at him.

"Are you sure about this?"

"I am."

"You're taking a big risk."

"The whole world is at risk."

Boucher let himself smile. "You're a better man than most."

"We'll see."

"And when the world comes knocking at our doorstep tomorrow morning? They'll expect to hear from you again, you know."

"I'll be back in time for breakfast."

Boucher rolled his neck, popping a few vertebrae. "And if you're not?"

"If I'm not back? Then it won't matter, will it?"

A frown creased beneath Boucher's mustache. "No. It won't."

They resumed walking, leaving the recorded Duncan behind as he continued to urge calm. After two flights of stairs they entered an underground parking garage that exited four blocks away inside what appeared to be a personal garage. An array of black SUVs and stretch limos filled the space, all heavily armored and ready to speed the president away in the event of an emergency that Marine One, the president's personal helicopter, couldn't handle (should Washington's airspace become compromised).

But Duncan didn't approach the black vehicles. Instead he walked up to an unassuming Hyundai Entourage. It was as heavily armored as the rest of the vehicles in the garage, but when he drove it with a baseball cap on his head and dummy children strapped into the backseat, no one would recognize him for who he was.

Boucher handed him the keys. "Never pictured you as a family man."

The van's lights blinked twice as Duncan unlocked the doors. "Never too late to start, right?" He climbed onto the driver's seat.

"Superdad."

"Dom, listen," Duncan said, his voice low so the Secret Service men guarding the garage entrance couldn't hear. "If things get worse, lock down the cities. Keep people from moving. If people are smart, we can keep this thing contained."

"Anything else?"

"Yeah, ask the FBI to send some guys with guns to Fox and let them know what it's like to have fear shoved down their throats."

Boucher smiled. "My pleasure, sir."

Duncan started the van, rolled down the window, and steered for the exit. He leaned out the window as he passed Boucher. "Up, up, and away."

FIFTY-SIX

Mount Meru—Vietnam

Major General Trung could sense the enemy surrounding him and thirty of his best—all that remained of his original strike force. They had launched a successful sneak attack on a small group of the hairy beasts, but the noise had attracted more. Many more. And they found themselves suddenly outnumbered and encircled.

The jungle had gone silent, save for the wind shaking the tree branches above and warning of an approaching storm. But on occasion, the branches would sway and creak without a breeze present, and sometimes the tall trees would bend against the wind.

They're coming. He recognized the signs he had missed prior to his first encounter with the creatures in 2009.

And, he thought with anger, *the most recent ambush.* They had lost the American prisoners. More important, they had lost the scientist they had gone to so much trouble to acquire.

But what had started out as a slaughter had turned into a victory when his men—the men who now shared the jungle floor with him—pushed the enemy back.

Their prize had been lost, but she would no doubt be found.

He only hoped she would still be alive at that point.

A shift in the breeze bent the jungle toward his position, surely hiding the approaching force above their heads. But it also carried their foul scent.

They were close.

But Trung was ready. He signaled to his men. Half of them raised their weapons to their shoulders and aimed. Up. The rest crouched to one knee and swept their weapons back and forth, forming an impenetrable, three-hundred-sixty-degree perimeter.

Trung squinted into the humid haze lit by the few streams of light filtering down from above. As the wind picked up, the light moved and danced on the forest floor. In the space between light and shadow, he detected movement of another sort, but couldn't trace it. His index finger tightened on his AK-47's trigger.

The enemy had arrived.

But they were waiting.

His thoughts turned to Queen. He wondered for a moment if it was she who was now stalking him. His breath caught in his throat as he pictured her face, ripe with ferocity and bearing the bloodred insignia of his Death Volunteers. Trung flinched back as a loud voice filled the forest.

"You shouldn't have come back!"

Trung recognized the voice as the same he'd heard in 2009, and again during the ambush on the VPLA camp. It was the voice of his enemy, and his enemy was American.

"Give me the woman, and we will leave," Trung said. It was the truth. He had no desire to fight this man, and his . . . brood, again. Having the location carpet bombed would be a much easier solution.

Movement dead ahead caught his attention. He focused on it.

The man emerged.

"Don't shoot," he said with raised arms.

Trung held his fire and his men followed his lead. The man was tall, rising a foot above Trung's tallest soldier. He was also nearly naked, clothed only in some kind of loin-cloth, and had a fresh bite wound on his shoulder, like some kind of primitive.

"I'm afraid that's not possible," the man said.

Trung did not respond, allowing his silence to ask the questions. Why?

"She belongs to me," was the answer.

Belongs to him? Though he could plainly see the man's reversion to a primal lifestyle (despite the glasses on his face), Trung was stunned by the man's cavemanlike asser-tion that he now owned the woman.

He scanned the forest, looking for others, and saw none. But he knew the man was not alone. One man on his own could not create such a stink as now swirled around them. "She is important to the people of Vietnam," Trung said, doing his best to hide his growing animosity.

"Of that I am sure," the man said. "But you cannot have her."

Trung squinted as he took aim at the man's head, but the subtle change in facial expression did not go unnoticed.

He tracked the man as he ducked, never losing aim as his finger applied pressure to the trigger. Despite being focused on his quarry, he saw a shadow shift in his peripheral vision. Something was rising up *behind* the man.

Trung's finger depressed the trigger and three shots rattled off, but his aim was sourly off now that he, too, was diving to the jungle floor. A thick-bodied hairy woman had risen up behind the man, spear in hand, and had let it fly with a mighty heave. He heard the shaft cutting through the thick air as it slid past his cheek. It struck, with a wet smack, dead center in the back of the man who had been covering the group's rear position.

The soldier fell to the ground silently, his spinal cord severed.

Chaos erupted as his twenty-nine remaining men opened fire, first at nothing, then at the large hairy bodies emerging from the forest. They came from the trees and the jungle floor simultaneously. The first to arrive were already dead—falling from above as they were plucked from the trees like rotted fruit. Each landed with a thud and an explosion of brush, filling the air with plumes of crushed leaf litter.

Trung squeezed off a quick three-round burst. One of the creatures pitched forward, tumbled, and fell, sliding to a stop at his feet. But the stumbling body had concealed the man's approach. He charged forward, spear raised high in one hand, a knife in the other. The look in his eyes was wild. Frenzied. Any sense of the man willing to let them leave after a simple conversation had vanished.

Then the spear was in the air and Trung was ducking once more. But he was not the intended target. The rod struck the man next to Trung, knocking him off his feet and pinning him to a tree.

Trung's eyes widened. The savage man was a warrior.

With a whistle, the major general called six of his men to his side while the others continued to fire into the encroaching mass of bodies. His plan would take timing, finesse, and sacrifice.

A pause in the gunfire signified clips running dry. The soldiers were adept at changing the spent clips out for fresh ones, but the few-second delay was all the enemy needed. The white man raised his knife in the air with a battle cry. This was the moment Trung was waiting for.

He released the grenade from his hand with a sideways toss, letting it bounce, mostly concealed, across the jungle floor.

"Get down!" he shouted to his men. Before ducking behind a fallen tree, he saw, with pleasure, the caveman's spectacled eyes widen. The man shouted a warning and dove to the side, but the battle cries of his brutish brethren and the reports of the VPLA weapons drowned out his voice.

The explosion sent shrapnel and a wave of pressure into anyone standing in range. Trung stood from his position without pause. When the caveman and his brethren picked themselves up and rejoined the battle, they would find Trung and nine of his men gone. The old tunnel discovered on a Vietcong map would lead them past the battleground. They emerged like snakes from a den, the sounds of battle behind them.

They had breached the front line. And the city gates were next.

Trung left the majority of his men behind. They would either win the day or die in combat—the way of the Death Volunteer. It was a price they all accepted, and often the cost of success. When the jungle cleared, he knew the sacrifice had not been made in vain. A village had been constructed at the base of a mountain, which rose high above them. A village populated by more of the man-creatures. But these were not warriors, and fled into the jungle at the sight of them.

Trung paused at the village center while his men searched the huts. They reported to him quickly. The village was empty. One of the men pointed out a large cave descending into the mountain. Torchlight licked the walls.

Trung ordered his men in.

Moments later, the gunfire in the jungle ceased. It was followed by the roar of a man.

Having heard the angry howl, Trung paused at the cave's mouth. The caveman was coming.

FIFTY-SEVEN

Moments passed. The cardioverter defibrillator never activated. As Sara feared, it had been fried by the torture King had endured. Without knowing it, the major general had arranged King's death the first time he held that stun gun to his chest and blasted him with eight hundred thousand volts.

Sara wept for King quietly, containing her sobs for fear of being discovered. Her body arched as she convulsed with tears. She had seen people die before, but never someone she knew well. Her last surviving grandmother had died when she was ten. But she'd hardly known her. Granted, she had only recently met King, but she now knew that it wasn't absence that made the heart grow fonder, it was suffering. And they'd endured a lifetime in the past few days.

Kneeling over King's lifeless form on the first stair down toward the fish pool, looking into his blank stare, Sara could no longer hold herself up. She fell forward, gripping King's wet shirt with one hand and his leg with the other as she continued to sob, each exhalation pushing out her will to fight on, each inhalation sucking in anxiety and hopelessness.

How could she escape without King? How could she evade Weston and Lucy? Or the hordes of other hybrids, for that matter. Even if she could escape she still had to survive in the jungle. And for how long? Days? Months? She had no idea which direction to go. She might walk right into a hybrid lair or into the hands of the Death Volunteers. Enemies surrounded her. She was thousands of miles from home. Hidden in an ancient city buried beneath a mountain, surrounded by enemies, and holding the one thing that could save the human race from extinction within her body.

"Damnit!" Sara screamed it, not caring who might hear. And she punched King's limp leg. A sharp pain shot through her hand as she struck something hard. Turning to the offending pant leg, and about to let out another curse, a question struck home in Sara's consciousness. What did King have in his cargo pant pocket that Weston or his goons would overlook? Certainly not a gun. Perhaps a radio? Maybe she could contact help?

A tingle of hope took root as she fished into the pocket. She pulled out a small device. Her hopes came crashing down. It wasn't a radio. Then she recognized the device. A solid black body featuring a single button and two metal prongs. The stun gun!

Sara gasped and sat up straight. Would it work? She shook the device next to her ear and didn't hear any water inside. It had to work! Gasping and grunting in desperation, Sara yanked King's shirt open, found the stitched-up incision where the cardioverter defibrillator had been implanted, and placed the stun gun against his bare skin.

She pushed the button, sending eight hundred thousand volts into King's body. Much of the charge filtered out across his skin, through his organs and muscles, but the proximity of the charge and the severe voltage of it caused King's heart to beat.

Once.

Sara growled loudly and pushed the button again, pushing the prongs down hard against his skin.

The second shock had the same effect. The heart, responding to the pulse of electricity, beat.

And then beat again.

And again.

King's eyes shifted and blinked.

Sara dropped the stun gun and covered her mouth as she cried. King was alive! The device that had sealed his fate had saved him from it. She wanted to throw herself on top of him, to squeeze him, hug him, thank him for coming back. But she just sat there crying, afraid to touch him for fear that his life would shrink away.

But King's heart was healthy. His whole body hale. And he lived once again.

King looked up into Sara's terrified yet relieved wet eyes. He'd been dead. And she had saved him. He looked to the side, for the object she had dropped when he came to. He found it. The stun gun. She'd shocked him back to life. But the cardio . . . King remembered the last time he'd felt the sting of the stun gun and realized the same thing Sara had. His cardioverter defibrillator no longer worked.

"Thanks," he said, and then smiled. "Rook was full of shit. . . ."

Sara wrinkled her forehead. *What?*

"This is way worse than heartburn."

Sara smiled, laughed, and then caught her breath. King's eyes went wide and he grabbed her wrist, staring at the outbreak meter's red glow. "No," he whispered, and then closed his eyes and lay still again. Panic began clawing at her insides. She lunged out a hand and checked for a pulse on his neck. The beat was regular and strong.

But he was unconscious, and helpless.

FIFTY-EIGHT

When King opened his eyes again, he was no longer staring up at the giant mountain crystals through the atrium-style ceiling of the fish pool room. The firm surface of the top stair no longer supported him.

Instead, he lay on a bed. A handmade mattress covered the surface. Its leaf-stuffed cushion crunched beneath him as he shifted his weight. Not exactly a Sealy Posturepedic, but certainly more comfortable than the stone floor. Looking to the side he found a small window—the room's only source of light, through which the now-dull crystal light glowed. The sun must be setting, he thought, and then what? Pitch dark?

A chill swept over King's body, not from thoughts of the dark or what might linger in it, but from his body. He looked down and found himself nearly naked, covered only by a large dry leaf, like the classic Adam.

He looked around for a clue of what was going on. As his eyes adjusted to the low light, the room around him began to take shape. There were crude shelves formed from freshly cut wood. A table. Several stools. A woodpile. An unused fire pit. A rope had been strung up across the room and on it, clothes hung. He couldn't tell, but assumed they were his clothes, hung to dry after his dip in the ancient fishpond. Beyond the clothes, hidden in the shadows, he saw something else . . . someone else.

"It's a bedroom." Sara's voice came from the dark corner.

"In the temple?" King asked. He wanted to be as far away from that hub of evil as he could get.

"In the city. Third gallery. Crowded little neighborhood . . . as weird as that sounds. Should take them forever to find us. How are you feeling?"

King smiled despite the fact that his body ached. "Exposed."

"Sorry, there weren't any blankets."

"Why are you in the corner?" King asked.

"Didn't want to freak you out."

"Because I'm naked?"

"No . . ." Sara leaned forward, entering the stream of light coming in from the window. He could only see the top half of her torso. The rest of her sat in darkness. Her hands covered her small breasts, but her shoulders, collarbone, and smooth skin were stunning on their own. "Because I am."

"Don't worry. I'm used to sharing a locker room with a buxom blonde, remember? I'm good at controlling my libido."

She smiled. "Well, I'm not." She shifted, feeling awkward. "I mean, I'm not used to sharing a locker room. Not with a blonde. I didn't mean controlling—"

King laughed and then winced as his chest ached. "Don't worry. I knew what you meant."

Sara sighed with relief, because *she* wasn't sure what she'd meant.

King sat up, and made sure the leaf stayed put. Despite his locker room claims, he was starting to feel a bit underdressed. Queen might be a babe, but he'd never had feelings for her, not like he was beginning to feel for Sara. "How did you get away from Weston? That must have been—"

"Never mind that," Sara said. "It's what I took from him."

King could see the excitement in her eyes. "You have the cure?"

"I *am* the cure."

He stared at her for a moment. "I don't understand."

"It's a virus, transferred through blood like an STD, but it *cures* Brugada. There are other symptoms associated with the virus, but I haven't presented any yet. He got it from the old mothers when they . . . you know . . . and it was passed down to all their children."

Sara looked confused by King's angry expression. She then realized what she had implied. "Oh, he didn't do anything. Don't worry." She took hold of her lower lip and bent it out, revealing her split lip. "I took it from him. Bit him."

She'd done it. Sara the twitchy scientist had weathered the worst this jungle and history had to throw at her and did whatever it took to get the job done. Now they just needed to escape in one piece.

He realized that he could still drop dead from Brugada and Sara might not be able to bring him back a second time. "I don't suppose you'd mind donating some blood over here. I'd really rather not need to get shocked again."

"Already taken care of," Sara said, motioning for him to check his lower lip.

King felt the inside of his mouth with his tongue. There was a fresh wound, already starting to heal thanks to the enzymes in his saliva.

"You were really out. I bit your lip, reopened mine, and planted a big bloody wet one on you."

"Could've waited for me to wake up. Would've been more fun."

"*If* you woke up at all," she said.

"Right. Thanks." King stood, holding the large leaf in place. He reached out and felt his boxers. *Dry enough,* he thought. He pulled them down, dropped the leaf, and began dressing.

Then it hit him, like a forgotten headache that returns with sudden movement. Sara's watch. The red glow. As he dressed more quickly, he asked, "When did the meter change?"

Sara looked at her wrist. "When I was with Weston."

"How long was I unconscious?"

"A few hours."

King's expression turned sour. A few hours at the onset of a pandemic could save thousands of lives. Maybe more.

But Sara already knew that. "I tried waking you up a few times, but . . ."

"Don't worry about it," he said. "But we need to get you out of here as quick as possible."

"What about the rest of the team?" Sara asked.

King hated to say it, but there was no choice. They might already be too late. "They can fend for themselves."

"That might be true," a voice came from the entrance to the room, "but I think you could use some help."

Sara stood quickly, holding Weston's handgun. She pointed the gun toward the door. A shadow entered the room, parted the clothes, and stepped into the light.

Queen stood before them, wearing only her fatigues and boots, but covered, absolutely covered, in weapons. Multiple belts held knives and handguns of all kinds. To her back were strapped four AK-47s, an RPG, and a satchel full of ammo clips. She held a backpack in one hand and a radio in the other.

"How did you find us?" Sara asked, afraid that if Queen had found them so easily, perhaps others could as well.

"I saw you from above as I came down. Followed some wet footprints to start. Then searched house to house. Now help me out of this. It weighs a ton."

They helped her remove the cache of weapons and lined them up on the bed. Queen handed King one of the belts from her waist. "This one's for you."

King noticed the knife handle and drew it. "My knife?"

Queen nodded.

"Thanks," King said.

"Consider it a wedding gift," Queen said with a smirk. "Besides, she's part of the family now." Queen's smile disappeared. "And there's an opening on the team."

"Bishop," King said.

Queen nodded. "Rook is captured. Knight is injured, but hiding somewhere. Pawn Two is dead."

King closed his eyes. He knew about Bishop. But Rook and Knight being missing in action and Somi dead were news to him. Bad news. No single mission in his entire career had cost him so much. He fought back his growing despair and turned the energy from sadness to anger. Sadness clouded the mind, made soldiers slow. Anger sharpened like flint to a knife. "What happened to Rook?"

"I was with him. We came in together." Queen shook her head. "He was taken by the original Neanderthal women. Shorter, but much more nasty. They're the ones we encountered at Anh Dung. Rook was alive when they took him . . . but I'm not sure for how long."

"Why did they take him?" Sara asked.

Queen picked Sara's now-dry sports bra off the line. "Mind if I borrow this?"

"No . . . go ahead."

Queen slipped into the bra, shoving her larger breasts into it, flattening them out. "A little tight." Queen bounced up and down. Her chest didn't budge. "But it will do." She looked at King, her eyes suddenly cold. "They took Rook to replace Weston."

King and Sara knew exactly what that meant. Weston, being the father of the Neanderthal women's children, had given them a family again. Now they wanted to start a new family . . . with Rook.

"Oh, God," Sara said.

"If we don't find him now, we'll come back for him," King said. "But first we need to get Sara back to the States."

Queen looked up. "Why?"

"I have the cure," Sara said. "It's in my blood. Have any open wounds?"

Queen put a finger on her forehead and pushed. The dry swollen skin cracked and bled. Sara squeezed her lip, cracking the skin once more. She walked to Queen and kissed her forehead gently, but lingered, allowing their blood to mingle, not just on the surface, but in the wound as well, allowing the cure to enter her bloodstream. When she pulled away, Sara's lips were bright red as though coated in lip-stick. She wiped the blood on King's black pants. "There," she said. "Now you have the cure, too."

Queen nodded and picked up the radio she'd brought and clicked it on. A loud hiss filled the room, but it was garbled with static. "Let's take off the kid gloves, get the hell out of this mountain, and call for a ride."

A loud barrage of gunfire blasted down toward them—distant but amplified by the walled-in chamber. They rushed to the small window and peeked out. Far above, small figures, soldiers dressed in dark brown and black camouflaged uniforms, at least ten, moved along the staircase, blasting away at a few hybrids in pursuit. The hybrids, totally exposed, were cut down under the accurate barrage. The soldiers were good.

Elite.

A brilliant flash of lightning entered through the ring of mountain holes and was amplified by the giant crystals. Rain poured through the holes next, hissing as it struck the city, watered the subterranean plants, and formed small streams on Meru's sloped stone streets. The wet stone smelled fresh and sweet.

King ground his teeth as another flash of light revealed the soldiers up above. They moved down the long stone staircase in a perfect retrograde maneuver. The man covering the rear ceased fire and ran to the front, while the new rear man took his position and opened fire. Then, he too ran to the front while the next man covered the rear. Always covered, always moving, always killing.

"Death Volunteers."

FIFTY-NINE

After dressing quickly in his black fatigues, King felt more like a soldier again, but still didn't quite look the part. His feet, like Sara's, were now bare. Sara joined King and Queen, dressed once again in all black, her short hair dried flat against her head.

After strapping on the belt to which his KA-BAR knife and a Smith & Wesson Model 39 9mm handgun were holstered, King took an AK-47 from Queen and slid five spare clips into his cargo pant pockets. Queen placed a satchel bag over her shoulder. It contained spare clips for her AK as well and two RPG rounds for the already loaded launcher lying on the bed.

"Where did you find all this?" King asked.

"Storage room in the caves above," Queen replied. "Looked like they'd been collecting weapons from a variety of forces since the Vietnam War."

He nudged the large backpack with his foot. "What's in here?"

Queen grinned and opened the backpack. Several bricks of C4 plastic explosives complete with wiring and a hand-held detonator were inside. "They must have bagged a demo team at some point."

King nodded and returned Queen's grin. "I have an idea."

"Thought you might," Queen said as she picked up the

RPG launcher and headed for the door. "I'll slow them down."

King held a weapon out to Sara. "This," he said, "is an AR-15 assault rifle. Fires eight hundred rounds per minute, so don't hold the trigger down. Short bursts with accurate aim is a hell of a lot more effective than praying and spraying." He quickly showed her the safety, how to hold the weapon against her shoulder, and how to reload it. He handed her the weapon and placed three spare ammo magazines in her cargo pant pockets. "Stay close to me. Do exactly what I say."

Sara nodded, nervousness beginning to swirl within her core. She'd been in several firefights since this mission began. Each had rattled her severely, but this one would be different. With only three members of the previously seven-man team present, *she* was expected to fight. King strapped a belt around her waist. It held a knife and handgun, just like King's.

"Safety is off on the handgun," King said. "If you need it, pull it out and squeeze the trigger. A round is already chambered."

A loud swish erupted from outside the stone building. King and Sara looked out the window. A trail of smoke traced through the open cavern behind an RPG. It shot in a straight line, headed for the stone staircase and the men descending it. Seconds later, the RPG struck the cavern wall and exploded. The sound rolled throughout the massive space and the orange light of the explosion blossomed throughout the cave, enhanced by the crystals. A portion of the staircase shattered and a pursuing hybrid fell off the side. But the VPLA soldiers continued down while the horde of hybrids paused at the edge of the gaping hole in the staircase.

Queen reloaded the launcher. "Better get a move on, King! If I can't hit these guys, they'll have our position."

The dull glow remaining in the cavern as the crystals filtered less and less light from the setting sun hidden by storm clouds outside made seeing and moving more difficult. But it also helped conceal them from enemy eyes.

A second RPG soared through the cave, this one spinning madly as the old RPG failed. It struck and crumbled a small building in the first gallery of the city. Queen whispered a string of curses and loaded the third and final RPG.

King took Sara by the wrist and pulled her toward the door. "Time to go." They exited the second-story room and descended a flight of stairs as a third stream of smoke shot into the air. This RPG, like the first, soared in a straight line. But, unlike the first, it generated sudden screams from the men still pounding down the long curved staircase. Queen's aim was true. The men lunged forward, some diving down the stairs, no doubt injuring themselves in the process. Most evaded the explosive, but two were caught as the RPG slammed home, shredding stone, flesh, and bone alike. Another man shot off the side of the staircase, propelled by the explosion's shock wave. He screamed the entire fifty feet down until striking the stone floor below. The seven remaining Death Volunteers continued on, bolting down the staircase without any concern for the hybrids still stuck behind the large gap.

One of the hybrids attempted to jump the distance, but fell short and careened to his death below. The others then retreated back up the staircase and disappeared from view.

Queen discarded the RPG launcher as King and Sara joined her. "Which way, boss?"

King motioned toward the temple, barely visible in the low light and looking more ominous than ever. "The temple."

They ran for several minutes, their bare feet allowing them to move in silence. As they reached the temple perimeter, facing the snake-covered balustrades, King stopped. He turned to Queen. "No one gets through that gate."

Queen nodded and took up position behind one of the balustrades. King looked at Sara. "No one."

Sara also nodded, with much less confidence, after realizing the order was intended for her and Queen. She mimicked Queen's prone position, aiming her AR-15 at the thirty-foot gate, praying no one would enter it before King returned. She looked back for King and saw him running up the temple stairs, the backpack full of C4 over his shoulder.

The dark outline of the main temple gate became harder to see as the rain pouring through the holes above poured into the chamber, striking the large crystals overhead and forming an honest to goodness subterranean monsoon. Water poured down the courtyard, flowed from the temple, and surged down through the large gate like a wide, shallow river. Knowing the general layout of the city, Sara knew the water would flow down the incline of the main street, through each of the five gallery gates, and into the horseshoe-shaped river surrounding the city.

"Nice knowing you, Pawn," Queen said to Sara.

A nervous laugh escaped Sara's mouth. "Thanks for the pep talk."

Sara marveled at how there always seemed to be a little levity before a fight. She'd seen smiles on the team's faces before every battle they knew was going to happen. No one seemed to appreciate the surprises. But before the Chess Team traded bullets and bombs with the enemy, they traded smiles. She realized the subtle last-moment mirth was actually some kind of warrior bonding. Before they put their lives in each other's hands they reaffirmed their camaraderie. That Queen was joking with her was a compliment. She decided to return it. "I'll try not to shoot you."

Queen cracked a wide grin, which quickly disappeared when the *thump, thump, thump* of approaching boots echoed up from the city, growing louder with every second.

The Death Volunteers were approaching the gate.

SIXTY

A scream rolled through the dark tunnels surrounding Meru. It was followed by a string of curses.

Rook stood with his back against a stone wall in a small, empty chamber that seemed to have no other function than to serve as a crossroads for four converging tunnels. He knew they were closer to the necropolis because the space glowed faint green from a thin coating of algae. What he didn't know was what the hell the old wenches wanted with him.

Despite the fact that he had killed several of them, they seemed to have no intention of returning the favor. That wasn't to say they weren't being aggressive. Several slashes across his chest seeped blood over his waist. But they could have killed him in an instant. Unless they were playing with him, or punishing him. But something in their eyes said otherwise. He didn't see malice or hatred. He saw excitement.

He tried to step forward, but was shoved back quickly, hitting his head against the wall. "Son of a bitch!"

"Not nice words!" Red shouted. "You be nice to mothers."

Red grunted at one of the others. Without hesitation, the Neanderthal woman leaped forward, landing on Rook, wrapping her legs around his waist and holding on to his neck.

Before Rook could move he felt immense pressure on his shoulder, then twin pops of pain as two large canines pierced his skin.

Rook shouted out for a moment before his training kicked in. They might be stronger, but he had leverage, reach, and the best hand-to-hand combat sparring partner in the world—Queen. He reached both hands around the beast's head and pressed both thumbs into its eyes, holding nothing back. The Neanderthal reared up with a roar and loosened its grip. He spun, pulling the heavy body off him, and heaved it like a giant shot put. The body crashed into two of the others and sent them all to the floor.

A fourth charged him like a Pamplona bull. He waited, then stepped to the side, took hold of a fistful of hair on the back of its skull, and added a strong shove to the Neanderthal's already considerable speed. It struck the wall head-on and collapsed into an immobilized heap.

Surging with adrenaline and confidence, Rook faced the rest of the old wenches, opened his arms, and shouted. He didn't say any words, just vocalized his rage. He'd been kidnapped by a bunch of hairy freaks who wanted to manhandle him and make him their bitch. And that was *not* going to happen. He would fight to the death before giving up.

To his surprise, the mob backed off, loosening the circle around him. The Neanderthal at his feet stirred, came to, and ran away on all fours, hiding behind the others. His show of strength and ferocity seemed to have made an impression.

Red stepped forward. She stood tall, sniffing the air, then sat squat, staring at him with her piercing yellow eyes. She grunted twice, then said, "Big man, new father."

"Not a chance," Rook said.

"Big man, yes!" She pounded the floor with her fists.

Rook thought for a moment. They wanted him to be the father. The *new* father. Weston's *replacement*. If he said no, they might just kill him on the spot. But if he said yes, what then? Would the merriment continue until he couldn't fight or he died anyway? Either way ended in death. Or was there some wiggle room? He decided to try some Neanderthal logic.

"Weston, father."

"No, *you* father."

"Me Rook. Weston father."

"Rook father!"

"There can be only one father," Rook said, holding up his index finger. "And Weston *is* father."

Red seemed to ponder this, chewing her bottom lip. Rook wondered if she would come to the conclusion he was hoping for.

"Then . . . we kill father."

"That's a girl," Rook said, then caught his breath. "Wait, which one?"

"Weston father."

"And when Weston is dead," Rook said, "I will be father. But not until then. Understand?"

The brood of Neanderthals tensed suddenly, moving away from the far tunnel. What happened next took Rook totally off guard. They formed a protective circle around him, guarding him from whatever was approaching. He was pushed low while they stood tall and ready. Shadows approached. Voices spoke quietly.

Human voices.

English.

Rook couldn't see them, but when one of the voices paused midsentence and said, "Oh no," he recognized the voice. As the old mothers hooted and charged, Rook stood tall behind them and shouted, "Stop!"

They listened, freezing in place only feet from the two newcomers. Rook laughed when he saw them, faces blanched and bewildered—Bishop with Knight clinging to his back like a baby monkey. The Neanderthals parted for Rook and allowed him to approach his confused teammates. But it was Rook who was even more confused. Bishop was alive . . . and *well*. Very well, it seemed.

"Bishop, how? I saw your head come off."

Bishop grinned. He actually grinned. Then shrugged. "I guess it didn't come all the way off."

"And you feel okay? You're not, you know, feeling extra hungry?"

"He was," Knight said. "You don't even want to know what he threw up back there."

Bishop fished the crystal from his pocket. "Something about the crystals here make it go away. I feel better than I have in years."

Rook chuckled. "Well, I don't give a crap what's doing it. I'm just happy to see you guys alive." He clapped both of their shoulders.

"So . . ." Knight cleared his throat. "Would you like to introduce us to your harem?"

"Watch it, little man." Rook turned to the group of Neanderthal women, still poised to attack. He motioned to Knight and Bishop. "Friends."

"Dangerous," Red said, her hackles raised high on her back.

"No. Bishop. Knight. Friends."

Some of them began growling. A low hoot came from the back of the group.

"Assert your dominance," Knight whispered. "Big and loud."

Rook pushed down his embarrassment at having to do this in front of his friends, but there was no other choice. He took a deep breath and bellowed, "No, damnit!" He turned fully to the mothers, snarled, and opened his arms, ready for a fight. "*I* am the father. They are friends! You will *not* hurt them!"

The group backed off as one. Red nodded, hackles lowering.

Geez, Rook thought, *talk about dysfunctional.*

Knight looked over Bishop's shoulder and gave Rook a smile. "I found Weston's journal. He discovered how to control them years ago. I was going to have Bishop try that out, but you fit the role so much better."

Rook looked back with a wicked grin. "Stuff it before I tell them to put you back in the meat locker." He turned to the old mothers. "Now then, let's go find Weston."

Red smiled. "Yes, Father."

SIXTY-ONE

From high up on the temple's first staircase, King had a clear view over the fifth gallery wall. He could see the city laid out before him in the dim light cast by the absolutely gargantuan crystals hanging precariously above. Worse, he could see the advancing VPLA troops as they charged through the fourth gallery gate, weapons sweeping for enemies. They moved with confidence, not just in their actions, but in their direction, as though they knew where to find them. But he would do the same. The center of the city, with its tall walls and single entrance, was the most defensible position and clearly the optimal place to make a last stand.

King worked faster, squishing the last chunk of C4 into a fissure at the top of the stairs. C4, unlike the way it's portrayed in movies, cannot detonate from being manhandled, shot, or burned. It's extremely safe and pliable; that is, until a blast cap or detonator is inserted, which King did next, pushing the two detonator pins deep into the putty as he had with the ten other explosives, filling gaps along the stairs and temple walls surrounding the cruciform-capped giant fish tank.

King activated the small wireless detonator in his hand, its single light blinking green. The explosives were armed and the electrical detonator would set off the explosives in a millisecond. The detonator in his hand had only one safety feature. The lone red button at the top of the pen-sized device needed to be pushed once, which would raise the trigger up, and then pushed again, which would send a signal to the receivers imbedded in the C4, signaling the detonation. Of course, switching it off, by twisting the base, could undo the first push of a button and reset the trigger. All in all, it was an advanced little device. King wondered if Weston might have actually taken it from the VPLA.

Reminded of the approaching force, King looked up again. Through the downpour he could no longer see the soldiers. They'd either entered the city's side streets . . . or reached the gate.

A blast of gunfire from below confirmed the latter.

King bounded down the steep temple stairs toward the courtyard full of palm trees and flowers below. Along the way he wondered if the shock wave from all that C4 would be enough to crack the crystals high above. Would they crash down on them all? Would the deluge unleashed from the massive subcity fishpond wipe away the city? He didn't know. But he did know the chaos would become his ally.

He hit the courtyard floor at a run, readying his AK-47.

A second burst of gunfire lit up the balustrades before him. Queen was firing warning shots, letting the VPLA know that the first man to enter would be the first man to die. The gate created a convenient bottleneck for them.

He reached the balustrades and crouched next to Queen, who no longer lay in her original position. Neither was Sara. She'd moved farther to the left.

Queen had changed positions twice, once after each burst of gunfire. First to make it appear they had a larger force defending the temple, but also to misdirect the aim of the man peeking in, who no doubt would soon lob a grenade in their direction.

King took aim at the gate. "Situation?"

"They're peeking and I'm trying to convince them to stop," Queen said, looking over the sight of her AK-47. "All set?"

"I just rigged the temple behind us." King showed her the detonator. "It's going to be a fast, wet ride out of here."

Queen fired a burst as a man poked his head around the gate. Stone and sparks flew as the three rounds just missed the man's head. King and Queen stood together and ran toward Sara. They stopped halfway there and took aim again. She motioned to Sara, who looked nervous, but kept her aim and concentration on the gate. "What about her?"

King looked at Sara, soaking wet and grimacing, yet somehow still beautiful. For a moment, he wasn't sure what Queen was asking him. Was this mission related, or about the fact that Queen had been reading him like an open book since he'd first seen Sara? "What *about* her?"

"How is she holding up?"

King tried to hide his relief, but was sure Queen would see through that charade as well. "She's a natural."

"You sure about that?"

A three-round burst rang out behind him. A man shouted from behind the gate. Had he been hit? He looked back and saw Sara jump to her feet and move toward them, her aim never veering from the gate as she weaved in and out of the double set of balustrades. King smiled. She *was* a natural.

Queen slapped King on the shoulder as she stood up. "I'll be damned."

The group rejoined each other at the center of the balustrades.

"What's the plan?" Sara asked.

"Move!" King shouted as the sound of multiple grenades clacking against stone filled the space between the balustrades and the gate. King yanked Sara up and the three of them ran back into the courtyard. The balustrades shattered and launched into the air as five separate grenades detonated at once. The tactic, similar to that of the Chess Team when facing the initial VPA regular army attack, was slightly smaller in scope yet no less effective as it eradicated the balustrades and created a shock wave that sent King, Queen, and Sara toppling to the hard courtyard floor.

King scrambled to his feet and ducked behind a raised garden at the back end of the courtyard. It held beds of red and yellow flowers and four palm trees. The position was defensible yet only twenty feet from the explosive-laden staircase. Far too close to attempt what he had planned.

Queen and Sara took cover behind an identical garden on the opposite side of the courtyard. Sara kneeled behind a palm tree and took aim. Queen lay flat behind the garden's foot-high stone wall and took aim around the corner. They were like a pair of cats, bouncing back, ready to fight. And just in time, too.

Through the gate to the courtyard, a wall of debris marked the location where the balustrades had been. Seven soldiers bounded over the wall, weapons up and firing. Bullets pinged all around the courtyard as the VPLA men laid down suppressing fire and took up positions behind the raised gardens at the front of the courtyard.

King leaned out from behind the garden wall and fired four separate three-round bursts at two locations. The first six rounds ripped into the side of a palm tree. The second six rounds found only stone, exploding sparks into the air. Finding targets in the dim light would be a challenge since the only way to see them through the rain and darkness was to look when they were returning fire. And that was a very dangerous technique.

Queen and Sara popped out of their hiding places just after King ceased firing, causing the VPLA soldiers to duck back down. King used the distraction to bolt across the courtyard and dive for cover next to Queen.

"Sara!" King shouted.

Sara turned to him as she ducked down behind the broad palm tree providing her cover. "What?"

"Do you know where they are? Can you tell?"

Sara knew what he was asking. Could she *sense* them? A few days ago she would have found it a ridiculous question. But now, in the heat of battle, she wished she could answer it in the affirmative. The problem was, she couldn't. "No! The crystals are screwing me up . . . or making me right. However you want to put it. Something about them realigns the neural pathways in the nervous system. My senses are as normal as yours now. I'm blind, so to speak."

Damnit, King thought. He could have used the advantage Sara's odd senses could provide. Old-fashioned tactics would have to do the trick. In many firefights a pattern emerged. One side fired and ducked, the other retaliated in kind. Sometimes a slow reaction or a misstep in the timing of the dance would result in a death. But breaking the timing on purpose guaranteed it. There just wasn't any way of knowing who would be shot . . . unless you rigged the system.

King lay low as Queen and Sara continued the fight. King counted as volleys of bullets were traded. He listened as bullets struck the tree blocking Sara and pinged against the wall where Queen hid. The VPLA soldiers had their positions pegged and it wouldn't be long before a grenade tumbled in their direction.

Sliding to the side, King reached the opposite end of the garden's short wall. He waited as Queen and Sara fired a barrage. Then as the last tracer ripped through the air, he rose from his position, just as the seven VPLA soldiers were doing the same. But they were aiming for Sara and Queen, and not one of them saw King until it was too late. Two of the Death Volunteers took three bullets each and fell to the floor. King wounded a third, striking only his right arm—his throwing arm. The man screamed, not just in pain, but because the bullet that had pierced his forearm had severed the tendons that controlled his fingers. With the tendons snapped, the fingers fell loose and the live grenade the man was about to lob fell to the stone courtyard at his feet. Seconds later it exploded, reducing the soldier to globs of flesh and sending metal and stone shrapnel into the heads and chests of two others.

Five down. Two to go. The odds had just turned in their favor.

Then a flash of lightning from outside the mountain pulsed through the open portals, struck the crystals, and filled the city with light.

King froze as though staring into the eyes of Medusa.

Standing on the eight-foot wall that surrounded the courtyard and separated them from the columns of balustrades was an army of hybrids, tense and ready for action. The two remaining Death Volunteers saw them, too, taking aim at the surrounding force. As Queen and Sara saw the group, they stood together with King, aim lowered, knowing that should a single shot be fired, the fight would end in seconds, with their deaths.

King tossed his AK-47 to the floor and held up his hands. Queen and Sara followed suit. As did the Death Volunteers.

Blazing fires plumed all around the saturated city. Orange light struck the crystals from below, and doubled in intensity. The light looked like a Southern California sunset, orange and pleasant. The rain falling through the mountain portals glowed like liquid Creamsicle as it fell and flowed through the city.

They turned toward the sound of wet footsteps. Weston walked down the stairs with Lucy at his side. A torrent of water flowed down the stairs from above, licking at their feet.

King fingered the detonator in his pocket. He could erase Weston from existence. But he would bury them in the process. King walked into the center of the courtyard and moved back toward the two VPLA soldiers, hoping they weren't stupid enough to attempt taking a shot at him. Weston reached the bottom of the stairs and walked toward them. He stopped ten feet away as his army of hybrids hopped down from the walls and encircled the five soldiers, Delta Force and VPLA alike.

"What will you do with us?" Sara asked, stepping forward.

Weston smiled. "You two," he said, pointing at King and Sara, "belong to Lucy."

Lucy clapped, hooted, and then bared her inch-long canines at the two. There would be no fooling her again.

"As for the rest," Weston said, then motioned to the circle of angry hybrids. "You belong to them."

SIXTY-TWO

As the group of hybrids closed in around King, Queen, Sara, and the two remaining Death Volunteers, they formed a tight, twenty-foot circle, bringing the group of combatants, who just seconds ago were trying to kill each other, into close proximity. The closeness and orange glow from the giant torches lit around the city revealed Major General Trung as one of the two remaining soldiers.

Queen saw him and frowned. She still had a gun and knife strapped to her waist. It would have been easy for her to kill him using either weapon, but the sudden action might be misconstrued as an attack on the hybrids. And that would do them all in. She decided to rely on the weapons she found most reliable and least likely to trigger an assault from the enemies surrounding them. She walked around King and Sara, facing Trung.

He saw her instantly. His eyes went wide with the memory of the terrible things he had done to her, to the woman whose ferocity and fortitude dwarfed any man he'd ever trained or served with, himself included. The bright red brand on her forehead burned fear into him. His companion saw Queen, too, and stepped aside.

"Don't do anything foolish," Trung said, his hand resting on his holstered gun. "You might set them—"

Queen reached out with both hands before Trung could

think to draw his pistol. She took hold of him by the front of his shirt and yanked him to her. She simultaneously thrust the glowing red Death Volunteer brand on her forehead toward him. Her skull collided with his face, resulting in a loud crunch as his nose and cheekbones gave in to the powerful head butt. He fell limp, dead from the single blow. A bloodred, smudged version of the VPLA star-and-skull symbol was stamped onto his forehead.

She dropped Trung in a heap and regarded the hybrids closest to her. They stepped back for a moment before turning their attention to the last VPLA soldier. With a speed equaling Queen's they reached out and snagged the soldier. He cried out, but a quick twist of his neck from one of the hybrids silenced him. The act was quick and easy, like unscrewing the cap from a Pepsi bottle. King drew his sidearm. Sara and Queen followed his lead, drawing their weapons.

A staring match ensued with neither side wanting to make the first move. There was no doubt that when the battle began, both sides would have casualties.

But the hybrids had numbers, strength, and speed on their side.

Weston stepped back, allowing Lucy to step in front of him. "I'm sorry, but the world will have to get along without you," he said, moving farther back away from the impending fight.

The circle of hybrids closed in tight around them.

The attack would come soon. King knew that if the hybrids made the first move he and Queen might get off a few shots, but the fight would be over quickly. Their only chance was to act first.

"Shock and awe," King said.

"What?" Weston asked.

Queen nodded.

"What does that—"

King and Queen took aim and pulled triggers. In a few seconds both had emptied their clips. Ten of the hybrids slumped over dead.

Lucy turned toward Weston. "Father . . ." She placed her hand inside the gaping wound in her chest.

The sudden act of violence shocked the remaining hybrids into stunned silence. They looked around at their fallen brothers and sisters, amazed at how quickly so many of them had fallen.

Weston's jaw shook and his eyes filled with tears. Lucy slid from Weston's arms and fell to the stone floor. Blood seeped from two gunshot wounds in her chest. "Lucy. My princess. No . . ." He became rage personified, his cheeks shaking as he shouted. "Kill them! Kill every last one of them!"

King took Sara's pistol from her hand and grabbed her by the wrist. He fired and began running. Sara followed, watching as he blazed a trail through the bodies blocking their way. He led them straight toward the courtyard exit. A moment later they burst from the circle like a nucleus being withdrawn from a cell.

The hybrids snapped out of their daze and launched after the three. The hair on their backs rose up. Their teeth gnashed. Their voices growled. They became as inhuman as the mothers . . . or grandmothers . . . who suddenly appeared at the courtyard exit, partly concealed in shadow.

King, Queen, and Sara slid to a stop on the wet courtyard floor. King looked back at the temple as he stopped. They were still too close, though the inch-deep water already flowing quickly past their feet was a good sign. The problem was that they would be torn to shreds before his plan could come to fruition. Either way they would be killed.

Still, he thought, *I may have to risk it.* He pulled the wireless detonator from his pocket and held it tight.

The hybrids stopped as well, confused by the sudden appearance of their ancestors.

Without pause, the old mothers charged.

King took aim despite the situation now being totally hopeless.

But he held his fire. Something wasn't right.

The wall of charging Neanderthal women wasn't converging on their position. In fact, the wall of fur opened up as it passed by them. The mothers were charging Weston and the hybrids!

King spun, watching as Weston's and the hybrids' shock turned to anger. This fight had been a long time coming. The two forces stopped short, sizing each other up and calling out like a horde of angry apes. Weston stepped back, looking fearfully at the mothers . . . and his children.

A heavy hand took King's shoulder. He spun and raised the weapon between a pair of blue eyes that hovered above a wide smile.

"What do you think of my cavalry?"

Rook.

He was shirtless and bore a bloody bite mark on his shoulder and three broad slices across his chest. King lowered the weapon and smiled.

A second large body stepped out from behind him. "We should go."

Bishop.

The hooting reached a crescendo, but the mothers were still waiting for something. As King wondered what they were waiting for, Rook stepped forward and shouted, "Now!"

King watched in shock as the old mothers followed Rook's command and launched forward, fifteen five-foot-tall demolition balls. Their hair raised up, shimmering with wetness, and bouncing with every confident stride. Their yellow eyes glowed in the wet orange light delivered by the crystals through the still-falling torrent of rain.

Some of the younger and smaller hybrids ran straight off. As did Weston. But the larger males stood their ground. The old mothers launched at them, biting, swiping, and leaping from the larger males as though they were trees. Screams of pain and roars of anger rolled up through the cavern and cut through the sound of the falling rain.

"C'mon!" Rook shouted. "Knight is waiting for us by the river."

They climbed over the ruined balustrades and made for the large gate, its massive opening a beacon of hope.

As they ran, Queen looked at Rook, his bleeding chest glowing orange in the surreal light. She looked at the bite wound on his shoulder. "You didn't actually . . ."

Rook looked incredulous. "Hell no! I just made all sorts of promises I couldn't keep, blah blah blah."

"Like most of your relationships," King added.

Rook smiled and nodded. "What can I say? I'm a ladies' man."

They passed through the gate as the hoots of hybrids in pursuit sounded out behind and around them. The city was *alive*. Full of hybrids. They would never escape, even with the help of the old mothers, who would most likely die as well.

As they neared the fourth gallery gate, five hybrids launched into the street, stalking toward them. King led the group to one of the nearby houses, pushing the button on the detonator once. When the team was off the street and headed up the stairs behind him, he stopped and let the others pass.

He looked out at the amazing city, lost for thousands of years and home to a forgotten civilization. The beauty and history of the place made King cringe at what he was about to do. This wonder could not be duplicated. It couldn't be replaced.

But neither could the human race. Seeing no other option for escape, he shook his head, closed his eyes, and pushed the detonator button a second time.

SIXTY-THREE

The four hybrids charging up the street toward the team's position on the staircase stumbled and fell as the massive amount of explosives planted by King detonated. The temple burst like a volcano, raining Volkswagen-sized chunks of the temple around the city. Buildings imploded as the giant pieces of wall, stairs, and balustrades descended like missiles. The fragments launched from the center of the blast shot up and struck the great crystals above.

From the outside, Mount Meru really did look like a volcano as smoke filtered out of the holes in the mountainside. But not all of the smoke made it out. Torrents of rain mingled with the smoke and fell back inside, collecting on the city walls as sludge.

The ground shook violently as a deafening shock wave shot out from the blast and ricocheted off the cavern walls, lingering painfully in the ears of everyone in Meru—human and Nguoi Rung alike. As the shock wave subsided, a new rumble filled the air, this one slower yet growing in volume. The hybrids in the street stood, still dazed. They looked at each other, then, as a group, retreated toward the outskirts of the city.

After watching the hybrids retreat, King entered the small second-floor room, rejoining Queen, Bishop, Rook, and Sara. They were looking out a window. Through it, a massive plume of smoke rose from the temple. Chunks of stone still fell around the city, mixed with the rain.

Portions of the temple twisted and fell, the sound of their collapse mingling with the still-expanding roar.

Sara turned away from the spectacle suddenly, looking at King. "Weston's close."

"Your senses are back?" King asked.

"I can smell *him*!"

King sniffed. His nose filled with an odor close to that of a spoiled French onion soup. He turned toward the door just as Weston entered wielding a pistol. He fired.

King grunted in pain and fell to the floor, grasping his shoulder.

"What have you done?" Weston shouted, moving toward the window while waving his gun at the team, forcing them away. He looked out the window, at the smoldering, ruined temple. The city began to shake around them. The rumble grew louder.

"No . . . ," Weston said quietly as the source of the steadily growing vibrations surged into view. A river of water spilled from the fifth gallery gate, flowing down the main street. At its front rolled stone debris, ruined balustrades, and the bodies of more than fifty hybrids and a few of the old mothers. Mixed in with their bodies were scores of bright orange and white fish. The subterranean fishpond had been emptied. Merging with the already considerable flow of rainwater, the torrent washed quickly down through the inclined city.

A loud snap, like the crack of a falling tree amplified through loudspeakers, drew Weston's attention up, above the temple. One of the large crystals that grew from ceiling to the city floor cracked and slowly fell.

The size and weight of the crystal was that of two 747s end to end. It struck the city below, crushing what remained of the temple with a force above and beyond the C4 explosion King had created. The shock wave flattened the fifth gallery wall, crumbled several buildings throughout the city, added force and speed to the river flowing down the main street, and loosened the other crystals above.

Meru was coming undone.

With wild eyes, Weston turned his gaze from the city to the team. He shook. Sweat beaded and dripped down his face. The gun moved from Sara, kneeling by the door with King, who was just now sitting up, to Rook, Bishop, and Queen on the other side of the room, seeing the three of them as more of an immediate threat.

The gun stopped at Bishop. Weston stared at him with wide, fear-filled eyes. "I—I saw you die." He pulled the gun's hammer back. "You should be dead."

Bishop grinned. "I've heard that before."

Then he charged.

Weston put two bullets in Bishop's chest before the two collided. They stumbled back together, toppling out of the large rectangular window just moments after the stone-filled front line of the river flowed past. They fell into a six-foot-deep, fast-moving river.

King launched to his feet and ran to the window. "Let's move," he said, and jumped in. Sara, Queen, and Rook followed at his heels.

The raging waters slid through the city streets like a giant snake, swerving with the bends and surging down inclines. The team, and Weston, were at its mercy. Swimming did nothing, so they simply tried to stay above water and avoid being crushed by the churning debris or smashed into the side of a structure or gate as they were whisked through the city.

Bounding across rooftops, several hybrids raced alongside the river yelling, "Father! Father!" as they attempted to free Weston from the river's grasp. One of them leaned from a stone overpass and pulled Weston up by his arm. The Chess Team flowed quickly past. He didn't want to be rescued. He wanted vengeance. "Put me back in!" Weston shouted.

The hybrid looked confused. "Father?"

Weston yanked himself free and fell back in. He was swept away, in pursuit of his enemies, the destroyers of Meru, the killers of his family. Of Lucy.

The Chess Team quickly passed through Meru's third and second gates in thirty seconds. As they approached the first and final gate, Knight waved to them from atop a statue, then leaped into the water. He'd seen the destruction from below, witnessed the city falling apart, and had a clear view of the hybrid horde fleeing over the rooftops. Diving into the raging water, even with an injured ankle, was far preferable to staying any longer. After passing through the final and smallest of the gates, they were free of the city. The flow spread wide and slowed as they entered the stone clearing between city . . . and river. Sara swam to King, who struggled to stay above water with his wounded shoulder.

"Do you need he—!" Sara's words were cut off as King shoved her underwater.

Weston took aim from twenty feet back and fired twice. King ducked down as the water around them absorbed the bullets. When he came up he saw Weston again, but then the water fell out from under them and they were tumbling through the air.

They landed in the twisting moat that flowed around the city and were pushed down deep by the river falling from above. King fought the current with his good arm, to no avail. He tried using his injured arm, but the blinding pain that came with the movement almost sapped his consciousness. Then he was pulled up. Sara again. She took him by the shirt and pulled him away from the newly formed waterfall.

The normally calm river flowing around the city raged with white water, fueled by the monsoon outside and the fresh addition of the temple's fishpond. As they were swept away and around the city, Queen, Bishop, Rook, and Knight pounded through the water and rejoined them.

"We have to get out of here," Knight said, looking toward the river exit, which was now full to the ceiling. There would be no surfacing in the underwater river. But the smooth vertical walls of the river offered no purchase or chance of escape. They'd been *designed* to sweep enemies away.

"Stay close and stay down!" King shouted as they neared the river exit. "Deep breath and curl up!"

The team began taking very fast breaths, saturating their bodies with oxygen. Sara mimicked them as best she could. Ten feet from the exit, three shots pinged off the stone around them. Weston, still behind, still enraged, shook the gun at them and swam closer. He shouted to the hybrids still running along the river's banks. "Get them outside! Go. Now!"

The hybrids obeyed, breaking off the chase and heading for the city's other, more secretive exits.

King looked back at Meru and saw more of the giant crystals falling from above. The whole mountain was coming down. Groups of hybrids and a few of the old mothers fled, funneling out through small tunnels he hadn't seen before. He turned back toward the tunnel exit. It loomed above them like jaws of the underworld.

"Go under!" King shouted.

The Chess Team pushed under the water and curled into fetal positions. The orange glow of the fire-fueled crystal light disappeared moments later as they were plunged into the pitch-dark underground river.

SIXTY-FOUR

Cold, wet darkness surrounded Sara. She felt herself pushed and pulled as the water encasing her flowed like a roller coaster through the interior of the mountain. Her back slammed into the stone roof. As she screamed out in pain, the air in her lungs escaped. The benefit was that her body became more naturally buoyant and sank down to the center of the flow. The downside was that she now needed to take a breath.

Her lungs and battered back burned. Nausea pulsed through her body, generated from the impact, the fear of death, and the rapid undulations of the river. She opened her eyes and saw only darkness. The others might have been feet away, but it was like they no longer existed. She'd entered some kind of torturous limbo where there was no up or down. Unlike limbo, there was plenty of pain to go around.

Sara clenched her hands over her mouth and nose, fighting her body's natural urge to suck in air. Her foot struck bottom and spun her body. She opened her eyes again and saw a bright sphere floating ahead. Within the sphere she saw five silhouettes kicking toward the light. They were headed for an exit!

Moonlight glowed above her through a clearing in the fading storm's clouds. Her equilibrium returned. Facing up, she shoved her feet down against the silt-coated river bottom and launched to the surface. She broke through the water gasping and gagging. The river slowed and deepened, allowing the team to collect themselves.

King, Queen, and Rook swam together at the center of the river. Sara, still ten feet behind, lay back and looked at the storm above. It wasn't the swirling dark clouds, the bullet-sized raindrops, or the sweet smell of the storm that held her attention, it was the way she experienced them. A flash of lighting arced through the sky. She saw it with her eyes . . . and *felt* it in her chest. She could hear the wind whipping through the forest, scratching leaves. The sound tickled the back of her neck. She was experiencing the world as she knew it again. And it was beautiful.

King swam to her. "You okay?"

Sara smiled. "You have no—" A splash, different from the deep resonating river, entered her ears and created a tension in her shoulders. Something had risen from the water, behind her. The smell told her who. A metallic click caused a deep tickle in her back. "Get down!"

Sara and King ducked beneath the water as three shots rang out. They kicked farther downriver, staying underwater, and surfaced next to the other four members of the team.

"We can't keep dodging bullets!" Rook said. "He's going to get lucky sooner or later."

They needed to get out of the river. King looked up. The walls around them ranged between forty and fifty feet tall—too high to scale, unless they wanted to make themselves easy targets. And there was no shoreline to speak of. If one existed earlier, it had been covered by the deepening water level. They were stuck. At the mercy of the river and the pistol-wielding Weston.

Sara grasped King's arm. He grunted in pain.

"Sorry," she said, then pointed up.

A group of hybrids ran along the cliff's edge, forty feet above the river, keeping pace with the team, watching and waiting for them to exit. He looked to the other side and shook his head. Five of the old mothers, including Red, pounded through the wet brush as they too kept pace with the group being carried downriver.

With enemies on both sides and behind, their only option was to let the river take them and pray the crocodiles didn't like to feed during a storm. King looked back and found Weston missing. He'd been far behind them, aiming his gun but never firing. Now, he had vanished. "Where's Weston?" he shouted.

The team looked for him, too, but found nothing.

"Did he bug out?" Knight asked.

King doubted it, looking for Weston among his progeny. But he was nowhere to be seen.

Lightning crisscrossed through the sky and struck in the forest nearby. The pulse of thunder that followed as the globules of rain superheated in a flash ripped through the air around them. The intense sensory backlash shot a pain through Sara's chest. She fled from it, ducking underwater.

King followed her under, afraid she had succumbed to a cramp, but found her treading water just below the surface.

Lightning flashed again, illuminating the underwater world. Fish freed from the giant pond, some living, some dead, moved through the water with them. A hybrid body bounced along below. Dead. A glint of silver far ahead, glowing brightly in the sudden light, caught King's eye.

He kicked toward the light, but a tug on his foot turned him around. He expected to see one of the fish attempting to once again make a meal of his body, but instead found Weston's face, twisted with anger. He'd taken hold of his ankle! King kicked and twisted, wrenching his leg free. He shot to the surface.

"Weston's surfacing!" he shouted, then dove back under. The team followed him under as Weston, and his pistol, surfaced.

Weston growled loudly then ducked back under. He could see the Chess Team several feet ahead of him. He slid back toward the surface, waiting for one of them to run out of air. He would surface with them and then fire. It would be easy.

King turned forward and swam hard ahead of the group, making for the glint of metal he'd seen. Lightning shot through the sky again and he saw it just beneath him. He reached out, fumbled, and then wrapped his hands around the familiar object. He turned forward just as the team headed for the surface.

The Chess Team's tactic had been to rise as one, possibly confusing Weston by giving him multiple targets, but as they watched him rise with them, each one of them realized his aim would be true.

Sara would fall first.

But if they didn't rise to take a breath, all would drown.

King pushed hard against the river bottom and shot up like a torpedo. He breached the surface before the others and took aim with Rook's lost .50-caliber Desert Eagle, clutching it in both hands.

The taste of silty fresh water filled his mouth as he took a breath. His eyes caught sight of Weston's head cresting like a rising submarine as Sara neared the surface. The sight of Weston's head rising held his gaze with laserlike focus. He pulled the trigger as Weston rose, pulling his own trigger a fraction of a second later. Weston's shot went wild as he was flung backward.

All but Sara rose from the river in time to see Weston's face implode and exit through the back of his skull. His body fell flat and shifted to the side of the river, where it bounced off the wall.

The hybrids above wailed, calling out for their father. But his body, now stuck against a branch, lay still and unmoving.

Their father was dead.

They stood still at the cliff's edge, their pursuit forgotten, and mourned him.

The old mothers, however, barely flinched. They weren't interested in the father. Their eyes were on Rook.

Sara surfaced, sputtering and looking for danger. King joined her.

"It's okay," he said.

"Where's Weston?"

King held up the magnum and checked the magazine. Empty. "Dead." Returning his gaze to the old mothers, he wondered when they would make a move. By the time they freed themselves from the river, they'd be too exhausted to run very far, let alone fight.

"Knight," King called out. "Where does this river go?"

"It runs southwest through Laos and into Cambodia."

"Past Anh Dung?"

Knight thought about it, recalling the map he'd taken from the maze chamber and cross-referencing it mentally with the maps of the region he'd memorized on the flight over. "Yeah, it does."

King nodded. That's where they'd stand their ground against the old mothers.

Birthplace of Brugada.

A village plagued by death.

Unwitting guinea pigs to Weston's observations.

Home to a field full of land mines.

Anh Dung.

They would finish this where it all began.

SIXTY-FIVE

The chase turned into a surreal, slow-moving event. The river had widened and the flow had dwindled to the speed of a casual Sunday drive. The Neanderthal women ambled along the riverside cliff casually, now only ten feet above the water, as they gave chase to what Rook now referred to as their "Great White Hope," aka himself.

The storm had ebbed some in the past ten minutes, but flashes of lightning still lit up the sky, shaking the world around them and filling the air with the scent of ozone.

Since Weston's death there hadn't been any sign of the hybrids.

The group had taken to lying flat on their backs, going with the flow and trying to rest before they made their move. And that moment seemed to grow closer every second as water poured into the river from hundreds of fast-moving rivulets, each contributing to the rising water level. They'd passed under several fallen trees that the Neanderthals most likely used to cross the river. Each time they'd passed under, the old mothers tried plucking them from the water. But their short arms couldn't reach. With the water level rising, however, they would soon be able to pluck the team out of the water like pickles from a jar.

King estimated they'd traveled at least two miles from the mountain and the ancient hidden city of Meru. Thunder rumbled again, but sounded different somehow. Distant, yet continuous, and somehow odd. Then it occurred to King that the thunder hadn't been preceded by a flash of lightning.

Queen said aloud what he was thinking. "That's not thunder."

The group leaned up and began to tread water again, looking upriver. They couldn't feel it in the water, but they could see it. A wave of energy flew through the ground, shaking trees and loosening soil from the banks of the river where it fell in clumps. Lighting filled the sky above, shifting through the clouds, illuminating the world below. For an instant, Mount Meru exploded into view. It looked as though a meteor had struck. The mountain rose up on the sides to half its previous height. It had collapsed. Meru, home of the gods, the last refuge of the Neanderthal species, had been buried.

At first Sara felt sad that such a historic and incredible place had been lost, but then she remembered what it felt like there. Beyond her senses being blinded, the place struck her as evil. The curses against humanity. The hate that had gone into laying those stones was still palpable. Meru was an evil place and Weston's time there had made him indifferent to the fate of the human race. The world was better off never knowing about it.

King saw the situation differently. Two things were about to happen. First, the collapse of the mountain would send a river-fueled tidal wave in their direction. Second, if the debris carried forward by the wall of water didn't kill them, the river, now blocked by the fallen mountain, would run dry, allowing the old mothers easy access to them.

Shifting his view toward shore, King saw their salvation ahead. A portion of the riverside cliff had been knocked down and a long beach had been formed on the opposite shore of the river from the Neanderthal women. He judged the distance traveled, the direction of the shoreline, and the objects—a rotting reed basket, a tattered T-shirt, and a half-submerged canoe—littering the shoreline.

Anh Dung. It had to be.

"There!" King shouted, pointing toward the shore.

As the six Chess Team members swam for the shore, the old mothers, who could clearly not swim, hooted and hollered.

"Rook!" Red shouted. "You father! Rook!"

Then they were off and running down the opposite shoreline, no doubt headed for another fallen tree. They'd be on top of them in no time. The group crawled onto the shore just as a surge of water caught their feet.

Rook looked back. "Move, move, move!"

As Bishop scooped up Knight and ran, the others ignored their wobbly legs and ran up the track of sand, entering the jungle just as a wall of water pounded down the river, eating up the shoreline as it moved. A loud swishing filled the forest. The raging waters had moved outside the confines of the river. Trees cracked and leaves swished as the river flowed through the jungle.

They ran, unable to see the oncoming wall of water.

But Sara could feel it. Huge and fast, slowed only by the trunks of hundreds of trees, yet moving steadily forward.

"Faster!" she urged them, feeling the water gaining on them, pushing through the darkness. But there was something else moving with the trees . . . in the trees. The hybrids. Over their initial shock, they had rejoined the chase. Out for vengeance.

As Sara felt the cool tickle of the first splash of water at her feet, she felt the earth beneath her rise up. She stumbled up the incline, clawing her way up through the sopping-wet earth and loose leaves. Clear of the water, she fell flat on her stomach and took several deep breaths.

Then King's hand took hers from above. "Not yet," he said, yanking her back to her feet.

They ran again, and then, as suddenly as the river had carried them from the mountain, they cleared the jungle and entered a clearing. Lightning lit the scene—a field full of tall grass. A series of bright orange flags placed by Bishop only days ago, each marking the position of a land mine, led into the reeds. The field was full of them.

"Follow the markers," King said, "but do *not* step anywhere near them."

They launched into the grass, leaving the cover of jungle and exposing themselves to the whipping rain, wind, and the hybrids moving through the trees.

Loud whoops filled the air behind them. The hybrids were coming.

A roar, followed by a loud "Rook!" sounded from their right. Red and the old mothers had crossed the river before the flood as well. The chess board was set and the pieces were moving.

The tall, thick grass slapped against Sara's face as she ran, but was a mere distraction to the pain in her back from when she had been crushed against the underwater cave ceiling. Her torn shirt revealed several gouges pouring warm blood down her back. Trying to ignore the pain she focused on the one thing lighting her path—Rook's bare white back.

She saw Rook's body leap up suddenly. When he came back down, an orange flag came into view between them. Too close to react quickly, Sara stumbled, jumped, and landed in a heap. She looked up and saw King leap over the small mound she'd nearly fallen on top of. He pulled her up and pushed her forward, just as the grass at the back edge of the field burst with the sound of running bodies.

Following Rook and Queen's plowed path, King, Sara, and Bishop holding Knight moved quickly through the field, though there was no doubt that the hybrids and old mothers were moving even faster. Rook's white form came into view again as Sara gained on him.

Snarls emerged from the grass around them. The enemy

closed in. Hybrid or fully Neanderthal, it was impossible to tell. Until a gentle click to their right signified the triggering of a buried land mine.

King dove on Sara as the mine exploded. A legless hybrid screamed as it was launched overhead. The single explosion seemed to set off a chain reaction. All over the field, as hybrids charged forward without sense of the danger, mines burst, hybrids screamed, and limbs tore away from bodies.

King was up and running again with Sara when the grass behind him collapsed. Red burst out at his heels. Hair raised, teeth bared. She was a creature out of mankind's past and King wasn't sure even a mine could stop her.

"King!"

Sara's voice spun him around and he just barely caught sight of the orange flag before stepping down. He jumped, rolled, and got back to his feet. Looking back, he saw Red jump the flag as well.

Smarter than she looks, King thought.

"They're all around us!" Sara shouted, feeling the presence of more than fifty individuals closing in from every direction . . . except for straight ahead. As Sara's attention turned forward, she felt more bodies approaching. They were surrounded. "Up ahead! There are more up ahead!"

A sudden shock wave coupled with a loud *whump* generated by a hybrid stepping on a nearby land mine sent Sara and King flying. They shot forward, crashing into Rook just as he and Queen exited the field. Bishop and Knight fell behind them. The team climbed to their feet. Sara pulled her knife, as did King and Queen, ready to fight for their lives. Rook, nearly naked and weaponless, clenched his fists. Bishop put Knight down behind the others and then stood on point, ready to let his body take the brunt of the attack.

Then they saw the group waiting for them in the village of Anh Dung. Too many to count and far more deadly than

Weston, Red, the hybrids, or the Death Volunteers. They did the only thing they could—dropped to their knees and waited for the end. It came quickly, as the mass of men before them opened fire.

SIXTY-SIX

Staccato gunfire ripped through the air, illuminating Anh Dung and the large field with muzzle flashes and glowing tracer rounds. Sara blocked her ears, though she couldn't help but watch the tracers soaring over her head, cutting into the field and mowing it down. It was as though they had been transported back in time to when their mission began so badly. Bullets flying. Tracers glowing. People dying. The only difference was that this time she didn't scream. She barely flinched.

Hybrids and old mothers wailed out as high-powered bullets slashed through their bodies as easily as they did the grass. Land mines exploded as those not cut down by the bullets fled through the field. The fight, if it could be called that, lasted only ten seconds.

King turned from the carnage and looked at the attacking force. Fifty men, dressed head to toe in black, lacking any insignia or marking of any kind. With eyes hidden behind rounded goggles and odd-looking face masks covering noses and mouths, their identities were cloaked. But King knew exactly who they were. He'd worn the very same gear on several missions.

"Cease fire!"

Delta.

And a lot of them.

Floodlights behind the line of soldiers flashed on. The field, now lit as though by the sun, revealed its carnage. Blood and chunks of flesh clung to thick reeds of grass. Depressions in the field marked where bodies had fallen. The Neanderthals, both hybrid and original model, hadn't stood a chance.

Weston was right, Sara thought, nature selected one of the races to extinction, but it wasn't humanity at the hands of Brugada. Humanity was far too good at killing to lose this fight. Even if Weston hadn't let them go, this massive force of men would have stormed the halls of Mount Meru until the cure was found. And nothing Weston did could have changed that.

The Chess Team stood together as the soldiers descended on their position. The others kept watch on the decimated field.

A single black-clothed soldier stepped in front of the rest, approaching King.

"You have the cure?" The voice was deep, modulated to disguise the identity of the man speaking.

King stared back in silence, trying to figure out if he knew the man behind the mask. Something in the modulated voice sounded familiar.

"After all this time, you don't trust me?" There it was. King recognized the sarcasm as the one member of the team missing since this debacle of a mission began.

"Deep Blue?"

Deep Blue nodded. "We'll catch up on the way home . . . if you've got the cure. If not, I've brought some friends to make sure we do."

"Could have used them a few days ago."

"I know," Deep Blue said. "I'm sorry." He looked over the group standing before him. Rook, beaten and bleeding from gashes on his chest and what looked like a bite wound on his shoulder. Queen, sporting a swollen red brand on her forehead. Knight, standing on one leg. Bishop, looking hale as ever, but different. More . . . at peace. Pawn, the civilian, her back bleeding beneath her torn shirt. And King, a bullet wound in his shoulder. He noted the missing member.

"Pawn Two?"

"Gone," King said. "Killed."

Deep Blue's head hung for a moment. "And the cure?"

"We have it."

A rustle of grass brought fifty assault rifles to bear on a single location at the edge of the field. A lone figure stumbled into view.

Red.

Her body bled from three bullet wounds, one in her arm, two in a thigh. She hobbled a few feet from the grass and stopped, looking at the silhouettes lined up in front of the blazing bright light. She heard a few of the men curse and say, "What the hell?" She ignored them, looking for only one person. "Rook."

Two more figures emerged from the field, also wounded, but not mortally. Two hybrids, male and female. They stood by Red, placing their hands on her thick mane.

"Rook!" Red shouted with a snarl.

"On my mark," Deep Blue said.

"Wait!" Rook shouted, stepping out of the bright light and moving toward Red and the hybrids.

"Rook," King said, his voice a warning.

Rook held up his hand, signaling them to wait. He stepped down the slight grade, stopping a few feet in front of Red. He crouched down.

"You father," Red said.

Rook nodded. "Weston is dead."

"You come now."

"No."

Red roared, pounded the ground, and charged forward.

Rook side-stepped, took the injured old mother by the back of her neck, and flung her to the ground. He knew if she hadn't been injured the result might have been different, but dominance had to be established.

He stood above her.

She looked up at him, her chest heaving with each breath.

"Leave. Now." He motioned to the hybrids. "And take them."

Red huffed and got back to her feet. She growled for a moment, then frowned. "Rook come again?"

"Not a chance."

Red looked at the soldiers aiming their weapons at her, then shook her head and turned around. She limped back into the grass, followed by her two children. They disappeared into the field.

"Rook," Queen said, her voice tinged with annoyance. "We can't let them leave. They've killed people. The villagers here. Somi."

"This is their home," Rook said. "It was before there was a human race. They were just protecting their home. We do the same thing every day on the job."

"Sir!" A man ran toward the group, wearing all black like the others but sporting a pilot's helmet. "We've got two MIG-21 inbound on our position."

"ETA?" Deep Blue asked.

"Five minutes."

"All right," Deep Blue shouted. "Pack it up. It's time to disappear."

The soldiers sprang into action, falling back toward the floodlights.

"You six are with me," Deep Blue said, leading them past the ravaged huts of Anh Dung where five UH-100S stealth Blackhawk transport helicopters waited, rotors beginning to spin.

Thirty seconds later, the reunited and complete Chess Team were cruising low over the jungle, headed south over Cambodia to the South China Sea, where they would rendezvous with the USS *Kitty Hawk* carrier group conducting "routine exercises."

An hour later, the five stealth Blackhawks chopped over the open ocean. The central Blackhawk in the V-shaped formation contained the Chess Team. Each wrapped in a thick wool blanket, they began to relax for the first time in days. If they hadn't been so intent on telling their story, the droning chop of the helicopter rotors would have lulled them to sleep. But the story begged to be told. They recounted their experiences with the Neo Khmer, the VPLA, Weston, the Neanderthals, and their half-breed brood. Deep Blue listened silently, all hints of whether or not he believed the tale hidden behind his mask.

When their story concluded with the confrontation in the field, Deep Blue nodded. "Glad we arrived when we did."

"If you don't mind me asking," Queen said, "what the hell took so long?"

"I was indisposed."

The six people sitting around him, who had been dipped in shit and come out clean, looked at him with dubious eyes. He'd have to do better than that.

Deep Blue sat still for a moment, his thoughts impossible to perceive while his mystery face was hidden from them. He glanced into the cockpit, made sure the pilots weren't looking, and turned back to the others. "I was infected . . . *am* infected with Brugada. And I am the reason you were sent on this mission."

He reached back and pulled his mask up and over his head. A handsome face all of them recognized immediately smiled at them.

President Duncan.

"Holy—," Rook said.

"I don't believe it," Knight whispered.

Sara was more stunned than the rest. "Mr. President," she said, offering her hand. Out of the six, she was the only one to have met him before, virtually, as she briefed the quarantined White House via video conference.

He shook her hand. "Nice to finally meet you in person." He turned to King. "I was going to tell you last week. At the barbeque." He shrugged. "Something came up."

"Can we get a rain check on that barbeque?" Queen asked.

Duncan smiled. "As far as I'm concerned, you all can have anything you want."

King leaned his head back and closed his eyes. "A barbeque will do."

Sara looked over at the Chess Team. She had started to feel like she might have the potential to be like them. And she'd fought her way through the jungle, been captured, beaten, and shot at. She'd bit a man to get the cure to Brugada. She'd fought with mankind's ancient enemy gone feral, whether from genetic assimilation or hyperevolution she'd never know. And had no desire to find out. She didn't want a barbeque, she wanted a million dollars, a yacht, and full-time masseuse. But these five, all they wanted was a cold beer and some ribs. Their commitment to their country, to all of humanity, went beyond anything she could conceive. They'd saved the world and wanted nothing for it. Despite all the failings she saw in them when she first met them, she saw them for what they truly were: heroes.

EPILOGUE

Siletz Reservation—Oregon

King shook his head as he entered the small town of Siletz. After a six-hour flight to Portland and a two-and-a-half-hour drive in a cramped Chevy Aveo rental, he was really starting to look forward to the long-awaited barbeque at Camp David, scheduled for the following week. The team had been on leave since Vietnam, for six weeks, recovering from battle wounds and debriefing an ungodly number of military and government officials.

Sara and a team from the CDC quickly isolated the herpes virus that triggered the gene alteration responsible for shutting down Brugada. The resulting inoculation—BGS, referred to as the "Bugs" vaccine, which was truly gene therapy—was tested on ten White House staff volunteers whose hearts had already stopped and been kick-started by the implanted cardioverters. They were all eager for a potential cure. A quick echocardiogram showed success and the Bugs vaccine was administered to the rest of the quarantined White House—no blood swapping or rash scratching required. Inoculating the rest of the infected outside the White House had been a logistical nightmare. Many came forward, fueled by fear, and claimed to have the disease. Demanding immediate treatment. While some, never knowing they were infected, fell

over dead. But in the end, BGS was mass produced and made
a mandatory vaccine. It would take time to inoculate the entire country, but with the outbreak contained, there were no
more reported cases. Furthermore, Duncan made sure samples of BGS were sent around the world to all governments
and health organizations. Brugada, both new and old strains,
would be made obsolete.

When Duncan finally addressed the press, all hell broke
loose. Accusations flew. Pundits ranted. A minority of the
population demanded his resignation, but with the details of
the events surrounding the assassination attempt on his life,
national pride and anger toward the offending nation qui-
eted the dissenters.

An investigation by the Vietnamese government (who
claimed ignorance) discovered Trung's hand in the plot to
weaponize the disease. His research, samples, and laboratory were incinerated under the watch of a team from the 20th
Support Command out of Fort Meade that oversees and
eliminates chemical, biological, radioactive, nuclear, and explosives (CBRNE) hazards. The scientists involved faced
jail time. And Trung, well, he was buried beneath the ruins
of Mount Meru, but only a handful of people knew about the
circumstances of his death, or the involvement of Weston,
the Nguoi Rung, and the last surviving Neanderthals. Their
world would remain a secret, per Rook's request to Duncan.

King would have been happy to spend the next week relaxing at Fort Bragg with the rest of the team. They were in high
spirits and at nearly one hundred percent strength again. They
had once again come up against the worst the world had to
offer and come out scarred, but alive, and more bonded to each
other than before. Except Bishop, of course; he had returned
healthier than before—his body free to regenerate without
fear of insanity so long as the crystal stayed around his neck.
Once they had their long-awaited barbeque, they would be
ready for a mission.

What King regretted most about the past six weeks was
not being able to see Sara nearly enough. They had en-

sconced themselves in hotels on a few occasions, when de-
briefs brought them together, but time had been short. With
life returning to normal, King looked forward to seeing her
on a more regular basis. In many ways she was his opposite,
but she was smart and witty, and having survived the horrors of Mount Meru, understood him like no other woman
could.

But fate, it seemed, would keep them apart for a little
while longer. He had received a cryptic e-mail from George
Pierce, his lifelong friend, former fiancé of his deceased
sister, an archaeologist and a victim of Manifold Genetics,
the company who turned Bishop into a self-healing regen.
Like Bishop, Pierce had been experimented on, giving him
regenerative abilities. The difference between them was that
the formula used on Pierce was developed from the DNA of
the mythological Hydra. Pierce's transformation had been
physically dramatic—green scales, yellow eyes, sharp claws.
But it had also been reversible thanks to an ancient serum
used by the historical Hercules to defeat Hydra twenty-five
hundred years previous.

King had seen Pierce only once since the dramatic events
of the previous year, but their bond was stronger than ever.
So when Pierce's short, but explicit, e-mail appeared in his
box, and there was no reply on his home phone or cell, he
did the only thing he could do—followed the instructions
sent by Pierce:

> *Jack,*
> *Find Fiona Lane and her grandmother Delores. They*
> *need your brand of help. Siletz, Oregon. Quickly.*
> *Please.*
>
> *-George-*

King had found their address easily enough, and had
booked a flight for the next morning. That morning. It had
only been fifteen hours since he'd received Pierce's e-mail and
he hoped he'd been fast enough to help them with whatever

problem existed. He knew that Fiona and her grandmother were both members of the Siletz tribe, living on the reservation, but nothing else about them stood out as interesting. Nothing. They were regular Americans doing regular American things. PTA. Girl Scouts. Basketball. Fiona's parents— Delores's full-blooded tribal son and a white, cornbread-loving woman from Texas—had been killed in a boating accident when Fiona was two. She'd been raised on the reservation by her grandmother since, and was now ten. What these two needed *his* help for was anyone's guess.

King passed a sign that read:

WELCOME TO SILETZ—POPULATION 3,000

King shook his head and thought, *George, this better not be a wild-goose chase . . . and I better be home in time for my barbeque.*

The road leading into town skirted pines on either side. King rolled down the window, letting the cool, late-September air fill the small car's cabin. He breathed deep. Then paused.

Smoke.

Just a hint.

And it wasn't a campfire.

A low cloud of soot billowed across the road and filtered up to the sky. After rolling up his window, King gunned the four-cylinder engine and cut through the smoke. He looked for a road that would lead to the source of the fire, but saw nothing. He didn't remember any roads close behind him, so he continued on at a fast clip. He rounded a corner atop a hill and saw the small town spread out below.

It was in ruins.

Smoke poured from several buildings.

Downed electrical lines snaked and sparked.

Bodies, so many bodies, filled the streets.

Without hesitation, King tore down the street. He worked his way into town, looking for motion, for someone to talk to, to help. But no one moved. He stopped three times to check bodies, but no one was alive. And their injuries were extensive. He hadn't seen anything like this since entering Anh Dung. But that was dozens of people.

This was thousands.

What was George involved in?

King jumped back in the car and followed the directions he'd printed out. After passing fifty more dead bodies and several strange piles of what looked like ash, King arrived at the house. It was a small white building with singed vinyl siding and a huge hole where the front door used to be. It looked like a wrecking ball had taken a swing at the residence. King drew his Sig Sauer and headed for the home.

He stood in the doorway, stunned. The hole in the front of the house ran straight through to the back. Something had pierced the building like a .50-caliber bullet through a skull and torn a larger hole right out the back. Debris from the impact had been scattered throughout the small backyard. A yellow, rusted swing set at the back of the yard was toppled and bent. All around it was another large pile of ash, as though whatever had struck the house had come to a stop and burned to dust.

King stepped into the living room and found what remained of Delores. The old woman's body had been crushed. Given the number of wood and vinyl siding fragments protruding from her body, he guessed she'd been killed by the initial impact of whatever had torn through the house.

Damnit, King thought. If only Pierce had been more specific. Had said an entire town was threatened. He could have had hundreds of boots on the ground in two hours, not one Delta operator in fifteen! He had no idea what had happened to this town, but he believed it could have been stopped. If only he'd known. If only there had been time.

King left the home and headed back to the car. He removed his cell phone and dialed his direct line to Deep Blue, which was very different from his direct line to President Duncan. But he never hit Send. A body caught his eye. A body *in the backseat of his car.*

He raised his handgun and searched the area. He saw no one. Other than fire, smoke, and live wires, nothing moved.

He opened the door and aimed inside. The body remained motionless, but even if she had been awake, the ten-year-old girl inside the car with lightly tanned skin, dark black pony-tailed hair, and a *Dexter's Laboratory* backpack would have posed no threat. A note had been pinned to her T-shirt, but King ignored it, checking for a pulse. It was strong and regular. He gave her a quick visual inspection and felt her limbs for breaks. She seemed unharmed.

King took the note and read it, knowing as he did that the barbeque with the president and a rendezvous with Sara would have to wait.

King—This one is for you. I've gone after the rest.

He'd seen the symbol a year previous, in a cave hidden beneath Gibraltar—a cave that had been the hiding place of a secretive and ancient order known as the Herculean Society—and the man they protected.

Alexander Diotrephes.

Hercules.

Read on for an excerpt from Jeremy Robinson's next book

THRESHOLD

Coming soon in hardcover from
Thomas Dunne Books / St. Martin's Press

Fort Bragg, North Carolina

"Get down, they see you."

"I can't see them."

"Above you. Flood infections!"

"Oh no . . . ahh! They're everywhere. I think I'm dead."

"Lew. Lew! They killed Lew. Ugh!" Fiona paused the game, put down the Xbox remote, and threw her hands up. "Every time, Lew."

Lewis Aleman smiled as he stood. "Sorry kiddo. If they designed joysticks as guns we'd be all set. I was great at Duck Hunt."

"Duck Hunt? Seriously? You *are* old."

"Forty-one isn't old," he said, moving from the sparsely decorated lounge to the small kitchenette. The college dorm–like space typically held a good number of off-duty soldiers playing pool, cards, or watching TV, but Lewis had made sure the space would be empty. A room full of soldiers looking to relax and have fun was not typically the right environment for a tween, boy or girl.

"If you weren't born in the nineteen-eighties or sooner, you're old." Fiona was dressed in all black pajamas and slippers—her favorite, she said, because they looked like special ops nighttime gear. The only aberration on her smooth, slender little body was a small rectangular lump on her hip. Hidden beneath her shirt, clipped to her waist, was the insulin pump that kept her blood sugar levels optimal. With a curtain of straight black hair hanging down around her head, only her brown hands and face weren't shrouded in darkness. "Popcorn time?"

The loud rattle of popcorn swirling around in an air popper answered her question. "You know how to use that?" she shouted over the loud tornado of corn kernels.

"Popcorn is my specialty!"

"You said you were good at Halo, too."

"Going to use a whole stick of butter. Can't go wrong."

"Might need to get your cholesterol checked," she mumbled.

"What?"

"Nothing! Nothing." Fiona stood by the large window that overlooked a large parking lot below and the expansive Fort Bragg that had become her new home. The nonstop movement of the base consisted of a mix of military and normal life. Men and women in uniform mixed with those in plainclothes. Jeeps shared the roads with SUVs and minivans. From her view in the barracks lounge she could also see the other barracks, their redbrick walls aglow from the setting sun.

She caught her reflection in the window and its distorted shape made her look like her grandmother, who even in old age had a youthful face. Her eyes grew wet as she remembered the woman who had raised her. Who had sung songs to her and taught her the traditions and language of a people who no longer existed. According to King, she was the last true Siletz Native American left alive. There were other descendants to be sure, but they had long ago shirked the tribe, joined the larger American society, and forgotten the ancient culture altogether. King also explained that she was the sole heir to the Siletz Reservation. And when she was old enough, she could claim the land as her own.

She lay in bed most nights daydreaming about what she would do with the reservation. She couldn't live there. Not by herself. Not without the tribe. Too many ghosts on that land. A pair of statues was her answer, one a tribute to her people, the second to her grandmother and parents, perhaps with a single road leading to them. The rest, as her grandmother had taught her, belonged to nature.

The popcorn popper fell silent.

Fiona wiped her nose and turned from the window. This was an emotional trip she made on a daily basis and she was determined to get over it. To move on. Be emotionally solid. Like Dad. King.

As she stepped away from the window, she took one last look back, expecting to see the face of her grandmother once again. Instead, she saw right through herself as a bright orange glow in the distance caught her attention. She stepped forward and placed her hand on the glass.

It was shaking.

"Lew?"

She could hear him walking into the room and could smell the buttery popcorn.

Aleman heard the concern in her voice and quickened his pace. As he approached, Fiona recognized the growing yellow orb for what it was—a distant explosion. "Lew!"

Aleman had just a second to look out the glass pane, see the fireball, register the shaking beneath his feet, catch sight of the approaching shockwave as it flattened the grass on the baseball field across the parking lot.

The popcorn fell to the floor as Aleman picked Fiona up and dove behind the thick Ikea couch.

The window blew in just as they hit the thin rug, sending shards of glass stabbing into the opposite wall, the TV, and the room's furniture. The building shook for a moment as the shock wave passed, then fell silent.

Lewis rolled off Fiona and stood, shaking the glass from his back. His handgun was already drawn and at the ready. He looked down at Fiona, his eyes more serious than she had ever seen them. "You okay?"

She nodded.

"Get up," he said, and moved to the now glassless window. A second, small explosion plumed into the air. It was followed by the distant popping of small-arms fire. Then an alarm sounded. One he thought he would never hear used. It meant the unthinkable.

Fort Bragg was under attack.

He looked back at Fiona, whose skinny body looked frail in her black pajamas. She had her eyebrows furrowed, her fists clenched, and her lips down turned. She knew what was happening just as surely as he did.

They had come for her.

Aleman ran down the staircase with Fiona over his shoulder and his handgun in his hand. Surrounded by brick and concrete, the sounds of the battle raging outside were dulled, but he could still feel the shaking of explosions in his feet. The second-floor door sprang open as three Army Rangers entered the stairwell, ready for battle. Aleman recognized them and, outranking them, commandeered their protective services.

"They're after the girl," Aleman shouted. "Do not leave my side."

The front man nodded. They had all been briefed on Fiona and knew she was under the military's protection, though they did not know why. "Where to, sir?"

Aleman had been wracking his brain on this point. They had never assumed someone would actually infiltrate Fort Bragg and hadn't come up with a fail-safe plan for such an event. They needed to be safe, but more than anything, they needed to hide. Someplace dark. Someplace secure. "Nearest fallout shelter."

The three Rangers took the lead and descended the staircase first. They entered the short hallway at the end of the stairwell and made for the lobby. At the lobby door, the last of the three Rangers held out an open hand to Aleman.

He stopped in the doorway and waited for the men to give the all clear. One man was about to, but his voice caught in his throat as his eyes grew wide. Something outside the lobby had caught his attention, and there was no time to shout a warning.

The lobby imploded as a large projectile burst through one side, plowed over the three Rangers, and exploded out the other side of the building. Fiona screamed as Aleman turned and shielded her small body with his own, taking a chunk of concrete to the back of his head. He fell to one knee, felt his mind swirl, and then forced himself back onto his feet, ignoring the warm trickle of blood dripping down the back of his neck.

He ran into the destroyed lobby, holstered his handgun, and picked up one of the dead Ranger's MP5 submachine gun.

Fiona's second scream was directed straight in his ear and caused him to drop her. She landed on her slippered feet and tugged on his shirt frantically. She pointed through the ruined lobby wall, where the large projectile had exited. "Lew!"

He turned and looked through the opening. A large gray mass, perhaps one hundred feet away, was turning around.

It heard her scream, Aleman thought.

Then it charged. In the brief moment he took to look, Aleman saw that it ran on four legs and vaguely resembled a rhino, though perhaps twice the size.

Hoisting Fiona up again, Aleman ran out the opposite side of the building and into the parking lot. A garage full of Hummers ready to go stood on the far side of the parking lot. Once mobile in one of the tough vehicles, he would make his way to the fallout shelter—after losing the behemoth, which he could hear gaining on them.

Running down a thin alley of parked cars, Aleman did his best to keep their heads low. Bullets were flying. Buildings were exploding. Bragg had become a war zone. As he exited the sea of cars Aleman turned to look for the large hunter. He saw nothing. But it was there. A car on the far side of the lot exploded into the air. Moments later a second car followed. It was charging straight through the lot, flinging cars out of its way.

Aleman took hold of the garage doorknob and turned. But it didn't budge. "Damnit!" He put Fiona down and kicked the door. Once. Twice. His head began to spin as blood seeped from the back of his skull. Knowing he wouldn't get through the door in time, he turned to face the creature.

As cars in the middle of the lot were flung skyward, he turned to Fiona. "We're going to dive out of the way at the last second, okay?"

She nodded and tried to look tough, despite her shaking lower lip.

"We'll be okay."

"Don't die, Lew," she said with a quivering voice. "Not for real."

Aleman focused on the giant gray force approaching them and refused to promise something he knew he couldn't. "Just jump when I say."

The car at the edge of the parking lot shot into the air, spinning madly as the monster burst free and charged toward them. Aleman only had time to see that the creature looked more like a bull-rhino amalgam with bull horns on top of its head and a third horn rising from its snout. But the rest of the features were dull, as though worn by time. Aleman tried to see more, to get some kind of hint about what this thing was, but his vision was blurring.

Then something amazing happened. A man, dressed head to toe in Special Ops black, charged toward the creature from the side. For a moment Aleman thought it might have been King, but the man was too tall and what he did next, well, not even King could have pulled it off.

The man took the creature by two of its horns and pushed down. The face, if that's what it could be called, dug into the pavement. The beast's forward momentum thrust its backside up and it flipped tail over head, landing on its back with a ground-shaking impact.

The man continued toward them without looking back. In his fading vision, Aleman could see the beast trying to right itself. And when it made progress he thought he saw two large shadows descend upon it. But he couldn't be sure. His attention moved back to the approaching man. Pushing Fiona behind him, he raised the MP5.

"Lew . . ." Fiona whispered.

The man raised his hands. "There's no need for that."

"Just stay back."

"I can protect the girl."

Aleman's aim faltered for just a moment, but it was all the man needed. He stepped forward and twisted the MP5 out of his hands, tossing it to the side. Knowing he was about to fall unconscious, Aleman asked, "Who are you?"

He watched helplessly as the man scooped up Fiona, who had fallen limp, perhaps passed out, and said, "King will know." He stepped away, and then paused. "I hope he appreciates me breaking my promise."

With fading vision, Aleman watched the man retreat with Fiona in his arms. His last thought was of King and how the man would react to finding out his foster daughter had been kidnapped.